THE CARDINAL

Also by Alison Weir

Innocent Traitor
The Lady Elizabeth
The Captive Queen
A Dangerous Inheritance
The Marriage Game

Six Tudor Queens
Katherine of Aragon: The True Queen
Anne Boleyn: A King's Obsession
Jane Seymour: The Haunted Queen
Anna of Kleve: Queen of Secrets
Katheryn Howard: The Tainted Queen
Katharine Parr: The Sixth Wife
In the Shadow of Queens

The Tudor Rose trilogy
Elizabeth of York: The Last White Rose
Henry VIII: The Heart & The Crown
Mary I: Queen of Sorrows

Quick Reads
Traitors of the Tower

Non-fiction
Britain's Royal Families: The Complete Genealogy
The Six Wives of Henry VIII
The Princes in the Tower
Lancaster and York: The Wars of the Roses
Children of England: The Heirs of King Henry VIII 1547–1558
Elizabeth the Queen
Eleanor of Aquitaine
Henry VIII: King and Court
Mary Queen of Scots and the Murder of Lord Darnley
Isabella: She-Wolf of France, Queen of England
Katherine Swynford: The Story of John of Gaunt and His Scandalous Duchess
The Lady in the Tower: The Fall of Anne Boleyn
Mary Boleyn: 'The Great and Infamous Whore'
Elizabeth of York: The First Tudor Queen
The Lost Tudor Princess
Queens of the Conquest
Queens of the Crusades
Queens of the Age of Chivalry

As co-author
The Ring and the Crown: A History of Royal Weddings, 1066–2011
A Tudor Christmas

ALISON WEIR

THE CARDINAL

A NOVEL OF LOVE AND POWER

REVIEW

Copyright © 2025 Alison Weir

The right of Alison Weir to be identified as the Author of the Work has been asserted by her in accordance with the Copyright, Designs and Patents Act 1988.

First published in 2025 by
Headline Review
An imprint of Headline Publishing Group Limited

1

Apart from any use permitted under UK copyright law, this publication may only be reproduced, stored, or transmitted, in any form, or by any means, with prior permission in writing of the publishers or, in the case of reprographic production, in accordance with the terms of licences issued by the Copyright Licensing Agency.

All characters in this publication – apart from the obvious historical figures – are fictitious and any resemblance to real persons, living or dead, is purely coincidental.

Cataloguing in Publication Data is available from the British Library

Hardback ISBN 978 1 0354 1619 6
Trade Paperback ISBN 978 1 0354 1620 2

Typeset in 12.5/15pt Adobe Garamond Pro by Jouve (UK), Milton Keynes

Printed and bound in Great Britain by Clays Ltd, Elcograf S.p.A.

Headline's policy is to use papers that are natural, renewable and recyclable products and made from wood grown in well-managed forests and other controlled sources. The logging and manufacturing processes are expected to conform to the environmental regulations of the country of origin.

Headline Publishing Group Limited
An Hachette UK Company
Carmelite House
50 Victoria Embankment
London EC4Y 0DZ

The authorised representative in the EEA is Hachette Ireland,
8 Castlecourt Centre, Dublin 15, D15 XTP3, Ireland (email: info@hbgi.ie)

www.headline.co.uk
www.hachette.co.uk

THE CARDINAL

To my dear friends

Maria and Eileen Bosco
Siobhan Clarke and Roger Pheby
Philip and Christine Clucas
John and Linda Collins
David and Caroline Dennison
Lesley Edmeads
David and Janet Harris
Jean Hubbard
Elaine Knowles
Heather Macleod and Glen Lucas
Burnell and Tamsin Tucker

with love and thanks for all your support.

This Cardinal,
Though from an humble stock, undoubtedly
Was fashion'd to much honour from his cradle.
He was a scholar, and a ripe, and good one;
Exceeding wise, fair spoken, and persuading:
Lofty, and sour to them that lov'd him not,
But, to those men that sought him, sweet as summer.
And though he were unsatisfied in getting,
(Which was a sin), yet in bestowing—
He was most princely: ever witness for him
Ipswich and Oxford! one of which fell with him,
Unwilling to outlive the good that did it;
The other, though unfinish'd, yet so famous,
So excellent in art, and yet so rising,
That Christendom shall ever speak his virtue.
His overthrow heap'd happiness upon him;
For then, and not till then, he felt himself,
And found the blessedness of being little:
And, to add greater honours to his age
Than man could give him, he died fearing God.

Shakespeare, *Henry VIII*

Part One

'He was a scholar, and a ripe, and good one'

Chapter 1

1482

Tom was trying to concentrate. All around him, boys – most of them fifteen, four years older than he – were busy at their studies, but he was distracted by the noise of building works going on beyond the mullioned windows, and it was hard to drag his attention back to the Latin translation on which he was supposed to be labouring, for he was too busy thinking about the construction of the new buildings and wondering how such a project would be managed. How did one get all those men and materials in the right place at the right time? But the approach of the master, beak-nosed, cane in hand, had him bending, squinting, to his book and vigorously dipping his quill in the inkwell.

The master paused, peering over his shoulder, then nodded and passed along the form, presumably seeking out other victims. Tom had already seen how quick he was to lash out with that cane.

His translation was soon finished, but the other boys were still scratching away with their quills. Tom pretended to be reading over the passage, but in reality he was deciphering the graffiti carved into the desk, doubtless by past pupils steeped in misery. Learning, he thought, should be a pleasure, but the prospect of four years of this stern regime was daunting.

He had been so thrilled to be awarded a place at Oxford, had fallen in love at first sight with the city, its ornate colleges, its quads and spires and its teeming student population. He had yearned with a passion to delve deep into its famous libraries and immerse himself in the knowledge of centuries. But now he felt that the vibrant life of the university was passing him by, and he wondered if he would ever truly be a part of it.

The day yawned ahead. It was not yet seven o'clock, when they would all troop meekly to daily Mass, which would no doubt be followed by an interminable sermon exhorting them to virtuous behaviour. Then there would be lectures until commons, where the fare was invariably beef broth, pottage and weak ale, and after that, private study or tutorials until bed, which was at eight o'clock in winter and nine o'clock in summer. It was like being in a monastery, although monks and friars probably had more freedom.

It was just his luck to end up at an Oxford college run by a religious fanatic who was determined to purge boys of their natural instincts. It was all very well for Bishop Wayneflete. The old greybeard's juices had long since dried up, and he had apparently forgotten what it was like to enjoy the rough and tumble of life with a horde of lads just on the cusp of adulthood, all eager to laugh, jest and play pranks. Tom doubted that Wicked Wayneflete had ever played a prank in his life. No, he just enjoyed making their existence as miserable as possible, with his petty rules and his abhorrence of levity of any sort.

Tom had been shocked to find that he and his fellow scholars were not permitted to speak their mother tongue, apart from on feast days. They were made to converse in Latin, and woe betide any who lapsed into English. He winced at the memory of a beating he had received during his first week, when he had not quite realised how important the rule was. Of course, it wonderfully concentrated the mind. If they wanted to communicate effectively, the boys had to learn Latin quickly. Tom was deeply grateful for his innate talent for languages. Thanks to his grammar-school education, and his own quick mind, he was competent in Latin and fluent in French.

He had been beaten too for swearing. He had not thought he could be overheard, but the masters seemed to have ears like hunting dogs, always on the alert for transgressions.

The other boys had taken pity on him, for most were older than he was. When, at the end of his first arduous day, he had retreated to the dorter, ready to enjoy his limited leisure time, and taken his dice from his travelling chest, they had stared at him in horror.

'Put them away!' one boy cried. 'We are not allowed to play games of chance. Old Beaky could look in at any time.'

'And you should cut your hair,' another said.

'I know,' said Tom. 'They told me that when I arrived last night, but I haven't had a chance.'

'You should not delay. If they see you with long hair, you'll get the whip,' a slight youth said. 'I'll cut it for you.'

Tom was appalled to find himself quickly shorn of his chestnut locks, hacked none too tidily into obedience.

He'd been told off when he whispered to his neighbour during a lecture, and again for finding Caesar's commentary on the Gallic Wars funny.

'No laughing in lectures!' the master thundered, then rounded on a boy who had arrived late, waving his cane at him.

'Sorry, Sir, I was sick, Sir,' the boy faltered, looking terrified, and a little green.

'You look perfectly well to me!' rapped Beaky, and gave him six lashes on the hand. Tom could see that the boy was trying not to cry.

When he himself had asked to be excused attendance in chapel because of a headache that had suddenly descended, it was refused. 'It is mandatory that you be there,' he was told. 'Don't ask for leave of absence again. If you absent yourself, you will be flogged.'

Tom had bowed his head, trying to ignore its throbbing, and done his best to perform his devotions. He felt bruised, not wanting his masters to think him eager to miss chapel, for he loved God and desired to serve Him to the best of his ability.

But it was so easy to commit a transgression. Even now, after several weeks at college, he found himself breaking one of the many rules. Yesterday afternoon, he had left a beautifully illuminated manuscript from the college library open while he went to fetch more paper. Seconds later, there was Beaky, looking over his desk with a face like a storm.

'It is forbidden to leave costly books open!' he barked.

Tom shrank into himself, apologising profusely and anticipating a beating. But a miracle happened: the master let him off. 'Don't do it again,' he commanded.

* * *

Tom was relieved to get to bed that evening. Lying beside his restless companion – boys under fifteen had to share a bed – he could not stop thinking of home. He supposed he was lucky and ought to be grateful, but right now he wished he was back in Ipswich.

His parents' inn was not a poor abode by any means. It was solid, timbered, warm and welcoming. Father was a busy man who could, and often did, turn his hand to anything. He was the proprietor of both the inn and a butcher's shop, and a yeoman farmer. He owned land out at Sternfield, where he grazed his animals. Ships from Ipswich carried his wool to the English market at Calais, where it was sold on to Burgundy, a trade that had made Ipswich prosperous. Tom had acquired an early understanding of how important the wool business was to England; it had been drummed into him. But Father was not a member of a guild, or a man of the standing of Uncle Edmund. Tom's mother's brother was a very important man, a rich merchant and a burgess who represented Ipswich in Parliament itself. Indeed, if it had not been for Uncle Edmund, Tom would not be here now, lying on a thin mattress in this chilly dorter. Robert Wolsey, by contrast, was too irascible and uncompromising to win the confidence of influential men. And for as long as Tom could remember, he had been in and out of the courts.

For all his faults, though, Tom loved his father, who clearly wanted the best for him, his older brothers, sickly Rob and sweet-natured William, and who was not above showing them affection. Impatient with others, he would take the time to teach them how to milk a cow, chop meat or reckon bills; or he would take the whole family to the markets and fairs that were held on bustling Cornhill, where they lived. But Tom loved his mother more. He had heard it said, by people who probably thought he wasn't listening, that Father had married above him, and he supposed it was true, for Mother's family, the Daundys, were wealthy and influential yeoman stock from Thetford. Mother was not quite gentry, but she had gentle ways and there was a daintiness about her that other town wives lacked. She was kind, devout and generous-hearted. Tom adored her.

Both she and his father were eager to see him do well, and Uncle

Edmund was always there, saying that such a brilliant young mind must be nurtured.

Father knew the value of getting on in life. 'Education is the way to advancement,' he often said, and while he was not rich, he had somehow found the fees of 8d a quarter to send Tom to the grammar school in Ipswich. 'You're a bright and industrious boy,' he'd told him. 'I expect great things of you. All my hopes lie in you, for your brothers won't make half the man you'll be one day.'

It was more or less an order, for Father was an ambitious and strong-willed fellow who liked getting his own way. He cared little about what others thought of him. When he brought his animals from the farm to be slaughtered and sold in his butcher's shop, he let them run wild in the street, unheeding of complaints that they were a nuisance and spread dung and disease. The town council, fed up with his defiance of their increasingly angry demands that he fence the beasts, had finally summoned him before the mayor's court, which had fined him – not that he paid much notice. He'd been fined too for letting his house be used as a gambling den, for selling bad meat and short measures of ale, and for charging prices above those decreed by law. Tom had long suspected that this was why his father had never been made a freeman of Ipswich.

But he was fond of his difficult parent, was willing to turn a blind eye to the haphazard, insanitary way the inn was run, and found it easy to please him. An inquisitive boy with a quick mind, he was eager to learn, and it was no trouble to apply himself to his studies. Every day he took the short walk from his home to the schoolhouse by the gate of the Blackfriars, behind St Peter's Church. The grammar school had been founded by the guild of merchants to educate their sons, and it had such a fine reputation that the local nobles – who were of a class not noted for an interest in education – sent theirs there too. Under the benevolent yet stern auspices of Master Squyre, the head, Tom learned the alphabet and the basics of Latin. He came to know the psalms by heart and developed such a love of music that he was appointed one of the choristers who sang when the whole school congregated every morning at six o'clock for the Mass of Our Lady in the Blackfriars' church.

When he got home in the afternoons, he helped his father in the inn. He was well liked by the customers and good friends with an elderly neighbour, Edward Winter, who shared the building that housed the inn, and its well too. More than once, in his cups, Edward told Tom that he would go far.

'Heducation,' he slurred one evening, as Tom brought him a fresh mug of ale. 'Assa key to it, boy. They could do with brains like yours at Westminster.'

'Go on with you.' Tom had smiled, surprised that Master Winter was so keen on learning when he had had so little of it himself.

'No, don't be like me, boy. Had my chance and didn't take it. Had to stay at home and look after my old dad. Don't you end up like me.'

'You've not done so badly,' Tom said kindly. It was a mystery to him what Master Winter actually did for a living, but he seemed to lead a comfortable existence.

'Coulda done better,' the old man grunted. 'But you – you'll go far!'

'He won't if he doesn't wash up those dirty flagons,' grinned Robert Wolsey, stomping into the bar with a tray of new-baked pies.

Tom wrinkled his nose. The meat smelt off. Father was up to his old tricks.

It had been a good life, Tom reflected now, as he tried to find a comfortable position in the narrow dorter bed. He could not stop thinking back to the days when he had enjoyed accompanying his father to the cattle markets in Cornhill, and laughing at the travelling showmen and the bull-baitings held there. Once, he had witnessed a hanging, and had been horrified by the bulging eyes of the struggling wretch and the time it had taken him to die, writhing and kicking as the life was choked out of him. He would never forget it. He preferred to dwell on his small pilgrimages to the shrine of Our Lady of Grace in Lady Lane, where he could gaze in wonder at her beautiful jewel-encrusted statue, her radiant face and the golden-haired babe leaping in her arms. Best of all were the colourful processions to mark the annual guild feasts, and the tables set out in the streets so that all might partake of the festive fare. He always gorged himself until he felt sick! How he missed it now, that old life, in which everything was safe and familiar. Looking back, it seemed like a golden time.

He had been fortunate. He knew that. The Lord Bishop of Norwich, who was a great man in the service of King Edward, had always taken an interest in the grammar school, and Master Squyre had told him how Tom excelled at his lessons. When the Bishop next visited the school, he had summoned Tom to stand before him and tested him on his catechism and his Latin, prompting him to ever greater efforts. At length, he had nodded sagely and turned to Master Squyre. 'The boy's learning is exceptional. I have never known one so young to be so erudite. How old are you, Master Wolsey?'

'Eleven, my lord,' Tom replied.

'Hmm.' The Bishop considered for a moment. 'It so happens that I have in my gift four places annually at Magdalen College School in Oxford. You will know of it, I am sure, Master Squyre. It was founded by my lord Bishop Wayneflete of Winchester about a dozen years back as a feeder school for Magdalen College, his other foundation. If the boy's family can meet the fees, I am happy to put him forward for one of the places.'

Tom had stared at him, amazed at the prospect. To go to Oxford! Young as he was, he knew that a university degree could open the door to any number of successful careers.

'By a happy coincidence,' Master Squyre was saying, 'my brother Laurence teaches at Oxford, and he has nothing but praise for Magdalen College. Master Wolsey, this is a wonderful opportunity for you, and you should be sensible of the favour shown you by my lord Bishop.'

'Oh, I am, my lord, I am! I am most grateful,' Tom cried, but he was in trepidation, fearing that his father would not be able to afford to send him to Oxford. 'Might I ask what the school fees are?'

'They are four pounds per annum.' The Bishop smiled. 'Do you think your father can afford that?'

Tom's hopes plummeted. 'Oh, yes,' he managed to say. 'I'm sure he can.' It was a lie, for he knew that such a large sum might well be beyond Robert Wolsey's means. But Father would have to find the money somehow – he must! So much depended on it.

'The Church has need of brilliant minds like yours,' the Bishop said. 'Most scholars at Oxford go into the Church. Indeed, most take holy orders in preparation for it. And if you do well, there are limitless opportunities. Even boys from humble backgrounds, like yourself, can rise to the highest offices in the land. Did you know that half the King's Privy Council are bishops?' He paused and looked out of the latticed window to the empty courtyard beyond. 'Now, Master Wolsey, I see that the other pupils have left. Go home to your father and tell him what I have said. Ask if he can afford the fees. Then let Master Squyre know if you would like me to put your name forward. I am sure that I can persuade the school to accept you.'

Tom had run home at the speed of a Greek athlete, determined to convince his father that it would be money well invested. He would tell his parents the good news first, that he had a chance of a place in Oxford. Then he would make his plea.

Father and Mother were so nearly bursting with pride that even the prospect of expensive school fees did not deflate their joy. Of course, Uncle Edmund had to be summoned, and a council of war was held.

'It is clear that the Bishop thinks Tom is destined for the Church,' Father said, as they sat around the big table in the inn.

'And how do you feel about that, my boy?' Uncle Edmund enquired.

'I like the idea, Sir,' Tom replied. 'It could lead to advancement for me and prosperity for the family.'

'Indeed it could! And are you prepared to work hard to ensure a successful career in the future?'

'Oh, yes, Sir,' Tom said fervently. 'I would consider myself unbelievably fortunate to have the opportunity.' In his mind's eye, he could see Oxford beckoning, shining like some great golden city of myth.

'There can be no doubt that he has the will to succeed, and that Oxford is the right place for him,' Uncle Edmund said. 'The question is, Robert, can you afford to send him there?'

Father frowned briefly. 'I have been doing some sums and thinking about where I can make savings.'

'You could stop suing people and taking them to court,' Mother said tartly.

Father glared at her. 'I have to do that to get paid and protect my rights,' he growled.

'What you are saying, I believe, is that to send Tom to Oxford, you would need to make sacrifices,' Uncle Edmund said.

'I am willing to do that,' Father told him.

'There is no need,' Uncle Edmund replied, clapping him on the shoulder. 'I myself will pay the boy's fees. I have a strong feeling that he will make his mark in the world.'

So Tom had gone to Magdalen College School, liked it and thrived there. Yes, the master had been strict – what master wasn't? – and academic expectations high, but despite having to work hard, he and his fellows had had fun. There had been many opportunities for making mischief, and he tried not to smile when he remembered what they had got away with. The head never had found out who had broken the window in the chapel with an ill-judged throw of a ball, or daubed a rude message on the wall of his house. It hadn't been Tom, but he'd been there when the crimes were committed, splitting his sides with his laughing friends. That was when he hadn't been slaving away at Latin and the classics. Well, 'slaving' was perhaps the wrong word, for he had always thrived on hard work, and he enjoyed immersing himself in the works of the ancient Greeks and Romans. He liked rhetoric; he shone at grammar. His master, habitually critical, had been full of praise for him, declaring he had never had so apt a pupil, and one so forward for his age.

'Not many boys of eleven have a fine brain like yours,' he'd told him.

Yes, Tom had loved Magdalen College School, but his time there had been all too short. He had studied there for just two terms when the head informed him that his progress had been so outstanding that they were sending him up to the university.

'You must decide whether to study for a Bachelor's degree in theology or canon law,' he said.

Tom was reeling. Leave this school, when he had only just settled in and begun to make friends? He had thought that university would be three or four years in the future. And yet, deep inside him there was a thrill of excitement. He had justified everyone's hopes, and far exceeded them. He was good enough to go to university earlier than most boys. He would study theology; he was fascinated by the Scriptures, and he loved debate. A glorious future beckoned.

Lying in the dorter now, he tried hard to recapture the feeling of euphoria that had overwhelmed him when he first arrived in Oxford, yet it was difficult. He had never dreamed that life here would be so gruelling, coming to this half-built college and finding himself the youngest among a thousand scholars. But he must put up with it, work hard and make the best of things if he wanted to fulfil his family's hopes and expectations – and indeed his own. If this was what it took to build a bright future, he would do it, and he would not falter.

Chapter 2

1486

As time passed, the rigours of university life became less important because the beckoning future seemed so bright and worth striving for. Tom had proved himself to be an outstanding scholar, and his tutors were delighted to have such an apt student. At fifteen, he was awarded his degree – which was almost unheard of – after which his admiring fellows, and even the masters, took to calling him the 'Boy Bachelor'.

When he rode home that summer and told them the news, his parents were overjoyed, and a proud Uncle Edmund laid on a great feast in his honour, which was attended by half the town, it seemed. But Tom's pleasure in the praise being heaped on him was diluted by concern for his brother Rob, who was sitting at the end of the high table, toying with his food. At twenty-five, Rob should have been helping their father with his many businesses, yet he had never been robust and was now wasting away with a hacking cough. Their mother made light of it, but Tom could see the fear in her eyes, and wondered if he should tell her that he had noticed spots of bright blood on Rob's kerchief. She must know, he told himself.

As the remains of the food were removed and goblets were replenished, Rob got up, smiled a discreet farewell and disappeared, bent as an old man. It had to be faced: his brother could not be long for this world – and what would happen then? Thank goodness for William, now twenty-three and next in line. The last thing Tom wanted was to follow in his father's footsteps. He had ambitions of his own.

He dragged himself back to the present. The talk at table had turned to the new King, Henry VII, who had defeated King Richard last year at the Battle of Bosworth.

'I don't care what Parliament says.' Robert Wolsey was in full flight. 'His claim to the throne is weak. He won't last.'

'That's treason, my friend,' Uncle Edmund observed. 'I'd watch your tongue. Besides, the King has married the heiress of York.'

'*She's* the rightful Queen!' Mother declared.

Uncle Edmund chortled. 'We can't have a woman ruling, sister!'

'Heaven forbid!' Father echoed.

'A woman might make a much better job of it than some of the kings we've had,' Joan retorted. 'King Richard had his nephews murdered. King Edward had his women. King Henry before him was mad. I rest my case.'

'We don't know that King Richard had his nephews murdered, Mother,' Tom put in. 'It's mere gossip.'

'Then where are they?' she retorted.

'I don't know,' he had to admit. 'Maybe they are still in the Tower.'

'It's unlikely,' Uncle Edmund said. 'I personally believe that they were murdered. What choice did Richard have? They were always a threat to him.'

'But the rumours that he killed them were a worse threat,' a town councillor said. 'They lost him vital support.'

'Well, I hope this new King will bring stability to England,' Edmund replied. 'But with all this talk of a pretender, who knows what will happen?'

'There wouldn't be any talk if Elizabeth of York was queen,' Joan declared.

'Hush your mouth, woman,' Robert muttered. 'You're not qualified to have an opinion.'

Tom was growing weary of the conversation. He liked what he had heard of Henry VII and wished him well. It was a view not shared by many at Magdalen, for the late King Richard had been a friend to the college – and generous. But one could not judge him on that alone, Tom felt. And Magdalen had already benefited from King Henry's bounty.

Anyway, the talk had drifted away from the reason why they were all gathered here – his own achievement. It was time to bring it back.

'Magdalen is now one of the richest colleges in Oxford,' he said.

'Its library is splendid, thanks to the beneficence of Bishop Wayneflete. He was much mourned when he died this year, and I have many reasons to be grateful to him.'

'You'll miss university life, Tom,' his mother said.

'Not at all,' he smiled, 'for I am going back to take my Master of Arts degree. It's all arranged. If, of course, Uncle, you can continue to support me?'

Mother had looked a little crestfallen, but Father rose splendidly to the occasion. 'Of course, my boy. You must capitalise on your success.'

'Indeed you must,' Uncle Edmund added. 'One day, I feel sure, the name of Wolsey will be famous. We're all counting on you, Tom.'

Tom smiled, contented again. 'Thank you, Uncle. I will try to live up to your expectations.'

It was after midnight when they returned to the inn, with Father staggering along the cobbled street and Mother tutting her disapproval. 'I don't like the boys seeing you like this, husband!'

'Oh, shut your mouth,' Robert slurred.

Once inside the building, William disappeared upstairs. Mother huffed off to the kitchen. Tom declined his father's offer of a nightcap and climbed the stairs himself, wincing when they creaked, for he was sure that Rob would be asleep. But when he entered the chamber they shared, the candle was still burning and he could see, in the light of the dancing flame, his brother's staring eyes.

'Father! Mother!' he cried out. 'Come quickly!'

He would never forget his mother's screams when she saw the lifeless body of her firstborn.

Of course, he could not return to university until after the funeral. When he did get back, he was glad to meet up with those of his fellow bachelors who were staying on with him. In their nightly forays to the inns and stews of Oxford, which often ended in their returning to college after the doors were locked, then having to scale the wall to get in, he could forget his grief, forget the memory of his brother's pale, shrunken body lying in the bed.

Chapter 3

1496

Tom read the letter from Master Winter with mounting dismay. He was to come home, for his father was ill. His mother was asking for him.

He stared unseeing through the window of his room, which overlooked the quad. His first concern was that she would expect him to stay in Ipswich and take over from his father, which was the last thing he wanted. He was twenty-five now, and the university was his life. He did not intend it to be so for ever, as he was ambitious and his mind was set on higher things, but he was contented here and had done well, although not as well as he had hoped.

He had gone back to Magdalen College and obtained his Master of Arts degree three years later. Since then, he had remained at the university, continuing his studies in theology, and last year he had been made a fellow of Magdalen.

Yes, he had done well, but it wasn't what he wanted. He longed for advancement, for an outlet for his capabilities in organisation and administration, which could not be given full rein in the rarefied world of the university. His ambition was to gain high public office in some capacity, and the best way to achieve it was through the Church. At eleven, that had seemed the obvious choice, but he had not then been of an age fully to understood what the vows of the priesthood would mean. Now he was a man and had tasted the sweet joys of the flesh. When the students were up, the brothels of Oxford did a brisk trade, of which he had sometimes availed himself. And since his graduation, he had acquired a liking for the finer things in life, through eating with the fellows, who kept a good table and lived in some comfort.

By doing the odd bit of tutoring, and spending some of the money kind Uncle Edmund regularly sent him, he'd been able to afford the occasional good meal in the better kind of inn, and to furnish his spartan room with painted hangings and small items of plate. He did not want to swear vows of chastity, poverty and obedience, did not want to surrender his will to a superior. He had not yet been able to bring himself to take that final step and enter the Church.

But his family clearly longed for him to do so.

'It's what we had you educated for,' his father had said plaintively on his last visit home, and he had looked so old, so diminished, that Tom had felt deep pangs of guilt, especially when he saw Uncle Edmund nodding at him sadly.

'You're past twenty-four now,' he said.

Tom nodded. He was aware that they had expected him to be ordained at twenty-four, the earliest age at which a young man could be accepted into the priesthood.

But it wasn't their life or their decision! And why should his father worry? Tom was confident that, in time, he would attract the interest of an important patron and begin to rise in the world without having to take holy orders. King Henry, by all reports, was keen to promote 'new men', men of ability rather than of noble birth. One day, Tom told himself, that could be him. Why not?

Yet now that prospect seemed to be fading from view. Was he really destined to give up all the pleasures of the world to find some preferment of which his father would approve? And if he refused to become a priest, would he be compelled to come home to spend his days running the inn? Was all his learning destined to go to waste?

His father was bedridden when he got home, his mother tearful and clingy. He was gratified to see that his brother William was running the inn, the farm and the butcher's shop quite competently. His young sister, Bess, was helping their mother keep house. His family didn't need him, and they clearly didn't want him interfering.

He sat beside his father's bed, marvelling at how skeletal this once big, brawny man had become.

'I have made my will,' Robert Wolsey croaked. 'I want to be buried in the churchyard of Our Lady St Mary of Newmarket, beside your brother Robert, and I want the church of St Nicholas to have my painting of the Archangel. Your mother is to have all my lands and goods, and they will come to William on her death. As for you, Tom . . .' He paused to gather his breath. 'You know how I have longed for you to enter the Church, for it is the quickest route to advancement.' Tom's heart plummeted, but his father remained oblivious. 'I have provided that if you be ordained a priest within a year of my death, and sing Masses for me for another year, you shall have for your salary ten marks.' Tom drew in his breath. It was a staggering sum; he had not known that his father had that kind of money or dreamed that he so wanted him to enter the Church. 'And if you will not be a priest,' Robert went on, 'then I have willed that another honest priest shall sing Masses for me and receive payment for it. You must wait for your mother to die before you get any more of my bounty.'

The old voice was fading. A change was coming over the weary features. Thomas jumped up.

'Mother!' he shouted. Then he turned to his father. But it was too late to make any promises.

After the funeral, he went back to Oxford with Joan Wolsey's blessing. He was resolved to defer any decision on joining the priesthood. For now, he would continue to pursue his academic career and study for a doctorate in theology. It was a relief to return to his rooms in the shadow of the rising Magdalen Tower, to get together for convivial dinners with his fellow dons and to exult in the heavenly singing of the choir in the chapel. He did not mind the constant shouts and hammering of the workmen building the new cloister; it would be an oasis of peace once it was finished, although he did wonder if he would still be at Oxford by then.

It was not long before he was offered the post of master of Magdalen College School, which he accepted eagerly because of the opportunities it offered to win patronage, for it was becoming fashionable for the gentry and nobility to send their sons to Oxford. All he needed in order to take that first vital step to a brilliant career was just a single influential patron.

Chapter 4

1498–9

Tom could not sleep. Tomorrow he was going to take the momentous step of entering the priesthood. He was still not sure that he was doing the right thing. His flesh continued to stir with the natural lusts implanted by God. He was unwilling to embrace chastity or poverty, still less obedience, and he often wondered why God required such sacrifices. But this was the way to advancement in the Church – and to claim his father's legacy. The old man would be pleased, he reflected. God would be pleased, even though He must know that His servant was not wholehearted in his commitment. Mother was certainly pleased. She had sent a small gold crucifix on a chain as a gift to mark Tom's ordination. It must have cost her a lot of money, as it contained a piece of the True Cross.

The longed-for patron had never materialised. No noble lord visiting Oxford had looked on the master of their son's school and seen his potential. They must have thought him entrenched in the university, fulfilled by his office and perhaps lacking in ambition. All his efforts to make himself noticed had come to naught. So now here he was, not getting any younger, and with no choice but to take the only road left open to him.

At one point, tears threatened. It was like a bereavement, giving up the old life and surrendering his freedom to a higher authority. With a mighty effort, he controlled himself. He would do what was necessary, put the past behind him and do his best for God. He would try to master his instincts. He suspected, though, that he would be fighting a lost battle.

* * *

He knelt beneath the great chancel arch of St Peter's Church in Marlborough. Before him, framed by the huge stained-glass window through which the March sun was blazing, sat enthroned the Bishop of Lydda, my lord Bishop of Salisbury's suffragan. A laying-on of hands, some fervent prayers, and then the vows he had agonised so long about taking. When he stood up, he did so as the priest his father had wanted him to be.

His ordination made very little difference to his life. Lacking a patron, he had no avenues towards preferment in the Church. He returned to Oxford, where they appointed him the college's bursar. He welcomed the chance to learn more about the administration of the college's funds. He found he was very good at it. As bursar, he got involved with the completing of the great college tower, but then he was accused of misappropriating funds and was dismissed from office. It was unfair and unjust, for he had thought it quite legitimate to use the money for the works, and he had not taken any for himself, as some would have done. It had been an honest mistake, nothing more, and so he had vehemently argued, facing the college authorities across a table. In the end, they had acknowledged his innocence and allowed him to keep his fellowship and his post as master of the school, but the incident left him burning with humiliation. He threw himself into teaching and wrote to every bishop he could think of, urging that he be given some sort of ministry, however minor. He hoped he didn't sound too pleading.

When he received the letter offering him the office of rural dean of Norwich, he was pleased rather than elated. It would bring in a stipend, even if it would not cover him in glory, and his duties would not be onerous, for all he had to do was act as a liaison between the local clergy of the diocese and the Bishop. He could carry that out from Oxford, riding out once or twice a month, or exchanging letters. He would do well, he would make sure of that, and make the Bishop notice him, and then promotion might just, finally, be in his sights.

In the meantime, he went about the college as if he had not a care in the world, taking pains to ensure that no one could see his discomfiture. He hosted dinners in his rooms for his friends and soothed his bruised pride with the occasional whore, not troubling his conscience with remorse. His priestly status had made little difference to his life at Magdalen College, and he was only occasionally called upon to take Mass in the chapel, for there were many fellows in holy orders. Sometimes, he found it hard to remember that he was a priest – and when he did, he felt a sense of disappointment, it seemed that nothing had changed. He was still at the university, stagnating.

Despite everything, Tom enjoyed teaching. It was deeply satisfying to know that he was influencing the minds of the next generation and, indeed, the future ruling classes. For in his charge were various little noble sprigs; some were insufferable spoiled brats, but others had obviously been taught the proper courtesies and deference due to their elders. Among the latter were John, Leonard and George Grey, the three youngest sons of Thomas Grey, my lord Marquess of Dorset. The Marquess, an affable, handsome man with fair hair and a fine reputation as a jouster, was eager to place his trust in Tom. He was a good father, a frequent visitor to the school, and always exhorting his boys to be virtuous and diligent in their learning.

He ranked only second after the mighty Duke of Buckingham among the peers of the realm, yet he treated Tom as an equal. Unlike Buckingham, he could boast no royal blood, for he was merely the son of the late King Edward's widow by her first husband. Yet he was half-brother-in-law to King Henry, and uncle to the royal children. Here, Tom prayed, was the patron he had longed for.

When the Michaelmas term ended in December 1499, the Marquess came in person to Oxford to take his sons home. Having inspected their work, and professed himself delighted with it, he accompanied Tom to his study for a goblet of wine and they fell into easy conversation.

'I'm building myself a great house, Master Wolsey,' his lordship revealed. 'It's in Bradgate Park, in Leicestershire, but the foundations aren't even down yet. The delays are frustrating, but it will be worth the wait, I don't doubt. In the meantime, I've had Astley Castle refurbished, where my lady is busy planning the Christmas festivities.' He smiled. 'I was wondering, would you consider joining us at Astley for Yuletide? The boys, I am sure, would love to have you. You've made quite an impression on them, and I feel I owe you some reward for what you have done for them.'

Here it was, the patronage Tom had longed for.

'It would be an honour,' he said, without hesitation.

As he hurriedly stuffed his clothes into a leather bag, he could barely contain his elation. To be asked to keep Christmas in a lordly household was an honour indeed. Who knew where it might lead?

He made time to dispatch a messenger to Ipswich, where his mother and her second husband were running the farm, having left William in charge of the inn. Bess was now twelve and of marriageable age, but Tom doubted whether she was ready for a husband, being small for her years, and hoped it would be some time yet before one was found for her. He was sorry not to be able to be with his family at Christmas, and he knew his mother would be disappointed, but she would understand, for she had always wanted to see him getting on in life.

That done, he hastened downstairs to join the Marquess's retinue.

Astley Castle wasn't so much a castle as a fortified manor house surrounded by gardens and parkland, all shrouded by snow. It had been a long, arduous journey and Tom was relieved to see flares lighting their way to the big house. He smiled as the boys slid off their horses and raced ahead, whooping, to greet their mother, who was waiting by the mounting block.

After hugging them and kissing her lord, Cecily Bonville, the Marchioness, welcomed Tom warmly. He was a little in awe of her, for she had been famed as the wealthiest heiress in England when Dorset married her, yet there was no false pride in her as she showed him to a bedchamber the likes of which he had never seen. It contained a handsome tester bed with hangings of fine red wool, a capacious carved chest for his belongings, a high-backed chair with an embroidered cushion, and a painting of the Virgin and Child. A ewer of wine and a goblet stood on a small table and there was stained glass in the diamond-paned windows. Warm coals crackled merrily in a brazier. Pulling aside the counterpane, Tom saw that the bed was made up with a soft feather mattress, bleached linen sheets and a plump bolster. Here was luxury indeed! He had never been housed so comfortably.

The castle was even more splendid downstairs. When he joined the family for supper in the great parlour, he could not but marvel at the fine furniture, the tapestries, the gold and silver plate and the plentiful choice fare that was served to him. He thanked God that good manners had been drummed into him, so that he knew how to conduct himself in lordly company.

He had never spent such wonderful days. After the austerity of the university, the feasting, the jollity and the entertainments were balm to his stifled soul. He joined in with the rest as the Yule log crackled merrily on the fire and everyone in the household – masters and servants, with the barriers of rank cast down – threw themselves into the games and festivities. When he saw his three pupils wide-eyed at the sight of their zealous master letting down his guard and romping with the rest, he laughed out loud.

He felt very privileged when the Marquess bade him sit beside him at the high table as if he was the most honoured guest, and talked to him as if they had known each other for years.

'I have not always been in high favour at court,' he told Tom, 'and I'm not sure that I even am now!' He laughed self-deprecatingly. 'Everything seemed set fair for me when the Queen my mother was married to King Edward. But when he died and King Richard usurped the throne, I felt I had to take some action, because of the way he disparaged my mother and declared my half-brothers bastards.'

'And did worse, if rumour speaks truth,' Tom ventured.

The Marquess bent to his ear. 'I believe it does, and that he had the boys murdered in the Tower. It was regicide, no less! That was why I joined the Duke of Buckingham in rebellion against Richard. When that failed, I fled across the sea to Brittany to the Earl of Richmond, our present King Henry of happy fame. No one rejoiced more than I did when the usurper was killed at Bosworth Field and Richmond took the crown. And I rejoiced too when he married my half-sister Elizabeth.'

'As did we all.' Tom nodded. 'I was but fifteen, yet I well remember the celebrations in Oxford.'

The Marquess refilled their goblets and sighed. 'Alas, the King is a suspicious man, and he made it clear early on that he does not trust me. He had me imprisoned when the pretender Lambert Simnel made his bid for the throne – as if I would have done or countenanced anything to displace my sister! Even after I was freed, I was required to give guarantees of my loyalty to the King and make my son Thomas his ward.'

'But you have prospered since,' Tom observed, flattered to be discussing such important matters with a great peer of the realm.

'I have indeed.'

'Then, my lord, that is all that should matter now.'

The Marquess clapped him on the back. 'Do you know, Master Wolsey, you speak truth!'

That Christmas, surrounded by the good cheer and luxury of a noble establishment, Tom felt a deep inner yearning to live in such splendour. For a moment, no more, he could see himself presiding over such a household, then had to laugh at his presumption. But as he chatted to his host, he could not help but wonder if the Marquess was preparing to extend to him his patronage. If not, he surely had influential contacts at court. Would he be willing to approach them on Tom's behalf? Would it be appropriate to ask? Why not? Whatever he did, it must wait until Christmas had passed. For now, he was going to enjoy himself!

Chapter 5

1500–1

'I am well contented with the way you have tutored my sons,' Dorset said on the last evening of Tom's visit. Twelfth Night had been riotously celebrated, and now the decorations were down and the new year already felt flat.

Tomorrow morning, Tom would be departing for Oxford, and so far nothing had been said about opportunities for preferment. Now he was seated at table with the Marquess and Marchioness, the board had been cleared and the cards and dice lay before them. Soon, there would be no time left for him to make his suit.

'It is an honour,' he said. 'My lord—'

But Dorset interrupted him. 'Indeed! You have pleased me so well that I wish to reward you.'

Tom's heart began to beat faster.

'I have a benefice in my gift, the parish of Lymington, which is currently vacant, and I would like you to have it, Master Wolsey, in reward for your diligence. When my boys go to school in the Michaelmas term, they will have a new teacher, for you shall be installed as rector of Lymington. It's a pleasant living, for it is a prosperous market town in the New Forest and St Thomas's Church is right in the centre. There's an annual fair and the coast is nearby, so it's a busy port. You will be comfortable there, I have no doubt, and having your own parish will give you the independence you lack at Oxford.'

It was not what Tom wanted. He yearned for a place at court, to be at the centre of things, to have a role in which he could use to the full his knowledge, his talents and his administrative skills. Stuck out at

Lymington, far from London, he would have little chance of making the contacts that were so vital to his ambitions.

He made himself smile and thank his beaming patron profusely. Then he knocked back the rest of his wine to drown his disappointment.

'With your leave, my lord, I must go to my room and pack, for I have an early start tomorrow.'

He fled upstairs, feeling dangerously near to tears.

Life resumed its usual monotonous course. He taught, he studied, he made two journeys home to Ipswich, saying nothing about Lymington, for he knew his family would urge him to take it – and be pleased for him. He burned with frustration. He even thought about turning down the Marquess's offer, reasoning that he stood a better chance of getting the preferment he wanted at Oxford. Yet how long had he been here now, since his graduation? Fourteen years, and not a patron in sight until now. He would be better off going to Lymington and proving how capable he was. It might fortune that the Bishop of Bath and Wells would take notice of him and offer him something more suited to his abilities. Tom was not a vain man, but he knew his worth.

The months dragged by, but finally it was October. He left Oxford with few regrets; he had been there too long and regretted wasting his young years living an almost monkish existence. He had enjoyed his studies, and teaching, but it was time to move on. He had been honing his administrative skills in running the school, and was itching to put them into practice in a wider capacity. He bade farewell to his colleagues and his pupils with a light heart, and set off on his way south, his possessions bundled up on a sumpter mule that dutifully trotted behind his horse. The weather was fair, the leaves turning all kinds of glorious shades of red or gold. Despite his reservations, he felt a sense of anticipation.

The Marquess had been right. Lymington was a comfortable parish. Once he had been instituted as rector and shown the ropes of his new living, Tom was able to look around himself with some satisfaction. The rectory was well appointed and spacious, standing in pretty gardens near the church. That was a fine edifice, thanks to the bounty of the pious dead who lay entombed within it. He found he enjoyed taking services, administering the sacraments, getting to know his parishioners, charming the chief among them – even the stern sheriff, Sir Amyas Paulet – and winning their trust. He began tutoring their sons for a small fee. Soon, he began to realise that getting on in life was not all about preferment to high office, but also about helping people, particularly at times of crisis, and making them aware of God's love.

Sitting at his desk by the latticed window, he wrote to the Bishop, trying without boasting to inform him that he had improved the living and was running it efficiently. Yet still he craved advancement.

Tom had been at Lymington for nearly a year when a letter arrived. He read it in disbelief. The Marquess of Dorset, his good patron, had departed this life. The news gave him a jolt and left him feeling rudderless. Trying to get his head together, he took stock of his situation. Much depended, of course, on whether the new Marquess was disposed to look kindly on him. He prayed that would be the case, as the young man was a prominent courtier and could do much for him. Besides, Tom had nowhere else to go.

He was in turmoil. He could not quieten his anxieties. Needing some distraction, he threw on his cloak and went out. The autumn fair was in progress and the town was busy. He wandered among the stalls, his ears assailed by sellers crying their wares, the lowing of the cattle brought for sale, and the hubbub of the crowds. He pushed through them, unheeding of their greetings and the surprise on their faces when he ignored them. He had rarely felt so low. Was he destined for ever to strive for preferment and not be given it? Had all those years at university been in vain?

The smell of fried fish from a pan over a fire made him feel sick. At the stall where a vintner was selling fine wines from France, he paused to accept a small cup to taste. It was strong and heady, and immediately made him feel better, so he paid for a large goblet and downed it in a few gulps. Then he had another, and another. Dabbing his mouth and feeling a satisfying sense of well-being, with his troubles now seeming insignificant, he began to make his way back to the rectory, none too steadily. Weaving through the throng, he found himself bumping into people, who turned irately, then stared when they recognised him.

He did not see the stone in the road that sent him flying. What he did see as he crouched there on stinging knees, his cassock covered in dust, was a pair of leather boots. His eye travelled upwards to find that the figure looming over him was none other than a glowering Sir Amyas Paulet.

'Shame on you!' he growled. 'Call yourself a priest? You're a disgrace. My lord Marquess will hear about this!'

'No, I pray you,' Tom begged, hauling himself to his feet, instantly sober. 'I will lose my living.'

'It's no more than you deserve,' barked Sir Amyas.

'I just heard that his old lordship had died,' Tom gabbled. 'I was so downcast I chose to drown my sorrows, but I am not used to strong wine. I beg your forgiveness, and all of yours.' He spoke to those who had gathered to stare. He felt utterly humiliated.

Sir Amyas was impervious. 'It is unbecoming in one of your calling to behave in such a gross manner. I will not let this go unpunished.'

He summoned the constable, and, to his mortification, Tom was hauled back to the marketplace and clapped in the stocks, his abasement complete. The shoppers closed in around him, some of them jeering. But others had heard what he had said to Sir Amyas and they were having none of it.

'Give the poor man some grace!' cried one. 'He wasn't to know how potent the wine was. It could happen to any of us.'

'Aye,' chimed in the vintner. 'It is strong. I wish now I'd warned him.'

'He's a good man, Father Wolsey,' a woman declared angrily to Sir Amyas, who was standing sentinel by the stocks. 'He takes care of our souls unstintingly and he teaches our children.'

'It's not Christian to treat him like this!' cried another.

Sir Amyas was seen to be wavering. The mood of the crowd was getting ugly. Someone threw a piece of offal, not at Tom in the stocks, as would have been expected, but at the sheriff himself, who stared aghast at the bits of gristle adorning his fine black gown.

He turned to the constable. 'Release him,' he snapped. 'And you, Rector, go home and remember well the lesson I taught you!'

As Tom was set free, the people cheered, even those who had booed him at first.

He was never more pleased to reach the sanctuary of his house. Leaning against the front door, he felt his heart pounding as indignation vied with embarrassment in his mind. He would have a nasty headache later, he knew. One day, he vowed, he would get even with Sir Amyas Paulet.

Chapter 6

1502

Tom had not needed to worry. The new Marquess evidently never learned of the events at the fair. In fact, he must have had good reports of Tom, for he proved as good a patron as his father had been. But advancement, strangely enough, did not come through him. It came from Oxford, where one of the fellows, meeting the Archbishop of Canterbury when the Primate visited Magdalen College, learned that his Grace was looking for a new chaplain, and recommended his industrious old friend, Father Wolsey. Soon, Tom was catapulted to the centre of national affairs, dividing his time between Canterbury and Lambeth Palace. He was able to make only the occasional visit to Lymington, which he was entitled to retain. It was not unusual for a priest who held more than one church office to be absent, and he soothed his conscience – which was nagging him for virtually abandoning his loyal flock – by telling himself that his new duties were far more important. Not only was he serving as spiritual adviser to the Archbishop, but he was also playing an active part in dealing with the many administrative matters that came to his attention.

He liked the amiable Archbishop Henry Deane immensely. Deane was sixty, twice Tom's age, but he was an Oxford man and they had much in common, although the Archbishop had studied law rather than theology. Like Tom, he had come from a modest background, but he had risen through the clerical ranks to enjoy a distinguished career in politics, and had only recently been consecrated to the highest position in the English Church. He was highly regarded by the King, who had made him Lord Keeper of the Privy Seal.

Tom was in awe of this formidably able, yet humble, man, for whose soul he was now responsible. He watched and took note as Deane set vigorously about his administrative duties, and learned a great deal from scrutinising the plans for his many building projects. What must it be like to have the means to accomplish such works, and to live in extravagant splendour, as the Archbishop did? Tom could not suppress pangs of envy. Yet he owed Deane much, especially when, in March, he was taken to the court at Westminster and presented to the King himself. He thought himself in Heaven as he entered the presence chamber and saw the monarch enthroned at the far end. This was where he wanted – and was destined, he was sure – to be.

On first sight, King Henry VII was unimpressive. He was tall and gaunt, with wispy grey hair and suspicious eyes. A monkey sat on his shoulder. 'Father Wolsey,' he said in a dry voice, 'I have been hearing good things about you. If my lord Archbishop can ever bear to part with you, there will be a post for you here at court.'

Tom took just a moment to craft his reply. 'I thank your Grace,' he murmured. 'Truly, I would be torn, for I know not where else I would ever find two such distinguished patrons.'

'You have a honeyed tongue,' the King commented, smiling at last. 'Are you a flatterer, Father Wolsey?'

Tom felt himself flush. 'I should hope not, your Grace. I ask only to serve where I am best needed.'

'Such humility is rare,' the King observed.

'Father Wolsey is a talented and able man, indefatigable in getting things done,' the Archbishop told him.

'I am sure he would have been useful in assisting you in negotiations for this Treaty of Perpetual Peace we have just signed, and with arrangements for the two royal weddings.'

'Aye, Sire. His help would have been invaluable.'

Tom knew all about the treaty, which it was hoped would bring a lasting peace between England and Scotland. It had been sealed in January by the marriage of the King's daughter, the Princess Margaret, to King James IV. He wished he could have been involved in those negotiations, and with the arrangements for the wedding of Arthur, Prince of Wales, the heir to the throne, to the Spanish Infanta, Katherine of Aragon, which had been lavishly celebrated, by all accounts, last November. He perceived that these alliances were triumphs of diplomacy, and burned to know more about how such treaties were negotiated and formulated. He felt sure that, in bringing his own organisational skills to the table, he could be more than useful in a diplomatic role.

The King rose from his throne and beckoned them into a window embrasure, where they could be more private, away from the ranks of courtiers who thronged the presence chamber. 'The Prince is not well,' he said in a low voice. 'Frankly, I am worried by the reports sent to me from Ludlow Castle by his physician.'

The Archbishop crossed himself devoutly. 'I will pray that he is soon restored to health, Sir. Remember, he is in God's keeping.'

Tom wondered what was wrong with Prince Arthur. He had heard no rumour that the youth was ill.

'He has need of your prayers,' the King said, his eyes suddenly brimming. 'They say he has consumption. He has become like a skeleton.'

Deane shook his head. 'Let us hope they are wrong. He is such a promising young man.'

Tom knew he must make his presence felt. 'I feel for your Grace and the Queen,' he said. 'I too will pray daily for the Prince, and if there is anything else I can do to help, I will do it most willingly.'

'I thank you,' the King said. 'I will remember your kindness.'

They spoke of other, less sensitive matters, and then the audience was over. The Archbishop and Tom bowed and departed, passing through galleries hung with beautiful tapestries. One day, Tom vowed to himself, this magnificent world would be his.

Passing a stone-mullioned window, he saw a garden below, in which sat two children, looking at a book: a big, handsome, robust boy and an exquisitely pretty little girl.

'The King's younger children,' Deane told him. 'That's Prince Henry, the Duke of York, and the Princess Mary. If, God forfend, anything ill befalls Prince Arthur, Henry is next in line.'

Tom peered down at the boy. There was something about him, an innate vitality, even at rest. And when he laughed, the effect was charming. A son to be proud of, he thought, and felt a pang because he would have liked such a son himself.

On the boat back to Lambeth, he thought about matters of the flesh. He had not kept himself chaste these past years. He had broken his vow of celibacy several times, but the women involved had been no more than passing fancies. He had used them, he had to admit. What else was a virile man of thirty supposed to do? He still thought the vow of chastity to be an abomination. It was ridiculous to expect men to abstain from indulging the natural instincts implanted by God, ridiculous to deny them a family and children. And so many churchmen did not deny themselves, that much he had learned. He knew of bishops who kept mistresses and called their bastards their nephews. No one was fooled.

It would be better all round, he thought, if priests were allowed to marry. That might sound like blasphemy, but it would give them a better understanding of the human condition and put paid to illicit fornication. Yet he doubted that the Church would ever come around to that way of thinking. And even if it did, he knew no woman he might want to marry. None of those he had known in the biblical sense had stirred his heart.

When he looked in the chipped mirror he used for shaving, he saw a plump-cheeked, pleasant-faced fellow with large wide-set eyes, full, sensuous lips and – to his dismay – the beginnings of a double chin, the result of too much overindulgence in good food and wine. But he liked his food; it was one of life's great pleasures, and if the price of enjoying it was an expanding waistline, so be it. There was no one to nag him or criticise, no woman for whom he wanted to look good naked.

He glanced at the Archbishop, sitting beside him in the boat. What would Deane say if he knew what his chaplain was thinking? A cleric of the old school, he might be shocked, but Tom doubted it. It would be the near-heresy that shocked him, not lustful thoughts. Deane was too much a man of the world to be outraged by those, for he had confessed to having had them himself.

They climbed out of the boat at Lambeth Stairs and walked through the gardens to the palace. Following on from his earlier thoughts, Tom was conscious of an emptiness within himself, a space that should be filled with love, an emotion he had never truly experienced, aside from his love for his family. But he had been too focused on his ambitions to think much on such things. He had so much else in his life that gave him satisfaction, and further preferment would be coming his way, he was sure of it. No man could have everything he wanted.

Muffled against the February chill, Tom entered the chapel at Lambeth Palace and sat down in his usual place. Unfolding his stole, he kissed it and placed it around his neck. Then he waited. And waited. Where was the Archbishop? He was usually punctual for his confessions, as he was in all matters, which Tom knew well, having served him for more than a year now. They had worked happily together, and Tom was grateful for the experience he had gained in attending to important episcopal affairs, and for the many chances he had been afforded to prove his worth. Deane had often praised his efficiency and his energy in completing tasks.

When the bell chimed the hour, Tom got up, removed the stole and went in search of his master. He found him in his study, slumped over the prayer desk. One searching look told him that Deane was dead.

The funeral was held in Canterbury Cathedral. Tom was there to pay his last respects, his heart heavy. He had existed in a daze of depression since his revered master had died, not just because he grieved for the man himself, but also because he himself had been cut adrift. No replacement for Deane had been chosen, so there was no role for Tom in the archiepiscopal household. It seemed cruel of Fate to have raised him to such a pinnacle for so brief a time, and then to cast him down again. He would have to find another patron, he thought wearily.

But this time it would be different. He moved in different circles now, knew people, had contacts. And it chanced that, as he left the cathedral among the throng of black-clad mourners, he found himself walking next to an elderly well-dressed man whom he did not recognise.

'A beautiful service,' he said courteously.

'Aye, and for a great man,' said his companion. 'And a great loss to England. I wonder who will replace him.'

'The word is that it will be Warham, our new Bishop of London.'

Warham was Master of the Rolls, a diplomat and lawyer who had proved himself useful to the King.

'I've not heard that,' said the older man. 'Are you employed in the Archbishop's household?'

'I was,' replied Tom wistfully. 'I was his Grace's chaplain. Thomas Wolsey at your service, Sir.'

'Wolsey! I've heard of you – good things, I might add.'

'I'm gratified to hear that.'

'It's said that you have a talent for getting things done. Very useful in a chaplain. I'm so sorry, I should have introduced myself. I'm Sir Richard Nanfan. You probably won't have heard of me, as I've been away these past ten years in Calais, where I serve the King's Lord Deputy as treasurer. I've come home on leave, but I'll be going back soon.'

They were approaching the Christchurch Gate. 'It has been a pleasure to meet you, Sir Richard,' Tom said. 'I must go back to my lodging and pack my things, as I have to vacate it tomorrow.'

'Do you have somewhere to go?' the old knight asked kindly.

'Not really. I will probably go back to Lymington and stay there while I decide what to do.' Tom was aware that he sounded downcast. He could not help it.

'I'm surprised that a man of your ability and reputation hasn't been snapped up,' exclaimed Sir Richard.

'It's early days yet,' Tom said. 'No one really knows what is happening.'

'I don't suppose . . . No, I'm sure you wouldn't consider it.' His new friend hesitated.

'Consider what?' Tom was intrigued.

'Well, an important young man like you probably wouldn't want to serve an old fellow like me.' Sir Richard smiled. 'I can't offer you much in the way of preferment, but I am in need of a chaplain, and Calais is as good a place as any in which to live. There, you would certainly attract the attention of Sir Edward Poynings, the Lord Deputy. He is a distinguished man with a long record of service to the Crown, and high in favour with the King.'

Tom was instantly alert. All sorts of possibilities were opening out before him. And going to Calais would be a high adventure, even if it was in a relatively humble capacity. He had always wanted to travel abroad.

'I would be honoured, Sir Richard,' he said, his heart feeling a hundred times lighter.

He had been warned that the English Channel could be rough and unpredictable, but he enjoyed the voyage from Dover, exhilarated by the stately rolling of the ship and intrigued by the misty coastline ahead. The Pale of Calais was not France, but an outpost of England, won from the French a hundred and fifty years earlier in the Hundred Years War.

'This is all we have left of our empire,' said Sir Richard mournfully, coming to stand beside Tom on the forecastle. 'Aquitaine was lost fifty years ago. It galls me to think that after all those battles, the French won in the end and took what was rightfully ours. It seems to me a shame that King Henry has no desire to win it back, but he hates war and will not spend money unless he absolutely has to.'

'I hear what you say,' Tom said, 'but does it not strike you that peace between our two nations is better than any war? I agree with the King, who may quarter the French lilies with his own leopards on his coat of arms, but is clearly too wise and prudent a ruler to press his claim to France by force of arms. The cost can be high in lives too, not just money.'

Sir Richard grinned. 'It's rare to hear an Englishman say that. Most of them long for a return to the glory days and great victories such as Crécy, Poitiers and Agincourt.'

'You speak truth,' Tom agreed, 'but the advantages of peace are manifold. Trade can flourish, and culture. Think of all those marvels that are happening in Italy – the art, the architecture! In Oxford, we were aware of it, and the Archbishop had books of building plans from France, where they are copying Italian models. If war intervened, that would all go out of the window.'

'It will be interesting to see what my Lord Deputy makes of you, Master Wolsey!'

'I look forward to meeting him!'

The towers of the Citadel and, beyond it, the soaring clock tower of the town hall were impressive sights as Tom disembarked with Sir Richard's small retinue before the massive Lantern Gate, the chief entrance to the walled town of Calais. The fortress had stood sentinel here for nearly three hundred years, his patron told him. For miles around the town lay the Pale, the land owned by the kings of England. The harbour in which the ship had docked was packed with vessels of all kinds, with goods being stowed away or unloaded. Tom could now understand why Calais was called the brightest jewel in the English crown.

As they rode through narrow streets lined with fine timbered houses, and market squares bustling with soldiers of the garrison, merchants, traders and townsfolk, Tom saw that the place was prosperous. Soon they came to the imposing palace of the Exchequer, the governor's residence, which stood opposite the beautiful church of St Nicholas. This would be Tom's home for the foreseeable future, and he was pleasantly surprised to find himself allocated a spacious lodging with a comfortable bed with blue woollen hangings. There was even glass in the shuttered windows and a carved bench in front of the fireplace.

He settled quickly into life in Sir Richard's entourage. He took care to serve his master wisely and discreetly, working all hours to prove his worth. For he was more than just a chaplain: before long, his patron realised that he could entrust all kinds of administrative matters to him, and made good use of his financial acumen. Soon, the two men had become firm friends. In some ways, the ageing knight was a father figure, looking to Tom's interests and keeping a benevolent paternal eye on him.

Tom liked Sir Edward Poynings on sight, recognising him as an experienced man of the world, trustworthy and wise. Before long, on Sir Richard's recommendation, he was undertaking duties for Sir Edward too, and being praised for doing them well. It was now taken as read that whenever Sir Richard was a guest at the Lord Deputy's supper table, Tom would be there too.

Tom thrived on their conversation. It was breath of life to him to be privy to such high politics.

'The French have always had their greedy eyes on Calais,' Sir Edward said one evening, as they ate in his ornate dining parlour. 'They are determined to get it back.'

'But that is a vain hope, surely?' said one of the eight guests. 'It is so well defended.'

'In terms of the garrison, yes, but these stout fortifications are expensive to maintain. Those who rule at Westminster may love the glory of holding Calais, but they do not want to pay for the privilege. My budget, alas, is always strained.'

'But surely trade here is thriving?' Tom asked.

'Yes, but a lot of the profits go to the Crown.' His host grimaced.

'Aye,' Sir Richard chimed in. 'If only we could see some of them.'

Tom would have liked to voice the unthinkable, that England would do well to give Calais back to the French and charge them a high price for the favour, but he sensed that would not be welcomed.

The conversation moved on to King Louis and the scandals of the French court.

'At least Calais is no longer being fought over by France and Burgundy,' Sir Richard said.

'No, if only because France now has the duchy of Burgundy. I hear that slippery fox Maximilian of Austria is greatly disgruntled.' Sir Edward turned to explain, although Tom had taken care to learn all he could of the political world on his doorstep. 'He was married to Burgundy's last duchess, and took care to wed his son to Juana of Castile, who may well be queen of Spain if the sovereigns Ferdinand

and Isabella do not provide her with a brother. Of course, the French won't like that! They loathe the Spaniards, always have. And it's said that Juana is unstable.'

'My feeling is that the Spaniards will set her aside in favour of her heir, the Infante Charles,' Sir Richard said.

'Then they'll be making more trouble for themselves,' Tom chimed in, 'since he is but three years old!'

'Ah, but one day he will be a great prince, for he stands to inherit not only Spain, but possibly all the Habsburg territories, and if his grandfather Maximilian becomes Holy Roman Emperor—'

'Which he has been pining for ever since they elected him King of the Romans eighteen years ago,' interrupted Sir Edward. 'And yes, Charles may yet win the Imperial crown.'

Tom listened to their talk, filing away the details. Even here, he was inhabiting the world of kings and emperors. In fact, he was closer to the affairs of Christendom here. Paris was not two hundred miles away, just four days' journey with fast horses. One day, he hoped to visit the city. But for now, he was contented in Calais. He had a kindly patron in Sir Richard and an influential contact in Sir Edward. He could happily bide his time here – for now.

Part Two
'From poverty to plenty'

Chapter 7

1507–8

Tom knelt by the bed, with the Nanfan family on their knees around him. He bent his head and prayed for the soul of Sir Richard, who had just departed this life, emaciated and riddled with a canker. The tears that ran down Tom's cheeks were unfeigned, for he had grown to love the old man in the five years he had served him. He knew that love had been reciprocated and that Sir Richard had fully appreciated his usefulness, his wit, his gravity and his conduct. He had gradually delegated all his duties as treasurer to Tom, and when, in consideration of his great age, he was discharged from office and allowed to return to England to live out his life in quietness, he had taken his beloved chaplain with him and named him his executor.

And that was how, last year, Tom had come to live in the picturesque moated manor house at Birtsmorton in Worcestershire that Sir Richard had built for himself some decades previously. Once more, he had found himself outside the orbit of public affairs. It was frustrating, at thirty-five, when the sands were spilling ever more rapidly through the hourglass, yet he owed a debt of gratitude to his patron and grieved sincerely for him.

Now he was free – again – to follow his own path. As soon as the estate was wound up, he would go home to Ipswich to take stock of his life.

But he was forestalled. Sir Richard had rewarded him beyond his wildest dreams. Tom knew nothing of it until a letter bearing the royal seal arrived at Birtsmorton, so soon after Sir Richard's death that the news must not yet have reached London. The King thanked

Sir Richard for his recommendation. He was indeed in need of a chaplain, and Father Wolsey would be most suitable for the position.

Tom could hardly believe his luck. Despite his grief, his spirits soared. This was what he had been waiting for all his adult life. He was going to court to serve the monarch himself!

The palace of Richmond was new and shining in the sunlight, its gilded pinnacles and onion domes rising above the River Thames like a citadel out of legend. Tom spurred his horse. As he approached the great gatehouse, he was swallowed up in a restless queue of courtiers, clerics, merchants and servants, all waiting to state their business to the guards on duty and be waved through.

When he finally emerged into the broad outer courtyard, an usher was there to greet him and show him to his lodgings. They ascended a stair and walked along a gallery, at the end of which the usher opened an oak door.

'Your rooms, Father,' he said. 'His Grace wishes to see you in his study when you have refreshed yourself. I will wait outside and escort you to him.'

Light from the diamond-paned window flooded the chamber. It contained a table and bench, a chest and a brazier. The walls were whitewashed and there was rush matting on the floor. Tom walked through the open door and discovered a bedchamber with a tester bed and a prayer desk. There was even a privy in the corner, for which he thanked God.

He must not keep the King waiting. He placed his luggage on the bed and washed his face and hands using the ewer of water and basin that had been left for him on the wide windowsill. Then he shrugged off his travelling cloak, hung it on a peg on the wall and dusted down his cassock, adjusting his mother's gold crucifix around his neck. He was ready.

'I bid you welcome, Father Wolsey,' King Henry said. Seated behind a desk laden with ledgers and papers, he looked far more gaunt and shrunken than Tom remembered, yet his manner was amiable.

Tom bowed, then remembered to raise a hand in blessing. The King crossed himself.

'Father Wolsey, I was saddened to hear of the death of my good servant Sir Richard Nanfan. He recommended you most warmly, you know.'

'I am humbled to hear it, your Grace.'

The King regarded Tom searchingly. 'I am sure you need no instruction in your duties as chaplain, but you should know that I hear Mass at seven every morning in my private closet, which is next door to this one, and I make confession once a week on Saturdays. You will attend me in the Chapel Royal on Sundays and feast days. I am told that you are good with administrative matters, so I may require your help as necessary, but otherwise your time is your own, unless I need to consult you on a spiritual matter. The Lord Steward will explain what bouche of court you will get and show you where your horse is stabled.'

It had all sounded straightforward, but . . . 'Your Grace, what is bouche of court?'

To Tom's dismay, the King was seized with a dreadful bout of coughing. It was a harsh, hacking cough that left him with a rasping voice, when he could finally speak. 'It is the daily allowance of bread, ale, meat, wood and coal,' he gasped. 'Stop that, Sir!' This last was addressed to the monkey that had just jumped up on the desk and begun nibbling at the ledger on which its master had been working.

The King batted it away. 'He's a terrible beast. He once ate my account book, much to my courtiers' amusement. They think it unkingly for a monarch to check accounts. They also think I'm a miser, and while there may be some truth in that, Father Wolsey, I believe that being prudent with money brings prosperity to a kingdom – and I know when to spend it when I have to.' He gave a self-deprecating smile. 'Now I am sure you wish to get settled in. I will see you at Mass in the morning.'

Tom bowed. As he left the study, he nearly collided with a gigantic well-dressed youth with handsome features, a Roman nose and long red hair. With him were two black-gowned older men.

'I beg your pardon, Sir,' he said, bowing instinctively, for there was an air of authority and importance in the young man, who could not have been more than sixteen or seventeen.

'No matter.' He smiled at Tom. 'The Prince of Wales, at your service. Are you my father's new chaplain?'

Tom bowed again. He had not recognised Prince Henry, the former Duke of York, who had become heir to the throne on his brother Arthur's death five years before. The Prince had looked robust then, but he was magnificent now. A son any man would be proud of.

'Yes, your Grace. I am Thomas Wolsey.'

'I wish you well in your new office. You will need it. My father is not a well man, and he was never the easiest of people at the best of times.' The Prince rolled his eyes.

One of the older men frowned. 'Your Grace, we should make haste to the King.'

'Oh, yes,' sighed the boy. 'He wants to see my Latin translations. Well, I will challenge him to find fault with them. Aristotle himself couldn't have done better!'

With that he was off, barging into the study. As Tom hastened away, he heard the King's dry voice saying, 'Now go out and come back in again properly, boy!'

His new duties placed him firmly at the very centre of affairs. He saw King Henry daily, first when he said Mass for him in his private closet, and sometimes later if his Grace wanted advice on a moral or spiritual matter, and these meetings became more frequent as Henry increasingly opened his heart to Tom in confession. Soon, their conversations began to focus on politics.

'You have a fresh approach, Thomas,' the King would say, having taken to using Tom's Christian name as they became more familiar with each other. Tom could not quite believe that he was sitting in the King's study discussing the situation in Europe or taxation in England – or that, in confession, he had the power to influence his sovereign's thinking.

He could have spent the rest of his time in idleness; instead he used it to cultivate the friendship of the principal members of the King's Council, especially those most in favour with the monarch, and in particular Dr Foxe, Bishop of Winchester, Secretary of State and Lord Privy Seal, and Sir Thomas Lovell, Master of the King's Wards and Constable of the Tower of London. He took care to seek out their opinions and advice, and even ventured to ask them to dine with him, invitations they gladly accepted. As he presided over a table set with silver plate and the choicest food he could afford, he could sense that these eminent men clearly appreciated and enjoyed his company, his conversation and his wisdom. And he learned from them, for they were willing to pass on valuable lessons in statecraft and opinions on the King's other advisers. As time went by, they lowered their guard and confided to him state secrets – even going so far as to confess their fears about the King's declining health. Tom listened gravely, taking care to let them know that his discretion was inviolable.

'His Grace cannot live long,' Foxe murmured. 'That cough is dreadful. I fear it could be consumption.'

An image of his dead brother came immediately to Tom's mind. He banished it resolutely. 'Isn't that what carried off Prince Arthur?' he asked.

'Aye,' Lovell replied, 'but I hope the King survives until the Prince attains manhood.'

'If only he didn't keep the boy so sheltered,' Foxe said.

'He fears him. Young Henry is suggestible. Put an idea in his head, and you'll never get it out. And there are those who would be only too willing to pour sedition into his ear.'

Dr Foxe sighed. 'The King is not popular, so it is not surprising that there are those who wish to see his son on the throne. There is much resentment against his forced loans – or benevolences, as he likes to call them.'

'We can thank Sir Richard Empson and Edmund Dudley for those. His Grace will not listen to the opinions of his other councillors when it comes to raking in money and taxes.'

'That is why he is so rich,' Tom observed, having been absorbing all this with interest. Knowledge was power – you could never have too much of it. 'I see now why the King keeps his heir so closely supervised.'

When he went to the door of his lodging to bid his guests farewell, he saw Thomas Larke on the landing. Tom got on well with the other royal chaplains, especially Larke, a highly cultivated and respected colleague who also hailed from the eastern shires. Their families knew each other distantly, for the Larkes had business interests throughout the region. Larke smiled and disappeared into his chamber.

'There goes a sound man,' Dr Foxe said. 'His Grace is blessed in his chaplains. And you ought to be preferred to greater things, Father Wolsey.'

'I have no doubt that you will be before too long,' chimed in Lovell.

'If God wills,' Tom said, deeply gratified. 'I bid you goodnight, gentlemen.'

Knowing that Tom had time on his hands, Foxe made him his secretary, a post Tom could easily combine with his duty to the King. Sage and learned, the Bishop was also a Magdalen man who came from yeoman stock, so they had much in common.

'We are lucky,' he told Tom as they took a brief stroll in the palace gardens after dinner, cassocks flapping in the late-spring breeze. 'The King prefers new men like us to the nobility. He does not trust the peers, and has banned them from keeping private armies, as they did in the time of the late wars between Lancaster and York. He will not risk them rising against him or succouring his enemies, such as those who have aspirations to the throne. He has suffered enough from pretenders.'

Tom nodded knowingly. While he was at university, it had seemed there was a constant threat from men who claimed to be scions of the late House of York, which had been overthrown at Bosworth.

'His Grace is ready and eager to favour men of ability, whatever their backgrounds,' the Bishop was saying. 'Men like you, with dedication, industry and a willingness to take on onerous tasks. Yes, you have come to court at the right time, Father Wolsey.'

* * *

As the months passed, it seemed to Tom that he went from strength to strength. He strove to be prodigiously thorough, hard-working and indispensable, and it paid off. In February 1508, the King rewarded him for his diligent and faithful service with the deanery of Lincoln.

'It is the next best thing to being made a bishop,' Sir Thomas Lovell said, congratulating him over a good dinner in Dr Foxe's rooms.

'And that will be next, mark my words,' Foxe added. 'I have never seen a man grow so rapidly in royal esteem and in authority. Father Wolsey, I shall recommend you for the office of royal almoner. His Grace has need of one, and the duties are not too demanding. You would be responsible for distributing the King's charity to the poor.'

Within a week, the post was Tom's. He was now Dean of Lincoln and Master Almoner.

Evidently the King was impressed with his grasp of politics and his diplomatic potential, because in March he sent him to Scotland. The Treaty of Perpetual Peace had failed to realise its objective, which Tom thought sad, and now there was talk that King James wanted to revive Scotland's Auld Alliance with France.

'Remind him that he is wed to England,' King Henry exhorted. 'Persuade him to abandon his pursuit of France. We do not want a war on two fronts.'

'I will do my best, Sir,' Tom promised, delighted to be chosen for this crucial mission.

It was a long and weary trek up to Edinburgh, and once he and his small party were past York, they were obliged to hire local guides to escort them through wild and lawless border country. The roads were terrible and ill-kept, the inns few and far between, and often insalubrious, and it was well-nigh impossible to communicate with men whose dialect was incomprehensible. Tom was heartily glad to reach the Scottish capital – only to be told that King James was at Stirling Castle. His shoulders sagged with frustration.

When he did finally catch up with the King and managed to have a conversation with him, he was impressed by the man's broad knowledge and his diverse interests. But James would not be moved on the matter of the French alliance.

'It is regrettable, Sir, that two neighbouring kingdoms cannot be friends,' Tom observed sadly.

'It has ever been so.' James sounded resigned. 'Scotland has always suffered from England's aggression.'

'But King Henry offers you friendship. He is eager for it. Your Grace is, after all, his son-in-law.'

'His friendship comes with conditions. He treats me as a junior partner. It is not to be borne. No, Master Almoner, I will not change my mind, but I appreciate your efforts to bring about a peace.'

Tom could do no more. He had learned that there were times when you just had to accept defeat.

Before he left Stirling, he sought an audience of the young Queen Margaret, King Henry having charged him to enquire after her health. She received him warmly, avid for news of home. She was pretty, with a round face and a wealth of auburn hair, but he sensed that she was not happy. All her babies had died, and she was probably aware of her husband's many mistresses, for the gossip had reached England and probably beyond the sea. But at least Tom would be able to tell her father that she was in good health.

He returned south burdened with a sense of failure, but King Henry was philosophical. 'If anyone could have prevailed with James, it would have been you, Thomas. If you couldn't succeed, no one could. He's as slippery as an eel.' He burst out coughing, and when the fit subsided, it left him breathless.

'Sir, have you consulted your physicians about that cough?' Tom ventured.

'Yes,' the King croaked, and for a moment the mask slipped. 'It's a consumption of the lungs, just like Arthur had. I know I am not long for this world. And that brings me to a subject I need to discuss. My son Harry.'

Tom was not surprised. He knew about the friction between the King and his heir. 'Would your Grace like to make confession?' he asked.

'No – maybe later. But the boy is impossible. Always chafing at the bit. He wants to rule; he covets my crown. And he makes it clear that, when he is king, he will do things his way. All my careful housekeeping will be overthrown. He needs to be curbed, and today I told him so. He was so disrespectful that I seized my dagger and I fear I would have killed him had not his tutors restrained me. I don't know who was the more shocked, Harry or me. Of course, I feel bad about it now.'

Tom hesitated. 'Sir, forgive me for speaking out, but you keep the Prince cloistered, like a girl. No one can access his chamber except through your privy apartments. Whenever I see him, he is always with his tutors. It is not a healthy life for an energetic and intelligent seventeen-year-old. He is bound to feel frustrated. And young men of his age are prone to rebelling against authority anyway. The Prince needs an outlet for his energies and his talents. If your Grace could perhaps allow him more freedom, that might go a long way to restoring harmony between you.'

The King was frowning, and Tom feared he had gone too far. But when Henry spoke, there was pain in his voice. 'Thomas, I have but the one son left to me. Should I lose him, and die without an heir, there would be a return to civil war, since so many descendants of the House of York have a claim to the throne. So I have to take every precaution to keep Harry safe – and that means saying no to him when he wants to go jousting and indulge in other dangerous sports.' He sighed. 'It grieves me, but is regrettably a necessity. And I understand why he resents the constrictions.'

'Maybe if he were to be married, matters would improve. It would give him a sense of responsibility.' The Prince had been betrothed to his brother's widow, Katherine of Aragon, for years, and still there was no wedding in view. Tom had seen the Princess and her ladies about the court from time to time, all of them dressed in shabby, threadbare clothes. She always looked forlorn.

King Henry rose and started to pace the room. 'Alas, even that path is closed to me. The Princess Katherine's father, King Ferdinand, has failed to pay her dowry, and she has sold some of the gold and silver plate that was meant to form part of it. Until that matter is resolved, the marriage cannot go ahead, but Ferdinand is proving monstrously uncooperative.' He sat down abruptly, coughing again.

Tom tried again. 'Maybe giving the Prince his own household would resolve the conflict between you. It would give him some autonomy as he comes to manhood.'

The King buried his face in his hands. 'Everything you say is true, Thomas. But the truth is, I do not trust Harry. He is eager for a crown and highly impressionable. He has charm and the common touch, whereas I am hated because my policies do not bring glory to England in the field of battle, and the price of peace and prosperity is high taxation. My fear is that unscrupulous persons will use Harry to topple me. So I must keep him under my eye, lest mischief ensue. But,' he wheezed, raising red-rimmed eyes, 'it will not be for long. Soon, everything he desires will be his.'

Tom felt the King's pain. 'I am sure that the Prince truly loves your Grace and that he would do nothing to undermine you.'

Henry gave him an odd look, as if implying that Tom was naïve if he believed that, but he said no more, apart from bidding him keep the matter confidential.

Tom was astonished when, one autumn morning at Richmond, the King suddenly announced, 'I have a mind to marry again.'

Only yesterday, he had been speaking again of dying.

'It would make sense,' he went on. 'I could forge a foreign alliance and get myself more sons.'

'It would indeed,' Tom said. 'Who does your Grace have in mind?'

'Margaret of Austria, Regent of the Netherlands; the Emperor Maximilian's daughter. By all accounts, she is a splendid woman, capable of ruling as well as a man, and accomplished in learning and other qualities.'

Tom had heard all this too. The Archduchess was renowned for her intelligence and her wise rule. There was a portrait of her in one of the palace galleries, which showed her with stolid Flemish features, full lips and laughing eyes. Rumour had it that she had worn out the second of her three deceased husbands in the marriage bed. What would she make of the ailing and ageing King Henry?'

Tom was flattered to be chosen to go Flanders to solicit Maximilian's consent to the match and negotiate a marriage contract. He was grateful to Foxe and Lovell for suggesting him for the mission.

'His Imperial Majesty is currently staying near Calais,' the King explained, handing Tom a safe-conduct. He proceeded to outline the aim of the mission. 'It is because of your wit and integrity that I am entrusting you with it. Be sure to make good speed and repair to me as soon as possible.'

'Very good, your Grace.' Tom was determined to prove to King Henry just how useful and efficient he could be.

At noon, he boarded a boat to London, where he caught the four o'clock barge to Gravesend, making good speed thanks to a prosperous tide and wind. He was in Gravesend within three hours, and stayed only as long as it took to provide himself and his new servant, William, with post horses, which were readily available at the dock. They raced for Dover as if the hounds of Hell were at their heels, arriving early the next morning. Tom thanked God that he needed so little sleep.

At Dover, a ship bound for Calais was waiting with its sails unfurled, so he leapt aboard and paid his fare. By noon, he was in Calais, whence he galloped to Maximilian's lodging outside the town. When he arrived, he asked if the Emperor would see him urgently, as he came on the King of England's business, and was instantly granted an audience.

The Holy Roman Emperor cut an extraordinary figure, with his mass of long blonde hair, his great hooked nose and his lavish gown of black and yellow.

'Master Almoner, you are most welcome,' he said warmly, speaking in French. 'I will always make time for an emissary of the King of England, for whom I have such a great affection.'

His smile did not waver when Tom conveyed King Henry's

proposal of marriage to his daughter. 'We would be overjoyed to have his Majesty as a son-in-law. I will put the proposal to the Archduchess, and we will consider it favourably, I assure you.'

The audience lasted for fifteen minutes. Tom emerged into the sunlight, not having expected to have fulfilled his mission so quickly and with what looked to be a happy outcome. He was eagerly anticipating telling King Henry that his business was successfully accomplished.

Without delay, he summoned William, jumped on his horse and rode back to Calais, arriving at dusk to find that his ship was ready to return to England. This time, the crossing was rougher, but he was in Dover by ten o'clock the next morning, and back at Richmond by midnight. Utterly weary, he fell into his bed and slept soundly until it was time to rise for Mass.

The King was just coming out of his bedchamber when Tom arrived at the closet door.

'Aren't you supposed to be in Calais?' Henry barked.

'Sir,' Tom said, 'if it pleases your Highness, I have already been with the Emperor and dispatched your affairs, I trust to your Grace's satisfaction.'

He related to the King what had passed at the audience.

Henry gaped at him, then quickly collected himself. 'We give you our princely thanks for your good and speedy exploit. Now you must take your rest. You can return here after dinner to tell me about your embassy. I will summon another chaplain to take Mass.'

Tom felt too restless to sleep, so he ate breakfast then sought out his friends, Foxe and Lovell, waiting for them outside the council chamber. They congratulated him on how quickly he had accomplished his mission.

'His Grace has already mentioned it to us,' Foxe told him. 'He thinks it a wonderful achievement and praised you most highly.'

'And that praise reflects on us,' beamed Lovell, 'because we recommended you to his Grace for this. He will not forget what you have done.'

That afternoon, King Henry bade Tom go before the Council, and sat nodding appreciatively as he related the details of his meeting with the Emperor. Afterwards, the lords gathered round to commend him.

'I would have thought such an expedition to be almost beyond the capacity of any man!' exclaimed the Earl of Surrey.

Tom barely slept that night. He could not stop thinking of the King's delighted reaction when he said he was back already from Calais. He had a strong feeling that further promotion would soon be in store for him.

He was right. Soon afterwards, Henry appointed him Dean of Hereford, Registrar of the Order of the Bath and a canon of St George's Chapel in Windsor Castle. Suddenly, his workload was greater, but he did not complain. He was not afraid of hard work or of delegating. What he wanted was power – and everything that went with it.

Chapter 8

1509

There was no more talk of the Archduchess. The King was lying ill at Richmond. His health had deteriorated over Christmas and there was much covert speculation at court that he would not last until the spring. He was thin and drawn, and Tom found it painful to witness him coughing so violently that there was blood on the kerchief afterwards. He had grown fond of the old fox, learned how to gauge Henry's temper and meet his expectations. You could almost have said that they had become friends, if kings ever made friends with mere mortals.

But the pragmatic soul in Tom also realised that he must look to the future, and that meant cultivating the favour of the next king – no easy task, since the Prince remained as inaccessible as ever. When he did encounter him, Tom took care to make himself as pleasant as possible. He did not want young Harry lumping him together with his father's other advisers. The King had confided that he and his son had clashed over policy and those who helped to formulate it. The Prince had urged him to get rid of the unpopular councillors Empson and Dudley, but his father had told him it was no concern of his.

Tom had been appalled to hear, though, that Harry had never been allowed to see a single state paper. He would have challenged the King on this, but for the fact that it would have been evident that he was thinking of a time when his master would be no more. All he could do was intimate to the Prince that he would be at his service should he need him.

Rain lashed the window of Tom's chamber overlooking the courtyard at Richmond. He sat at his desk, staring at the letter that had just been delivered. It had been sent by his stepfather.

His mother was dying; she was asking for him.

He had long felt guilty for rarely making the time to travel to Ipswich to visit her, and he longed to see her just one more time before death claimed her, yet he was deeply loath to leave court just now, with the King's health so precarious. He dared not risk being absent when the monarch died. It was imperative that he was at court to support the new King, and that he was not left out when there was the anticipated redistribution of offices. Moreover, it was April and very wet. The roads had turned to quagmires. Progress would be slow. How cruel of Fate to present him with this dilemma at such a time! Yet he could not ignore his mother's plea.

In the end, duty – and love – triumphed over inclination.

Soon, with the trusty William in attendance, he was riding north to Suffolk, wrapped in two cloaks, every mile taking him further from where he wanted to be. He felt like screaming with frustration and he had to keep reminding himself that the King had seemed no worse when he had given him leave to depart. God grant that he remained stable, at least for the next week.

When Tom reached the farm, William and Bess embraced him with welling eyes, and he knew to expect the worst. He climbed the stairs to the best bedchamber and was shocked to see his poor mother looking so emaciated. Her chest was heaving and her breath rattled in her throat as she held out her arms with an effort and bade him kiss her.

He bent, tears in his own eyes and guilt washing over him. How could he have neglected her, his gentle, loving mother who had always shown him nothing but kindness? He was suddenly glad that he had come. The court seemed far away now; in fact, it seemed that the world had shrunk to this one candlelit room.

When his stepfather went downstairs to fetch him a mug of ale, Tom sat beside his mother and, at her eager behest, told her of his advancement, his life at court and his friendship with the King. Her old eyes widened, shining with pride.

'I always knew you would make your mark in the world,' she whispered. 'There was something special about you. You have more than fulfilled that early promise. Now I can die happy, my boy.'

Tom bowed his head. His instinct was to say there was no need to talk about dying, but he could not, would not lie to her. Instead, he took her thin hand and stroked it. 'Rest now,' he said. 'I am here.'

She died in the morning, peacefully, as a flower closes its petals at dusk. Tom wept as he said the prayers that would see her into the next world, where he was sure her few sins would be dealt with lightly. Then he went to the church and spoke to the vicar and the sexton, since his stricken stepfather was in no fit state to attend to practicalities.

He stayed a week for the funeral, feeling as if his heart would break as the coffin was lowered into the damp earth. Afterwards, he greeted friends and neighbours who had come to partake of the funeral meats at the farmhouse, people he had not seen in years. Uncle Edmund was there, with several of the Daundys; he had aged, but he was full of plans for the almshouses he intended to build in Ipswich.

'They'll be a permanent monument to me, better than any tomb,' he told Tom. 'But when your time comes, Ipswich will raise a greater monument to you, my boy. I hear that you are doing brilliantly at court. I always said you'd go far.'

'It's all thanks to you, Uncle,' Tom said.

'Aye, and I congratulate myself on having the perception to see the potential in you. Your mother was so proud, God rest her soul.' He wiped away a tear.

Tom moved on through the throng. He recognised several people, some from the old days in the inn, among them Edward Winter, who embraced him in arms that had grown very frail. The old man looked a hundred years old.

'Come and meet my cousin,' he said. With halting steps, he led Tom across the room to a group of people deep in conversation, and tugged the sleeve of a tall man in clerical garb. When the man turned, Tom recognised him at once.

'Thomas Larke!' he exclaimed. 'I did not dream I would meet you here!'

Father Larke smiled. 'I had hoped to see you, Tom.'

'Of course, you know that Thomas's family come from Norfolk,'

Winter explained. 'They have property in Thetford and Yarmouth. They're much grander than me! I'm just the poor relation.' He grinned. 'But it's good to see some of them here today.'

'I only met your dear mother a few times, but she was always most kind and hospitable,' Father Larke said. 'Forgive me, I am being discourteous. Let me introduce you to my kinsfolk.' Tom greeted Larke's brothers, but his eyes were drawn to the only woman in the group.

Slender in her black gown, with hands like a child's, she could not have been more than twenty. She had a sweet face and glossy brown hair worn unbound, proclaiming her maidenhood. Her eyes were blue and luminous, her lips soft and her nose ever so slightly tilted. With looks like hers, it was surprising that she had not been snapped up by a husband. By God, if he'd not taken vows . . . He could not take his gaze off her; there was wisdom and kindness in those blue eyes – and allure. He was barely aware of Larke introducing her.

'Father Wolsey, this is my sister Joan.'

He smiled at her, remembering his manners. As the conversation resumed, he kept stealing glances at her, and soon became aware that she was looking at him too, with barely concealed interest. When her brothers moved away to talk to other mourners, he edged closer to her.

'Can I fetch you more ale or a plate of food, Mistress Larke?' he offered, liking the way her eyes locked with his, not boldly, but with warmth.

'No thank you, Father.' Her voice was melodious, like a bell. 'You too are a chaplain to the King?' He suspected that she might be a little in awe of him.

'Yes,' he said. 'I have that privilege.'

She laughed suddenly. 'Well, that's debatable, from what I've heard!' Not in awe, then. 'That old skinflint taxes us half to death.'

Tom was taken aback by her candour. 'You should not speak ill of the King. Some revere him as a second Solomon for his wisdom.'

'I speak as I find,' she said fearlessly, but with such charm that he could not be cross with her.

She was curious about the court, and he readily answered all her questions, wishing to prolong his enjoyment of her company. Soon, they were exchanging their life histories. Her father, she told him, was a grazier and farmer, and had twice been mayor of Thetford. Her family had lived in Norfolk since ancient times. Tom felt unusually comfortable with her, perhaps because they shared similar backgrounds. She was so easy to talk to. And he had never been attracted so powerfully to a woman.

At length, he steeled himself to ask the question that had been nagging at him.

'Are you betrothed, Mistress Larke?'

She smiled; the effect was enchanting. 'No, Father. I have had suitors, but my father did not think them good enough.'

No man would be good enough for you.

'I imagine they are queuing up!' Tom smiled. 'You are very beautiful.'

Joan laughed. 'And you, Father, are a flatterer!'

'I speak from the heart,' he declared.

'You must come and visit us in Yarmouth,' she said, and there was more than an invitation in her eyes.

'I will do that,' he said, grasping her hands. Just touching her skin sent his senses flying. Then he dragged himself away, aware that he ought to be circulating.

Alone in his bedchamber beneath the eaves, Tom could not stop thinking about Joan Larke. He had never wanted a woman so much. Could it be that, middle-aged man that he was, with his juices supposedly drying up, he had fallen in love at first sight?

He pulled off his clothes and folded them, then dragged on his nightgown. Even if it was love, he had taken a vow of chastity and was forbidden to do anything about it. Yet he could not help but wonder if Joan felt the same way about him. Dare he risk declaring himself? No! he admonished himself. No sane man would do such a thing.

The truth was, though, that he could not deny his feelings. This, he recognised, was the madness of which the poets wrote, this all-consuming longing for the object of his desire. It went against all reason that he should even consider embroiling himself in a love affair that could undermine everything he had worked for, and risking the scandal, for he had been at court long enough to know that those who were envious of his success would not hesitate to exploit any weakness in his character – and he could not have that, not when he had waited so long to enjoy the position that was now his. Yet when he asked himself what he wanted most, love or power, the answer, right at this moment, was love. And not love in the abstract, but the love of the beautiful, the wondrous, the fatally alluring Joan Larke!

As he climbed into bed and doused the candle, he reminded himself that he was here in Ipswich for his mother's funeral and should not be having carnal thoughts for that reason alone. And he was a priest – he shouldn't even be thinking of love, especially since it was unlikely that anything could ever come of it. Marriage was out of the question, so what had he to offer Joan? Nothing but shame!

No, he told himself, turning to face the wall, he would be a fool to take things any further. It must be grief that was making him so emotional. He had always prided himself on being a rational fellow. He could not allow lust for a woman to dominate his life. Giving in to his fantasies could, if pursued to a conclusion, lead to the ruin of his reputation and even his career – the career that meant everything to him. Besides, he was no lovestruck boy but a mature man, one of the King's most trusted chaplains. He could not let his passions run away with him.

Suddenly, he was weeping as the enormity of his loss overwhelmed him and reality struck. He fell asleep thinking of his mother, the love she had so selflessly given him and the pride she had taken in him. In life, he had not been as diligent a son as he could have been. In death, he could not let her down by compromising his integrity.

When he arrived back at Richmond, he found the court shrouded in gloom. The King was dying. People were speaking openly of it. Yet he could not help thinking of Joan and the promise in her eyes.

Resolutely quelling his teeming thoughts, he hastened to the royal lodgings, only to be told that his Grace was sleeping. He tried again that evening to see his master, but was asked to come back in the morning. When he rose at six to get ready for Mass at seven, he made his way to the King's privy closet, only to find Father Larke already there.

'We are to say Mass in the King's bedchamber,' he said. Tom robed himself in his vestments and followed him along the gallery.

The room was crowded, foetid with the smell of sickness and humanity pressed too close together. Privy councillors, physicians, courtiers and clerks had gathered around the vast bed. At its head sat the Prince of Wales, holding his father's hand, his eyes anxious. The King's eyes were closed and his face was waxen, as white as his pillows, but he looked peaceful.

Everyone drew back to let Tom and Father Larke approach and knelt in unison when they administered the Sacrament of Extreme Unction to the dying man. Then it was just a matter of watching and waiting. The Prince seemed distressed and edgy. Tom tried not to think of a pair of inviting eyes and a cape of shining hair. It was almost impossible to banish Joan from his mind.

Suddenly, the King's eyes opened and focused on his son. He waved a weak hand. 'Go, my boy. You'll be more useful to me in chapel, praying for my deliverance from my pains.' The Prince rose with alacrity and departed. Outside, a church bell chimed the hour. Tom knelt and prayed for a happy death for his master.

After a while, the King's voice quavered, 'Send for my son. Bid him return. I can feel a change coming upon me.'

Tom pushed through the ranks of courtiers and hastened to the Prince's chamber, where he found him staring unseeing at an open book. He looked up warily.

'My lord Prince, the King your father is asking for you,' Tom said gently. 'Come quickly, for he is *in extremis*.'

'Why was I not called sooner?' the young man asked. 'This touches me more than anyone.'

'I am sorry, Sir, but his Grace has suffered a sudden deterioration. Let us make haste!'

The Prince seemed reluctant to approach the bed. He was wrinkling his nose against the stale air. Tom knew he hated anything to do with illness and death. Yet the King was reaching out to him with skeletal hands.

'Harry, my boy!' he rasped. 'Heed me!'

The Prince knelt and took his hand. 'Father?'

'I am dying, my son. Soon you will be king. My councillors have sworn to ensure a smooth succession.' The hoarse voice grew fainter. 'Before I go to meet my Maker, I expressly command you to take in marriage the Lady Katherine.'

'I will, Sir,' his son promised. But the King was beyond comprehending, having been seized by a violent paroxysm of coughing, followed by a gush of blood from his mouth. When it subsided, he lay gasping. John Fisher, Bishop of Rochester, chaplain to Henry's mother, the Lady Margaret, held a jewelled crucifix before the dying man's eyes. The King reached feebly for it and beat it against his chest.

It was time for Tom to step forward. 'Into thy hands, O Lord, I commend my spirit,' he recited, 'in the name of the Father, the Son and the Holy Spirit.' As he spoke, the King dropped the crucifix and his head fell to one side.

Everyone knelt in respect for the passing of a soul. Bishop Fisher made the sign of the Cross over the body. 'Eternal rest grant unto him, O Lord, and let perpetual light shine upon him,' he intoned.

The Prince remained on his knees, head bent. 'Amen,' he said when the prayer was finished, then he rose to his feet, staring at the bent heads around him. For everyone else had remained kneeling and now shifted around to face him.

'The King is dead,' the Earl of Surrey said. 'Long live the King!'

'Long live the King!' Tom echoed with the rest.

Having long yearned to be at the centre of court life, Tom had never thought to find himself riding through the City of London in a royal procession, but here he was, some way ahead of the King with the other clerics, on his way to the Tower of London through streets lined by cheering crowds. Of course, the acclaim was not for him. It was for the young King, already the darling of the people not a week after his proclamation.

Earlier in the day, Tom had stood at a respectful distance as King Henry VIII, resplendent in cloth of silver and the midnight-blue velvet of royal mourning, paid his respects to his father's corpse, which was now lying in state in the Chapel Royal at Richmond Palace, where it would remain until it could be taken to Westminster Abbey for burial. Before the body was cold, the new monarch had asked Tom to make the arrangements for the obsequies and the state funeral.

'My father was full of praise for your organisational skills,' he said. 'I know I can rely on you in this important matter.'

Tom had thrown himself into what he did best, managing and planning, although he had never had to do it on such a grand scale. It distracted him from dangerous fantasies about Joan Larke, and he found he was enjoying himself. He determined to do well, for if he did, surely greater things might come his way. His post of almoner had lapsed with Henry VII's death, but Henry VIII had kept him on as chaplain.

It was abundantly clear from the ecstatic cheering that few mourned the dead King's passing. Tom knew that if he were in Henry's shoes, he would be feeling overwhelmed, for the acclaim was deafening. The forthright Joan had spoken truth. Henry VII might have brought peace and good government to England, but he had been hated as a miser and an extortionist. The contrast between him and his heir could not have been greater.

But let us not forget, Tom reflected, as the Tower came into view ahead, that the late King had left England with such an impressive reputation that all Christian nations were eager to forge alliances with her. He had also left the treasury full of the riches he had accumulated over the years, and in this wealth lay the realm's strength and security. Tom believed that people had always underestimated Henry VII's greatness. They saw him as a dark, suspicious prince – and God knew he had had reason, with continual threats to his throne – and not to be trusted. They did not see the wise founder of a strong dynasty and the guardian of peace. Look at them, rejoicing at his passing!

The new King had nicely judged the public mood and wasted no time in making it clear that he was determined to dissociate himself from his father's unpopular policies. Today, he'd had a universal amnesty proclaimed – and he had ordered the arrests of the hated Empson and Dudley. Their heads would seal his popularity. He wanted to show his subjects that he would never allow his ministers to practise such wicked extortions. Tom could envisage his prim little mouth set in virtuous determination.

Tower Hill was packed with happy crowds, all waving and calling down blessings on their new monarch. The great procession halted, and Tom watched as the Constable of the Tower came forward with a cushion bearing the keys to the fortress, which he presented on bended knee to the King, who then rode through the great Lion Tower and into the outer ward, where the Yeomen Warders were struggling to keep the people back. It was the same when he entered the royal palace, where the court had assembled and the state chambers were crammed to bursting point, with everyone straining to catch sight of him or present a petition. He was the fount of honour and patronage now; he could make or break men as it pleased him, a heady prospect for so young a man, especially one who had been so frustratingly cloistered. Tom prayed he would use his power wisely and remember that a good prince cultivated those who could be useful to him and rewarded those who gave good service – like himself.

Bowing to left and right, the King moved through the throng, preceded by the Yeomen of the Guard, and ascended the throne set beneath a rich canopy of estate embroidered with the royal arms of England. Sitting tall and straight, hand on hip, beardless chin held high, he addressed the company.

'My lords, welcome! We thank you for your warm greetings, and we wish you and all men to know that we mean to rule over you wisely and well. We are a lover of justice and goodness, and bear much affection to the learned, who will always be welcome at our court. Know that we do not desire gold, gems or precious metals, but virtue, glory and immortality!'

Tom was impressed. As the courtiers thundered their ovation, the young King flushed with exaltation. He rose, raising a majestic hand in acknowledgement of the cheers, then withdrew. As the courtiers dispersed, Tom found his lodging, a cramped chamber in the Salt Tower, and unpacked his few belongings, thinking that he too had made a good beginning, having won his new master's confidence and been entrusted with an important task.

He had not been able to stop dreaming about Joan. No woman had ever captured his imagination so powerfully, and now he was finding it hard to put his scruples before his longing for her. It had got to the point where he had begun to wonder when he might find an opportunity to see her again. Could he be so bold as to take her up on her invitation to visit Yarmouth? And had he really read the invitation in her eyes correctly? Yet he dared not be away from the court just yet. He had to entrench himself, make himself indispensable to the King.

There was a solemn feast that night in the great hall of the Tower, and although the court was in mourning, the King appeared in splendour. Young as he was, he understood that to be seen as a great sovereign, it was essential to look the part and make a display of magnificence. And he *was* magnificent – he didn't even have to make an effort, unlike his father. In his person, he was the embodiment of kingship. More than six feet tall, he was majestic, strong and the epitome of male beauty, with his narrow waist, broad shoulders, fair skin and auburn hair worn chin-length and straight in the French fashion. He had a broad face, penetrating eyes and a high-bridged, imperial nose. Many were saying he was the handsomest prince they had ever seen. Our new Octavius, Tom thought, who – God willing – would restore the popularity of the monarchy and bring peace and prosperity to England. It felt like the start of a golden age.

Harry – for so Tom now thought of him, having heard the late King habitually refer to him by that name – kept Tom busy over the next few days. He made no secret of his admiration for his chaplain's energy and brilliance, and his willingness to do his new master's will. Tom made sure he knew that if he wanted something done, he himself was the man to ask. He flattered Harry, especially when the young King demonstrated that he had a good grasp of affairs and showed himself masterful and statesmanlike.

'We are blessed to have a prince who behaves wisely, loves justice and goodness and bears such affection to learned men,' he said one day to one of the lords spilling out of the council chamber into the gallery, extolling their master's virtues. 'It is no wonder that the whole kingdom is rejoicing in the possession of so great a king.'

'Amen to that,' murmured the Earl of Surrey. Harry heard him and smiled, accepting the compliments as his due. But the Duke of Buckingham and one or two other peers were staring balefully at Tom, as if he was a piece of dirt beneath their shoes. It did not trouble him. Brains before blood! He knew he was far more useful to the King than the Duke and his cronies would ever be. He could afford to ignore their hostility.

'I think your Grace is most prudent to say you will not be making any decisions until you have slept upon a matter,' Surrey was saying.

Harry beamed at him. 'You will find, my lord, that once I do make my mind up, I judge myself to be in the right, as a divinely appointed king.'

'Naturally, for your Grace is invested with a wisdom beyond ordinary mortals,' Tom observed.

'By St George, you speak truth!' Harry replied, clapping an arm around Tom's shoulders.

'My councillors were difficult today,' the King sniffed, as he bade Tom be seated in his closet. They were there to discuss the coming funeral, but he seemed more disposed to grumble. 'My father left me an overflowing treasury.'

It was true. Few kings had started their reigns in possession of such a staggering fortune.

'I have many plans on how to spend it!' His eyes lit up. 'I want to make my court the most magnificent in Christendom. And I want to conquer France, which is rightfully mine. My father was against the idea, but I know I can lead my people to victory, and I'm not going to let those old greybeards on my Council dissuade me.'

Tom's heart sank. The last thing England needed was a war that would inevitably deplete her resources. 'Your Grace,' he said gently, 'your father left this realm strong and wealthy, and at peace after decades of civil strife. Why waste money on another war?'

Harry fixed a steely gaze on him. 'You're as bad as the rest of them, Thomas. But when I am crowned at Rheims, I will remind you all that you tried to dissuade me. I will hear no more protests.'

Tom knew when to keep silent. He bowed his head and moved on to the list of those who were to be invited to the funeral.

Tom was pleased that the King had finally married the Princess Katherine. They had been united in a quiet ceremony at Greenwich with little pomp. Tom himself had made the arrangements. Two weeks later, on Midsummer Day, the young couple went to their crowning. Tom had not been invited – he had not expected it – but he stood in Westminster Hall that morning and fell to his knees with everyone else when the King made his entrance, a vision in royal robes of crimson furred with ermine. There was a flurry as people scrambled to get into place for the procession to Westminster Abbey. When Harry passed by, Tom turned to John Fisher, Bishop of Rochester.

'This day consecrates a young man who is the everlasting glory of our age,' he enthused.

'Aye,' smiled the gaunt-faced Fisher. 'This day is the end of our slavery, the fount of our liberty, the beginning of joy. Watch how the people run before their King with bright faces, celebrating their liberation!'

The King had overheard them. He paused and grasped each man by the hand.

'Thank you,' he beamed.

Suddenly, the new Queen appeared, golden-haired and beautiful in her crimson robes, smiling at him with eyes of love, which caused Tom a few pangs. If only he could be living a parallel life in which he and Joan were able to be together. He watched enviously as Harry took Katherine's hand and, preceded by the nobility in furred gowns of scarlet, they walked together to Westminster Abbey. From outside could be heard a mighty roar of cheers.

* * *

Harry was unstoppable, ardent in the pursuit of enhancing his glory. Tom knew that he wanted to impress his subjects with dazzling displays of elaborate ceremonial and pageantry. He was always talking of plans for building or beautifying palaces that would serve as settings for his princely magnificence. He let it be known that architects, artists, musicians and scholars were welcome at his court, and talented men came flocking, adding to his prestige.

'I'm going to style myself "your Majesty" in the continental manner,' he said, looking up from an old treatise on kingship as Tom entered his study. Tom suspected that most people would continue to use the traditional titles of 'your Grace' or 'your Highness'.

In many ways, he saw, Harry was immature and naïve, but his learning was impressive. He had wholeheartedly embraced humanist teachings on sovereignty and liked to expound on them.

'The perfect ruler,' he declared to Tom, when they were out riding in the park, 'should be a prince of splendour and generosity, giving freely to everyone. He should hold banquets, festivals, games and public shows. And I will, you can count on it! I would outshine my rivals, the King of France and the Emperor. People expect marvels of me. '

'I don't doubt that your Grace will satisfy them,' Tom smiled.

'I hate sitting in council,' Harry said. 'I prefer to delegate to my ministers and leave them to work out the details of my policies, but I mean to remain very much in control and keep my own counsel. And I am resolved to play a prominent role in Christendom. I do mean to win back the lands my predecessors lost in France; they are mine by right!' He frowned and shook his head. 'My councillors think I just seek glory. They say the King of France is richer in resources and manpower than I am. But did that deter Henry V or the Black Prince? By St George, they didn't have to contend with old women like Surrey pouring scorn on their endeavours! King Ferdinand is my ally, but they think he is using me to fight his wars for him! I know what people were saying, that Spain is ruling England at one remove, through the Queen and her father. But I will not be taken for a fool – I can make up my own mind!'

He spurred his horse. 'My interests and Ferdinand's are one and the same in this matter of conquering France! France is his ancient enemy as she is mine. With her vanquished, we will both be the stronger. And yet when I say this to my councillors, they won't listen. Thomas, I know my subjects. They want victories like Agincourt. Yet my lords urge me to be patient. They tell me I must not risk myself, since I do not yet have an heir.'

'That is wise advice, Sir,' Tom ventured, when Harry paused for breath. 'If you were to die in battle, this kingdom might be plunged into another civil war, for there would be many with a claim to succeed you. I counsel you as a friend. Wait until you have a son, then pursue your enterprise against France.'

The King snorted. 'This is so frustrating!' he muttered. 'If only the Queen could bear me an heir!'

Tom smiled. 'Sir, I will pray that your hopes are realised, and soon.' Inwardly, he was worried. Harry was young and headstrong. The lords were right. It *would* be prudent to wait a while before going to war, if only to test the loyalty of that fox Ferdinand.

Tom was in the roomy linenfold-panelled closet he used as a study, seated at his solid oak desk by the latticed window and staring at the pile of paperwork awaiting his attention. Harry, eager to be off hunting, had asked him to go through it and bring any matter of import to his attention. The documents had come from the clerk to the Council. As Tom sifted through them, he saw that most related to routine business, apart from a request to the Archbishop of Canterbury to order prayers and intercessions for the Queen, now that it was known that she was with child. That was quick work, Tom thought, smiling to himself, then feeling the familiar pang of longing for Joan. But his smile soon faded as a letter marked 'copy' caught his eye.

He drew in his breath. The King must be informed of this immediately.

As soon as he heard that Harry had returned, Tom hastened to his study, where he found his master reading his summary of the Council's proceedings.

He did not waste words. 'Your Grace, it has come to my knowledge that some of your councillors have written in your name to King Louis, offering friendship and peace. I thought you should know.' He handed over the draft of the letter.

An angry flush rose from Harry's neck as he read it. 'How dare they usurp my prerogative!' he seethed. 'Summon them!' He was working himself into a frenzy.

Tom did not envy the lords when, half an hour later, the King stormed into the council chamber. He stayed in the gallery, near enough to hear his master shouting at them. Moments later, Harry crashed out of the room.

'Attend me, Thomas!' he barked, striding fast along the gallery. 'Find the French ambassador. Invite him to watch the jousts this afternoon. I intend to take part and display my martial prowess.'

'Is that wise, your Grace? You should not risk yourself—'

'Are you going to forbid it too? No, Thomas, my mind is made up. Oh, and make sure there is nowhere for the ambassador to sit. Let him feel the full blast of our enmity towards his King. Then, when he has learned what it is to feel conspicuous and embarrassed, you may provide him with a cushion.'

'Your Grace, it will be seen as an insult.'

'That,' Harry smiled grimly, 'is the intention.'

Tom winced as he witnessed the discomfiture of the French ambassador, and the amused reactions of the courtiers. He understood that Harry wanted to be adored by his people and have them know he shared their sentiments about England's ancient enemy. After the jousts, in which the King covered himself in glory and thankfully escaped without a scratch, Tom made his way to Harry's tent, following as the King walked along the lists, chatting and laughing with the spectators, clapping a man on the shoulder or chucking a woman under the chin. He knew just how to play a crowd – and how they loved him! They seemed to see him not as a person of this world, but as one descended from Heaven. If he could keep this up, he would have a successful reign.

'Your Grace shows himself more of a companion than a king,' Tom said, as Harry approached. 'You understand the value of being accessible to your subjects.'

'I want to see them, and be seen by them,' the King replied. 'They are welcome to come into my palaces to watch tournaments and court entertainments. And I mean to go on progress annually to meet those who live farther off in my kingdom.'

Tom hesitated, knowing that what he had to say would not be well received. But he had been giving a lot of thought to the matter and knew it to be important. 'Sir, since the Queen is with child, and the campaigning season ends in October, it might be best to defer the French venture until next year at the very earliest. You will need time to prepare well, if it is to succeed. And by then, you will have your heir.'

'Hmm.' Harry thought about it, frowning. Then his face lightened. 'I can always rely on you, Tom, to give me excellent counsel. My councillors know it too; you are highly thought of.'

Yes, Tom thought, but by the new men, not the old nobility.

'France will have to wait,' the King sighed. 'It won't be for long, God willing.'

Chapter 9

1509

With the King given over to pleasure and the summer stretching gloriously ahead, Tom realised that he could get away. Joan had been constantly on his mind. He could not banish the image of her from his head – not that he wanted to, for no other woman had ever felt so special. He had been drawn in by her forthrightness, her sincerity and her wit as much as by her beauty. Had he been free, and living in Ipswich, following in his father's footsteps, he would have been pressing her to marry him.

But he was not free. He was bound by his vows to God and his priesthood. It seemed ironic that the career he had ardently pursued all his life, which had brought him to his present pinnacle of success, was the one thing that prevented him from having something he had not until now, this late in life, known he wanted – and that was the love of a woman. Yet again he asked himself what he could offer Joan. She was not like the whores he had occasionally bedded, and he could not dishonour her by asking her to give herself to him. It might spoil her for marriage with some man who could provide her with a decent life.

Despite his qualms, he found himself packing his old leather bag, donning his riding clothes, saddling his mount and taking the horse ferry at Lambeth across the Thames, then spurring eastwards to Essex, telling himself – and everyone else – that he was going to see his family.

As he rode, he became aware of another need that had recently surfaced in him, that basic human instinct to reproduce and leave something of himself behind. Indulging his fantasy, he let his mind run riot, imagining the children he might have had with a woman like Joan: a strong boy to follow in his footsteps, and at least one pretty, vital girl who would be the image of her mother. Again, he pulled himself up. Any children he had would be bastards, unable to inherit his new-found wealth, shunned by society. But he did so want a son, a fine boy of his own flesh and blood – in fact, a boy who would grow up into a man just like King Harry. For Tom was coming to feel a deep and almost paternal affection and admiration for his young master. At thirty-eight, Tom was old enough to be Harry's father and felt quite protective towards him. He recognised the feeling as love. But it would be a hundred times more intense for a son of his own.

He got as far as Ipswich, but then turned north. He could not resist the lure of seeing Joan. After spending a night in an uncomfortable inn and having to stop several times to ask for directions, he finally found the Larkes' farm nestling on the banks of the River Yare, outside the town of Yarmouth. It was well kept and looked prosperous. Dismounting in the yard, he looped his horse's reins over a fence post and leaned through the open door of the timbered farmhouse. There, standing at a table in the flagstoned kitchen, was Joan, kneading pastry, a large pie dish beside her. She looked so fine, even wearing her apron and with her lovely hair confined by a white coif. She stared at him open-mouthed.

'Father Wolsey!' she exclaimed.

'I could not stay away,' he said hoarsely, drinking in the sight of her. She was even more beautiful than he remembered.

Her face flushed with pleasure. And those eyes! They were an open invitation. The urge to make love to her was suddenly powerful in him.

His voice shook. 'Forgive me for this unexpected visit. I can't quite believe that I came, or that I am here. I pray I did not misread your invitation.'

Joan's hands had ceased kneading. 'You did not. But believe me, I do not usually make such invitations. I am not that kind of woman.' She held his gaze. 'You may think me forward, but I have no patience with petty social niceties. We have but one life and should live it as we wish. I am tired of waiting for my father to find me a husband. I want to live – now!'

Tom was amazed. He had read her aright! He could hardly contain his joy. Now he knew that the poets were right, and that there was such a thing as love at first sight.

'You think me forward!' She smiled, blushing a little. 'It is not maidenly for a girl to voice her desires!'

'Ah, if only I could declare mine!' he blurted out, astonished at himself. 'But what of my vows – and your reputation?'

She regarded him steadily with those beautiful eyes. 'My brother is a learned man, and even he says there is nothing in Scripture that says a priest should be celibate. It is a demand imposed on you by a corrupt church. And where there is love, there can be no sin.'

Tom's amazement grew. He had never heard a woman speak so freely or boldly, or express such controversial opinions. He felt himself melting under her gaze.

When he could speak, his voice was hoarse. 'Then know that beneath this cassock, there is a man who now wishes he had never embraced the priesthood. I am but human: I like to dance, to hunt and be merry, and I appreciate a fair maiden.'

'If you were not in holy orders, Father Wolsey, I would be encouraging your suit.' Again, there was an unfeigned sincerity in her humour. He knew she meant it.

'And I would be pressing it,' he said.

In two strides, he crossed the distance between them and folded her in his arms. She lifted her face for his kiss, and he bent to her lips. She tasted so sweet. He felt himself harden against her apron. When he finally broke away, he gazed at her in wonder. He had never known a feeling like it.

'I don't understand what has come over me,' he said, for once at a loss for words.

'I think there's no doubt!' She smiled.

'I haven't stopped thinking about you,' he told her. 'I have been longing to come to you, but my duties at court kept me from doing so.'

'No matter. You are here now. And the sight of you does my heart good.' She kissed him again, playfully this time.

'Your father, your brothers . . . Are they here? I shall say that I came at your brother's invitation, and that I shall stop and see my family in Ipswich when I return.' He felt cheapened by the lies.

'Let us not think about your return just now,' Joan said. 'My father is out in the fields. He will be back at sundown. And if I don't get this pie in the oven, he'll give me a right scolding.' She loosened herself from Tom's arms and turned back to the table. 'How long are you staying?'

'That's rather up to you,' he said, holding his breath.

'Stay as long as you like,' she replied, almost nonchalantly, laying the pastry over the pie dish and cutting it to shape at the rim. She laid down the knife and looked at him. Her eyes told him everything he needed to know.

Peter Larke was a jovial man, apple-cheeked and leathery-skinned from a life spent in the open air. He welcomed Tom warmly and bade him sit beside him at dinner. The pie was delicious, but Tom struggled to eat any of it. He was too aware of Joan sitting further along the board with her brothers. He wondered what her father would say if he knew why he was really here.

'It was good of you to come so far out of your way to see us,' Larke said.

'It was no trouble.' Tom smiled.

'And our young King, what do you make of him?'

'I'm deeply impressed,' he replied.

'Flatterer!' Joan shot at him.

'Not at all,' he protested. 'He is extraordinary. In the future, I have no doubt that the whole world will talk of him. And I am proud to serve him.'

As they plied him with questions about the King and the court, Tom suddenly found himself worrying what Harry would say if he discovered that his chaplain was embarking on an illicit love affair. He could just see that prudish little mouth pursed with disapproval.

Oh, God, what had he started? And yet, stealing glances at Joan serving preserved quinces with dollops of thick yellow cream, he feared he would not be able to resist her.

The box bed in the attic room at the top of the house was cosy. Joan had made it up with clean sheets, a plump bolster and a woollen counterpane. Tom blew out his candle and climbed in, then lay there wondering how he was going to take things further with her. He was lost, beyond redemption. His body paid no heed to his conscience. Desire was rampant in him.

The house was still. The Larkes retired early, to be ready to rise with the dawn. Outside, he heard the distant call of an owl. Then there was the lightest of creaks and the door swung open. Joan slipped in, softly closing it behind her. Tom had not drawn the curtains, and a shaft of silvery moonlight bathed her slim figure, clothed in a thin white smock. Her hair hung loose down her back. He had never seen anything so lovely. He could not speak for longing.

She held a finger to her lips and came to him. He opened his arms, and she went into them, snuggling down beside him in the bed. He kissed her, his tongue probing deeply, and she responded with fervour.

'I've never felt like this about any man,' she whispered.

'And I have never wanted a woman so much,' he declared. 'It seems incredible that we can feel like this on such a short acquaintance. I never believed in love at first sight until now.'

'You are talking of love, Master Wolsey?'

'Tom, I beg you, Mistress Joan! And yes, I am talking of love. I know this for what it is.' He swept her into his arms again, casting caution to the winds.

'Yes,' she said. 'When you know, there is no room for doubt.' There were tears of joy in her eyes.

Tom felt a spike of anguish deep within him. 'I should not be doing this or taking advantage of you. It's selfish of me. I'm a priest, and I'm twenty years older than you. I can offer you nothing.'

'You can offer me yourself,' Joan said simply. 'I don't care about your being a priest or how old you are. You should see our vicar – his housekeeper, for so he calls her, has six children by him. And he's not the only one. It's not natural for a man to be celibate. The Church shouldn't ask it of you.'

Tom marvelled again at her candour. 'But society nevertheless judges and condemns,' he protested. 'And people talk.'

'Let them!' She snapped her fingers, twisting out of his embrace and kneeling up on the bed. 'They are ignorant fools. What matters in this life, Thomas Wolsey, is love, and how people treat each other. I keep the commandments. I don't recall there being anything in them about celibacy!'

'Hush,' he breathed. 'That's almost heresy.'

'Here, my dearest, we speak our minds freely. There's no one to listen. My father holds the same views as I do, and Thomas.'

'But they would draw the line at my compromising your reputation.'

Joan smiled. 'I think not. Father is ambitious. He's heard a lot about you from Thomas. He'll probably see advantages to be gained from your compromising my reputation, as you put it.'

Tom shook his head. 'It's not right, however well he takes it or what he hopes for.'

'Then why are you here?' she challenged, her blue eyes flashing.

'I'm here because I could not stay away,' he said. 'Because I am gripped by a kind of madness.'

'Love is a gift from God,' she replied, taking his hands.

'And lust is the work of the Devil,' he retorted, hearing his voice waver.

'Well, you can leave now if you're not ready to accept God's gift with grateful hands!' Joan made to climb off the bed.

Tom pulled her back into his arms, feeling like a callow youth, not the worldly, experienced churchman he had thought himself until today.

He was suddenly resolved.

'I'd like to stay,' he said.

When she left before dawn, they had not enjoyed each other properly, but had lain awake for much of the night clasped in a tight embrace, murmuring of love and exploring each other's bodies. Tom had been aching to make Joan fully his, but still his troubled conscience held him back.

At breakfast, he took care not to meet her eye lest he give himself away before her menfolk. He felt shamefaced in the presence of her father, who evidently thought highly of him, and whose trust he had betrayed, under the man's very roof. But he stifled such thoughts; they must not sully what he had with Joan.

He stayed for three days, during which Joan came to his bed each night. Still he reined in his desire. It was sheer bliss just to hold her, caress her and talk with her. He was almost certain that Peter Larke and his sons were completely unaware of what was happening. Nevertheless, guilt weighed on him. By any standards, he was behaving badly. But Joan would not listen.

'What can be wrong with two people loving each other?' she soothed, pressing the length of her body to his. 'Cease your fretting. If I'm not bothered, you shouldn't be.'

And, of course, he was only too willing to heed her. It was only in the cold light of day that his qualms surfaced.

'Do you have to go back so soon?' Joan asked, sitting up in bed, her long tresses cloaking her breasts.

'Aye, though I wish I didn't,' Tom sighed. 'I'd stay here for ever if I could. But duty calls. The King expects my return.'

He packed his things reluctantly, knowing he would miss this peaceful place and the warmth and kindness extended to him. Above all, he could not bear to leave Joan.

'Come again,' Peter said, extending a hand, as they gathered around the mounting block. 'You are always welcome here, Father Wolsey.'

'I will,' Tom said, not daring to look at Joan. 'Thank you all for your hospitality.'

He got on his horse and spurred it towards the gate. Footsteps squelching in the mud sounded behind him. He looked around and there was Joan, running after him.

'You forgot this!' she cried, handing him a warm pie wrapped in a cloth. 'I baked it for your noon-piece. And here's an apple.'

He reined to a halt and she handed them up to him. Their fingers touched.

'God keep you,' she murmured, and turned back to where her father and brothers were waiting before Tom could thank her.

'I am heartily pleased to see you, Thomas,' the King beamed, rising from his desk. 'I've missed having your advice and support. I trust that your family are well?'

'Thank you, your Grace. They are very well.' He had not seen them at all.

Harry clapped him on the back. 'Good, good. You'll be pleased to hear that Bishop Foxe has recommended that you be reappointed almoner and given a seat on the Privy Council, and I entirely agree!'

Tom felt himself flushing with pleasure. 'I cannot thank your Grace sufficiently,' he said. 'My only wish is to serve you.' Inwardly, he was rejoicing to be given this golden opportunity to attain greater prominence and power, to exercise influence at the highest level and grow in good estimation and favour with the King. It was a heady prospect. How could he ever have dreamed of jeopardising the glittering future that assuredly lay ahead of him?

'Walk with me, Thomas,' the King invited, heading down the spiral stair to his privy garden. 'I mean to appoint to my Council those who are sympathetic to my views. Foxe and Warham are good men, wise and experienced, but they're too cautious and conservative, and they expect me to be like my father. But I am not my father. Caution and carefulness never won great victories! I get so bored sitting there listening to their homilies. It's a waste of my time when I could be out hunting or tilting.'

Tom seized the moment. 'Your Grace knows that you can rely on me to shoulder the burdens of state you find onerous.' He could see himself as the power behind the throne, while his young master rode in the lists, planned glorious but impractical campaigns, indulged in revelry and wrote love songs. Somewhere in this scenario, Joan vaguely featured, but in what way he could not imagine.

'Ah, Thomas, I am lucky to have such a servant,' Harry said, striding along between the flower beds. 'I cannot wait to see how you handle yourself in Council.'

'I look forward to being of service to your Grace,' Tom said humbly. Inside, he was exulting. Yet, as he followed the King down towards the river embankment, the thought of Joan nagged at him. How hard might it be to find time to visit Yarmouth now that he was a Privy Councillor? Well, he would think about that later. He would find a solution; he always did, when presented with a problem. Nothing must be allowed to mar this day of triumph.

He took to the Privy Council as a duck to water. Several of his fellow councillors, mainly those who came from humbler backgrounds like himself, made him welcome. The nobles still looked down their noses at him. It did not bother him. He knew he was more than their match in intellect and industry. He could tie them in knots if he had a mind to it. Instead, when it came to discussing business, he employed his wits and his eloquence to persuade everyone at the board to follow his advice.

Sometimes, he felt that he dominated the meetings. Yet they listened; they heeded him, even Foxe and Warham. Before long, they asked him to be their emissary to the King in all their proceedings. Because Harry was rarely present, having more exciting things to do, he expected to be given a summary of what had passed after every session. Then he would issue orders or dictate policy.

'You've shaken them up a bit,' he told Tom, as they left the council chamber one morning when he had put in a rare appearance at the head of the board. 'It's what they needed. I know I can trust you to make them get things done, and done the way I want them! No one among my councillors is more earnest and ready to advance my will and pleasure.'

Tom now found himself attending on the King daily. Harry made no secret of the fact that he genuinely liked him; he called him his friend and walked with his arm about his shoulders. Tom rejoiced in his affection, for he now regarded this golden young man almost as a son. Each day he grew more fond of him, and when he worked like a slave to please him, it was not just with an eye to his own advancement.

His pride swelled when Harry drew a cameo ring from his finger and gave to him.

'I will send you this token whenever I want you to be certain that confidential orders come direct from me, and not from some clerk or middle man,' he said. 'It shall be the outward symbol of my trust in you.'

The courtiers rapidly took note, and Tom soon found himself besieged by those who sought his patronage and begged him to make suit for them to the King for favours and preferment – and who were willing to pay handsomely for the privilege. Some councillors looked on jealously, resenting the attention shown to him, especially when, of them all, it was always Tom whom the King kept near to him. Harry made no secret of his estimation for his almoner, or of how highly he regarded his abilities.

Buckingham had no compunction about voicing his grievances. One afternoon, as Tom entered the council chamber, the Duke was holding forth to a group of other lords. 'He's put us all out of our accustomed favour. The King commits all his will and pleasure to Wolsey. A butcher's boy!'

Tom smiled at him. 'Good day, my lord. I assure you that my only endeavour is to satisfy the King's mind. He is young and lusty, disposed all to mirth and pleasure, and wishes to follow his desire and appetite rather than travail in the busy affairs of his realm. I but do my best to disburden him of such weighty and troublesome business, enabling him to spare time for his pleasures. It is with his authority and commandment that I try to see all matters sufficiently expedited and perfected.'

The Duke grunted and took his place. 'Methinks there is a whiff of the slaughterhouse in here, sirs,' he muttered.

Tom ignored him. He was not worth the bother of rising to the bait.

Tom stared at Thomas Larke, unable to believe his ears – and his good fortune.

'You're bringing Joan to court?' he echoed.

'Yes,' said Larke, clearly unaware of his friend's inner turmoil. 'She was asking about the court when I last visited, and I thought she would like to see the pageant next week. She's so looking forward to it!'

Tom began counting down the days, the hours and the minutes. He had yearned to see Joan again and felt sure that she was longing to see him too. Had she contrived this visit for that purpose? He would not be surprised.

The White Hall at Westminster was crammed with people avid to see the spectacle. At the far end of the room stood the empty throne on the dais. Courtiers occupied the benches along the walls, or crowded in behind, and the common people were packed into the space in front of the screens passage. In the centre of the vast chamber stood a mock hillock made of papier mâché with realistic trees and flowers. Around it sat young chattering maids-of-honour dressed in flowing white gowns banded with gold, their long hair loose. Above, in the gallery, minstrels were tuning their instruments. An air of expectancy pervaded the room.

Seated at the side, Tom had been searching the new arrivals for a glimpse of Joan. And now here she was, looking very becoming in a low-cut black gown that showed to advantage her slender figure. Her dark hair flowed about her shoulders and she wore a fine gold cross around her neck. Her simple outfit looked striking against the gaudier clothes worn by the court ladies.

She was holding her brother's hand and gazing around with interest. Tom hastened over to greet them and caught his breath when her eyes met his.

'This is a great pleasure,' he declared, beaming. 'Let me find us a place where we can get a good view of the pageant.' There were no spaces left on the benches, so the three of them stood by the tapestried wall. Tom was acutely aware of Joan beside him. Discreetly, he reached for her hand and squeezed it. She returned the pressure.

He found it hard to focus on the pageant. All he wanted was to be alone with his love. He remembered the softness of her body, her response to his touch, and longed to know such joy again. But Joan was seemingly engrossed in the spectacle before her, applauding with the rest as a group of masked young men staged a mock battle and the young ladies danced with the victors. She cheered with delight when the masks were thrown off and the King revealed himself.

'He's as handsome as they say,' she observed.

'He is a marvel,' Tom said, feeling a touch jealous of Harry's effortless ability to attract women, even the down-to-earth Joan. He himself had never been as handsome, and his youth was long gone. He began to wonder miserably what she saw in him. Was it his position and his prospects? God, let it be more than that!

After the pageant ended, drinks of heady spiced wine were served, and then there were games of blind man's buff, oranges and lemons and hide-and-seek. When the Master of the Revels announced that the latter would be played all over the ground floor of the palace, Tom seized his opportunity. 'Allow me to show you a good hiding place,' he offered, taking Joan's hand. Giggling, and flushed from the heat and the wine, she let him pull her away, out into the coolness of a gallery and into the warren of rooms that faced the river.

'Where are you taking me?' she cried, laughing.

'Somewhere we can be alone!' he told her. Drawing her into the closet he used as a study, he shut the door behind them, bolted it and took her into his arms. 'Dear God, I have longed for this!' he breathed, kissing her hungrily.

'And I too!' she whispered. 'Oh, Tom . . .'

He felt the change in her, knew she would not resist him – knew too that he would not be able to resist her this time. He lowered her down onto the table, devouring her with his mouth, his hands insistent at her skirts. And she, catching his passion, lifted them high and showed herself to him. Losing control, he entered her. It was not the quick relief he had felt with others, but an explosion of joy.

Afterwards, as they made themselves decent, Tom wondered why he felt no shame. And why should he? It was for bliss such as this that men and women were made. And what was so wrong with what they had done?

'I love you,' he said. He had said it in the heat of their coming together, but now, sanity restored, he wanted Joan to know that it was true.

'I love you too, Thomas Wolsey.' She smiled. 'But we must get back. My brother will be looking for me.'

'Before we go back, know this,' Tom said, seizing her hand, 'that I will find you again and contrive some way for us to be together. I vow it.'

'I should like that very much,' Joan told him, her eyes shining.

They hastened back towards the hall. To Tom's relief, the game was still going on, and the galleries and chambers were full of people seeking each other. They found Larke seated at a bench, chatting to some courtiers.

'Ah, there you are.' He grinned.

'I got lost!' Joan told him. 'Tom rescued me.'

'I loathe paperwork,' Harry complained, looking longingly out of the window of his study. 'Writing is to me somewhat tedious and painful.'

Tom had been entertaining erotic thoughts about Joan – he yearned for her constantly, now that she had gone home – and reluctantly dragged himself back to the present, his heart sinking. The King had virtually to be forced to write letters.

'If your Grace would just pen a message to the Queen of Scots.'

'Must I?' Harry looked peevish.

'She is your sister, Sir, and women must be pleased.'

He often wondered how the King could be such a great scholar yet hated putting pen to paper. Even now, he pursued his studies. Some called him a universal genius. On his desk lay works by Duns Scotus, Thomas Aquinas and the early Church Fathers. Tom had recommended that he read them, and was touched to see that his advice had been taken.

'Very well!' Harry conceded.

Tom beamed at him. 'Now, Sir, I want to tell you what happened in Council today, and then perhaps you would let me know your mind and pleasure so that I can expedite things.'

He went through the notes he had made and the proposals he wished to suggest, to each of which his master nodded. 'Approved,' he said, looking wonderfully pleased to have the business over and done with so quickly. 'Am I free now?'

'Of course, your Grace.'

'I wish all my councillors were like you.' Harry was rummaging in a cupboard crammed with balls, dog leads, arrows and swords. 'They are forever nagging me to sit through their boring debates, which pleases me not at all, but now I have you.' He looked like a cat that had been served a great fish.

Tom shook his head. The lords should know better; they should be aware that their King hated being constrained to do anything contrary to his royal will, which was something that he himself always bore in mind. They were fools if they thought they could persuade Harry to leave his pleasure and attend to the affairs of his realm.

'There is no need for your Grace to be present in Council all the time,' he said.

'Again, you remind me of how much reason I have to love you,' the King told him.

It soon became clear that, by making himself invaluable to the King, Tom ruled all. It was in his power to bring about what he decided was best. Who was now in high favour but Master Almoner? To whom did the petitioners come but Master Almoner? Whatever he advised or asked for came to pass. When he requested a post at court for his brother, the King readily agreed and appointed William a gentleman of the Privy Chamber, a great honour.

Tom would have asked for a good marriage for his sister, Bess, but she was ailing and often feverish, and he feared he might never see her again. It was so hard to find time to get home. The demands and needs of the King always came first. He promised himself that he would try to get to Ipswich as soon as possible, if not to Yarmouth to assuage his constant longing for Joan. If only there were a way for her to come to London again . . .

Chapter 10

1510

Tom knelt before his sovereign, who bent to invest him with the insignia of the Order of the Garter, the highest order of chivalry in England. It was St George's Day, and they were at Windsor for the first proper Garter Day celebration of the reign, the previous year's having been overshadowed by the death of the late King.

Tom rose and bowed, then took his place with the other knights in the stalls of St George's Chapel. Some were regarding him with open, undisguised resentment. A butcher's boy! they would be thinking, jealous of their privileged circle being invaded by someone so lowly. He was growing used to it now and did not let it bother him. If the King liked him, and wished to reward him for his hard work, why should he care? Besides, he had something far more important to think about.

As he walked in procession to St George's Hall, blue velvet mantle and ostrich plumes flapping in the April breeze, Tom's mind was in turmoil. He had tried to still his raging thoughts during the ceremony, not wanting anything to spoil this triumphant day, but now they had assaulted him again.

Joan was with child. His child. Larke had revealed that she had confided the news to him during a visit to Yarmouth. Tom had expected him to be angry and censorious, but he had taken a measured view.

'I was shocked at first,' he said, 'but then she told me that it was she who pursued you and that she cared not a fig for convention. She said she did not blame you at all.'

Tom had stood there trembling, wild thoughts of seeking release from his vows spinning in his head. 'I have felt guilty for taking advantage of her ever since,' he confessed. 'I wish I could do the right thing by her. I know I have trebly offended, in breaking my vows to God, dishonouring your family and compromising her reputation. I hold myself wholly to blame. Yet how can I put things right? If I were not in holy orders, I would marry her without hesitation. I love her.'

'You cannot marry her, but you can support her and minimise the difficulties she will face,' Thomas said, a touch sternly.

'Of course I will,' Tom had replied firmly. 'I am not poor, as you well know. And I want to do all I can for her and our child.' Now that the shock was wearing off, he could feel excitement at the prospect of becoming a father. He was picturing himself with a sturdy little boy who looked just like King Harry. But the prospect was bittersweet. It was a crying pity that he would never be able to acknowledge his offspring openly.

'What of your father?' he ventured. 'He will be out for my blood.'

Thomas sighed. 'My father is a pragmatic man, and an ambitious one. He has already realised that you can do far more for Joan than the kind of man she might have married could ever do. And you come from a similar background. I too wish you were free to marry her, yet I know you will look after her and not let her down.'

'Never,' Tom had vowed.

But now, short of sending money, he was agonising over how he could support her and – more importantly – how he could be with her. The miles that separated them seemed so many that she might as well be on the moon. He did not want to be apart from her at this time; he wanted to be nearby when she gave birth, so that he would know at once that she had come through it safely; and he could not bear to miss seeing his son grow up. He wanted the boy to have a mother and a father.

Some would have said that the proper thing to do would be to relinquish Joan so that she could wed a man who would save her reputation and give her child a name. Tom had enough money now to make it worth some man's while. Yet he could not bring himself even to contemplate it. The thought of her in another man's arms, his son calling another man father, was anathema to him. If Joan wanted it, though, he would have agreed, even if it killed him. Yet she had told Thomas that she did not, and that the only man she wanted was Tom. She too had known that God had intended them for each other.

So where could they be together? He could not install a mistress in his lodgings at court. The King, who famously prided himself on being a virtuous man, most certainly would not approve, for it would reflect badly on him. Moreover, this would not be the right time to broach the subject, for the Queen had just borne a stillborn daughter. Harry had been devastated, having pinned all his hopes on her presenting him with a son and heir, and now everyone was avoiding mentioning children or pregnancy in his hearing. And if Tom bought a house in London for Joan, Harry might well have something to say about that, for it was hard to keep anything secret in the gossiping world of the court.

Yet it was the King who unwittingly came to his aid.

'I have a fine house for you, my friend,' he said, one sunny day in May, as they were finishing the morning's business before dinner. 'It's the old rectory of the church of St Bride, by Fleet Street, and it was leased by my father to Sir Richard Empson.' Empson who, with Edmund Dudley, still lay in the Tower under sentence of death, their property having been declared forfeit to the Crown.

'I'm assigning the remainder of the lease to you,' the King went on. 'It's a princely dwelling, with an orchard and twelve gardens. You have earned it, Tom, and it is my pleasure to give it to you.'

He handed Tom a bunch of keys dangling from a chain and a patent confirming the grant. 'There are five years left on the lease.'

'Sir, I know not what to say,' Tom stammered, momentarily overwhelmed. 'I had never looked to own such a house. I cannot sufficiently express my gratitude.'

'No need, Thomas.' Harry beamed. 'It is I who should be grateful for all you do for me. No king ever had such a tireless servant.'

Tom skipped dinner and took a barge to Blackfriars, alighting at the confluence of the Fleet river and the Thames. There stood his new residence, rising tall and stately amid gardens that stretched down to the riverbank. Here, by a miracle, was the place where he could bring Joan and rear their child. Discretion would not be a problem.

Having raced around the house, delighted at its lofty hall, its well-appointed chambers, the fine furnishings that had been left untouched for months, he hurried back to Westminster and wrote to Joan at once, telling her of their good fortune and bidding her come to London as soon as she could. He enclosed money for her journey, and to pay one of her brothers to escort her. Then he tried hard to concentrate on his afternoon tasks. If God willed it, she would be here with him soon, and then they would be together for good. Some might call it living in sin, but could sin ever make you feel so ecstatically happy? Being with Joan would make him a better man, bring added zest to his life. What could be wrong with that?

But then doubts began to plague him. What if she decided that the life he had offered her was not for her? And if she did come to him, how would he keep her existence a secret? Servants could be sworn to secrecy, but everyone knew that they were notorious gossips. Except . . . well, he had several who could be trusted to keep his secrets, and they could act as buffers against the rest. Discretion must be his watchword. He would have to explain to Joan that they could not show affection for each other when any servant was present, and that she must remain out of sight when visitors came. Other churchmen kept mistresses – why should not he?

She was here! He was waiting for her when she arrived, standing in the hall of the rectory, eager to see her face when she saw the splendour in which she would now be living, the fine new tapestries he had purchased, the plate and pewter displayed on the massive court cupboard. But as she scrambled out of the litter and almost ran into his arms, he knew that none of these things mattered and that all the treasure he had in the world was gazing up at him, the living mound of the life they had created moving between them.

'Dear Tom, how I have missed you!' she breathed. 'It has seemed an eternity since we were together. And this? Oh, my God.' She drew back and stared around her in wonder. 'I know not what to say. I never dreamed . . .'

'Welcome to St Bride's Inn, your own house, my sweet darling,' he said, barely able to take his eyes off her. 'I have longed for this moment, for us to be truly together. And now here we are.'

Putting his arm around her shoulder, he led her to the two tall chairs behind the high table on the dais and summoned one of his servants to bring wine and some little cakes he had had specially prepared against Joan's coming.

'They are roasting a goodly joint of beef for supper,' he told her, 'but this will stay you after your journey. And then I will show you the property and after that you can rest.'

Joan loved the house. She looked around her in wonder, could not stop exclaiming about how marvellous it was. 'I cannot believe I will be living here!'

They ascended the stairs. In his bedchamber, she ran her fingers over the ornate carvings, damask curtains and counterpane of the great oak tester bed he had bought for them. 'I'll feel like a queen in this.'

'But my darling, I cannot risk my manservants finding you here,' he said, hating to disappoint her. 'Your room is up this secret stair.' He drew aside a curtain and led the way up to the floor above, where a very pretty bedchamber had been prepared for her, with a smaller tester bed and hangings embroidered with flowers. There was a stone fireplace on the opposite wall, with a high-backed chair on either side.

'I will come to you here,' he said.

Joan was smiling. 'It's beautiful.'

Tom opened a small door in the corner. 'I thought this room would serve for a nursery.' He led her into a spacious panelled chamber. 'My steward will order a cradle and the necessary furniture – and find a nurse and rockers.'

Joan laughed. 'It's as well you have a steward, for I would not be competent to act as mistress of this lordly house!'

'You would be perfect,' he said, kissing her hungrily, wondering if it was permissible to make love with a pregnant woman. His need for her was almost painful. 'Alas, that would be too public a role for you, my darling. You do understand the need for discretion?'

'I do, Thomas Wolsey,' Joan said. 'If it is the price of loving you, I am willing to pay it.'

Their eyes met and they fell into an embrace. 'I have wanted you so much,' he murmured.

'Then take me,' she whispered.

'But the babe . . .'

'Oh, they say you shouldn't, but I can't see how it can hurt. As long as you're gentle.'

'I'd never forgive myself . . .'

'Enough of that. Let's christen my new bed!'

Tom had never felt so happy. God had been good to him, and although he feared there might be a reckoning, he would not let that worry him now.

Of course, much of his time was spent at court, and he wasn't able to be with Joan as often as he would have liked, but most evenings, as soon as his duties were done, he would hurry to the jetty, hail a boat and hasten home to her. Then they would sit either side of the hearth in her bedchamber, she sewing, he discoursing on his day, both of them content in the other's quiet company, until one would suddenly look at the other, desire flowering, and they would fall to lovemaking, secure in the knowledge that no one would disturb them. The servants knew who – and what – Joan was, but so far, it seemed, they had respected her privacy, and Tom's. For, with her kind and practical nature, she had quickly endeared herself to them. And that was why she now enjoyed the run of the rectory and the gardens, where she and Tom went strolling as the evenings grew warmer and she became heavier with child.

Seeing Joan about the house – their house – bustling around, ordering the servants, or sewing by the hearth, resting her hands on her swelling belly, or preparing the nursery, or just holding hands with him across the dinner table, made Tom fit to burst with joy and pride. And lying with her at night, lost in transports of passion, or just being close to her, was the greatest joy of all. He felt like a man reborn.

She had brought her cat from Yarmouth, the sweetest little tabby called Cocksparrow. Some people, Tom knew, didn't like cats and even associated them with witches, but he was fascinated by the playful creature and laughed out loud whenever it danced sideways when encountering an imaginary enemy. When he sat working in his study, it slept at his feet. Life was bliss, pure contentment – and it could only get better.

Inevitably, there were times when council meetings ran late or the King wanted him to be present at a feast or revel. He was torn when that happened, yet he loved his work and knew that his future prosperity depended on pleasing his master. And Joan was easy about it. She never complained. Naturally, she was used to her menfolk working long hours on the farm, and she was still enjoying the novelty of living in such a grand house.

Yet she kept him grounded. She refused to let him glory in his growing wealth and power. 'Pride comes before a fall, Thomas Wolsey!' she would remind him when he came home boasting of some praise the King had bestowed on him, or some new honour. 'Never take his favour for granted. Just be grateful for what you've been given in life.'

She was right, he knew, but he did so want her to be proud of him, and he cared deeply for her good opinion, because she was intelligent and wise in her judgements and always spoke her mind. He found himself confiding in her matters he had been discussing in Council, and even asking for her views on them, because he soon learned that her advice was sure and wise. And she never hesitated to tell him if she thought he had acted wrongly. He had chosen well, he knew. They were well matched.

When Joan went into labour that summer, the midwife – paid handsomely to keep her mouth shut – shooed Tom out of the bedchamber and down the stairs to his own.

'I don't have men in my birthing chambers!' she squawked.

Pacing up and down in fear and agitation, he tried to shut his ears to Joan's screams, and when he could bear it no longer, he ran upstairs and begged to be allowed to see her, so that he would know what was happening. For all he knew, she might be dying in there. But the midwife shut the door in his face.

'All is progressing well!' she shouted. It didn't sound like it.

When, finally, she emerged, beaming, with a linen-wrapped bundle in her arms, and told him he had a son, Tom wept at the wonder of it, and with relief that Joan had come safely through her ordeal. His first view of his child was through a blur of tears.

When he finally saw Joan, lying clean and tidy in bed with the swaddled infant in her arms, and Cocksparrow curled up at her feet, she was rosy-cheeked and smiling, and he marvelled at how resilient women could be. He was so utterly relieved to see her that he swept her and the babe into an embrace and kissed her heartily. 'Thank God you're safe!' he cried, ignoring the shocked faces of the midwife and the maids.

When they were finally alone, he sat by the bed, nursing a goblet of wine, and admired their son, who fortunately favoured his mother rather than his father in looks.

'He's wonderful, isn't he?' Tom murmured.

'Yes! See, he's looking all around him and taking notice already.' Joan loosened her smock, revealing a swollen, blue-veined breast, and began suckling her son. Tom felt tears welling again, the sight so moved him.

'I'd like to call him Thomas after you and my brother,' Joan said.

He smiled at her proudly. 'Thomas it is, then!'

'And can we have my brother as one of the godfathers?'

'Of course we can.'

There was a knock on the door. It was the steward, looking flustered.

'Master Almoner, the King is here!'

'The King?' Tom had never dreamed that Harry would come to visit him here. If something momentous had occurred, surely he would have sent for him?

'Don't worry,' he said to Joan, rising and setting down his goblet. 'I'll see you later.'

The King was waiting for him in the hall, dressed in a voluminous cloak and a broad hat with a feather. He appeared to have come alone, but Tom knew there would be guards posted outside. As he bowed, Harry raised him.

'No ceremony, Tom! This is just one friend calling on another. I came to see how you are settling in.' His gaze took in the new tapestries and the plate-laden buffet. 'It all looks very fine!'

'All that I have comes from your Grace's bounty,' Tom said. 'I'm still getting used to living in such a splendid house. But I am forgetting myself. Would you care for some wine?'

The steward was hovering. 'A cup would be most welcome,' Harry said, and the man hurried away.

'Pray be seated.' Tom indicated the master's chair by the fireside.

The wine was brought, and Harry asked if Tom had any other plans for the house.

'Nothing major, Sir. It's so well appointed that there is no need. I was thinking of building a summer house in—' He stopped mid-sentence, because the wail of a baby could clearly be heard.

The King frowned. 'What is that?'

The cry came again.

'My housekeeper has just given birth to a son,' Tom said, thinking quickly, and remembering too late that a priest's mistress was often referred to as his 'housekeeper'.

Harry's eyes narrowed. 'Your housekeeper? Why employ a housekeeper if you have a steward? Thomas, is there something I should know?'

Again, Tom gathered his wits. If he lied to the King now and the truth came out later, things would go worse for him.

'Sir, I beg you to forgive the lie, but knowing how virtuous you are, I did not want to tell you, yet I must reluctantly confess that it is my mistress who has just borne a son. My son.'

He looked at Harry nervously, and fleetingly glimpsed the longing that flashed in the King's eyes. He wished he had kept his mouth shut, remembering that stillborn princess. But the Queen was with child again now, although few would know it until she had quickened and all looked well. Harry would not risk another failure becoming public knowledge.

As Tom had feared, the King's mouth pursed in displeasure. 'A son. Well, Tom, may I congratulate you.' There was little warmth in his voice.

'I fear I have disappointed your Grace,' Tom murmured.

'I don't want any scandal,' Harry said.

'There won't be any, I assure you,' Tom promised.

The King nodded. 'I know I can rely on you, Thomas. You've never let me down, and I value that. I envy you your son. It's a pity that you cannot acknowledge him as your own.'

Tom stared at him. In the euphoria of new parenthood, he had fondly, and naïvely, envisaged little Thomas growing up in this fine house, being nurtured by himself and Joan, his paternity known only to their trusted servants. But the King's words had pulled him up short.

'You must know, my friend,' Harry said, 'that keeping the babe's presence a secret would be impossible. There can be no place for a child in a clergyman's establishment.'

Later, when the King had gone, his usual good humour restored by two goblets of fine wine, Tom looked in on Joan and was relieved to find her asleep. It was as well, because he was reeling from what the King had said and needed time to think before he faced her again.

He retired to his study with another brimming goblet of wine and sat down at his desk. What was he to do?

The right, the proper, thing would be to have the child fostered or adopted, and soon. That was what he would have advised anyone else in his situation. But how could he tell his darling Joan that their precious son must be sent away, literally dragged from her arms? What had he embroiled her in by getting her with child? It had just been made horribly clear that all he could give her was pain.

He threw himself flat on his bed in a turmoil. Dare he defy the King's implicit command and keep young Thomas here, at least until he grew older? But it would be impossible. Harry clearly expected him to use the house for entertaining courtiers and foreign dignitaries; he had as good as ordered him to avoid any scandal, and Tom dared not risk the child's presence being exposed, as it had been this evening. Yet he could not bear the thought of strangers raising his precious son.

Dear God, what could he do?

He was expected at court early the next morning, so he did not disturb Joan. His head aching, he sat through the council meeting in a daze, drawing curious glances from some of the lords, and no wonder, because he usually found himself contributing more to the conversation than anyone else and making his views known persuasively. But today, he could not concentrate. He excused himself, pleading the pain in his temples.

He had barely escaped from the meeting when the King sent for him, inviting him to dine with him in the Queen's chamber, a great privilege. So although he wanted to do nothing more than lie down and sleep, he tidied himself and made his way there.

He was disgruntled to find that the Duke of Buckingham had been invited too, and the hearty Charles Brandon, the King's physical double, jousting partner and close friend. Though Brandon greeted Tom with the warmth he displayed to everyone, the Duke's nod was frosty. But Queen Katherine received Tom graciously, and the King welcomed him as if last night's conversation had never taken place.

The food was good, with fifteen dishes served at each course and a great stand of oranges for the remove, but Tom could not fancy any of it because he was feeling so ill and fretting about what he must say to Joan. But no one seemed to notice. The wine was flowing freely and they were all laughing and joking, as the Queen looked on serenely. To Tom's relief, Harry kept deferring to him and seeking his opinion, which he readily gave, making a real effort to be his usual eager self.

'I'm going to insist on invading France as soon as possible,' Harry announced.

'Bravo!' cried Brandon.

It was still too soon, Tom thought. Harry's enthusiasm often ran away with him; he had a tendency to rush into things. He took a breath. 'Greater victories are made in diplomacy than on the battlefield, Sir,' he said.

'There speaks a churchman!' Harry laughed. 'Thomas, I mean to win great victories for England! By right, I am king of France, and I mean to conquer it.'

Tom knew when he was defeated. 'Then I will assist your Grace in every way I can,' he said.

Along the table, the Duke of Buckingham leaned forward. 'Your Grace may rely on your nobility to support you,' he said pointedly, implying that a butcher's boy should not be stealing the glory. But Harry ignored the barb and simply raised his goblet to Buckingham.

'We'll have some fun in France, eh, Ned!'

'It will be a wonderful day when your Grace is crowned at Rheims,' the Queen said, looking adoringly at her husband. Her country and France were great enemies; she had an emotional investment in this venture.

'And with you beside me, my love.' Harry smiled, raising her hand to his lips. 'How delighted your father will be!'

Tom said nothing. The King was in love with his pretty wife and might well listen to her above his councillors. It clearly hadn't occurred to him that it might one day be to England's advantage to seek France's friendship. He watched the royal couple together, worried about Katherine's influence. The King's subjects would not think kindly on being ruled by a foreign power.

There came a moment when the Queen placed Harry's hand on her belly. He grinned, evidently having felt the babe kick.

'A fine general we have in there, my love! He will be Prince of Wales and, God willing, Dauphin of France!'

Tom felt sick when he rose from the table and thanked the Queen for her hospitality. It was time to go back to St Bride's Inn and face an unsuspecting Joan.

As he sat in the boat carrying him downstream, he thought it might be best if she took Thomas back to Yarmouth. He would miss them dreadfully, but at least Thomas would be with his mother, while the farm was a healthy place for a growing child. And he could visit from time to time without courting scandal. It seemed the most workable solution.

But Joan did not agree. Sitting up in bed nursing the baby, her beautiful hair about her shoulders, she looked aghast when Tom told her what the King had said and how he proposed to resolve the problem.

'No!' she cried, clasping Thomas closer to her breast.

'But it is the only way, sweetheart.'

Her eyes flashed. 'I will not be parted from you, Thomas Wolsey!'

'Then what are we to do? There can be no question now of Thomas staying here. You must take him back to the farm.'

'I will not! My place is with you.'

'Your place is with our son.' He was a little shocked that she would put him first.

'But I love *you*; I cannot bear to be apart from you. This little stranger — I must confess that my heart is not yet fully his. It will hurt me to part with him, but he will know no better if we find a wet nurse who can foster him. And I can visit him as often as I want.' Tears filled her eyes. She was being brave, he knew it, and for his sake. He was humbled in the face of such love.

With his heart breaking, he made discreet enquiries and was recommended to a Mistress Barlow, who lived with her husband and large brood of children in Willesden, north-west of London. Her last baby had not survived, and her milk had not dried up.

Tom travelled out to see her and was impressed. The house was spacious, the family happy and the woman herself clean and motherly. He told her only that Thomas was his nephew and that he had promised the child's widowed mother that he would find a wet nurse for him. The lies slipped easily from his tongue. He was not sure if she believed him.

He told her that the baby's name was Thomas Winter, having given him the surname in honour of Edward Winter, who had been instrumental in bringing Tom and Joan together. It was bitter gall to him that he could not give his son his own name.

A quarterly fee was agreed, and it was arranged that Tom would bring Thomas to Willesden on the morrow.

'The only drawback,' he told Joan on his return, 'is that it's ten miles away, a long round journey if you mean to visit him frequently.'

'I don't mind,' Joan said stoutly. 'It will be worth it. And it's important that we find the right people to care for him.'

That last night with Thomas, Tom could not sleep. He was aware of Joan lying wakeful – and silently tearful – beside him. It was unbelievable that tomorrow he must give up his son. But he would not be giving him up. He too would visit him and keep a protective eye on him. He would do everything he could to make the boy's life an easy and enjoyable one. He would lack for nothing. And when he was older, Tom would find him a place in his household and preferment at court or in the Church.

But for now, parting with the winning little fellow, flesh of his flesh, was going to be the hardest thing he had ever had to do. He toyed with the idea of abandoning his career at court and taking himself and his loved ones off to Lymington, where he could live out his life in untroubled obscurity, a provincial priest and a family man. Yet he knew that Harry would never let him go and, if he was strictly honest with himself, that he could never give up all that he had earned. If Thomas was to have a good life, he had to stay.

Dawn found him still wakeful, sitting by the hearth in Joan's bedchamber, drinking in the sight of his son sleeping soundly in the cradle. Later, when he took the child from Joan's arms, his heart broke again to see her sobbing so pitifully. The ride to Willesden passed in a blur, obscured by his own tears. It was the worst day of his life.

Chapter 11

1511–12

The celebrations for the birth of the Prince of Wales had gone on for days. There had been a great tournament at Westminster, banquets, feasts and endless revelry. Now they were at Greenwich, where the ebullient young father was presiding over yet another lavish feast. Tom was glad for him, for he knew how crucial the birth of a male heir was to the future welfare of England. He rejoiced to see a triumphant Harry's delight in the boy, even as he felt a searing envy of him, for this child would never have to be hidden away.

'Now I can fight the French and claim what is rightfully mine!' Harry was saying, kissing the Queen on the cheek and clinking goblets with her. She was flushed with pleasure.

Tom saw the Earl of Surrey enter the hall and head through the revellers in his direction. The old man's face was grim. 'I must speak with you, Master Almoner,' he said, drawing Tom aside into an oriel window. 'I've just heard from Richmond. The Prince is dead.'

Tom felt the news like a punch. He could not imagine what it would do to Harry – and the Queen. He felt like weeping, but controlled himself.

'How?' he asked.

'A fever, I am told. And now I must break it to the King. I think I'd rather face the French in battle.'

'Should I tell him, as his almoner?'

'No, I will do it. I've never yet shirked an unpleasant duty. I'll see him in private.'

Tom watched Surrey make his way to the dais, bend down and

whisper in the King's ear. Frowning, Harry rose and led him through the door to the royal apartments. Tom got up and followed.

He had not quite caught up with them when he heard an anguished howl coming from the King's study. 'No! No! God would not be so cruel . . .'

Without hesitating, Tom stepped into the room to find Harry collapsed in his chair, weeping bitterly.

Tom could imagine his master's agony, for his own, lesser grief was raw. He laid a hand on the King's heaving shoulder. 'And God shall wipe away all tears from their eyes; and there shall be no more death, neither sorrow nor crying, neither shall there be any more pain. Blessed are they that mourn, for they shall be comforted.'

Harry raised a ravaged face. He looked as if the world had crashed down on his shoulders.

'Why?' he asked. 'Why?'

'It was a fever, such as carries off so many infants,' Surrey told him. 'The physicians were summoned at once, but there was nothing anyone could do.'

'The Queen,' Harry blurted out. 'Does she know?'

'Not yet,' Tom said gently. His eyes met Surrey's. 'We thought it best for your Grace to break the news to her. I will send her to you. Then you and she can share your sorrow together in private.'

He hurried away, dreading to think how the Queen would take it. She had already lost one child. It would be hard for her. Yet it was a cross too many parents had to bear. He could not imagine what it would be like to lose young Thomas.

He found her still in the hall, laughing with the guests. He bent down to her. 'Madam, the King wishes you to join him in his closet.'

She looked at him enquiringly, then rose and made a dignified exit, her ladies following. Tom offered up a fervent prayer that God would give her and the King the strength to bear their loss.

After the pomp of the state funeral, Harry wore black for three months. It was obvious to Tom and everyone else that he was suffering, but he threw himself into state affairs with a determination that surprised them all.

Pope Julius had been pressing him to join the Holy League, an alliance between the Vatican, Spain and Venice against King Louis, who had aggressive territorial ambitions in Italy. Tom was all for it, but since it accorded well with Harry's own ambitions, the King needed no persuasion. At Easter, the Pope bestowed on him a Golden Rose he himself had blessed, which symbolised the Passion of Christ – a token of high apostolic favour.

Harry was bursting with excitement at the prospect of war. Starting on May Day, he jousted for three whole days, taking on all comers, showing off his martial prowess. He sat for hours planning military campaigns. Tom understood. This was the King's way of coping with his grief.

He was now Harry's right-hand man and unofficial secretary. He took care to be always ready with sage, fatherly advice and priestly words of comfort. Many were the happy sessions they spent together in the King's study, discussing the affairs of the realm and the world at large. Tom took an international view of things and he found that Harry was quick to see the bigger picture. They talked about diverse subjects, even mundane domestic matters. Tom made it his business to know everything that went on at court, who was at odds, who was in love, who was behaving unfittingly – all useful knowledge to have at hand. He had started to use paid informers, and soon realised that it was money well invested.

When Harry appointed him a prebendary of York, a canon of Windsor and registrar of the Order of the Bath, Tom showed himself profusely grateful. His wealth was mounting, as was his status in the land, but he knew he was capable of rising further. He might live like a nobleman these days, but he deserved it! So what if the lords sneered at him for having ambitions above his station in life? He served his King well. Why should he not be well rewarded?

That summer, when Harry took the Queen away on a summer progress through the Midlands, Tom stayed at court, attending diligently to business, keeping in touch with his master by letter and looking to the advancement of Joan's family. She had not been her normal joyous self since Thomas had gone away, and it had become her habit to spend much of her time at Willesden, where she was always made very welcome.

'I see Thomas nearly as much as I would if he were here,' she told Tom on her return one evening, throwing her cloak across the chair in her bedchamber. It was almost as if she was saying it to comfort herself. 'And he knows me now, knows me for his mother.'

Tom watched her being brave and positive, and his heart bled for her. He drew her into his arms. 'I am glad he knows you, my darling.' He did not trust himself to say more.

They never spoke of the hard choice they had had to make, or the fact that they had put their love and Tom's career before Thomas's needs. Miss his son though he did, Tom now felt he had made the right decision, for clearly the child was thriving. And it was not unusual for even great ladies to send their babes out to be nursed.

Nevertheless, he felt the constant need to make it up to Joan for depriving her of the normal life of a mother. In using his power to help her family, he satisfied his conscience to a degree. He spoke highly of Thomas Larke to the King whenever he could, with an eye to obtaining greater preferment for him. And it would come, for Larke was cultured and sincere. Tom revered him and was glad that his liaison with Joan had not affected their friendship. He appointed Larke his confessor and made him a canon of St Stephen's Chapel in the palace of Westminster.

It occurred to him that a priest such as Larke would expect him to confess the sins of breaking his vows and keeping Joan as his mistress, yet he could not bring himself to do so, because it would mean having to promise never to commit those sins again, and he had no intention of giving Joan up. Nor would he be a hypocrite.

He wondered if she was tempted to confess to her own sin. He dared not ask, for he feared to hear the answer. Did she, like him, wonder if being deprived of Thomas was a punishment for what they had done? Being unable to talk about it with her, a woman who was usually so forthright, was an indication of how heavily their misfortune lay between them. Yet how could love such as theirs be a sin? Surely, it was a gift from God.

He continued his reparation by helping Joan's other brothers. John and Edmund had also entered the Church, and Tom secured for them several lucrative benefices. He persuaded his friend John Kite, Archbishop of Armagh, to employ young Peter, and helped William to establish himself as a draper. Joan was so grateful, so appreciative. Looking at her smiling face, he wanted to say he would do anything for her – but he couldn't, because it would not be true.

When she told him she was with child again, his heart leapt, yet his joy was tempered by sorrow that this child too would have to be given up. Again, he vowed that he would be the best father he could be to it. Joan said little. What was there to say? She knew what had to happen.

When the King returned from his progress that autumn, he reverted to spending his days in pursuit of amusement, content to leave matters of state in Tom's hands.

'Thomas knows my mind on most things,' he told his Council. 'I'm giving him the authority to make decisions without reference to me.'

Tom bowed his head modestly, but not before he had seen the glowering faces of Buckingham and others. Yet he felt himself invincible. He knew all their weaknesses – and their secrets. Warham's bastards and Buckingham's intense jealousy of Harry, for example! The King relied on him increasingly, for he was the readiest among all the councillors to advance his will and pleasure. Unlike those greybeards Foxe, Warham and Surrey, he appreciated that Harry, being young, was bored by administrative matters. Tom was happy to shoulder the weighty and troublesome business his master loathed, whereas the others nagged him to attend to it. Tom also shared the King's lavish tastes in building, art, music, learning and revelry; he understood him. They had much in common.

Now, to Tom's satisfaction, England was to join the Holy League, in alliance with Pope Julius, the Senate of Venice, King Ferdinand and the Emperor Maximilian, a powerful coalition united against

France, their common enemy. Tom had once been against war, always arguing that peaceful means were the best way of settling quarrels between princes, yet now, with the King so set on invading France, he had caught his enthusiasm and supported him wholeheartedly.

'This will be a holy war!' he declared to the Council. 'We must put our strength behind his Grace, for his cause is righteous!' He glared at Warham and Foxe, who were rigidly opposed to war and rapidly falling from favour. 'Why such long faces, my lords? Our King is a good son of the Church. He wishes to please his Holiness. Look how he has commanded us all to curb our extravagance and dress soberly; my lords all, you have abandoned your silks in a holy cause.'

In November, Harry signed the Treaty of Westminster, which enshrined the aims of the Holy League; and he and Ferdinand agreed that England and Spain would jointly attack France in the spring. Harry was ecstatic. All his talk was of war and the glory he would win. He was so grateful to Tom, the architect of the pact.

Tom basked in his sovereign's praise. Seeing him riding so high in favour, courtiers and petitioners came flocking, craving his patronage. He was inundated with gifts, some of them substantial inducements. He knew he should not be accepting bribes for favours, but it was the way of the world. He was always adding to his store of treasure. Fortune had smiled on him, yet he was aware that her wheel could turn. It was best to provide for the future.

The new baby was a girl, born in the chill of February. Tom's heart melted as he cradled his tiny daughter, a great lump in his throat. Peering through the bedroom door, he saw Joan lying exhausted in the bed, her head turned away.

'Don't let me see her.' She had said it all along. 'It is best that she is taken away at once.'

The wet nurse was waiting, and soon the litter stood ready by the front door, packed with hot bricks wrapped in flannel against the cold.

'Her name is Dorothy,' Tom told the woman, choked. 'Today is St Dorothy's Day. She could have no better example than the virgin martyr.' And her mother, he would have liked to say. But this little

Dorothy would never know her mother. She was going to be adopted by one of Tom's clients, an alderman of Worcester called John Clausey, and it had been agreed that when she was old enough, she would be placed in the convent of Shaftesbury, where she would be assured of the finest education a girl could have in England, with a view to becoming a nun. Tom had promised a handsome dowry.

Giving her up was a terrible wrench. One final look at her sweet face and he had to turn away and clamp his mouth shut, fighting the urge to howl. When the litter had disappeared from sight, he dragged himself back upstairs to comfort Joan, praying that relinquishing this second child would not drive too deep a wedge between them. Yet how could they ever get past this searing sense of loss?

King Harry could have no idea how much he had asked of his faithful servant.

Joan had locked the nursery door. For her, the pain of her terrible loss was something she lived with inwardly. Fortunately, Tom had plenty to distract him, for the powers in Europe were hot for war.

'His Holiness has withdrawn King Louis' title of "Most Christian King" and bestowed the kingdom of France upon *me*,' Harry announced to the Council in March. 'All I have to do now is win it! So there must be no more delays. I am going to war.'

His steely gaze raked along the board. Tom noted the dismay on the faces of some of the lords. They started as the King banged his fist on the table.

'I'll brook no opposition. We invade France this summer.'

'I will put preparations in train, your Grace,' Tom said smoothly, as the others glared at him. 'But might I suggest that, given everyone's concerns about your safety and the succession, the expedition be led by some noble commander on your behalf? If he is victorious, the triumph will still be yours.'

Harry frowned.

'That is wise advice,' said Warham.

'I'm sure her Grace would agree,' said Buckingham.

'She will be all for the war,' Foxe murmured in Tom's ear.

That evening, Harry summoned Tom to his closet. 'Her Grace agrees with you,' he said. 'Her father has declared war on King Louis, and she tells me he is urging me to win praise and glory in reclaiming what is rightfully mine, yet she too fears for my safety and has begged me to appoint a commander. And so,' he sighed, 'reluctantly I have agreed. What matters is that the invasion goes ahead.'

In April, England declared war on France. The Lord Admiral, Sir Edward Howard, was commissioned to command a fleet of eighteen ships with Harry's magnificent *Mary Rose* as its flagship, his instructions being to harass French shipping and threaten the French coast to prevent any naval attack on England.

One sunny morning, Tom was seated at his desk at Greenwich, drawing up lists of provisions for the army, when he looked up and saw through the diamond-paned window a shifting orange glow in the sky.

'There must be a big fire somewhere,' he observed to his clerk, opening the casement and leaning out. Some way to the west, beyond the bend of the Thames, a great building was ablaze.

He shouted down to the boatmen on the Thames. 'What's burning?'

''Tis the palace of Westminster!' came the answer. 'It's caught hold, and no one can put it out!'

'By St Mary! God save us!' Tom hurried out of the room and collided with one of his servants.

'Father, I just returned from Westminster – the palace is up in flames. Some say it started in the kitchens. People have made heroic efforts to save it, but it's an inferno.'

Tom had gone, running to the royal apartments, where he found the King in his closet, shutting his writing desk.

'Your Grace, the Palace of Westminster is on fire!'

'What?' Harry was horrified. 'Is it bad?'

'Everyone is doing their best, I hear, but I fear it is out of control. The messenger said it started in the kitchens.'

'Have my barge brought to the jetty,' Harry ordered. 'I will see for myself. Attend me!'

As they hurried downstairs, Tom could not bring himself to believe that the ancient palace, the chief seat of government for centuries, was being consumed. When the barge passed the Isle of Dogs and rounded the bend in the river, he saw billowing black smoke in the sky some way ahead. By the time they reached the City of London, they could see flames leaping high and there were sparks in the wind.

'Dear God!' Harry groaned. 'All those treasures, all that history, gone.'

The bargemen could not approach too near the burning palace because of the fierce heat, so Harry and Tom had to watch helplessly from the Thames as the flames destroyed it. Desolately, Harry gave the order to return to Greenwich, unable to bear witnessing its complete destruction.

Tom returned to his study, but it was impossible to attend to business, for he was too churned up by the sight of the burning palace. In the afternoon, he sent his servants to see if anyone had perished in the fire and if anything had been salvaged from the ruins, then followed them to see for himself the extent of the damage.

He returned that evening, interrupting the King and Queen at supper. 'The fire is out, Sir, but I fear that much has been lost. Yet they have managed to save Westminster Hall, the Painted Chamber, the crypt of St Stephen's Chapel and the Jewel Tower.'

Harry looked devastated. 'So the royal lodgings are destroyed?'

'Yes, Sir. I have seen the damage myself, and they are past restoring, as are the service quarters. Will your Grace rebuild them?'

For once, Harry looked at a loss. 'Sit down, Thomas. Have a goblet of wine. You look as if you need it.'

Katherine smiled at Tom and poured him a drink, for which he thanked her profusely.

'I will have to give this some thought,' Harry said. 'It will take years to rebuild Westminster. In the meantime, Westminster Hall can still house the law courts and be used for ceremonies of state. But I will need an official residence in London.'

'There is Baynard's Castle,' Tom suggested. 'It is the Queen's own property.'

'It is beautiful,' she said. 'I stayed there with Prince Arthur.'

Harry frowned, possibly uncomfortable at being reminded of her first marriage, for he had been mightily jealous of his brother. 'It's too cramped for a court and there is no room to expand.'

'There is always the Tower of London, Sir,' Tom said. 'Your late father built splendid lodgings there.'

'It's also too small, and outdated. I will sleep on the matter.'

Tom saw Harry again in the morning.

'I have no choice but to accept a compromise,' the King said. 'If I can't live comfortably in London, I can still do so in royal style at Greenwich or Richmond, or Eltham Palace. They're all just a short boat ride away. As for Westminster, there is enough left for it to remain the seat of government.'

In June, the King sent a naval force commanded by Tom's erstwhile patron, the Marquess of Dorset, to Spain. The plan was that Dorset's men would join forces with the army of King Ferdinand and invade France from the south.

Harry could settle to nothing. Waiting for news was anathema to him. He longed to be at the centre of the action.

'If only I knew what was happening!' It was his constant complaint. 'Tom, you must let me know as soon as you receive word from Dorset, whatever time of day or night it is.'

'Naturally,' Tom said confidently, but the delay was making him uneasy too.

The messenger arrived that night, after Harry had retired. Tom read Dorset's letter with mounting dismay. King Ferdinand, that old fox, had persuaded him to deploy the English troops to aid him in conquering the kingdom of Navarre, which he considered to be rightfully his. *We shall easily prevail*, Dorset ended, *and then we shall advance into France.*

Tom could not credit Ferdinand's audacity. He was a temperate man, but anger now rose in him. The money for the army and its provisions had been raised by taxation for the specific purpose of conquering France, not to assist the King of Aragon in fighting a private war that was no business of England's. Dorset's forces should be in France by now! The King was going to be furious.

Hating to be the bearer of bad news, Tom made his reluctant way to the royal apartments, where the guards outside Harry's bedchamber door raised their crossed pikes and let him in. His master was sitting up in his massive bed, reading in the candlelight. He squinted at Tom.

'Thomas? What brings you here at this ungodly hour?'

'Your Grace.' Tom bowed, then broke the news.

'He did what?' Harry roared, leaping out of bed. 'He had no right! Send orders at once to Dorset, commanding him to invade France NOW, with or without Ferdinand.'

'At once, Sir!' Tom raced away.

The next news was even worse. His letter had not reached Dorset before Navarre was taken. Now Ferdinand had abandoned the English troops who had helped him, for they had drunk the contaminated water of Spain, and dysentery had cut a swathe through their ranks, aided by the stinking, insanitary conditions in their camp. Many had died. The rest were too ill to go on, and their prolonged stay had depleted their supplies. It was an inglorious end to what should have been a victorious campaign.

Harry was incandescent, cursing Dorset for his ineptitude and his failure to stand up to Ferdinand.

'I should have gone myself!' he thundered, glaring at his councillors. 'But I let you dissuade me, fool that I was. Now I am no nearer to conquering France than I was before, and England is covered in ignominy!'

'Sir,' Tom protested, 'we were concerned for your safety—'

'I don't want your excuses!' Harry interrupted. There was no reasoning with him in this mood. 'Summon Dorset home. He'll answer to me for his incompetence!'

He stumped around in a temper for days, snarling at everyone, even Tom. Tom suspected that the Queen was bearing the brunt of it, for it was her father who had caused this debacle. And when Dorset finally presented himself at court, looking gaunt and terrified, Tom stood by as the King shouted at him for the best part of a quarter-hour before he felt it incumbent upon him to step in and calm the waters.

'Sir,' he said, hastening after Harry as he crashed out of the council chamber. 'All is not lost. The Emperor Maximilian is hot against the French. King Ferdinand miscalculated in deciding to take Navarre before France, but it would be unwise to make an enemy of him, for he is still your friend. Next year, it will be a different story. We will raise a greater army – and you will lead it yourself!'

Gradually, Harry allowed himself to be mollified.

'It's always next year, next year,' he grumbled. He had no patience. 'How long must I wait to wear the crown of France?'

Chapter 12

1513

Harry was sitting at the head of the council board, not so rare an occurrence now that war was again in the air. 'I am fully resolved to invade France in person with a puissant army this summer,' he said, looking challengingly at the lords as if daring them to gainsay him. 'Therefore, it is necessary that this enterprise be speedily provided for in every detail.' He turned to Tom. 'And there is no man so fitted for the task as my well-beloved almoner here, so it is to him that I am committing my whole trust in the matter.'

Tom bowed his head. He could feel hostile eyes on him, but he truly doubted that any of them would be pleased to take on the amount of work the King had just heaped on him. And none would be so scrupulous about doing it properly.

'I shall be happy to take upon myself the whole charge and burden of this business,' he said.

'I knew I could rely on you, Thomas,' Harry declared happily.

Tom set to work. These days, he had a team of lawyers, secretaries and clerks to help him, but there was still too much to do. Numerous supplies and provisions had to be ordered for a large army, and there were so many things to organise that he found himself labouring away into the small hours.

He hardly saw Joan, and when he did manage to get home, he was too exhausted to make love to her, which he desperately wanted to do since he felt it would bridge the gulf that had opened between them after their children had been taken from them.

Joan had continued to put on a brave face; she was often over at Willesden, visiting Thomas, returning home full of his milestones and achievements – but there was a brittleness about her that frightened Tom. He feared he might be losing her, and that he could not have borne. She gave his life meaning. Yes, he loved the trappings of wealth and status that royal favour had brought him, but without anyone to share them with, he would be lonely indeed. Yet he had no time just now to make things right between them, and in the summer, he would be away in France. He was panicking at the thought.

One night, he came home feeling utterly weary, having spent the day wrestling with lists and figures. His body was crying out for rest. But there was Joan, sitting up late for him, looking a little like her old alluring self.

'I am so pleased to see you, my dear heart,' she said. 'I feel bereft when you are not here, and lately, when we have been together, I've been aware that I've not been good company.'

He hastened to her, knelt by her chair and took her in his arms. 'I know, I know,' he murmured. 'A heavy burden has been laid on us, and it is much the worse for you. It grieves me that you have been made to suffer so just for loving me. I cannot express how bad I feel, how deeply I wish it were otherwise. I would not blame you if you left me.' His voice broke.

She clung to him tightly. 'Don't be a fool, Thomas Wolsey! I love you. I will never leave you, even if the King commands it!' Her voice was fierce. She kissed him hard. 'Come to bed!' she invited, softer. 'Make me forget my sorrows.'

Her words invigorated him. He needed no second bidding. When they came together, it was more passionate, more violent, than ever before. He felt he had been lifted to a new level of ecstasy. And he knew, from Joan's ardent responses, that she felt it too. As they lay exhausted afterwards, bare limbs entwined among rumpled sheets, his eyes found hers and he knew that they were one again.

He returned to his work with a lighter step, tackling his multitude of tasks with greater enthusiasm. He knew he was doing a good job and that everything that could be done to ensure the success of the campaign was in hand. He was diligent in bringing all things to fruition and ensuring that the great royal army would be superbly equipped. He was indefatigable, getting everything done with good humour and efficiency.

'How you cope with it all is beyond me.' Harry watched, amazed, as Tom made sense of the piles of paperwork on his desk. 'It's sufficient to keep busy all the magistrates, offices and courts of Venice! Anyone else would be overwhelmed by it.'

'I thrive under pressure, Sir.' Tom smiled.

'You're a marvel,' Harry said. 'No king could have a servant more willing to please.'

One spring day, needing a break from work, Tom took himself out for a breath of air. Strolling through the palace gardens, he came upon the King and some courtiers playing bowls and paused to watch. Harry, of course, was winning – not because the others let him, but because he was very good at the game.

Presently, Tom became aware that the Queen was standing beside him. She acknowledged him with a gracious incline of her head, and he bowed. They stood together, applauding whenever someone scored.

Suddenly, she spoke, in a low voice that would not carry. 'Master Almoner, I have been told that you are trying to dissuade the King from invading France.'

Tom was surprised. 'Madam, who has told you that? The world knows that I am for peace, not war, but I see that this war is necessary. Heaven knows, I have been working hard to facilitate it.'

'My father's ambassador believes that you favour the French.' She was watching him closely.

'Then he is mistaken, Madam. I would not wish you to think that I am in any way hostile to Spain. My aim is to protect English interests. This is a small kingdom, and Christendom is dominated by two great powers, Spain and France. England's friendship tips the balance of power and preserves peace, so if the King favours Spain or France, he does so for a good reason.'

'I can hardly think that he will ever favour France when he is married to Spain,' Katherine said, sounding irritated.

'Naturally your Grace would think that, but history shows us that alliances can founder and shift.'

'Rest assured that I am doing everything in my power to preserve this one,' she said firmly.

Tom felt it best to change the subject. 'I see that Brandon is set to win,' he said, turning back to the game.

By June, everything was ready, and on a blazing hot day, the King left Greenwich for Dover, accompanied by the Queen, who was to remain as Regent. Tom had found it hard to say farewell to Joan that morning, and had left a little late, having been unable to resist the urge to make love to her one final time before the long separation that loomed ahead; but he was heartened to witness the splendour and pageantry of Harry's departure, which he himself had devised in concert with the royal heralds. And now here he was, a part of it, astride his mount in a great cavalcade that included no fewer than a score of peers. The heralds and trumpeters were riding ahead, announcing the King's presence to the crowds that had come flocking to see him as the colourful procession wended its way along the leafy roads of Kent. Behind him marched six hundred archers of the Yeomen of the Guard in their green and white liveries, making a splendid sight.

Tom smiled to see Harry waving at the people. How they adored him! The cheers were deafening in places. They would be even louder if he returned as a conqueror. Tom prayed that the invasion would be successful.

At Dover, he stood on the quayside as the Queen bade her husband farewell. Harry had confided to him that she was with child again, although the world did not as yet know it. The Earl of Surrey was to advise her Grace on all matters of state and had been deputed to escort her back to Greenwich.

It felt like a grand pageant rather than a war. After they docked in Calais, there were celebrations and tournaments, all aimed at impressing the French. Tom did not get much chance to attend, for he was busy supervising the checking of the vast stocks of provisions and munitions that he had had shipped from England. But finally, the task was completed, just in time for the King to march forward, his forces in battle order, through the Low Countries, to the well-fortified town of Thérouanne, where he met up with his ally, the Emperor Maximilian.

Together, they laid siege to the town. Tom was relieved to see that the small prefabricated palace he had designed to Harry's specification looked solid and was well furnished, offering every luxury a monarch might need. Not that the King was there often. He was too busy overseeing the repeated assaults on Thérouanne and throwing himself into the heat of battle with no thought for his safety.

The French retaliated by using diversionary tactics. In August, an army of fifteen thousand tried to engage the allied troops in an attempt to draw them away from Thérouanne, but were driven back so fiercely that they spurred their horses and galloped away at speed, leaving their tormentors jeering and laughing.

'We're calling it the Battle of the Spurs!' Harry spluttered, returning to the palace with Brandon, both of them in high spirits. 'By God, Thomas, you should have seen them fleeing!'

'I wish I had,' Tom said wistfully. 'Surely this will hasten the end of the siege?'

He was right. A week later, Thérouanne fell.

'It's all down to you, Thomas,' Harry enthused, happily donning his armour for his triumphal entry into the town to receive the keys. 'We couldn't have done it without your efficiency in ensuring that we had adequate supplies.'

'I thank your Grace,' Tom smiled, 'but I think our success was due in no small measure to your generalship.'

Harry grinned, taking his due. 'And to our brave soldiers. Armourer, burnish this breastplate – just there. I mean to give the French a good show today. They shall marvel at the magnificence of their conqueror – or rather, I should say, their saviour!'

Tom was with the victorious army when it marched into the town with the Imperial battalions, the victorious princes at its head. Harry looked jubilant, bursting with pride. It was a sight to send tremors down the spine. Yet he did not receive the welcome and ovation he had expected, for the townsfolk stood glowering at him in hostile silence. They looked pinched and starved. Tom felt chilled.

The King was in a foul mood when they got back to the temporary palace that evening. 'Set the soldiers to work pulling down the walls,' he ordered. 'Then burn the town, but turn the people out first. They shall not stay to harass the Emperor's territory another day.'

Tom made himself scarce and caught up with his correspondence. There were letters from the Council, and from the Queen, who begged to be assured of her husband's safety and was praying for his success. Tom was pleased to be able to inform her of the fall of Thérouanne. He frowned when he realised that someone had taken it upon himself to tell her that Harry had taken risks, which was patently untrue. She should not be fretting in her condition, when the future welfare of England hung on a good outcome to her pregnancy. He prayed that no one thought fit to inform her that her husband had been dallying with a young Frenchwoman, as had credibly been reported to him.

Tom found Harry at table with the Emperor, enjoying some fruit after dinner. Next to that slippery old snake Maximilian, the King looked like an innocent choirboy, with his fresh face and youthful good looks. Both men looked up expectantly.

Tom addressed his master. 'His Holiness has sent your Grace his congratulations.' He saw Harry glance at the Emperor, doubtless wondering if Pope Leo, who had succeeded the late Pope Julius, had sent him congratulations too. But Maximilian just sat there smiling.

'We are deeply honoured,' Harry said, flushed with his success.

'Oh, and Sir, the Queen has written again, desiring news of you. She asks after your health and trusts in God that you will come home shortly with tidings of another great victory. Your Grace, she says she can take no comfort or pleasure unless she hears from you.'

'I will write to her,' Harry promised. 'Is she keeping well?' Tom knew what he meant.

'It seems so.' He smiled. 'She says she has been horribly busy making standards, banners and badges to send to us.'

'We will have need of them when we take Boulogne,' Harry said. 'With that and Calais in our hands, we can command the Channel and use the ports as a bridgehead for bringing over more troops.'

'First, I think,' Maximilian interrupted, 'we should go to Lille to see my daughter, the Regent. She has followed our campaign with great interest and would be delighted to receive your Grace.'

Both Harry and Tom had corresponded with the Archduchess Margaret and been repeatedly surprised to be dealing with an intelligent woman on equal political footing – and to find themselves admiring her abilities, for she governed the Netherlands and Burgundy with wisdom and integrity. Yet Tom privately agreed with the King: it was against Nature for a woman to rule, for it overturned the natural order of the world. Women had not the capacity of men; they were inferior creatures, weak and emotional. Yet he had to admit that there were rare and honourable exceptions, such as Queen Isabella and this Archduchess – and his own Joan.

'Might I suggest,' continued Maximilian, 'that you then take the town of Tournai, which is near Lille, and consolidate our supremacy in the east.'

'But what of Boulogne?' Harry thought his plan was better.

'We march there afterwards!'

Tom was uneasy. It seemed that the Emperor, like Ferdinand, was looking to his own interests. It would be much more to his advantage than England's if Tournai fell. He sensed that Harry felt the same. But it could only mean a short delay, he told himself. There were weeks of the campaigning season left before winter set in, time enough to take Boulogne.

Towards the end of August, Harry and Maximilian rode to Lille, where they spent three days as the guests of the Regent Margaret. The Burgundian nobility had rushed to be presented to the King of England. Harry was supposed to be taking his ease, but he astonished Tom and everyone else with his energy. He jousted before the Archduchess and her young nephew, the Infante Charles of Castile, running courses against Brandon and the Emperor's champion and breaking many lances, to thunderous acclaim.

'I don't know how he does it,' Tom marvelled to a group of Flemish courtiers. 'He's fresher after this exertion than he was before.'

Harry was unstoppable, jousting and playing sports in the daytime, then dancing all night. But the revelry came to a sudden halt with the arrival of a letter from England.

'I must see the King!' Tom insisted to the guards outside the door of the royal suite. 'This cannot wait.'

He burst in and made a sketchy bow as Harry looked up, startled at his clumsy entrance.

'Your Grace, my apologies for the intrusion, but the Scots have invaded England.'

'By St George!' Harry leapt to his feet, dropping his lute. 'When? Where?'

'They crossed the northern border four days ago. It seems that King James is taking advantage of your Grace's absence. Scotland has ever been a friend to France, Sir. Undoubtedly, he thinks to distract you from your purpose.'

'I never did trust him!' Harry was pacing up and down. 'By God, I wish I was in England now! I'd trounce the Scots! What is their strength?'

'My intelligence estimates that King James has eighty thousand men.'

Harry's fair skin paled. He sat down heavily at his desk and reached for his pen. 'I shall write to the Queen and my Council and order them to prepare in all haste for the defence of England.'

'It appears that they are already doing so with great diligence,' Tom assured him.

News of the invasion swept through the camp. There were calls to retreat and go home, but the King resisted. 'We march on Tournai first,' he said, yet his voice lacked conviction. He was taut with anxiety, desperate to know what was happening on the other side of the Channel.

At last they received more news. Surrey had hastily raised an army and was marching north. The Queen was on her way to the town of Buckingham to rally his troops.

By now, Harry was in a fever of impatience, desperate to be back in England.

'I should not be here trying to take piddling little towns when my very throne is under threat,' he growled. 'It is more fitting that *I* should be riding at the head of Surrey's army to deal with the Scots as they deserve.' To his credit, he did spare a thought for his sister Margaret. 'When I think that her marriage to James was supposed to herald perpetual peace, I could strangle him!' he seethed.

Maximilian was supportive. 'Your Highness must do whatever is necessary,' he said. 'It would be a shame if you had to abandon this chance to take Tournai, but you yourself must decide where your priorities lie.' He placed a comforting hand on Harry's sleeve.

'What should I do?' Harry asked Tom late that night, when they were at last alone. 'My head is aching with the worry of it all.'

'Sir, I feel I should point out that if you take your army home now, you might arrive too late to defeat the Scots. By the time your Grace returns, Surrey will be in the north. He is a great soldier. Put your trust in him. With luck, God may give you victory over both your enemies.'

In the end, the decision was made for the King. Surrey had vanquished the Scots in a great battle on Flodden Moor in Northumberland. King James and many of his nobles had been slain.

Triumphant at the news, yet irritated because the Queen had effectively written that her victory was more important than his, and not a little jealous of Surrey – for Tom knew he felt that he himself should have been leading that army – Harry returned to his own war with renewed energy and laid siege to Tournai. From his chamber in the temporary palace, well behind the lines, Tom could hear the bombardment and the shouts of the besiegers. On 21 September, Tournai yielded.

When Harry returned to camp after taking possession of the town, he was in a jubilant mood.

'I could not have achieved such victories without you, Thomas!' he cried, throwing his arm around Tom's neck. 'I'm making you bishop of Tournai as a reward for all the pains you have taken on my behalf. Never has an army been better victualled and equipped!'

Tom flushed with pleasure. A bishop! 'I never thought to rise so high, Sir,' he said. 'I humbly thank your Grace.'

'Of course, you'll have to appoint a suffragan to act for you,' Harry said. 'I can't have you running over to France all the time.'

'Of course,' Tom agreed. He didn't want to be spending half his time abroad. Too many things took him away from Joan as it was. But he would be glad of his new status – and the revenues it would bring in.

Later, as he wrote to tell his beloved of his advancement and jokingly inform her that she must henceforth call him 'your Grace', he was thinking about those triumphs that Harry had accounted his victories. Two towns taken and a rout of the French. None of it had moved the King closer to fulfilling his dream. And now it was autumn, and the campaigning season was coming to an end. With winter approaching, there would be no opportunity to make further gains in France. Tom could not help feeling that all his efforts had been in vain.

Yet he had his bishopric, and he was glad to be going home. He could not wait to see Joan, to hold her in his arms, to claim her in bed. Not long to wait now! And he would visit young Thomas too and see how he had grown. One day, he vowed, he would reclaim him. Little Dorothy, however, was lost to him for ever. He could hardly bear to think about her.

In October, a new treaty was agreed at Lille. Harry, Ferdinand and Maximilian were to invade France the following year, and Harry's enchanting sister Mary, a vision of beauty at seventeen, was to marry the Infante Charles, Maximilian's grandson and Queen Katherine's nephew, who would one day inherit Spain and might even succeed Maximilian as emperor. A bright future surely awaited Mary, for if these things came to pass, her husband would be a new Caesar, the master of vast territories stretching from the Low Countries to Italy. And Harry was confident that next year, he himself would be crowned at Rheims.

At last they were headed for home. Late in October, the English fleet made port at Dover, and Tom was obliged to be one of the small company Harry took with him to Richmond, galloping at speed past the cheering, waving crowds who had come running to see the King.

'Look, Sir! Love for your Grace is universal with all who see you,' he cried, knowing that flattery was the breath of life to his master, and that it was important to say something to echo the mood of the occasion. 'To them you are not a person of this world, but one descended from Heaven!'

Harry grinned at him, turning to wave again at his subjects, a conqueror returning to a hero's welcome.

'Let us pray that the Queen crowns our joy with a son,' he said.

'That is my constant prayer,' Tom assured him. God, he was sure, would smile upon the King this time. He longed to see Harry a father.

He would have liked to escape to St Bride's Inn and Joan that evening, but despite the efforts of his subordinates in his absence, there was so much paperwork awaiting him that he needed time to sort it in order of priority. And there was a council meeting in the morning, so he doubted he would get away much before dinner time. Sighing, he called for water for washing, changed into clean clothes and descended to the great hall to find some supper.

Later, when he returned to his study to start clearing the urgent business, he was startled to find Surrey and Warham waiting for him. And they had some very bad news indeed.

The lords stood as Harry entered the council chamber and took his seat. Tom's heart was sinking.

'My lord of Surrey,' the King said, 'I owe you and your captains my hearty thanks for the victory at Flodden.'

The old warhorse bowed his head.

'In reward, you shall be restored to the dukedom of Norfolk,' Harry continued, as the Earl's craggy face lit up. Tom knew he had desired this for years, ever since his father had lost the dukedom, and his life, because he had fought for the losing side at Bosworth. The others were congratulating him, clapping him on the back.

'Join me for supper tonight,' Harry invited. 'The Queen and I would hear more of your victory.' He paused. 'Now, gentlemen, let us discuss the war with France.'

Tom felt sick.

'It has cost one million pounds so far,' Archbishop Warham said, 'and your Grace has taken two small towns to the benefit mainly of the Emperor.'

Tom drew in his breath.

'Graceless dogholes, they're calling 'em,' observed Lord Thomas Howard, Surrey's plain-spoken son.

Harry bridled. 'They were important strategic victories!' He looked like a lion about to pounce.

'I beg to disagree with your Grace,' Surrey countered. 'Tell him, Master Almoner.'

Tom was angry at being put on the spot. He should have known they would leave it to him to break the news. 'The fact is,' he said slowly, 'that your Grace need not have gone to war at all. We have just learned that King Louis made peace with Pope Leo before you even left England.' He did not need to explain that his Holiness would not now be bestowing the kingdom of France on Harry.

An angry flush infused Harry's cheeks. For a moment he seemed to have been robbed of speech. 'And neither Maximilian nor Ferdinand knew anything of it?' he growled. 'I find that hard to believe.'

'Evidently not, Sir,' Tom replied. 'They have been wrong-footed as much as your Grace has. And both are fully resolved to invade France with you next year.'

'Good! Louis shall answer for himself then! As for his Holiness, words fail me. He is as crafty as any Borgia!'

'Alas, the Holy See is not as holy as we might wish,' Tom observed. 'The Pope is a prince like any other, and protective of his landed interests.'

'Well, he too shall be taught a lesson about fidelity,' Harry seethed, his mouth setting in a prim line. 'I will not be deterred, even by Rome! I have acquitted myself well in France and, by St George, with the help of my allies, I will conquer it within a twelvemonth!'

As the meeting broke up and Tom was about to head off for St Bride's, the King detained him, making small talk until the rest had gone.

'Katherine has miscarried the child,' he said. 'I thought you should know.'

Tom could have wept for him.

'That's the fourth child she's lost,' Harry went on. 'I didn't tell you about the one last year. It was stillborn at five months.' Tom had known, in fact. One of the Queen's ladies was in his pay. 'In truth, I am in despair. A king needs a son to succeed him and inherit his kingdom. Why does God deny me that boon, when my need is greater than other men's?' There were tears in his eyes.

'Who can fathom the ways of the Lord?' Tom said gently. 'I wish I could offer some comfort to your Grace.'

'I've prayed and redoubled my prayers,' Harry said, regaining control of himself. 'I've gone on pilgrimage to Our Lady of Walsingham. I cannot believe that the Queen and I have done anything to deserve God's displeasure. By St George, she's fasted enough in penance, and she doesn't even know what she's done wrong!'

'Maybe if she fasts less, things will go better for you both,' Tom suggested.

'That sounds like good sense to me,' Harry said, his mood lightening. 'Thank you. I'll talk to her.'

Tom bowed and sped away. After waiting ages for a boat, he was finally on his way home. When Joan walked into the hall with Cocksparrow in her arms and saw him there, the look on her face was beyond price, and he almost thought it worth the long weeks of separation to see it. Then she was in his arms, and he melted into her, burying his face in her neck and rejoicing in the warmth and the closeness of her. He could not wait to get her to bed.

Chapter 13

1514

I am becoming used to living like this, Tom thought, as he stood looking around his hall at St Bride's Inn on a cold January day. It was much smaller than the King's hall at Greenwich, but almost as splendid, because Tom had filled it with sumptuous tapestries, elegant furnishings and a showy display of gleaming plate. He was steadily becoming very wealthy, rich enough to aspire to a standard of magnificence that imitated his master's. Joan went about clad in the finest silks and velvets, neither of them caring if she flouted the sumptuary laws, since Tom doubted that anyone would bother – or dare – to call them to book.

The whole time he had lived here, he had been conscious of time slipping by. Next year, the lease would expire. He ought to ask Harry if he would extend it. Yet he wasn't sure if he wanted that. St Bride's Inn was beautiful, but it was small, too small for entertaining in the way he ought to be entertaining, given his increasing importance in the land. He was beginning to think that he should be looking for somewhere grander, and more permanent.

Joan agreed. 'But not too far from London,' she said. 'I need to be able to see Thomas.'

'I will find out what might be available,' he promised. He would not refuse her anything, after she had given up so much on his account. He still desired her fiercely, still sought her opinions and confided in her, and yet he could not help but feel that there was a distance between them these days. The problem was that they were increasingly apart, thanks to the demands of his office. And Joan had too much time on her hands, time she spent at Willesden or buying luxury items to beautify their home. He knew she still loved him – her welcome after his return from France had been proof of that – but sometimes it seemed as if he might never recapture the full joy and wonder of their early years together.

The nursery door upstairs had remained locked. It was as if Dorothy and all memory of her had been shut away inside. But one morning, when Tom returned to Joan's bedchamber to retrieve a scrip he had left by his chair, he found her with her hand on the latch.

They stared at each other.

'Are you going to open it?' he asked at length.

'No,' she said, dropping her hand. 'I don't think so. It would be too painful. But,' and she beat her breast, suddenly vehement, 'she is here, here in my heart, and no one can ever take her away from me.'

He was beside her in two strides, folding her in his arms. 'And no one shall,' he said, deeply moved. 'She will always be yours. And rest assured, she is being well cared for. I make it my business to know.'

'You did not think to tell me?' Joan wrested herself free and looked at him accusingly.

'Forgive me! You never speak of her. I did not wish to raise a painful subject.'

'I am her mother!'

Tom sank into the chair, his face in his hands. 'I am sorry, truly sorry. I mourn her loss too, you know.'

'I know.' Her voice was softer now. 'Tom, we should talk about her. She is not dead, and even if she was, I would want to keep her memory alive. And you . . .' she knelt beside him, 'must stop punishing yourself. I made my choice.'

'But you could not have known what it would mean.' He put an arm around her shoulders and pressed her to him. 'And I feel responsible.'

'Stop blaming yourself, Thomas Wolsey!' she chided him, standing up. 'I love you. I wish things could have been different for us, but we are together, and that's important to me.'

'I love you too. You are everything to me,' he said, rising, and bent to kiss her, trying not to see the tears in her eyes.

* * *

His new house must be imposing; it must impress all who saw it and proclaim to the world that the man who lived there was of very high status indeed. It must be a place where he could aspire to a lifestyle emulating that of the King. Above all, it must be in a healthy location, for he still cherished hopes of bringing his son to live there with him. And, of course, it must be worthy of Joan, his beloved. Always he felt he had to make it up to her for what she had lost.

He consulted his physicians; he employed two of them now, careful to keep himself in good health. 'I want a prime site in wholesome air within twenty miles of London.'

After some searching, they told him that the Knights Hospitallers were looking to lease their manor at Hampton, which lay by the Thames, fifteen miles from Westminster. On a late January day, Tom went to view it, taking a boat from Blackfriars stairs. The walled plot contained a fairly new courtyard house, which he was told had been built by the previous tenant, Lord Daubeney. It was too small and would have to be demolished, but the riverside setting was perfect. He could envisage a palatial residence rising there, built of red brick in the Burgundian fashion, yet embellished with the very latest antick decoration in the new-fangled style that was flourishing in Italy but only just beginning to feature in English buildings. Tom was willing to wager that once Harry saw what he was planning, he would want a palace just like it!

'I'll take it,' he said, then hastened back to St Bride's to tell Joan about it. Her enthusiasm matched his, and that night they sat up late while she made a list of what she wanted for the house and he did the sums.

'There's enough in my treasure chest for me to employ the best craftsmen working in England,' he said, 'and if need be, I'll bring some over from abroad. And I'll send to Italy for some architectural pattern books. I'll build a palace such as the world has never seen!'

He wasted no time. Within two weeks, plans were drawn up, changed, drawn up again, then men were set to work to pull down the existing house. The King took an interest, asking to see the plans and the pattern books, and marvelled at Tom's vision.

'It will be a palace fit for a king,' he said, a touch wistfully.

'I would expect to offer your Grace nothing less when I entertain you,' Tom said. 'I am building apartments for you and the Queen, and they will have every comfort you could wish for.'

He was already looking forward to showing his new house to Harry. But he knew he would have to contain his excitement for many months yet.

The child, not yet four, stared up at Tom. His son had grown into a beautiful boy and was now losing the chubbiness of infancy. He became a playful little soul once he had got over his initial diffidence at seeing his visitor. Not that he was aware that the tall cleric who turned up every fortnight or so was his father, but he knew Joan and smiled broadly when he saw her, showing his baby teeth. He was growing up tall and strong, a son to be proud of. If only he did not have to be hidden away . . .

This situation could not go on, Tom decided. He could not have Joan coming back from her visits tearful and racked with longing for her own flesh and blood. He would speak to the King and do his best to end this torment.

The following afternoon, when he returned to court, he came upon Harry shooting with Charles Brandon at the butts.

The King smiled ruefully. 'Have the Council sent you to fetch me, Thomas? They were much put out when I said I had business to attend to.'

'I haven't seen them, Sir. I wanted—'

'But *you're* just the person I want to see,' Harry interrupted. 'When you move out next year, I'm going to demolish St Bride's Inn and build myself a new palace in its place.'

'That's a capital idea, Sir,' Tom said, suppressing a twinge of sadness at the coming destruction of the house that he and Joan had made their home. 'You need a palace in London and St Bride's is the perfect location.'

'It has all worked out perfectly,' Harry said, finishing the game and striding off towards the royal lodgings.

'It has, Sir, but for one thing. I have a request to make of you.' Tom found himself trembling. So much rode on this moment.

'Ask, and if it is in my power, I will grant it!'

'It concerns my son, Sir. His mother is longing to have him with her and grieves for his absence, and I too – I would play a father's part and nurture him under my roof. We did your Grace's pleasure in having him fostered, but he is such a toward child, and would benefit from what I can do for him and the example I want to set him. I pray you, could I bring him home? At Hampton, there will be room to spare, and his presence will not be compromising in any way.'

Harry's blue eyes narrowed. He slowed his pace. 'Thomas, I should not have to remind you of the need to avoid a scandal that would reflect on me. You are my chief minister, and that which was unbecoming in a dean is even less so now in a bishop. I wish I could grant your request, but I cannot risk bringing discredit on the Church, on your office – or on myself. I am sorry.'

Disappointment gripped Tom like a pain in the guts.

'I hope you understand my position, my friend,' Harry said. 'Tell the boy's mother that the Queen herself, if she had a son, would be obliged early on to place him in his own separate household. I myself was sent away to Eltham Palace when I was very young. I saw my mother only when she visited me, and on the rare occasions on which I came to court. It is the way of the world. I know that merchants and yeomen do things differently, but in your unique situation, you must needs be pragmatic.'

'Think no more of it, Sir,' Tom said, barely able to get the words out. He glanced sideways at the King, wondering if it would be wise to attempt a final plea, but was deterred by his set expression. He saw too that Harry had lost his usual healthy colour and was sweating in the January cold. He wondered if he might be ill.

They parted at the palace, and Tom hastened down to the landing stage to catch a boat home. He was thankful that he had not mentioned approaching the King to Joan, for he could not have borne her disappointment. Coping with his own was difficult enough.

'You're quiet tonight,' she said later, sitting in the candlelight, her embroidery tambour on her lap, Cocksparrow at her feet. 'Is all well?'

'Perfectly,' Tom said, looking up from the papers he had brought home. 'I'm just tired.' He was struggling to keep his voice from breaking.

As Tom had thought, the King had been developing a fever and was obliged to rest, but by the beginning of February, he had risen from his bed, fierce against France and eager to start campaigning again. He could not wait to return to the field. At Candlemas, after High Mass at Lambeth Palace, he created Charles Brandon duke of Suffolk and formally restored the dukedom of Norfolk to the valiant Surrey. The ceremony of ennoblement took place in the great chamber at Lambeth Palace. Tom was present, along with many peers.

When the King had gone, courtiers crowded around to congratulate the new-made dukes. As Tom had anticipated, it was nevertheless clear that the advancement of Brandon was not popular. He heard the words 'surprising' and 'upstart' and smiled to himself. He had expected nothing less from the older nobility. Buckingham, who had not troubled to hide his fury, was nowhere to be seen.

Tom had urged Brandon's ennoblement. 'Your Grace might render him more meet a husband for the Regent Margaret,' he had argued, remembering how Brandon had pursued the Regent at Lille the previous autumn, almost causing a scandal. But, as so often, Tom had another motive. Once Surrey was restored to his father's dukedom, his influence in Council, in concert with Buckingham's, would need to be counterbalanced by a grateful Brandon, who would be all too willing to ally with Tom, his benefactor. Fortunately, Harry had seen the wisdom in this.

'New blood and new men are what we need!' he'd declared.

Tom too had benefited from the royal largesse. Four days later, he was made bishop of Lincoln.

'We should drink to you too, my friend!' the King said, as they feasted one evening. Again, the vultures of the court looked ready to swoop.

'Good service deserves to be rewarded,' Harry continued, looking about him challengingly. 'I need men like Thomas and Suffolk, and you, Thomas Boleyn.' He nodded at the dark-haired diplomat standing by – another of those who had no time for Tom, which was unsurprising, given that Boleyn was married to Norfolk's daughter. 'You all serve me well, and you are all proof that an ancient pedigree is not necessarily a prerequisite for advancement at court.'

The expressions on the faces of Buckingham and Norfolk were priceless. As was that on Joan's when Tom came home at the end of the day and told her of his good fortune. She looked so pleased and proud, but – as ever – she kept him grounded.

'My lord Bishop! Well, there's a thing! Thomas Wolsey, you have done well and we shall celebrate with some good sack this evening,' she said, kissing him. 'But you should be wary of baiting the nobility. After all, they are the King's peers. It would not do to make more enemies than you already have.'

Tom gentled her, kissing the tip of her nose. 'They can't touch me,' he told her. 'I have the King's high favour – and they know it.'

'Never take that for granted,' she cautioned. 'You think you're invincible, yet there are no guarantees in this world. Take care, my dear heart.'

'I assure you that I keep my enemies in sight,' Tom said, thinking that she was fretting without cause. 'Now, let us toast my promotion!'

Before retiring to bed that night, he spent some time in prayer in his little oratory, rendering the thanks due to God, who was, he acknowledged, his true benefactor. My lord Bishop of Lincoln – and he an innkeeper's son! Well, well. He was truly grateful for the wits and ability that had enabled him to rise so high. Yes, he had done it chiefly by his own indefatigable efforts – and maybe God had called him to this eminence that he might do some good.

Sometimes, he found it hard to pray. He made time for the daily offices, of course; it was expected of him as almoner. Yet there was always too much happening in his life for him to feel a spiritual connection to his Maker. He was not – admit it – priestly material. He knew he would not be able to shoulder the burdens of his diocese and that he would have to appoint deputies, but wasn't that what a lot of bishops had been obliged to do? They were political animals, like himself, more at home in Parliament and court than in their cathedrals, ministering to their flocks – with honourable exceptions, of course.

God would understand, he told himself, for He had brought Tom this far, and He must have done it for a good reason. God, Tom felt sure, did not mean him to take up the sanctified life; no, He meant him to be in the world, working for peace – and the glory of England.

'This came for your Grace.' The clerk handed Tom a letter in code, with the translation written beneath. He waited. Tom waved him away and sat down at his desk to digest the report. He drew in his breath sharply as he read that, unbeknown to Harry, Ferdinand and Maximilian had signed a secret pact with King Louis. For weeks now, he had become increasingly anxious about Ferdinand's failure to commit to any plans for war.

Knowing that the King would attend Council, he entered the chamber beforehand with a heavy heart and delivered his news to the assembled lords, laying the reports before them. He could sense their outrage. For a moment, no one spoke. They didn't need to: their faces spoke for them.

Then Harry made his entrance, and Tom had to break the bad tidings all over again.

'What?' the King roared. 'Are you telling me that my allies have gone behind my back and signed secret treaties with Louis?'

'I fear it is true, your Grace,' Norfolk said. 'We have the reports here from your agents.'

'Then I have been made to look a fool!' Harry muttered, visibly seething, clenching his fists. His eyes angrily scanned the papers. 'I can see no faith in the world save in me only, and God, who knows this, will prosper my affairs,' he declared defiantly. It was said through gritted teeth.

Tom felt for him, for he had been made to look like a gullible halfwit, expecting Ferdinand and Maximilian to help make him king of France, when clearly neither of them had had any intention of doing that. They had played to his vanity, played him like an ignoramus, and now it was clear that they had secretly colluded with Louis in agreeing that he should be permitted one or two minor victories that would benefit them and hopefully satisfy his craving for glory. Tom's mind set to work rapidly, trying to devise a way to bring his master back from this.

Harry looked devastated. 'I trusted them,' he said. 'I thought them men of honour. Well, I will never be so trusting again.' His tone was bitter.

'The ramifications of this alliance breaking down are manifold,' Warham chimed in, unsparing of his master's distress. 'The Princess Mary's marriage to the Infante Charles cannot now go ahead, for it says here that Maximilian's council has refused to accept her as his bride.'

Another body blow for the King – and his sister.

'But preparations for the wedding are well advanced!' Harry cried. 'They are to be married in May, and I have spent a fortune on the Princess's trousseau, jewellery, furnishings and plate. Her retinue is already drawn up.'

'Sir, there can be no wedding,' Norfolk said gently.

Harry looked as if he was about to explode again, but Tom, whose quick thinking had presented him with a solution, sought to cheer him. 'Your Grace, there is an advantageous way to counteract this misfortune. You yourself might consider an alliance with France.'

Everyone stared at him.

'But we are at war with France!' Harry protested.

'Wars never bring prosperity,' Tom continued. 'Peace with France will save England's face and bring many benefits. And I hear that King Louis is looking for a wife.'

'No,' Harry said. 'France is mine and I mean to win it!'

'But without allies, it will be a long and costly struggle.' Tom leaned forward. 'I am not advocating abandoning your Grace's ambitions in that direction. I merely advise postponing the enterprise until you are in a position to pursue it. The Princess may yet be a queen – and I think Louis will be eager to come to terms.'

Some of the councillors, notably Warham and Suffolk, were nodding sagely. Harry glared at them in disgust.

'You can all forget that idea,' he said brusquely. 'As for the perfidy of Ferdinand and Maximilian, I will sleep on the matter and advise you tomorrow.'

From the King's angry demeanour the next morning, and the fact that the Queen had clearly been crying, as Tom saw when he briefly encountered her in the gallery that led to the royal apartments, there had been an almighty row between them. It required little imagination to deduce that Harry had sought a scapegoat for the betrayal of his allies, and who better than the faithless Ferdinand's daughter?

'I want a divorce!' he demanded as Tom entered his closet. 'Can it be accomplished? I will pay the Pope's price.'

Tom was shocked, but inwardly he was not displeased. He had never approved of the King being under his wife's influence in political matters, and now, evidently, Harry's trust in her had been shattered. And yet, what he was now asking was akin to wanting the moon. The difficulties could be tremendous.

'Your Grace, I urge caution. There are no grounds.'

'She has betrayed my trust, and she is barren! Are these not grounds enough?'

'Not in the eyes of the Church, Sire.'

'But is not her barrenness a sign that God does not smile on my marriage?'

'Her Grace has borne two sons; that they died is not her fault. And you are both young yet. There is plenty of time.'

'You're one to talk,' Harry snarled, pacing up and down like a caged lion. 'You advocate a peace with France, so why should you champion one who loves Spain?'

Tom held his gaze. 'Because of the great respect and affection I have for the Queen, Sir, and because putting away such a great lady will bring down the wrath of Spain and the Empire on you. But if you are bent on a divorce, I will put out discreet feelers as to how the matter would be viewed in Rome.'

'See to it!' Harry commanded.

Chapter 14

1514

Within a week, it was apparent that the King was coming around to favouring a French alliance. Tom had marshalled all his skills to persuade him and gradually worn down his objections. Even Suffolk had failed to do that. Harry might be firm friends with the Duke, but the man had no brain and could easily be bested.

The Howards were not bothering to hide their hatred of Tom. It was no secret that Norfolk was determined to unseat one he openly called a low-born upstart, and he was relentless in trying to poison Harry's mind against him. Tom, in turn, was doing his best to eclipse the Duke in the King's counsels and discredit him. It wasn't easy, given how grateful Harry was for Norfolk's victory at Flodden.

Fortunately, most of the councillors were now in agreement with Tom's pro-French policy. Weary of all the war talk, and aghast at the expense, they were ready to set aside their prejudices and work with him. Yet there remained Buckingham, who opposed everything Tom did on principle.

Buckingham made no secret of the fact that he loathed Tom, and those aggrieved lords who felt that the butcher's son was usurping their traditional privilege of being chief advisers to the King had rallied behind the Duke. There came the day when Harry sat down to dine with Wolsey in his privy chamber and it was Buckingham's turn to have the honour of presenting the golden basin in which the King would wash his hands. After Harry had finished, Wolsey smiled at his rival and dipped his fingers in the same water.

A look of outrage erupted on Buckingham's face. Water suddenly splashed out of the basin, soaking Tom's fine leather shoes.

'You did that deliberately, my lord!' Tom snapped.

'I, my lord Bishop? It was an accident,' Buckingham smirked.

'And I am supposed to believe that?'

'Gentlemen, please!' Harry intervened. 'I'm sure his Grace of Buckingham will apologise.' He looked up expectantly at his cousin.

'I apologise,' the Duke muttered, with ill grace.

Tom suppressed his fury. Buckingham was so obvious, so transparent in his overweening pride. It was this, with his aloof manner and his sheer incompetence, that had prevented him from rising to the kind of eminence he himself enjoyed. But he was too stupid, as his behaviour had just proved.

Later, when the Council convened, Tom noticed the insufferable fellow reeking of disapproval as he proceeded once more to enumerate to Harry all the good reasons why he ought to make peace with the French. Buckingham must be furious that the King was not including him in the conversation or asking for his opinion, but Harry had no need to. Like most of the older nobility, Buckingham hated the French, England's traditional enemy, and he would never bring himself to approve of Tom's foreign policy on principle. Tom knew that the King did not want peace with France either, but he was sensible enough to realise that Tom was giving him wise advice, and he always took a mischievous pleasure in discomfiting the Duke, for he believed that the empty-headed fool had secret designs on his throne. It was a ridiculous notion, because Buckingham's place in the royal family tree was so distant as to render his claim laughable – unless, of course, the man was idiotic and proud enough to take himself seriously.

'Very well,' Harry declared, 'I will make peace with the French. See to it, Thomas.'

Buckingham looked as if was about to suffer an apoplexy.

'As your Grace wishes,' Tom said smugly.

Harry was fond of his sister Mary and, at enormous cost, had provided her with a fabulous trousseau of sumptuous clothing, jewellery, furnishings and plate – all for the marriage that was not now going ahead. Regarding the bills and receipts, Tom shook his head and sighed at the outlay. It could not go to waste! He felt for the tall, graceful young woman, a beauty with the red-gold hair of her race and a charming, lively manner. Charles's advisers had done him no favours in rejecting her.

But all was not lost. There would be a wedding, he vowed, just with a different bridegroom. He sat down and began drafting a letter for Harry to send to the French King.

Tom's negotiations with France reached a speedy and successful conclusion in the summer, when King Louis formally asked for Mary's hand. A new treaty was signed, providing for Harry to keep Tournai and receive a pension from Louis. At the end of July, at the royal manor of Wanstead, the Princess formally renounced her betrothal to the Infante Charles. A week later, the peace with France was proclaimed, and it was announced that she was to marry King Louis. Harry could not sufficiently thank Tom for negotiating such a satisfactory settlement, one that would restore his greatness in Europe.

Then came news that Cardinal Bainbridge, the Archbishop of York, had died in Rome, where he had served as the King's ambassador to the Vatican. Tom and Harry were appalled when they learned that the Cardinal's servant had been thrown into prison, having confessed to poisoning his master.

'It says here that during a heated quarrel, the Cardinal dealt him a blow, so he sought his revenge.' Harry laid down the letter. 'That was behaviour most unbecoming in a man of the cloth, yet he did not deserve to be murdered for it.' He paused, deep in thought. 'Now I am left with a vacant see to fill. As far as I'm concerned, there is only one man for it, and that is you, Thomas. Will you be my new Archbishop of York?'

Archbishop? Tom felt light-headed with exultation. He had hardly drawn breath since he had been made bishop of Lincoln!

'I would be honoured, your Grace,' he said fervently, envisaging how thrilled Joan would be when he told her the good news. He had been absolutely right to build himself that fine house that was rising, brick by brick, at Hampton. It would be a fitting setting for an archbishop. Of course, there would be episcopal palaces up north, and there was an imposing house, York Place, near Westminster, which would more than make up for the loss of St Bride's Inn.

He prepared as fast as he could for his translation from Lincoln to York. Once consecrated archbishop, he ordered that his archiepiscopal cross be carried before him at court or wherever else he happened to be, even in the presence of Archbishop Warham, who bristled at the sight.

'My lord of York,' he said, bearing down angrily on Tom in the great hall. 'Might I remind you that you are under my obedience, for my office is superior to yours? I am Primate of all England and senior to all other bishops within this realm. I charge you now, in view of the ancient obedience of York to Canterbury, to cease the advancing of your cross in the presence of the cross of Canterbury.'

Tom glared at him. 'My lord, it is my understanding that Rome long ago decreed that each of us should carry his cross in the province of the other. Therefore I shall continue to have mine borne before me when we are together.'

Warham flushed an irate puce colour. The eyes of the courtiers were transfixed upon them. 'I am sure you are mistaken,' he hissed.

'And I am sure that I am right,' Tom said, knowing it was the truth, for he had checked the precedents.

The Archbishop turned on his heel and swept away, outrage emanating from him. Battle lines had been drawn, Tom realised. Another enemy.

He wasted no time in drawing up plans for lavish improvements to York Place, where he intended to live while Hampton Court was being built.

'Thanks to your Grace's bounty, I can transform it into a fine palace where I can entertain you in princely style,' he enthused as he guided the King around the rambling complex of buildings, where men were already at work, his new steward, Thomas Cromwell, hovering in their wake. He had liked this bullish-looking lawyer from the first. Cromwell was the son of a blacksmith, so they had their lowly birth in common, and the sense of achievement that came with rising through one's own abilities. But while Tom had opted for the ivory towers of Oxford, Cromwell had been a mercenary in Italy – and a ruffian, by his own testimony – before he had opted for the law. Tom had been prepared to overlook his chequered past, judging that he was a man of some ability.

Harry, who loved updating and improving his older residences, and building new ones, expressed his pleasure at seeing the project progress.

As they entered a gallery, a young woman stepped out of one of the doorways leading off it, carrying bolts of rich fabrics. It was Joan. She coloured when she saw who Tom was with, and hastily made a low curtsey.

Harry was eyeing her appreciatively.

'This is my good friend Mistress Larke, Sir,' Tom said, full of trepidation lest the King order him to banish her from his house to avoid scandal.

'Your Grace.' Joan bobbed again. 'Our families know each other. I'm just here today to help my lord Archbishop with ideas for furnishings.'

Harry was smiling. 'And by the look of those, you have excellent taste, Mistress Larke!'

Tom held his breath. Had the King swallowed the pretence – or was he choosing to ignore the implications of Joan's presence here?

But no, it seemed that he really did think Joan a family friend, for he moved on and said no more. Behind him, Tom threw Joan a look of relief over his shoulder as his heart rate slowed a little.

Later, he led her to a suite of rooms at some distance from the archiepiscopal apartments. 'After what happened today, my love, we cannot risk your being discovered here again. The King won't be deceived a second time. These are fine rooms. I think you should have them. Believe me, I hate hiding you away—'

'It's all right, Tom,' she interrupted, sliding into his arms. 'The last thing I want is to invite scandal and make things difficult for you. I just want to be with you, and if this is how it must be, then I am content.'

'You are a saint,' he breathed, his arms tightening around her. 'I don't deserve you.'

'After all you have done for me? Without you, I should not have lived in fine houses, dressed in silks, commanded a host of servants or enjoyed riches beyond my wildest dreams! And I would not have had you, the most important thing of all!'

'But I have brought you nothing but grief and ignominy!'

'You have loved me, and that is the greatest treasure I shall ever have.'

He shook his head, not convinced. 'Yes, but in loving you, I have deprived you of other important things in life. You're half my age. You should not be wasting your youth on an ageing man.'

Joan twisted out of his embrace. 'You're a great man, Thomas Wolsey, but a fool when it comes to love. Stop agonising and let me be the judge of what's important to me. These are beautiful rooms, and I will be happy to have them for my own. And maybe we should choose a similarly distanced apartment for me at Hampton Court.'

'What a woman you are!' he marvelled.

Still, he felt guilty. It was not fair on a lively young female like Joan to be hidden away like a shameful secret, even if she did live in some splendour. She could not be a wife, or a mother, or even mistress of her own household. She had no friends, save her maids. She was too intelligent to spend her days in gossip and sewing, but that was what she did. It could not be enough for her, surely.

Was she content? She had assured him repeatedly that she was, but sometimes he caught a hint of frustration or testiness. He wished he could offer her more, but it was more impossible than ever now.

'I have written to the Vatican, asking Pope Leo to appoint you a cardinal,' the King announced grandly the next morning, with a beaming smile. 'Your merits are such that I can do nothing of the least importance without you, and I want you to know that I esteem you among my dearest friends.'

Tom's heart was overflowing. He was dangerously near to tears. 'Your Grace's friendship means more to me than any cardinal's hat,' he said, knowing he sounded choked. 'But I am truly sensible of the honour, and very, very grateful.' He would have liked to tell Harry that he looked upon him, and loved him, like a son, that he would move mountains for him if he had to, but he felt that would be overstepping the respectful distance he must keep with his sovereign.

It was strange, he reflected as he returned to his office, that personal fulfilment could come from the most unexpected relationships, such as his illicit one with Joan and his deferential one with the King. He was blessed indeed to know them both. And he was jubilant at the prospect of being made a cardinal – a prince of the universal Church, a member of the Sacred College, only one step down from the throne of St Peter itself! What more could he ask for now? To be pope? He chuckled at the thought.

No, it would be enough to be a cardinal. It wasn't just the status, the power and the iconic red robes that appealed to him, although he knew he would revel in them all; it was his conviction that he had the skills and the ability to use the office for the good of England – and Christendom itself!

In the autumn, a reluctant Princess Mary sailed to France to marry King Louis. Tom had his suspicions about her antipathy towards the match arranged for her; he was sure it was not just down to the fact that Louis was so much older. He had noticed the way her face lit up whenever Suffolk entered a room, and how her eyes followed his tall, magnificent figure. It was sad that there could be no future in it, yet she was a princess and had been brought up to understand that any marriage she made must be for England's advantage. And to be fair, she had played her part well through all the great ceremonies of her betrothal. It had only been as the moment of departure loomed that she had begun to look miserable. Tom hoped that marriage would soon settle that, and that the French King would be kind to her.

Returning from seeing Mary off at Dover, Harry summoned Tom to his closet and told him about the great send-off he had afforded Mary, and what a fine sight the escorting fleet had been.

'It was hard parting with my little sister,' he said wistfully. 'We've always been close. But I feel I've done the right thing by her. She will be queen of France, and no other English princess has ever had that honour. And yet, on the quayside, as we said farewell, she told me she had only consented to marrying Louis for the peace of Christendom, and she asked me to promise her that if she survived him, she could marry whom she liked.' He drew in a breath. 'Did you know that she's in love with Brandon?'

'I had a slight suspicion, Sir,' Tom said carefully, 'but I put it down to a girlish fantasy, nothing to bother your Grace about.'

'It's more than that.' Harry frowned.

'Then I am sorry for her. Did your Grace give that promise?'

'Aye, I did, to pacify her. But let's hope that she'll have forgotten it by the time Louis dies.'

'She may well change her mind, for women can be very fickle,' Tom observed. 'And, much as I admire my lord of Suffolk, he has had two wives already and no one seems certain as to whether or not he was lawfully married to either of them, so it's as well that the Princess is now beyond his reach.'

'Indeed!' Harry guffawed. 'He's a rogue, is Brandon. I'd never have permitted him to wed her, not in a thousand years!'

By Christmas, Tom's army of workmen had made York Place ready for occupation, and as soon as they had gathered their tools and left, and the place had been thoroughly cleaned, Tom and Joan took a boat upriver to inspect it.

'It's a very fine palace,' Tom exclaimed, gazing up at the brick-faced edifice in wonder. 'Fit for entertaining the King in princely style!'

They walked through room after room, overawed by the fresh splendour of the hall, the chapel, the watching and dining chambers, then passed through eight luxurious rooms hung with tapestry until they reached the presence chamber, which was just like the King's throne room.

'I will hold audiences here,' Tom said.

'Are you sure you can afford all this?' Joan ventured.

'Easily, darling. Next to the King, I'm probably the richest man in

England, and it is only fitting that the display of wealth I make reflects the magnificence of my master.'

He walked on, telling her that he intended to have the tapestries changed every week, and the buffets blazing with plate. And all the while he was conscious of a chill that did not emanate from the as yet unheated rooms. It had suddenly struck him that when a man climbed so high, he had much further to fall. It was a disturbing thought. Was he tempting Fortune to turn her wheel by indulging his passion for riches and the fine things in life? No, he would not believe it. All that he was, all that he had, had come to him through sheer hard work and diligence – and the King's affection. He could not believe that Harry would ever turn his face from him. He was far too useful, and anyway, there was much love between them.

Well satisfied, he and Joan ascended a spiral stair to Tom's bed-chamber, where they found in place the great alabaster bed he had commissioned, bearing his coat of arms surrounded by an exquisite design of gilded flowers. Cocksparrow had already made himself at home and was stretched out luxuriously on the counterpane.

'You may be lodged in another part of the house,' Tom said, drawing Joan to him, 'but here we will be together. Come, my darling, come to me now.' His voice was hoarse, his desire suddenly urgent. 'Let us baptise it!'

He shooed the indignant cat away.

Part Three

'This great pomp and pride'

Chapter 15

1515

King Louis was dead. The news arrived early in the New Year. He had left his young Queen a widow after less than three months of marriage.

'It sounds as if she wore him out,' Harry said, seated at dinner in his privy chamber with Tom and the Queen, all of them wearing black.

'By all accounts he was not a well man,' Tom said. 'God rest him.' He crossed himself.

'This new King, Louis' cousin, Francis of Angoulême,' Harry said. 'What do we know of him?' His eyes narrowed. Tom had already deduced that Harry was jealous of this unknown younger rival, for that was how he must regard him.

'He is not king yet, Sir,' he reminded him. 'It is not yet known whether the Queen your sister is with child.'

A gleam came into Harry's eye. 'An English king on the French throne! And without the cost of going to war! That would suit me very well! She wrote that she had gone into seclusion.'

'Her Grace must keep to her chamber for forty days, by which time it will be known whether she is *enceinte* or not.'

'God send that she is!' Harry cried.

'Amen to that,' Katherine said. 'But I pity her. I have heard that in France the chamber of a widowed queen is hung with black, with even the windows covered, and that the only light permitted is from candles. And there must she lie, in her white mourning, with only her ladies for company.'

'I'll wager that Francis's mother is keeping an eagle eye on her,' Harry speculated.

'The ambitions of Madame Louise are well known,' Tom observed drily.

He wondered if the King remembered his promise to Mary. If she bore a son, as mother of the King she would be obliged to remain in France, whatever her personal wishes. But if not . . .

It was, regrettably, likely too soon for her feelings for Suffolk to have cooled. She might even be fantasising about wedding him – if, of course, he was willing. Tom had been watching him to see if there had been any abatement in his lusty flirtations with ladies, and had not been surprised to see him carrying on as normal. But the King's sister would be a great prize, worth forsaking his dissolute ways for. Yet the King would never allow Mary to marry the son of a standard-bearer, duke though he was. Tom could envisage trouble looming ahead, but he was too busy to dwell on the matter. He was virtually running the country. Harry was now leaving most business to him, and it was incumbent on him to rule everything wisely and prudently.

He knew his own worth. He was an able and efficient statesman, with a grasp of European affairs that was second to none. He now laid down a rule that anyone who wished to approach the King about a serious matter should first discuss it with him. That way, he could keep his finger on the pulse of what was happening. He paid informers to keep him apprised of the movements and conversations of his enemies. He made royal officials accountable to himself alone. He insisted on ambassadors showing him their dispatches before they sent them abroad. When the Papal Nuncio refused to do so, Tom threatened him with the rack. He would not have carried out the threat, of course, but the man had to be made to see that Tom needed to be kept informed.

It was true that he had a finger in every pie, but there had to be some cohesion for government to run smoothly – and one never knew when a fund of knowledge might be useful. He was aware that his increasing power and wealth provoked more jealous criticism than ever from both the nobles and the common people, and that much of it was calculated to alienate the King. But there was no hint that Harry resented the splendour in which his favoured minister lived; on the contrary, he often said that it reflected well upon his greatness to have such a distinguished servant.

What did bother Tom were the accusations of lechery and fornication that had recently been levelled at him and were spreading with alarming speed. His spies reported that there was talk – in the court and the streets – of his voluptuous life and abominable licentiousness, and that many considered his magnificence inappropriate for a man of the Church.

He prayed that this vitriol had nothing to do with Joan, for they had taken such great care to be discreet. But if he himself had spies, he could be certain that his enemies employed them too, although surely not on as grand a scale. And in the large household he now employed, there might easily be those who were not to be trusted. He watched Harry for signs that he had heard the gossip, waited for a disapproving homily, but the King remained apparently impervious. Tom felt, though, that he was living on a knife-edge. Let his foes dig up one clod of scandal about his private life, and his happiness would be under threat.

With a heavy heart, he realised that he could not visit young Thomas at Willesden as often as he had done hitherto. He dared not risk his secrets being discovered. So he confined his trips north of London to once a month; Joan, of course, went far more frequently. Sometimes, they went together, and those were the best times, for it felt like they were a proper family.

His son was five now, an engaging little fellow with a boundless capacity for mischief-making. He was wayward, yet lovable, and it was all too easy to smile at him indulgently. Yet he knew that such an approach was not in the boy's best interests. It was clear that Mistress Barlow was ineffective when it came to ruling Thomas. It was time for him to be breeched and placed in the charge of a tutor who would stand no nonsense.

Tom discussed it with the goodwife, and she was willing, for a handsome increment, to offer board and lodgings to a suitable gentleman. In truth, she seemed relieved that Tom had broached the matter.

'I didn't like to ask your Grace,' she said, 'but Master Thomas is becoming a terrible handful.'

'I can see that,' he said, frowning. 'Thomas, put down that marchpane! You've had three pieces already!'

The child eyed him slyly, opened his mouth and popped in the sweetmeat.

'Oh, no you don't!' Tom swooped and gave him a sharp smack on his rear. 'This is what happens to naughty boys who disobey their elders!' Thomas let out a wail, but Tom ignored it and turned to Mistress Barlow. 'Madam, if he misbehaves in future, he is to have a dose of the same medicine.' He wagged a finger at his son. 'In future, you will do as you are told, or I will know about it,' he said sternly.

Yes, it was time for a man to take control. He only wished he could do it himself, but that, of course, was impossible.

He wrote to Magdalen College, and was recommended to contact Maurice Birchinshaw, a young tutor who had graduated with distinction in canon law and grammar, and who also had an interest in church music. Birchinshaw was now teaching at St Paul's, the London school founded by Dean Colet, the renowned humanist scholar. He would be perfect – if he was willing.

Dr Birchinshaw was adamant. Thomas must come to the school. A place could be found for him as soon as he learned to read and write, and he would receive a Christian education. There would be no fees, since the school had been richly endowed, but he must be enrolled as a day boy and provide his own candles.

Tom went to view the school at St Paul's Churchyard. He was impressed with what he saw, but perplexed as to how Thomas could get to and from school daily, seeing that he lived in Willesden.

Sitting in his study, Dr Birchinshaw saw the problem.

'The boy could lodge with me, for a small consideration and his keep,' he said. 'I have rooms nearby in Ludgate. I will take you to see them.'

They were clean, neat and well furnished. The housekeeper was a ruddy-cheeked woman with a winning smile. A price was agreed, and Tom exhaled in relief.

Thomas was going to school.

When Tom returned to Willesden the next day and told his son of his good fortune in being found a place in the best school in London,

Joan expressed herself delighted, but Thomas stamped and stuck out his bottom lip. This, Tom thought grimly, was what came of too much smothering by women!

'You are going, my boy, and I'll brook no arguments,' he declared. 'Mistress Barlow, see that he attends to this.' He handed her a hornbook that he had bought from a bookseller by St Paul's. 'Hang it around his neck and make sure he learns his letters, his numbers and the Lord's Prayer and recites them every day. Now, nephew, cease your blubbering and kneel for my blessing. The next time I see you, you'll be at school, and I'll guarantee you'll be in your element.'

The following week, Tom travelled down to Hampton Court, where works were progressing, although not at the rate he would have liked. Even so, as the boat approached, he looked up in awe at what he knew would be the most splendid palace ever seen in England. It was rising tall and majestic, a grand red-brick house with mullioned windows, turrets and tall chimneys, like some heraldic beast crouched by the river.

Alighting, he bounded across the dry moat to what was to be the great gatehouse, then through the cobbled Base Court, which was already surrounded by foundations for the fine lodgings he had planned for visitors and staff. All around him, workmen were building, hammering, mixing mortar or carrying away barrowloads of waste materials. He wandered into the palace, seeking out the master of the bricklayers, then walked with him through the empty chambers, the extensive service quarters and the big kitchens.

'I'm planning to have some antick work in terracotta,' he said. 'I'm sending to Italy for craftsmen. My arms are to be placed above the tower gateway and be supported by *putti*, so leave a space for them; and I am commissioning medallions of Roman emperors for the facade. When do you think the palace will be ready for occupation?'

The master pulled at his beard. 'Hard to say, your Grace. Depends on the weather. Another two years, give or take a few months.'

'That long?' Tom gritted his teeth with frustration.

'It's a big house,' the master said. 'These things take time.'

They walked on through the muddy wastes where the gardens were to be laid out, and there met the engineer, who discussed the sophisticated system of pipes and drains that would bring water to Hampton Court from natural springs three miles away at Coombe Hill.

'The pipes will go under the Thames,' he explained, unrolling his plans and spreading them out on top of an unfinished wall.

'It's an astonishing feat of engineering.'

'Aye, your Grace. The supply will serve the whole palace, and every lodging will have a tap, while those for the King and Queen will have water piped into the bathrooms. The overflow from the cistern will supply the fountains, moats and fishponds.'

'That's excellent,' Tom said, examining the plans flapping in the spring breeze. 'Am I right in believing that no one has ever attempted such a scheme?'

'You are indeed!' the engineer said, grinning. 'And once in place, it will last for centuries.'

When Tom got back to court that afternoon, he found a letter on his desk. It bore the seal of the Duke of Suffolk.

He frowned. Suffolk had lately been sent to France to bring Queen Mary home. It had been established that she was not with child, and Harry was eager to have her back in England. Tom suspected that he was planning another advantageous marriage for her. After Suffolk's departure, the King had confided to Tom that he'd warned the Duke not even to think of marrying her himself. Clearly, he had remembered that his sister had cherished feelings for Suffolk.

Tom broke the seal and opened the letter.

The words danced before his disbelieving eyes. *I have married her heartily*, the Duke had written, *and lain with her, so that I fear she may be with child.* Evidently, from the tone of his missive, he had realised the enormity of what he had done.

Tom braced himself. The King would have to be told. Sweating, for it was an unseasonably warm March day, he girded his loins and hurried downstairs.

* * *

'Your Grace, I must speak with you,' he murmured in Harry's ear, interrupting an archery match.

'Can't it wait?' Harry raised his bow and drew his arm back.

'No, Sir.'

The arrow sped to the bullseye.

'Bravo!' The watching courtiers cheered, clapping their hands.

'Very well,' Harry said. 'Gentlemen, continue without me. I will be back soon.'

As they walked through the budding gardens to the palace, Harry glanced at Tom. 'You look troubled. What is wrong?'

Tom drew in his breath. 'Sir, Queen Mary has married the Duke of Suffolk.'

'What?' Harry shouted. Passing courtiers stared at him, almost cowering.

Tom swallowed. 'I've just received a letter from the Duke in which he confesses his offence and begs me to solicit your forgiveness. He writes that Queen Mary would never let him rest until he had agreed to marry her.'

'I'll have his head for this!' Harry seethed. 'How dare he! We must have the match annulled.'

'Alas, Sir, I fear it is too late for that, for he says he has lain with her and thinks she may be with child.'

Harry flushed with rage and stamped off towards the palace.

Breathing heavily, trying to keep up with him, Tom cried, 'Wait, Sir!'

The King slowed and glared at him. 'Yes?' he barked.

Tom braced himself. 'If my memory serves me correctly, Sir, you told me that you promised Queen Mary that she could choose her next husband when King Louis died.'

Harry's eyes narrowed. 'I don't remember saying that,' he muttered. He was lying. Tom could tell by his shifty demeanour. 'And even if I did, she should have asked if I approved.'

It was useless to argue with him when he was in this mood.

Entering the palace, Harry bawled out an order for the Council to convene at once. The lords were as outraged at Suffolk's presumption as he was, old jealousies surfacing fast.

'He should be executed, or at least imprisoned, since he has committed treason in marrying a princess of the blood without royal consent!' Norfolk thundered, as the other lords cried their agreement.

'Gentlemen, gentlemen,' Tom intervened, 'can we all calm down? Your Grace, given your love for Queen Mary and your affection for my lord of Suffolk, may I propose that you demand a large fine as punishment?'

There were rumbles of disagreement, but Harry's anger was clearly cooling and Tom hoped he was beginning to see the wisdom in what he had suggested. Furious as he was with Mary, he did love her, and Suffolk was closer to him than any of his other friends, even Tom himself.

'Yes,' the King said at length. 'A fine would compensate for the usurpation of my prerogative and the loss of an opportunity to marry the Queen to England's advantage.' He thought for a while. 'I think that twenty-four thousand pounds should be sufficient.'

There were sharp intakes of breath all along the table.

'That is a huge sum,' Buckingham said. 'Even Suffolk, with his new-found riches, won't be able to afford it.'

'They can pay it in instalments,' Harry said. 'They can sell some of the Queen's jewels. Better still, she can surrender to me all the jewels and plate Louis gave her, in part payment.' He was almost rubbing his hands in glee.

'I will write to her Grace and the Duke immediately,' Tom said, rising.

Tom was not surprised when the Suffolks accepted the terms with alacrity. Of course, they would have been expecting a far worse punishment. Greatly mollified at the prospect of all that money coming his way, Harry allowed Tom to persuade him to receive the couple back into favour, both of them ignoring the barbed comments of those who felt that Suffolk had got off too lightly.

Tom felt he had done well. Suffolk now had every reason to be grateful to him and to show him favour. He had cleverly transformed a rival into a client seeking patronage; from now on, the Duke would be obliged to co-operate and work more amicably with him. Which was as well, because now that he was the King's brother-in-law, Suffolk would have the second seat on the Privy Council after Tom, who naturally had the first. It would be good to have an ally to counterbalance the hostility of Buckingham and the Howards.

The King was grateful to Tom too. His sister and his beloved friend were coming home, and he sent Tom with a host of lords and ladies to meet them at Dover. It was early May, and the weather was beautiful. Tom enjoyed the journey through Kent, although not the condescension or frostiness of some of his aristocratic companions.

'Your Majesty,' he said as he bowed low before Mary, who extended a slender hand to be kissed. 'Welcome home.'

'My lord Archbishop, we are much beholden to you,' she said, smiling at him radiantly, tendrils of golden hair whipping at her French hood.

'Indeed, my lord, we cannot thank you sufficiently,' Suffolk added. They both looked supremely happy.

'Tomorrow we set off for the King's manor at Barking, where he will be waiting to receive you,' Tom told them. 'But first, let us go to Dover Castle, where food awaits you.'

Mary's joyous air gradually dissipated the nearer they got to Barking. Both she and Suffolk were tense. It was as if they could not quite believe that the King had been so merciful.

'His Grace is looking forward to seeing you,' Tom said soothingly, more than once, but still they looked worried. Only when they arrived at Barking and threw themselves to their knees, and were then raised and enfolded in Harry's warm embrace, did they start to relax and enjoy themselves.

'You shall be married in public,' Harry told them. 'My lord Archbishop is making the arrangements.'

Tom smiled at them. It was just another item in a long list of things to be done. But one of them was personal. He had long wanted to reward Joan's brother, his chaplain Thomas Larke, for his support of them both, and because he had given good service and deserved preferment. The Bishop of Ely had just died, and his various benefices had become vacant. One was the rich living of Winwick in Lancashire, and Tom was easily able to persuade the King to grant it to Father Larke.

'He'll be under the patronage of the Legh family,' Harry observed, once more astonishing Tom with his encyclopaedic knowledge of the gentry and nobility. 'They're sound people.'

Larke thanked Tom profusely for his good fortune and set off for his new post. Tom would miss him, for Lancashire was a long way off and it was unlikely that they would be able to visit each other often, if at all, but Joan was delighted.

'You're a good man, Tom,' she said, kissing him. 'Never forget it! You look to your own, and not many of those jackals at court can say that.'

Chapter 16

1515–16

In September, Tom learned that Pope Leo had made him a cardinal.

'I can hardly believe it!' he told Joan, who was as overwhelmed by the news as he was.

'My clever Tom,' she said, hugging him, her eyes filling. 'You deserve it. You work so hard.'

He kissed her, then, with his head spinning with jubilation, hastened to the court. He had the King to thank for this!

He found him playing bowls.

'Word has just come from Rome, your Grace. I am to be made a cardinal.'

Harry straightened to his majestic height and grasped Tom's hands. 'Thomas, I am heartily pleased for you. No man deserves such a high honour more. And your advancement to cardinal reflects well upon me – and upon England!'

'I am not deserving, Sir.' Tom felt that some self-effacement was called for. 'This is your doing and I cannot express—'

Harry slapped him on the shoulder. 'Nonsense, man! No prince ever had a better counsellor. So what's next for you, eh? The Papal throne?'

Tom hesitated. The idea had, of course, occurred to him. Now that he was a member of the Sacred College of Cardinals, it could become reality. He knew he had what it took to wear the Triple Tiara.

He had paused a moment too long.

'Oh, no,' Harry said, 'I could not bear to lose the ablest man in my kingdom – and my good friend. What would I do if you went to Rome?'

Tom had thought this through in the long reaches of the night when he had lain wakeful, his mind too busy to sleep. 'You would be very well served, Sir, with an Englishman sitting in the seat of St Peter. To my knowledge, there has only been one English Pope, and that long ago. Most popes serve only their own interests. But were I to be elected pontiff, I would put your interest and England's first, and continue to serve you in every way I can.'

Harry was frowning. 'Hmm. Well, that day may come, but I would rather have you here! Remember that. Tell me, did you ever hear back from Rome about my marriage?'

Tom had been hoping that the King wouldn't ask that question. He had not mentioned the subject again. Was he still contemplating an annulment?

'I did, Sir. I was told that should your Grace wish to apply to his Holiness to examine the case, he would study the matter with all diligence.'

Harry frowned. 'That commits him to nothing! But never mind. I intend to stay married to the Queen. She is a good woman.'

Tom nodded thankfully. 'Indeed she is.'

'Tell me, how is that new palace of yours progressing?'

'Hampton Court? Slowly, Sir! You know how workmen are.'

'Oh, I keep a close eye on those working for me,' Harry said. 'I often ask for plans or reports while building is going on, and I make a point of visiting the sites to make an inspection. I'll abide no slacking!'

'Methinks I must take a leaf out of your Grace's book.' Tom smiled.

Harry grinned at him. 'I'm happy to be of service. After all, you are building yourself a palace to outrival any of mine!' It was said only half in jest. Tom could sense, and had sensed for some time, that deep inside, the King was jealous.

'My dear mother used to stay at Hampton Court when Lord Daubeney owned it,' Harry was saying. 'She was there shortly before she passed away.' He looked momentarily pained. He had often spoken of his love for his mother, who had died when he was a child. These had been the only occasions when Tom had seen him betray a vulnerability.

'I fear that the old house has now been completely pulled down,' Tom told him. 'I've saved the clock from the tower, though.' He felt an instinctive need to placate Harry. 'When the new palace is built, there will be luxurious apartments for your Grace and the Queen, for when you honour me with a visit. I shall spare no expense in making you welcome.'

'Be assured I shall visit often!'

'That would only be fitting, for it is thanks to your Grace's munificence that I am able to enjoy such an abundance of riches.' He sat down at the table, eager to change the subject. 'Now, Sir, maybe you would like to see these reports of the French advance on Milan. King Francis is determined to conquer the duchy, but, as you know, it is occupied by the Swiss. I have asked our envoys in Italy to keep your Grace informed of events.'

The King scowled. 'Let us hope that the Swiss hold their ground!'

Tom was shocked to receive reports that his cardinal's hat, the worthy symbol of his new honour, dignity and authority, was being carried by some lowly Papal emissary who was reportedly dressed like a varlet! He could not allow his moment of triumph to be spoiled.

'I won't have my hat brought hither by a base person,' he raged to Joan, waving the report in her astonished face. 'It's an insult!'

'Calm down, my dearest,' she soothed, taking his hand. 'You're overreacting, and the problem is easily remedied. Send a messenger with new apparel in costly silks to stay the messenger and bid him put them on, so that he arrives in London looking like some high ambassador.'

Thanking her, and regretting his outburst, Tom did as she advised, and was gratified to learn that the emissary looked quite splendid when he was received at Blackheath by Archbishop Warham, who – even if he was seething inside at Tom's advancement – had gathered a great assembly of prelates and gallant gentlemen and conducted and conveyed him through London with such pomp that you would have thought the greatest prince of Christendom had come into the realm.

Honour was now satisfied, and on 22 December, clad in silk, velvet and ermine, Tom went in procession to St Paul's Cathedral to be invested as cardinal by Warham. As he knelt there beneath his old rival's disapproving gaze, he felt infused with a strong sense of power, elation and, yes, spiritual fulfilment. It was for this that he had been born. Somewhere among the congregation, Joan was watching. He hoped she had a good view of his triumph. He stood up, stately in his new red robes and hat, and blessed the people, trembling with the solemnity of it all. The choir's voices soared.

'Make way for my lord's Grace!' his gentlemen ushers cried out as he left the cathedral. Descending the steps, he mounted the mule he must now ride in imitation of Christ, although it was trapped in red and gold.

As his procession set off for York Place, he was preceded by his officers carrying silver crosses and pillars, poleaxes and a mace, and his cardinal's hat, raised up high so that all might see it. Taking up the rear, Tom held an orange stuffed with spices to his nose to ward off the smell of the unwashed populace. As he passed, lifting his hand in blessing, some fell to their knees, awestruck, although he did hear the odd shout of derision and see a few resentful faces. He hoped that those scurrilous rumours about his so-called lechery had been forgotten.

The next day, his cardinal's hat was displayed in a glittering ceremony in Westminster Abbey. The pomp was such that men said it could have been a coronation. Every bishop and abbot in, or within reach of, London was present, all wearing their rich mitres, copes and other costly ornaments. The hat was set on a cupboard with tapers about it, and all the nobility were required to make obeisance to it, even the greatest dukes in the land – who would surely have seen this as distasteful abasement. Tom was not there; it was not expected of him, but he heard of the proceedings from his chaplains, and his heart swelled with pride to think that all that ceremonial was for him, humble Tom Wolsey. He fingered his mother's crucifix, which he still wore daily. How he wished his parents had been alive to see his success. And it was all down to his own diligence – and his beloved Harry's favour. Was ever man so blessed?

After hosting a sumptuous banquet at York Place, he took Joan to bed, suppressing his qualms about whether it was right to indulge in carnal delights so soon after being made a cardinal. But he was feeling vigorous, omnipotent even, and needed to express it.

'Why, Tom, I do declare you've never been so passionate,' she giggled as he withdrew from her a second time.

'I marvel at myself,' he whispered.

'You *are* a marvel,' she said, kissing him. 'I shall look forward to more nightly romps with my lord Cardinal!'

He drew her close to him. 'You are a wonderful woman, and I am a lucky man. If only I could acknowledge you openly, but I dare not risk any more scandal.'

'Let us not dwell on that,' she reproved him. 'I am content as I am.'

Tom knew that his elevation had made him more unpopular than ever. When he rode abroad, the crowds came to stare, standing there sullen and hostile, some even booing him. The nobility despised him and were deeply and overtly jealous of the power he wielded. But at least one of his opponents would soon trouble him no longer – or not as much.

'Warham's resigned the chancellorship,' Harry told him one morning shortly before Christmas.

'Indeed?' Tom wasn't surprised. England and France had fallen out yet again, and neither Warham nor Foxe shared the King's revived enthusiasm for a war with the old enemy, so their positions on the Council had become increasingly untenable. Tom had clashed several times with Warham, who was clearly finding it increasingly difficult to assert his authority as Lord Chancellor and Primate of England in the face of Tom's superior power.

'He says he is weary of public life and wishes to retire to his diocese,' Harry went on. 'He's been a loyal servant, and of course he will continue to serve as Primate of England, but I must confess to being pleased that he is resigning. For some time now, I have been thinking that matters would run far more smoothly if you, Tom, were Lord Chancellor. You are my choice.'

Tom smiled. The promotion was well deserved. He knew all the strengths and weaknesses of his fellow councillors, and not one of them could do for Harry what he did.

'Your Grace does me too much honour,' he said.

'Nonsense!' the King barked. 'You've earned it on your own merits.'

And thus it was that on Christmas Eve, at Eltham Palace, Tom found himself on his knees before his sovereign, receiving the Great Seal of England in the presence of a throng of nobles and courtiers. He could sense the animosity emanating from them. He was aware that no subject had ever before held so many high offices in both Church and state, or commanded an income that enabled him to live like royalty. Of course, he would now have to employ more staff to manage his vast concerns, but competition for places in his service was rampant, and his wealth would easily allow for the increased cost.

Harry raised him to his feet. 'I know that you will serve me well, my lord Cardinal, and rule all things with your customary consummate ability and prudence. And be it known, good my lords, that in future, anyone treating of serious matters is to speak first to the Cardinal, and not to me. All visitors must kiss his hand before they seek an audience with me.'

Tom saw the clenched mouths and fists of some of the lords, felt their hostility as a tangible thing. Well, he would not let it trouble him. So complete was the King's confidence in him that none dared challenge his power. And he would make sure to discharge his duties so conspicuously as to surpass the hopes of his master and confound his enemies. He was back at his desk the next day, which was Christmas Day, aware that from now on he would be constantly occupied with the affairs of the kingdom, and that he would have even less time to spend with Joan.

By the New Year, Tom and Joan were living at York Place, where he soon found himself working to a punishing schedule. He was often obliged to rise at four o'clock, then to sit at his desk for twelve hours without stopping once to eat or use the privy. But it was essential to keep a firm hand on all aspects of government. The King expected it of him. He saw Harry only infrequently, visiting the court mainly on Sundays, but they remained in daily contact by letter and messenger.

Tom kept his loving master well informed, wrote out summaries of the letters and documents the King did not have the patience to read in their entirety, and drafted replies for him to sign, because Harry, at twenty-four, still liked the freedom to enjoy himself. Back would come the dispatches, marked where something required urgent attention or clarification, and often they arrived late at night, for the King was always off hunting or planning new revels by day.

Yet he did take more interest in affairs of state these days, and liked to have the final say in decision-making, even if he invariably took his Chancellor's advice. When, one morning, Tom wrote to him, *Your realm, our Lord be thanked, was never in such peace and tranquillity*, he smiled, for Harry would know whom he had to thank.

Tom was a rich man, wealthy enough to live lavishly, with his fees as Lord Chancellor augmenting the hefty revenues from his bishoprics. Long behind him were the days when he and Joan kept a small staff at Blackfriars. He now employed over a thousand servants, all clad in his livery of crimson velvet emblazoned with a cardinal's hat, while his cook, a man puffed up with importance, wore damask, with a great gold chain about his neck.

Of course, it was even more difficult now to keep his life with Joan a secret from the rest of the world, and the truth was that he felt so invincible that he decided it wasn't really necessary. The cat was probably out of the bag already. Did not Archbishop Warham keep a mistress and children quite openly? And he was not the only one! Yet, for Harry's sake, Tom maintained discretion, as before – and Joan, dear, generous soul that she was, went along with it, for she had never sought a public role.

On feast days and holidays, Tom dined alone beneath a rich cloth of estate and was served more dishes than were permitted by law to a nobleman. He dispensed alms that were far more lavish than the King's. Loving sacred music, he kept a choir in his extravagantly appointed chapel. He was aware of being guilty of the sins of pride and greed, yet he could not help himself. His life had changed unbelievably since he had entered the King's service and he still felt like pinching himself. He reckoned that his rewards were a fair return for the long hours of work and the responsibilities he shouldered.

One Sunday after Mass, Harry had expressed concern about the time he spent slaving away.

'My own good Cardinal,' he said, drawing Tom aside into a window embrasure, 'for God's sake, take some pastime and comfort, so that you may longer endure to serve me – and for your health's sake.' He looked genuinely concerned.

Tom did not want his master to think that, at the age of forty-four, he was losing his strength, for he was still bounding with energy and vigour, despite having put on weight with all the fine food he was eating. All the same, he was touched by the King's care for him.

'Yes, Sir, I should exercise more,' he said. 'Mine is such a sedentary life.'

So he danced and he hunted, and he bedded Joan most nights; even when he was dropping with fatigue, the old Adam was lively in him. Guilty again – of the sin of lechery! But how could something so beautiful and precious be wrong? As Joan said, whenever his conscience sometimes troubled him, God had fashioned men and women for love, so why should they deny themselves? They weren't hurting anyone. Indeed, as Joan herself had said, there was nothing in the Bible about priests being celibate. Yet in the eyes of the world, both of them would stand condemned. And neither of them could confess their sins, for then they would have to undertake not to commit them again. But how could he give up Joan, his love, his very life, the person he turned to when it all got too much for him?

He remained constantly aware of the need to avoid scandal, and that the higher one climbed, the further there was to fall. He knew his good fortune was entirely dependent on the King's will and favour. Since that awkward moment when they were discussing Hampton Court, there had been no sign that Harry resented the splendour in which his minister lived; on the contrary, he had made it clear that it reflected well upon his greatness to have such a distinguished servant. And Tom agreed. It was the perfect justification for all his wealth and display.

Chapter 17

1516

For some time now, the King had been growing increasingly concerned about the succession.

'Three boys and a girl, all dead,' he had said one evening at table, in a rare unguarded moment when he and Tom were dining alone. 'If I don't get a son to succeed me, England may face another civil war, like the late wars between Lancaster and York that my father brought to an end. God knows, I have enough Yorkist relations with a claim to the throne. If I died tomorrow, they'd be like wolves, fighting for the crown.' He'd sighed. 'Why does God take my sons? Why does He deny me an heir? I've prayed, long and hard.'

Tom hid his own concern. 'I am sure that God will grant your prayers,' he had said soothingly. And God had. The Queen was pregnant again and nearing her time, which was great cause for rejoicing.

Poor Joan, however, had just suffered a miscarriage, which was not, although Tom could not help feeling a guilty sense of relief that they would not be obliged to give up yet another child. Joan had taken it cheerfully, so he hoped she felt the same. When she had told him that there was to be another child, he had all but broken down. Yet she had been strong in the face of his misery.

'We may not be able to call him ours,' she'd said bravely, 'but we can be widowed mother and uncle again. I pray you, find foster parents who live nearby.' Now God had solved their problem, sparing them a greater anguish.

She was visiting Thomas at St Paul's School whenever Dr Birchinshaw permitted her, although Tom could not accompany her as often as he would have liked. Yet they were both pleased to see a change in the boy, whose high spirits and wilfulness seemed to have been somewhat suppressed by the discipline of school. It was enough just to be able to see him, even if Tom did have to keep up the fiction that the boy was his nephew, which he was sure nobody believed for a minute. Yet he knew that Joan pined, as he did, for the daughter who was irrevocably lost to them. He prayed there would be no more children, as he knew that neither of them could have borne another loss. He had taken to withdrawing before his climax, even though the Church deemed it a sin. Yet it seemed to him a greater sin that a child born of love should be torn from its parents.

The court was at Greenwich, where Katherine had ceremoniously taken to her chamber to await the birth, and everyone was in a state of suspension, all realising how crucial it was for her to present the King with a son. Now she was in labour.

'Stay with me, Thomas,' Harry asked, pacing up and down his privy chamber. 'I can't discuss intimate matters with my gentlemen.' They were lounging about him, playing dice or cards, strumming a lute or guffawing at jests; idle fools with too much power, the lot of them, Tom thought, and a bad influence on the King. But this was not the time to mention that.

When the news had lately reached England that King Ferdinand of Aragon was dead, Harry had been frantic.

'On no account must the Queen hear of her father's death,' he'd insisted. 'Not when her confinement is imminent. I do not want to risk any ill hap befalling her or the child from shock or grief.'

The old fox's death had left his daughter, Queen Juana of Castile, as his heir, but she was shut up in her convent, mad as Diogenes, so he had been succeeded by her sixteen-year-old son Charles, who was now king of all Spain. There would be time enough, Tom had concurred, for the Queen to learn this when she had recovered from her ordeal.

Harry now led the way to his closet.

'All will be well, Sir, I am sure,' Tom said soothingly.

'I'm worried,' the King confessed. 'They say she's having a hard travail. It's gone on for hours now. I sent for the holy girdle of her patron saint, St Catherine, to help things along, but it doesn't seem to have helped at all. By St George, I wish I could be with her. Even I, the King, am not allowed in the birthing chamber! Those midwives are dragons!'

The door opened and an usher brought in one of the dragons.

'Your Grace,' she said, curtseying, 'the Queen has borne a healthy daughter.'

'Thank God! Thank God!' Harry cried. By no sign did he betray that he was disappointed not to have a son. 'Thank God that they have both been spared. Come, Tom, attend me. Let us go and greet the child!'

Tom followed, a constriction in his throat. He fought back tears as he watched the King greet his wife lovingly and take the babe in his arms, showing delight in his daughter. This was how it should be for all parents, he thought. How it should have been for him and Joan. He could hardly hide his emotion.

Harry was making faces at his new daughter. 'We are both still young,' he said to Katherine, 'and if it is a girl this time, by God's grace, sons will follow.'

When she was three days old, the infant Princess was christened in the church of the Observant Friars and baptised Mary. Tom was honoured to have been chosen as one of the godparents, along with the Countess of Devon and the Duchess of Norfolk; like them, he bought a costly gift of plate for the child. The ceremony was conducted with great solemnity, and afterwards refreshments were served. The King and Queen were not present at the baptism, by tradition, for it was the godparents' day. When the Princess was returned in procession to her parents, who were waiting in Katherine's bedchamber, Tom again felt choked as they proudly took her, in turn, in their arms and gave her their blessings.

Hot upon the heels of Mary's christening came that of the Suffolks' first son, Henry. In gratitude for his saving them from Harry's wrath, the proud parents honoured Tom by choosing him as godfather alongside the King. Tom stood beside Harry at the lavish ceremony. It felt as if he was almost a member of the royal family.

* * *

Spring came in with a flourish, and Tom became aware that the King was showing increasing favour and friendship to the renowned humanist scholar Thomas More, whom he had persuaded to come to court the previous year to serve him as an unofficial secretary. That in itself was enough to make Tom see More as a rival. He knew him to be an intellectual with an international reputation, a man who understood and deplored the superficiality of court life and disdained the trappings of wealth and power – in great contrast to Tom himself, who was fearful that Harry would come to see his own wealth and power from More's doubtless disapproving point of view.

For Harry valued More's opinions. Tom had noticed how often he invited him to his private apartments to discuss astronomy, geometry, divinity and all the other interests they shared, most of which Tom did not have in common with them. On other occasions, the King and Queen asked More to make merry with them at table.

Tom felt excluded, even though he could think of no reason why Harry should not have more than one close friend. It was jealousy, pure and simple – and he must curb it, for he and More had to work together. So he made every effort to befriend the man, and found, to his surprise, that they got on well – so well, in fact, that one afternoon, as Tom was passing through the long room where the secretaries worked, he saw More lay down his quill, ready to leave for his house at Chelsea, and asked him to stay and share a tankard of ale.

The lawyer smiled that sweet smile of his. 'I should very much like to, my lord Cardinal.'

'You are enjoying life at court?' Tom asked, pouring.

More shook his head. 'Not really. I did not want a post here. You would hardly believe how unwilling I was to accept it.'

Tom raised his eyebrows. 'Yet you had proved yourself able and useful in two diplomatic missions for the King.'

'Aye, and how I regret it!' More smiled again. 'I should have made a fool of myself.'

'Well, his Grace and I are heartily glad that you are here. He tells me that you are soon to publish a book.'

More's face brightened. 'Yes. It is called *Utopia* and it describes the ideal state.'

'And how would you see that?' Tom was intrigued.

'As a neo-Platonic, absolute republic with laws based on the humanist ethos. I will give you a copy. It is being printed this week.'

'I shall look forward to it. Thank you.'

The book was waiting on Tom's desk six days later. He took an hour off work to peruse it, feeling increasingly disturbed, for it was essentially a powerful critique of English government and the vicious machinations of monarchs and courtiers. The Latin prose, however, was so elegant, and the scholarship so breathtaking, that the content might well barely register with some of the fools at court who might bother to read it just to keep up with the rest.

The book won nothing but praise in all quarters. Even Harry, to Tom's surprise, was full of it.

'I wish I had written it myself!' he declared.

'Does your Grace not find it a little subversive?' Tom ventured.

'It's just a concept, Thomas! It doesn't bear any relation to real life.'

Tom rather thought that was not what More had intended. But he held his tongue and told himself he was blessed to serve a king with such a liberal outlook.

'I'm preferring Master More to the Privy Council,' Harry announced. 'We need fine minds like his.'

Tom felt that familiar tremor of jealousy.

At last – at long last – Hampton Court was ready for occupation. It wasn't finished by any means, but the magnificent state apartments were complete, and the tower containing the royal lodgings for the King and Queen. Harry's chambers were on the first floor, the Queen's on the second floor, and there was a suite of rooms for the Princess Mary on the ground floor. On the day they were due to arrive and be shown around, Tom and Joan kept continual watch at the window, looking for the first glimpse of the cavalcade. As soon as they saw the outriders, Joan fled upstairs to her new apartment and Tom hastened to the great gatehouse, where he stood, restlessly shifting from foot to foot, eager to greet his august guests.

Harry was riding astride a great black horse, looking awestruck at the sight of the vast red-brick palace rising majestically above the Thames. 'By God, it's a wonder! I have nothing like this, and I'm the King!'

Tom shivered involuntarily. Had he overreached himself, a humble innkeeper's son, in building so lavishly and grandly? Had the sight of Hampton Court aroused his master's jealousy? But no, there was his good friend, dismounting in the Base Court, smiling broadly.

Tom bowed low. 'Your Grace, welcome to my humble abode.'

Harry was staring around the vast cobbled courtyard, which was surrounded by fine lodgings. He embraced Tom, who could not help noticing the disapproval in the Queen's eyes as she gave him her hand to kiss. But Harry himself gave no sign of displeasure. On the contrary, he flung an arm around Tom's shoulder and let himself be led across the courtyard.

'This accommodation, Sir, is for my household and guests,' Tom told him, waving an expansive hand at the fine brick ranges surrounding them. 'I keep two hundred and eighty beds with silk hangings made up in readiness for visitors.' He led the way through a second imposing gateway to another courtyard. 'Here you see my great hall, the banqueting chamber and the chapel.'

Harry squinted up at the large mullioned windows, the turrets, the tall chimneys, the sculpted new-fashioned antick work and the stone cherubs supporting Tom's coat of arms above the gateway.

'The decoration is inspired by the architecture of Italy,' Tom told him.

'I can see that. My father patronised Italian artists and sculptors, as I myself have done.'

'I must confess that I drew some inspiration from the architectural pattern books your Grace obtained from Italy,' Tom said.

'But you've created an excellent house in the Burgundian style,' Harry marvelled. 'It will be the wonder of Christendom.'

They had arrived at the entrance to the tower that housed the new royal lodgings, and Tom threw open the door. Everything looked new and luxurious, more than fit for a king. But Harry's eyes widened when he saw Tom's own apartments, which were even more sumptuous and sported moulded ceilings, carved friezes, paintings, priceless tapestries, sixty large carpets presented by the Venetian Senate, and furnishings of unprecedented splendour. The windows looked out over beautiful gardens, fishponds and two thousand acres of parkland. The smile faded.

'This palace will rival the one I'm building at Bridewell,' the King said peevishly. 'It's coming on apace, although not fast enough for my liking. It's going to be very like this, with red brick and two courtyards. The royal lodgings will be on the first floor, in the new French style, and they can be accessed by a processional stair. I'm building a long gallery, so that my courtiers can exercise indoors in wet weather, and there will be a tennis court and terraced gardens fronting the river. I've spent a fortune on it, but Hampton Court has given me new inspiration. Of course, there isn't the space at Bridewell to build on a scale like this.' He frowned. 'However, I'm going to enlarge and beautify Greenwich and Richmond and Eltham, and one day soon, I'll wager you, they will excel your Hampton Court in magnificence.'

The Queen had remained silent, not deigning to comment on the gilded linenfold panelling, the vast wall paintings by Italian masters, the ceilings delicately carved and painted in gold leaf and a host of other wonders. As Tom led the way into the chapel, however, he heard her murmur, 'Is it right for a servant to appear richer than his master?' The King muttered something in reply, but Tom could not make out the words. He was relieved when the royal couple took their leave and departed.

He hurried upstairs, eager to tell Joan about the visit and unburden himself.

She looked up from her sewing. 'Did it go well?'

'I think so. His Grace was deeply impressed.' He hesitated, then told her what the Queen had said. 'I wish I could have heard what the King replied.'

'You know he will hear nothing bad said about you.'

'Yes, but he might heed the Queen.'

'I doubt it. From what I hear, her influence is much diminished.

Now, if she was the mother of a son . . .' There was a wistful tone in Joan's voice.

'That's as may be, but the King might well agree with her. He has no palace to equal this one.'

She sighed. 'Tom, he himself enriched you.'

'Yes, but he may feel I have overreached myself.'

'If you were not so obsessed with riches, we would not be having this conversation.'

He stared at her, speechless. 'Do you not like the way we live? I have attained it through sheer hard work. You could be a queen!'

'I would be happy with you in a hut, Thomas Wolsey, and I am grateful for what you have given me, but I do fear where your ambition will lead you. Just beware. Your enemies are always ready to pounce, and the King is suggestible, as you know.'

'But you think that now I should not be worrying about his being jealous?'

'I wish I could reassure you, but I wasn't there.' Joan got up and poured some wine. 'I'm sure that you are worrying unnecessarily.'

Chapter 18

1517–18

Life at Hampton Court was everything Tom had hoped for. He lived like a king, was served like a king and held court like a king. Surrounded by sumptuous splendour, he took great pleasure in the overt envy of his enemies whenever state business required them to wait on him, and when he was alone – if one could ever be alone with a thousand servants in attendance – he would wander from chamber to chamber, admiring his possessions.

Joan, by contrast, preferred to keep to her rooms, which she had made cosy and welcoming. 'I do not wish to be cause for gossip by showing myself too often in public,' she said. 'I am quite content with my own company. Cocksparrow and I get on very well together.'

The cat, which had grown fat with cream and contentment, was purring loudly in its basket by the hearth.

'I wish I could spend more time with you,' Tom said, putting his arms around her.

'You come to me at night,' she giggled, and playfully bit his ear. 'Otherwise, I *would* be complaining!'

'Our nights are a joy,' he murmured. 'You cannot know how much I desire you.'

'Then prove it!' she challenged, laughing. For a short moment, Tom was torn between taking her at her word and the great pile of papers awaiting his attention, but he could not resist Joan – it had ever been like that between them. Giving way to his need, he tumbled her on the bed, pulling up her skirts and kissing her soundly.

* * *

By no word or deed had Harry given Tom any further cause to believe that he was jealous. On the contrary, he was continually praising him. Tom thanked God that the King knew his worth. He himself must never forget that. He had earned his riches and his palaces, and it was fitting that his glory reflected the prestige of his master. It was largely due to his efforts that peace now existed between the great European powers, a peace that had brought great benefits. Many foreigners had settled in London, set up businesses and prospered. Inevitably, there was resentment, for the English were insular and disliked strangers, but they would soon see that the newcomers enriched society in many ways and broadened men's horizons.

He was shocked, therefore, when, on May Day, while the King and Queen were out a-Maying and enjoying a picnic in the woods at Kensington, messengers came battering at his door with news that the simmering tensions in London had boiled over into violence.

'The apprentices have risen, my lord! Great mobs of them are fighting in the streets and attacking any foreigners they encounter.'

'If your Eminence doesn't act soon, there'll be a bloodbath!'

'My lord, they are threatening to kill the Lord Mayor and the aldermen!'

Tom did not hesitate. He could not act alone in this: he needed the King's sanction. Rounding up a posse of Privy Councillors, he hastened to the park, where he found his master dining beneath the trees.

'Your Grace,' he cried breathlessly, as soon as he came within earshot, 'there are riots in the City. The apprentices have risen against the foreigners.'

Harry jumped to his feet. He had been laughing, but his face was now like thunder. 'By God, how dare they? For years I've been encouraging foreign merchants to set up trade in London, yea, and seen they were made welcome.'

'Aye, Sir, and they have prospered. Many of them are her Grace's countrymen.' Tom bowed his head briefly in the Queen's direction.

'England has prospered because of it,' Harry said, flushed with anger. 'How dare these knaves attack those under my special protection!'

'Sir, there is much resentment. The people do not like foreigners stealing their business, as they see it. But whatever the rights and wrongs, we have to act. Mobs of apprentices are rampaging in the streets, and I fear for the safety of our foreign guests.'

'I will return to Richmond, make ready and leave for the City at once,' Harry declared. 'Send my guards ahead; tell them to bring the rioters under control as quickly as possible.'

Tom sped back to the palace and relayed the order. He watched from a window as the King departed, riding like fury to London. Then he waited for several anxious hours until they brought him news that the rioters had been brought swiftly under control. Many had been arrested and would certainly pay the ultimate penalty for their crimes. The King wanted Tom in London, at once.

Harry sat enthroned at the top of the steps at the end of Westminster Hall. Beside him sat the Queen. Tom stood behind them with the lords of the Council. Before the King, four hundred apprentices knelt, wearing halters around their necks. Most of them were mere boys, boys from a similar background to Tom himself. He could easily imagine how overawed they were by the terrible majesty of their sovereign's justice. Their terrified faces were upturned as one, beseechingly, to the King's implacable visage. Crammed in at the other end of the hall were their families and many wailing mothers, all in terror lest their sons meet the same fate as the ringleaders of the riots, who had been summarily hanged.

Harry would have executed the lot of them as an example to show those who were guests in his kingdom that he was determined to protect their interests. But the Queen had dissuaded him. Tom had been there, had seen her burst into tears.

'They are so young, Sir! They were probably led astray by those hotheads. Please, I beg of you, do not put them to death. Do not break their mothers' hearts!'

'Her Grace is wise to urge mercy, Sir,' Tom had said. 'Sometimes it is a finely judged decision. In this case, I think it would enhance your fame to pardon these silly youths.'

'Hmm.' Harry's anger had cooled somewhat, after meting out

instant harsh justice. 'Maybe I should show some mercy. But how would it look to the world at large?'

'Everyone would applaud you, Sir. Let the Queen and myself publicly plead for the lives of these wretches. Then you can show mercy without any loss of authority.'

Harry had agreed. Now he rose and addressed the quaking apprentices before him. 'You are all guilty of a most heinous and grievous crime against innocent persons who are under my royal protection, as guests in my kingdom. After this evil May Day, what foreign merchant would risk his business by coming to London? It must be made very plain to them that London is a safe place, and that they are welcomed by all. Those who have risen against them, and made a mockery of my protection, will be made an example of. I sentence every one of you to be hanged.'

The faces of the apprentices registered shock, as from the back of the vast hall came an outburst of the most pitiful weeping and keening.

The Queen seized the moment. 'Sir,' she said, falling to her knees before the King, 'for the sake of Our Lord Jesus Christ, and His Holy Mother, who knew what it was to lose a son, I beseech you, pardon these boys. They know they have done wrong, but I am sure they have learned their lesson. I beg of you, set them free to return to their loving families.'

As she raised her hands in supplication, Tom knelt too. 'May I add my plea to her Grace's?' he asked. 'Your Grace was ever a merciful prince. I too crave the lives of these youths, who have suffered sufficiently to atone for their crimes.'

Harry's eyes ranged around the hall, seeing faces turned pleadingly up to him. It was as if the collective breath and tears of the condemned wretches had been stilled in expectancy, as he looked down frowning on the two supplicants kneeling at his feet. Suddenly, he smiled, and it was as if the sun had come out. 'I can refuse you nothing,' he said to Katherine. Then he turned to Tom. 'Your prayers are heard, my faithful minister.' He looked sternly at the cowering felons before him. 'All of you are pardoned and restored to liberty. You young fellows may thank the Queen and the Cardinal for your lives. You are free to leave.'

There were great shouts of exultation as the apprentices threw their halters in the air for joy and fought their way through the throng to be reunited with their families, while their mothers rushed to embrace them, calling down blessings on the King's head. It was as if peals of joy were ringing through the hall.

'You have done a good day's work, Kate,' Harry said. 'And you too, Thomas.' He raised a hand, acknowledging the cheers for himself. There was little he loved more than the acclaim of his people. 'Now everyone is pleased, and no harm is done.'

There was little time for rejoicing, for the terrible disease known as the sweating sickness had once again visited England and people began falling like flies in London. Tom had had it once, long ago, and survived, but he remembered how ill he had felt and how terrified his mother had been for him. For what began with a little pain in the head and chest could very rapidly develop into a deadly sweat and kill within two or three hours. A man could be merry at dinner and dead at supper. The speed with which the disease struck was truly frightening. But once a whole day had passed, all danger was at an end.

Tom was convinced that panic inflated the threat. One rumour, his physician told him, could cause a thousand cases of the sweating sickness. 'Some suffer more from fear than others from the illness itself,' he added. 'My advice, if you get it, is to go to bed in a room with a roaring fire and sweat it out.'

Tom wasn't sure if that would be of any use. You would sweat anyway, whether you were in bed or not. He had heard that treacle could be efficacious, or exotic potions made from powdered sapphires or gold. The truth was that no one had the slightest idea of what might cure the disease. They were all at the mercy of God.

Harry was more fearful than most. He was petrified of anything to do with illness and death, especially the plague, of which there were outbreaks most summers in his hot, crowded, dirty capital, but the mere words 'sweating sickness' were so terrible to his ears that he refused to remain in any place near to the contagion. When the first cases were reported, he had ordered that no one who had been in contact with any infected person was to come to court, and immediately moved from London to Richmond; and then, when someone sickened there, to Greenwich.

Having had the sweat and recovered, Tom was immune and able to stay in London, holed up in York Place, looking after affairs. Joan kept to her rooms with Cocksparrow for company. All around them was illness and death. The streets were deserted. Tom offered up prayers for the afflicted. Too many people were dying. Many were saying that it was a judgement of God. But why would God visit such a punishment upon England now?

August, and the sickness was still raging. Tom was working from dawn to midnight, dealing with as much as he could on his own, for he had sent most of his household home to their families. Cromwell was one of those who had stayed: Cromwell, who was clearly eager to show himself indispensable. When Tom had suggested that Joan seek refuge at the farm, she refused to leave, and he had not pressed the matter. The King, meanwhile, had gone to Windsor, where he had shut himself up with the Queen, his priests, his favoured gentlemen and six physicians. No one else was allowed to come near him. All but the most necessary government business was being held in suspension.

Multitudes are dying around us, Tom wrote to him, whereupon the King immediately abandoned his plans for a summer progress, for who knew where the sweat might appear next? It was rampant in Oxford and Cambridge now, and the universities had sent their students down.

It was December before the pestilence began to abate. Tom took himself and Joan off to Richmond Palace to keep Christmas there, ensuring that they were well supplied with oranges, which opinion now held to be an antidote to the sweat. The King did not join him. He was too fearful to keep Christmas as usual. He would be having a dismal Yuletide, Tom reflected, watching the mummers from his high seat on the dais.

In January, Harry returned to Greenwich, but as a few poor souls were still dying of the sweat, he did not stay long and soon made plans to depart once more on his travels.

Tom had been pleased to see his master looking so well, if anxious and restless to be gone. He had not enjoyed the long separation from him and was sad to see him leave. But Harry continued to write regularly – from Eltham, Farnham, Reading, Wallingford and Abingdon, where the Suffolks had joined him. It was clear that he was beginning to relax a little, since no one was coming daily to tell him of another death. To be on the safe side, though, Tom advised him to restrict the numbers attending court at Easter. He urged him to pay heed, not only because of the sweat, but also because he had heard rumours from abroad that some unnamed noblemen were plotting against the King, and it was best that Harry took no risk until Tom had delved to the bottom of the matter.

Harry's secretary, Master Pace, replied that his Highness sent his most hearty thanks for Tom's warning and most lovingly appreciated the special regard he had for the safety of his royal person. Tom was gratified to read that.

He wrote back that it might be wise if his Grace ordered his Privy Councillors to stay away. Harry duly complied, as Tom had known he would, for his inherent suspicious streak was easily aroused. Indeed, he instructed Tom to keep watch on Suffolk, Buckingham, the earls of Northumberland, Derby and Wiltshire and anyone else he thought suspect. The letter was marked, *For none other but you or I.*

Tom raised his eyebrows when he read it. Things were coming to a pretty pass if Harry was entertaining suspicions of Suffolk, his good friend and brother-in-law. And he could hardly believe that the earls the King had mentioned would ever dream of plotting against their sovereign.

Of them all, though, Buckingham was the one most likely to plot treason. Tom had had his eye on him for some time, yet he was honest enough to admit to himself that suspicions might be coloured by the Duke's open resentment towards him. There was, in fact, no evidence that he was up to anything nefarious. Nevertheless, it was important to remain vigilant.

Tom was convinced that, rather than dwelling on imaginary threats from the great lords of his realm, Harry would do better to curb the power of the gentlemen of his Privy Chamber – the 'minions', as Tom privately called them. They were with the King twenty-four hours a day, waking, sleeping, eating, drinking, working and making merry. They had his ear, and their influence was considerable. Tom knew them to be, for the most part, expert and superbly qualified manipulators, and for that reason he feared them. He believed that some were working against him – and that could never be allowed to happen. Already he had secretly recruited more spies to keep watch on them.

One of the worst was Sir Nicholas Carew, whom Tom suspected of encouraging Harry to indulge in drinking, fornication and other vices. Not that Tom himself was guiltless, at least in regard to fornication, but Carew had also defied his orders and wishes on several occasions. Now that the King was away, Tom charged Carew with being overfamiliar with him without respect to his rank, and banished him from the court. Yet scarcely had the arrogant fellow left than he was back, by commandment of the King, and strutting around looking insufferably smug.

Tom knew himself bested – for now. But he would settle the score, when he could.

Tom smiled as he read again the Papal bull that conferred on him his new dignity. Henceforth, two crosses would be borne before him in procession. He was aware that he was guilty of the sin of pride. But no matter! It was a lovely, sunny May day, and he had achieved his desire. He had good reason to be proud. In April, King Francis had sued for peace with King Harry, and word came that the Pope had appointed a legate, Cardinal Campeggio, to come to England to help negotiate a treaty. Tom had bristled at that. He would not be relegated to second place behind Campeggio. He sent to say that the Cardinal Legate would not be allowed to enter the realm unless he himself was made Papal legate and could meet Campeggio on equal terms. Pope Leo had promptly complied.

The appointment gave Tom unprecedented authority over the English Church, even surpassing that of Archbishop Warham, before whom he now took precedence, much to Warham's chagrin, which was embarrassingly evident when he saw Tom making an entrance with his two crosses borne before him. He was to share his legatine powers with Campeggio, to whom he was senior in the College of Cardinals, and he now invited Campeggio into England. Tom found the man hard to like, although he tried, in Christian charity, so that they could work together amicably. His fellow legate was a gaunt-faced man with a long grey beard, and a clever lawyer. He had once been married, but his wife had tragically died and he had entered the Church. There was an innate reserve in him, an air of superiority that irked Tom, who resisted being made to feel very much a junior partner when he was in fact the elder by some years and invested with equal authority as legate. But when Campeggio began putting pressure on the King to join a new crusade against the Turks, Tom had to make it clear to him that his Grace was not interested. As a consolation, Harry bestowed on Campeggio the bishopric of Salisbury, whereupon he returned to Rome. After his departure, Tom continued to negotiate the treaty without his help.

The court had reassembled in its entirety in the beautiful new palace of Bridewell – not as large or as sumptuous as Hampton Court, Tom noted nervously but with some satisfaction – and Harry was glad to be working with him again. When Tom showed him the bull from Rome, he clapped him on the back. 'You deserve it, Thomas! You can be of even greater service to me now. They'll be wanting you for pope next!'

It was said in jest, but Tom knew that his appointment as legate was a step nearer to the Triple Tiara, and that his secret dream of becoming pope might one day become reality. Yet he was torn. He knew Harry's views on the matter, and that he himself would be loath to abandon his beloved master for Rome. And then there was Joan. How could he leave her, the true love of his life? He could take her with him, of course – it was well known that most popes kept mistresses – but her heart lay in England, with Thomas. Truth to tell, Tom did not know if he really wanted to leave England either.

Perhaps it was a fantasy, his dream of becoming pope. Even if he did decide to pursue it – and it would take a lot of money in bribes – he would need the backing of the King of France or the Emperor, and each would doubtless have their own candidates when the time came. Yet he knew he had the capacity to secure such support. Right now, as the wrangling for peace began, he had the opportunity to be the arbiter of Christendom. This would not be just to his master's benefit, but could also make him indispensable to those two great princes and rivals.

Over the next few weeks, with consummate skill and diplomacy, he transformed the mooted treaty with France into one of universal and perpetual peace between England, France and the Pope. Its purpose was to persuade Maximilian and the Infante Charles to agree to maintain peace throughout Christendom, a noble aim that they could surely not refuse. Of course, Harry took the credit, proclaiming himself the architect of this ambitious alliance, even though everyone knew that Tom had done most of the negotiating.

Tom knew he was at the pinnacle of his powers. He virtually ruled both the King and the kingdom. He could recall himself, only a few years ago, deferring in all things to Harry's judgement and will. 'His Majesty will do so and so,' he would say. Then, as his influence grew, he had said, 'We shall do so and so.' But now he was in a position to say, 'I shall do so and so.' He was, effectively, a king without a crown. And enjoying his power with his master's blessing was the wonderful thing about it, for it meant that his enemies could not touch him.

Tom had remained painfully aware of the contrast between his spectacular and successful public life and the private frustration he felt at having to keep his family a secret. Joan had always borne the loss of her children with fortitude; she had never reproached him for it. Only occasionally did he see her eyes mist over when she saw a babe in arms or an infant run to its mother. She visited Thomas often. The boy was eight now, strong and well built, yet he was idle and seemed insensible of the good education being afforded him. As his 'uncle', Tom could not be as strict with him as he would have liked, so he chose to encourage and praise him instead, all the while suspecting that Birchinshaw disapproved of his leniency – as well he might.

There was a deep well of emptiness in his heart when he thought of Dorothy, who was lost to him and Joan, gone for ever, although he still received discreet reports on her progress and they all told of a little girl who was well behaved and happy. But she had been deprived of her natural parents, and that was a terrible thing for a child. The wages of sin, he reflected, were worse than death.

Their dreadful losses could have broken him and Joan, but thankfully they had brought them closer than ever. No one apart from themselves could understand what the other was feeling. For some strange reason, tragedy had fired the passion that constantly flared between them, and the nights they lay together were filled with a unique magic. It was not just the breathless coming together, or the intense physical pleasure, but the complete openness of hearts. Tom could not get enough of his beloved, and his desire was fully reciprocated. He had tried to deny himself the ultimate satisfaction, for Joan's sake, but it had proved impossible. He could only pray that God, in His wisdom, would not send them any more children.

It was after one of these heart-stopping episodes of lovemaking that Tom mentioned to Joan that the Queen was again with child. He felt her stiffen and wished he had not said it, but she seemed more concerned for Katherine than for her own woes.

'How old is she now?' she asked.

'Thirty-two,' he told her.

'Well past her youth.' She sighed. 'I pray God heartily that it may be a prince, to the comfort of the King and the realm.'

'Amen to that,' Tom said fervently, cradling her in his arms. 'Her condition is to be kept secret, lest any mishap befall her. The King, of course, is delighted. He's desperate to have a son. I hope it's a boy, for her Grace's sake. I feel for her. She has borne so many losses.' Again, he wished his words unsaid.

But Joan did not react this time. 'You feel for her, yet she does not like you.'

He shrugged. 'I suppose she thinks me lacking in the humility desirable in a prince of the Church. She certainly thinks I favour France, and that I am working against the interests of Spain, when truly my aim is to see this universal peace come to fruition.'

'I think she believes you have usurped what she sees as her rightful place in the King's counsels.'

'Aye, probably. But her influence was undermined when her father broke faith with the King. If she had borne a prince, she might have regained it.'

'And might yet do so.'

'I don't think so. Her time has gone. The King loves and honours her, I am sure, but he pursues others.'

'Bessie Blount?' Joan chuckled.

'You know about that?'

'I've heard gossip. Servants talk.'

'His Grace would not be pleased. He takes great pains to be discreet.'

'Does the Queen know?'

'If you do, my love, then she probably does too.' He bent forward and kissed her, then remembered he had papers to read. 'Oh, well, duty calls. Try to sleep. I'll just look over these.'

He sat up, settled back against the pillows and reached for the documents from the table by the bed. Beside him, Joan lay with her hair spread out on the pillow, looking beautiful and peaceful, and no older than she had looked nine years ago when he had first made her his. His manhood stirred again. No, he must not give in to temptation. He had work to do.

In September, a grand French embassy arrived in England for the signing of the Treaty of Perpetual Peace. Tom stood in a place of honour in St Paul's Cathedral, watching as the King scrawled his signature in the presence of a vast concourse of nobles and dignitaries. Tom celebrated High Mass with splendid solemnity, after which the King's secretary, Master Pace, delivered a long oration praising his master, who sat beaming on a throne upholstered in cloth of gold.

Tom felt a profound sense of pride and achievement. This was his treaty, the fruit of his efforts. He, humble Tom Wolsey, had brought about peace in Europe and persuaded twenty nations to bind themselves to live in peace and not invade each other's territories. He had put England at the forefront of European diplomacy and made her a desirable ally.

It had been agreed that the treaty would be cemented by the betrothal of the two-year-old Princess Mary to the Dauphin of France. The Queen had made it obvious that she was not happy about this. Of course, she would hate the prospect of her precious only child being married off to France, Spain's ancient enemy, and her frosty manner towards Tom made it plain that she blamed him for brokering such an alliance. No doubt she was angry with Harry too, for signing the treaty. But surely even she could not deny that peace in Europe was preferable to war?

At York Place, Tom hosted a lavish supper for the ambassadors, and sat at the King's right hand at the high table.

'I do declare that such a wondrous feast was never given, even by Cleopatra or Caligula,' one of the ambassadors enthused, eyeing the spectacular array of dishes laid out before him.

When the feasting was over, the musicians struck up and Harry and his sister Mary led out twenty-four masked dancers. Tom spied Bessie Blount among them. She was a comely young woman and seemed very easy in the King's company. He noticed the Queen watching her, her lips pursed. She knew.

After the masque, Tom ordered that large bowls brimming with gold coins and dice be brought to the tables so that the company could settle down to some serious gambling. Then there was dancing, and Harry took to the floor with the lovely Bessie Blount. Tom knew that Joan would be watching the proceedings from the squint above the minstrels' gallery, and felt a pang of bitterness. How he would have loved to dance openly with her, his dearest darling. When, at midnight, the King retired, doubtless to steal a few precious hours alone with his mistress, Tom hastened to bed, eager to be with his own sweet lover.

Two days later, at Greenwich, the Princess Mary was formally betrothed to the Dauphin in the Queen's great chamber, in the presence of her parents, the ambassadors and the lords and ladies of the court, all of them decked out in glorious finery. As her godfather, Tom stood again in a place of honour, together with Cardinal Campeggio, who had recently returned to England – unopposed, this time.

The tiny Princess Mary looked exquisite in a gown of cloth of gold with a black bejewelled hood; at two years and eight months, she had learned to manage a court train without falling over. The Admiral of France stood proxy for her infant bridegroom, as Tom held the Princess in his arms and placed on her tiny finger a great diamond ring that was much too big for her.

'Are you the Dauphin of France?' Mary asked the Admiral. 'If you are, I want to kiss you!' Everyone laughed.

'That will have to wait a little!' Harry chuckled. 'No, sweeting, the Dauphin is in Paris, tucked up in his cradle.'

After Tom and Campeggio had blessed the little bride-to-be, she was carried off to bed and Harry led the company into the presence chamber for the betrothal feast, at which he was served by the dukes of Norfolk, Suffolk and Buckingham, the latter not troubling to conceal his disapproval of the alliance with France, much to the King's obvious irritation. Harry was clearly vexed with the Queen too. Tom thought she could have made some effort to conceal her hostility to the betrothal. She had barely smiled all day, and departed after the first course, saying that she was tired. She was great with child now, so it was a reasonable excuse.

The King's eyes narrowed as he watched her go, but soon he was carousing with the rest, his good mood restored. It was three o'clock in the morning before Tom finally fell into bed.

Two days later, the King took the visiting envoys hunting at Richmond, after which they rode to Hampton Court, where Tom entertained them at a great banquet. Neither expense nor labour had been spared to ensure that the French would make a glorious report to their master, to the King's honour and that of his realm. Tom's cooks had been working day and night to prepare the numerous dishes that were served in surroundings of breathtaking splendour. The French seemed overcome, looking about them as if they had entered a heavenly paradise.

Tom watched them with deep satisfaction. This was the culmination of his peace-making achievement. The King could bask in the glory, and he himself in the knowledge that it was he whom Harry had to thank.

The Queen's child was a girl, who did not live long enough to be baptised. Joan wept when Tom told her, but not as bitterly as Harry had. He had broken down in Tom's arms, raging at cruel Fate, who had denied him – and England – a prince. It had been impossible to find words of comfort to allay his pain. There could be no saying that next time all would be well, for there had been so many next times, and it now seemed unlikely that the Queen would bear another living child. So Tom had held his sovereign in sympathetic silence and let the storm pass over.

As Christmas approached, Harry was tense and troubled. Tom could sense it as he sat with him, going over the latest dispatches from England's ambassador in Paris. He assumed that his master was worried about the succession.

The King sighed, then hesitated. 'You're a man of the world, Thomas. I think that you of all people will understand when I explain the predicament in which I find myself. You may be aware that for some years now I have been courting Bessie Blount.'

Tom smiled. 'I am aware, Sir. But I have not seen her lately.'

'That is because she has left court. She is with child, Thomas. My child.'

Tom was not surprised, and certainly not shocked. 'Is she making demands upon your Grace?'

'Not at all!' Harry's fair cheeks were flushed. 'I wish to do the best for her, and the babe. She is staying with friends of her family, but I care not to trust to their discretion. I want to send her to a place where she can give birth in secrecy and comfort. I have many houses, but none will afford her the privacy this merits. I want no scandal!'

Tom had not needed to be told that. He had winced when the King had referred to his being a man of the world who would understand his problem. It meant that Harry had not forgotten his secret relationship with Joan or the fact that they had a child. Was he aware that Joan still lived with him, and that she had borne another babe? They had been so careful, but you never knew who was watching.

Calm down! he exhorted himself. If someone had talked, his enemies would have made political capital of it by now.

He turned his attention back to the matter they were discussing.

'Has your Grace considered Jericho?'

Harry reddened. He probably thought that Tom had not known about the house he had purchased from the priory at Blackmore in Essex, one of his secret houses of pleasure, where he had sometimes taken Bessie for covert trysts. Its moat was fed by the River Can, known locally as the River Jordan, which was how the house had acquired its name.

'Rest assured, Sir, that your visits there remain unknown to the world at large. I just happened to see the deeds among some papers and drew a few conclusions. But it is an ideal place for the lady to be confined. It's secluded and peaceful, and screened by high brick walls. I will see that everything is put in readiness and engage a midwife and servants. All will be sworn to secrecy, and of course they will have no idea who the father is. We shall say that Mistress Blount is a widow. No one will discover the truth.'

'Why didn't I think of Jericho?' Harry chuckled. 'It's a capital idea. But I couldn't be seen to be organising things there. The only one I can trust to do that is you, Thomas.'

Chapter 19

1519

'Is there any news?' Harry asked for the umpteenth time, bursting into Tom's closet on a cold February morning.

'No, your Grace, not yet.'

The Emperor Maximilian was dead. A new Holy Roman Emperor would now have to be elected. Harry had immediately put himself forward and sent the ever-diligent Master Pace to Germany to campaign on his behalf.

'Do you think I stand a good chance of being elected?' It was his constant refrain; he could not bear the thought of being passed over.

'I am quite optimistic,' Tom replied. 'But I don't think we will get the result this soon. Why don't you go hunting, Sir?'

Harry went, his head doubtless full of plans for what he would do when he became emperor.

Tom stood at his study window at York Place, gazing out unseeing at the bleak January gardens. He had been growing increasingly suspicious of the minions, those young and influential members of the King's Privy Chamber. Having infiltrated one Williams, his spy, into the sanctum as an usher, he was disturbed by what the man had to report.

'There is no doubt that they are doing their best to undermine your Eminence in the King's sight, and Master Carew is one of the worst,' Williams had said, standing before him, cap in hand. Of course. Carew had ever been a troublemaker. Well, he would find that Tom too could resort to underhand means.

'You have done well, Williams,' he said, pressing a purse of coins into the fellow's hand. 'I will now be able to deal with these varlets.'

In bed that night, he told Joan what he had learned. 'What I fear is the minions undermining me in the King's sight.'

'As I've told you before, the King knows which side his bread is buttered,' Joan replied sleepily, lying within the curve of his arm.

'Yes, but I fear they are spreading lies about me. Have you heard any rumours among the servants?'

'No,' she replied. 'Stop fretting, Thomas Wolsey. You're a match for their malice any day.'

He wished he could feel as confident about that as she did.

He made efforts to disperse the minions and get them away from the court. He gave them assignments that looked like honours but were really calculated to take them as far from Harry as possible. And he had a sound reason for doing that, if challenged by his master, because it was being whispered at court that the King had got into bad company. Tom knew all about what was going on because his spy brought him daily reports. He was shocked to hear that the King of England was donning disguises, roistering in the streets with his friends and generally behaving like an idiot. But the minions clearly thought nothing of encouraging him to join them in indulging in what Tom's man coyly described as French vices. He could imagine what that meant! Once, Harry would have silenced any brawlers, but now he was stooping to carouse and wench with these young bloods, when, at nearly twenty-eight, he should know better. It was not dignified. No wonder sober and discreet courtiers and clerics were eyeing their sovereign with disapproval. These minions were bringing scandal on the throne by encouraging such behaviour.

And his Harry was abetting them – the young man who had desired virtue, glory and immortality! Tom hoped that the Queen never got to hear of it.

Every day, his spy reported some new outrage.

'They give him evil counsel.'

'They encourage him to gamble away large sums.'

'They are too homely and familiar with him.'

'They forget themselves!'

Today, there was nothing new. 'They are poking fun at all the estates of England, even the ladies and gentlemen of the court,' the agent said, twisting his cap in embarrassment as he stood before Tom.

'Do they poke fun at the King?' Tom barked.

'No, but they spur him on to join in with them.'

Tom felt a pang of concern. He dared not ask if he was the butt of their vicious humour, or if Harry had laughed at him with them. He could not have borne that.

After St George's Day, when the court had moved to Greenwich, he confided his concerns to Thomas More, whose wisdom he had come to respect. More listened with his usual courteous consideration, his frown deepening.

'Your Eminence, I urge you to consult the Privy Council, but take good care not to criticise the King.'

Tom took this sound advice and was gratified to hear that many of the lords were also concerned about Harry coming under the influence of the minions.

'The Privy Chamber is now rivalling the Privy Council for power,' Norfolk snarled. 'We must put an end to the King associating with these young varlets. They're dangerous.'

Only Buckingham disagreed. 'You're all jealous,' he sniffed, looking pointedly at Tom.

The others jeered him down.

'I, for one, will be glad to see the back of these minions,' Norfolk said, to vigorous nods of agreement.

Tom, they agreed, should initially approach the King. No one was better placed to do so. He smiled grimly to himself. They were getting their own back once more, punishing him for being first in Harry's counsels.

He might as well get it over with now. With a heart like lead – for he was averse to doing anything that might make his beloved master like him less – he took himself off to the royal apartments, vowing that he was not going to deal with this all by himself. He would ask the King to grace the Council with his presence. There was safety in numbers.

Harry was in his privy chamber, roaring with mirth at something one of the minions had said. They all stared as Tom was announced. He made his way to where the King sat, then bent and murmured in his ear. 'Your Grace, might I crave a private word?'

'Of course,' Harry said genially. 'Begone, the lot of you! My friend and I have more weighty matters to discuss.'

There was no mistaking the resentment in the faces of the young men as they unwillingly scattered.

'How can I help you, Thomas?' Harry asked, when they had gone.

Tom took a deep breath. 'Sir, your councillors have expressed some deep concerns to me.' He was not going to say that he had concerns himself – not unless he had to. 'It concerns the gentlemen of your Privy Chamber, and it is about conduct that might be to the detriment, hurt and discredit of your Grace.'

The King was immediately alert. He cared about his reputation.

'If your Highness would grace the Council with your presence at tomorrow's meeting, I am sure that you could easily set their minds at rest.'

Harry nodded. 'I will be there.'

Of course, they made sure that he was the one to raise the matter. As soon as Harry was seated at the head of the board, his gaze raking them enquiringly, everyone looked at Tom.

He rose. 'Your Grace, we are all agreed that the Privy Chamber should be purged of young gentlemen who behave in a manner not in keeping with your dignity and honour.'

He was watching the councillors for their reactions, fearing that they might not support him after all, but for once, heads were nodding in unanimous agreement with him. He caught Norfolk's eye and was gratified to see the old Duke nod too.

Harry said nothing. His expression was hard to read.

Tom made himself go on. 'Sir, I am speaking of Sir Nicholas Carew, Francis Bryan, Sir Edward Neville and Sir Henry Guildford, to name but a few. They give your Grace evil counsel. They encourage you to gamble away large sums; they are too familiar and forget themselves. You patiently suffer these things, but because of your gentle nature, you neither rebuke nor reprove them.'

'These men are my friends,' Harry declared, yet he did not leap further to their defence. Maybe he too had had his concerns.

'Alas, Sir, they are not good friends. You may not be aware that recently, during a diplomatic mission to Paris, Neville and Bryan publicly disgraced themselves when accompanying King Francis as he rode in disguise through the streets. They threw eggs, stones and other trifles at the people.'

Harry flushed, doubtless remembering the times when he and his friends had visited taverns in London and got drunk and foolish. He could not know that Tom knew about that.

'And back home, they are all French in their eating, drinking, apparel and other vices,' the Earl of Surrey sniffed.

'It's true, Sir,' Norfolk chimed in. 'They sneer when they compare your court with that of France; they poke fun at older courtiers and venerable household officers, and generally comport themselves in a reprehensible manner.'

'Aye, Sir!' chorused the other councillors.

'We ask your Grace to put a stop to their behaviour, since it reflects badly upon you,' Tom pleaded.

Harry was visibly squirming. There was a long pause.

'Very well,' he said at last. 'My Lord Chamberlain, you will summon all the offenders, dismiss them from their posts and order them to leave court. But they can still make themselves useful to me. Carew and Neville can go to Calais to help man its defences; the rest can attend to their duties in their own counties.'

He had taken it better than any of them had anticipated. His honour and his reputation were always to be fiercely guarded.

He turned to Tom. 'I thank you, my lord Cardinal, for reminding me how a king ought to behave, and for preventing me from bringing himself and my court into disrepute.'

He rose and departed. The lords congratulated themselves – they even congratulated Tom – on the happy outcome to the meeting. It was rare for them to be in such concord.

In place of those who had been dismissed, Tom brought into the Privy Chamber some older, more sober knights whom Harry liked, men who could be relied upon to do Tom's bidding. But it was clear that Harry missed the others; his leisure hours were not so lively without them. Nevertheless, he told Tom that he meant now to lead a new mode of life, paying less attention to revelry and pastimes and more to state business. Tom and the other councillors were glad to hear it.

It was June and stiflingly hot when Tom hurried to Harry's study. The doors were opened for him; he never had to crave admission.

'Your Grace has a son! Let me be the first to congratulate your Grace!'

He saw the royal jaw drop as tears welled in his master's eyes.

'Truly?' Harry asked. 'Is he thriving?'

'Indeed, he is, Sir, and his mother too.'

Harry was in ecstasies. 'I must ride down to Essex to see him. Do you realise what this means, Thomas? It means that I myself am capable of siring a healthy boy! It proves that my lack of an heir is the Queen's fault, and that I am a man like other men!'

Clearly, he had been worrying about that.

'I never doubted it, Sir,' Tom said.

Harry was bursting with excitement. 'I shall call him Henry, of course, and give him the surname Fitzroy, which means son of the King.'

Tom was surprised. 'But won't that make it obvious whose child he is?'

'I want it to be obvious!' Harry declared, his eyes afire with purpose. 'I have a son, a healthy son! I want the world to know it.'

Tom was shocked. 'I advise your Grace to be discreet. You said you wanted to avoid scandal.'

'Not any more,' Harry said.

'No, Sir?'

'I see no reason for discretion. I want the world to know the truth.

Never again can it be said that there is some lack in me. I will not suffer any more slurs on my manhood.'

Tom nodded. He could understand how his master felt.

He could not help remembering how different the King's reaction had been when he himself had told him that he had a son, nine years ago now. He tried not to feel resentful. Yet Harry had had sound reasons for not wanting a scandal. He appreciated that. Hopefully now, the King would understand his position too.

When he got home, he hastened to his treasury and found a covered cup of silver gilt, beautifully chased.

As soon as Harry was back from Essex, Tom gave it to him.

'For the child,' he said. 'With my blessing.'

Harry embraced him, clearly touched. They walked together in the privy garden, where their conversation could not be overheard.

'My son is a goodly child of great beauty,' Harry enthused. 'I can see myself and Bessie in him. This is too fine a child to be kept hidden. I mean publicly to acknowledge him as mine!'

Tom suddenly felt sick. Here was Harry planning to give his bastard every advantage in life, whereas he had forced him and Joan to give up their precious children – only for Tom to discover now that, when it came to it, the King cared not a fig for any scandal. He felt so betrayed and cheated that it made him speak rashly.

'But a bastard cannot inherit your Grace's crown!'

Harry stared at him. 'Think you I do not know that? That my joy is not tempered with frustration? I have asked myself how God could be so cruel, when He knows that the thing I most desire, and need, is a son to succeed me. When I think of it, I could weep.'

Tom immediately regretted his impulsive words. He put a fatherly hand on the King's shoulder. 'It is an impossible situation for your Grace.'

Harry looked at him, his gaze intent. 'Tell me, is there any possibility that I could have the boy declared legitimate?'

Tom was thrown. Hurriedly he gathered his thoughts, knowing he should be taking time to think properly about this. 'Parliament could declare him legitimate. The Church might frown on it, though.'

'But you are Papal legate. You have authority over the Church in England.'

'Indeed I do. What I see as a stumbling block, though, is whether your Grace's subjects would accept a bastard as king.'

Harry thought for a while. 'Do you think they would?'

'I honestly do not know. But I am certain that your Plantagenet relatives would not, especially the Duke of Buckingham. I can foresee trouble there. Your Grace, my advice would be to shelve the matter while the child is young, and then bring him by stages to the public notice. When your subjects see what a fine boy he is, then will be the moment to start making it clear, by degrees, that he is fitted to be king, and that that is your intention. Then, hopefully, you will win the people's acceptance and approval. After all, no one wants to see a return to civil war. You have brought good government and peace to England, and your subjects will want that to continue.'

'By St George!' Harry exclaimed, brightening. 'You have the sow by the right ear, Thomas! I shall take your advice, for it is sound, as ever. And you shall be godfather to my son and guide him in the way he should go. I will make you responsible for his care.'

'Your Grace, I am deeply honoured,' Tom told him. It was a clever move, giving him a vested interest in a child who might one day be king; in return, he would be obliged to work hard to make the boy heir apparent. And hopefully, in the long run, the boy would be grateful.

'There is no one who deserves it more,' Harry said, clapping him on the back. 'While he is young, you may leave him with Mistress Blount. And I insist that she be called, and honoured as, "the mother of the King's son".'

'It would be politic, Sir, to arrange a good marriage for her.'

Harry's eyebrows rose. 'But I want her back at court. The King of France has *maîtresses-en-titre*, who openly consort with him. Why should I not have the same, now that Bessie is the mother of my son?'

'Because, Sir, your subjects will not tolerate it. The Queen is much loved. By all means continue to honour Mistress Blount with your attentions, but I pray you be discreet. Let a respectable marriage be a cover for your affection.'

Harry sank down on a stone bench. 'As always, Thomas, you are right. I see the wisdom in your words. You never fail me. Very well, arrange a marriage for her. But make it clear that it is to be in name only. And Thomas, I want you to go to Jericho now to organise the christening.'

Tom felt choked as he gazed down at the infant in his arms and presented him to the priest for baptism. His godson was a goodly babe with his father's red-gold hair and Roman nose, and he was wailing lustily. He was a son any man would be proud to own, the son the Queen should have borne Harry, and he should have been carried to the font in a glittering procession with the whole kingdom rejoicing, not borne covertly to this obscure priory church with only his nurse and his godfather present.

He was thinking too of his own son, whom he could not call his. It gave him a pang whenever he thought of the lost years when he and Joan should have been raising the boy at home with his sister. What a happy family they would have been. It did not bear thinking about.

Once the ceremony was over, the child was returned to his mother's arms for her blessing, and Tom went back to court, where he would explain that he had been called away on personal business. He would keep a discreet eye on his godson, as he did on his own children, and never – for now – betray to anyone the boy's august parentage. He hoped that the King now realised what he had asked of his dear friend!

Back at court, Tom worked quickly, casting his net wide for a suitable husband, one who would appreciate the advantages of being married to the King's mistress, but who was compliant enough to settle for a chaste bed.

As usual, he discussed the matter with Joan as they lingered after supper in her chamber.

'I feel sorry for Bessie Blount,' she declared, sipping her wine. 'How awful to be in her situation. I have heard that she truly loves the King, but he's treating her like a chattel.'

'He wants to avoid a scandal,' Tom said.

'He might well create one! Oh, my dearest, how glad I am that you never tried to marry me off for the sake of propriety!'

'It never occurred to me,' Tom told her, 'and besides, I love you too much to be able to contemplate sharing you with another man.'

'Even if he wasn't sleeping with me?'

'Not in any circumstances!' Tom got up, fetched the ewer of wine and refilled Joan's goblet. He touched her hair, glossy and fine beneath his fingers. She looked up at him, and he caught his breath. For one dreadful moment, he could glimpse a barren future without her.

He clutched her to his breast. 'I love you,' he said, and bent to kiss her, thanking God that he had been blessed with such a good woman. She tasted so sweet. He felt desire rising in him and grasped her hand. 'Come to bed, my darling.'

Within three months of Henry Fitzroy's birth, he found the right man in one of his wards, a wealthy young gentleman called Gilbert Tailboys, who had estates in Lincolnshire and Somerset. Tailboys was overjoyed by his good fortune, especially when Tom persuaded Parliament to assign Bessie a handsome dowry. He had a job to convince Harry that it was politic for her to leave court to live with her new husband, but promised him that he would arrange for him to visit her in secret, to avoid scandal.

'That is crucial, if you are to make Master Fitzroy your heir one day,' he urged. 'We do not want people remembering that you had a notorious liaison with his mother.'

Harry grudgingly conceded the point. He abandoned discretion and openly acknowledged his son, yet very soon perceived that Tom had counselled him well, for there was much whispering at court. But the impending marriage of Bessie Blount gave rise to an explosion of fevered gossip. No one dared openly to criticise the King, but there was furious resentment, particularly among the nobility, against Tom. He learned from his spies that he was being called 'the royal bawd' for facilitating a sinful liaison, and that he was encouraging fornication by rewarding Bessie with a good marriage.

He had been the target of vicious criticism anyway, of late. Harry's old tutor, the poet John Skelton, had written a scathing doggerel about him, and it was being repeated throughout the court to jeers and laughter.

> Why come ye not to court?
> To the King's court or to Hampton Court?
> The King's court hath the precedence,
> But Hampton Court hath the pre-eminence!

It was hurtful, given how hard he worked to provide the kingdom with good government and stability, but he knew who was behind it. Norfolk, in particular, was jealous of him, and of his fine palace, and Norfolk was Skelton's patron. It was almost certainly he who had bidden him compose his waspish attack. Anger rose in Tom. He could not move against Norfolk, but he could order Skelton's arrest, and was furious when he heard that the old man had evaded the guards and fled into sanctuary at Westminster Abbey. Well, he could rot there!

Harry had approved his arrest. He had been outraged by his old tutor's attack on his beloved minister. But he had evidently heard the gossip. They were walking in the gardens one day when he suddenly said, 'Well, my lord Cardinal, you can't have it both ways,' in a taunting tone of voice he had never used with him before.

Tom looked at him, uncomprehending.

'Ha!' Harry laughed. 'You dismiss my minions, as you were pleased to call them, for their misconduct, yet you openly make a mockery of marriage, or so your opponents say.'

'But I helped you, Sir.' Tom could not hide his dismay.

'You did, and I am grateful. But I am recalling my friends. I will not have it said that you are a hypocrite. And in doing that, I am helping you.' Harry grinned.

'Alas, Sir, you have outfoxed me,' Tom said, his heart sinking. He did not believe for a moment that the recalling of the minions was in any way an altruistic act on the King's part. Rather it smacked of opportunism!

'I will not have you slandered and libelled for my sake,' Harry said. He came to a halt, then turned and fixed a serious gaze on Tom. 'When I hear such savage criticism of the man who serves me best, I am bound to do my utmost to counteract it.' He hesitated. 'I have not liked to bring this up before, Thomas, but you know as well as I that this is not the first time that you have been accused of immorality. A king may have private failings and get away with it; a churchman cannot be seen as venal. Christ's minister must be above suspicion. Any hint of scandal, and your enemies will pounce. I can save you from *them*, but I cannot protect you from yourself.'

Tom stood there, frozen into immobility. This was what he had feared for many years, and he dreaded to hear what was coming next. He had thought there had been a tacit agreement between them that his private life was his own, so long as he was discreet. But no. Here was his King, his beloved Harry, himself the father of a bastard son, telling him that he must live his life above reproach. Harry, who had resisted his advice to send away the woman he desired, but who was now implying that Tom should do just that, to preserve *his* reputation. Anger gripped him.

'What exactly is your Grace implying?' he asked coldly.

'Do I need to spell it out?' Harry asked. 'It's an open secret that you keep a mistress. You think you're being discreet, but – as you well know – walls have ears. And I do not think you should be giving your enemies any further cause to try to ruin you.'

'I was not aware that I had actually given them any cause! I but tried to smooth the path for your Grace, and it has rebounded on me!'

'Indeed it has, and I am sorry for it, but Thomas, I am only trying to protect you. Do as I have done, as *you* advised me. Find her a suitable husband and send her away. Then take your own advice and see her in secret – not on your own turf. But it would be better if you broke with her completely.'

Tom was aghast. 'Is that an order, Sir?' he croaked.

'It's as much an order as you gave to me.' Harry's tone was terse.

'Then I stand to lose all I hold dear,' Tom said hoarsely. He was perilously near to weeping. He could not begin to contemplate the empty future looming ahead, bleak and incomprehensible in its magnitude. All he could think of was how he would break the news to Joan. Darling Joan. His beloved, whom he must give up, wholly against his will.

'We are men, Thomas, and we understand the realities of life,' Harry said, wrapping an arm around his shoulder. 'And as men, we must face them.'

If I am a man, Tom thought, I must be resolute and fight for my happiness – and for Joan's. She has lost enough through me.

He looked the King in the eye. 'I cannot do it,' he said. 'Your Grace may have all the rest of me, but my heart is hers alone.'

Harry's gaze was steely. 'Thomas, your mode of life reflects badly on you and on the Church – and it reflects on me. I am not suggesting you do this; I am commanding you.'

'I am your friend, Sir,' Tom said faintly.

'And I am insisting on this because I am yours!' Harry retorted.

There was nothing to be gained by arguing. He was not going to change the King's mind. They walked back to the palace in silence and parted in a strained fashion.

Chapter 20

1519

It was six hours before Tom would be free to return to Joan and tell her that they must part. He looked at the pile of papers on his desk and felt ill. How could he concentrate with this weight of sorrow, this dread, on his mind? The words were dancing before his eyes, meaningless.

He gave up. Summoning one of his secretaries, he barked a few instructions. 'Sort out what should have priority. I will be back tomorrow to deal with it. For now, I have a punishing headache and must go home to rest.'

He took his barge back to Hampton Court. As it neared the jetty, he looked up at the great palace. It meant nothing to him now. Somewhere within its walls, Joan would be passing a leisurely day, unsuspecting of what lay in store.

The sun shone down mockingly as he dragged his steps towards the gatehouse.

'Make way for my lord Cardinal!' the guards cried. It was a travesty, all the pomp and ceremony that surrounded him. His life was in ruins. Nothing would ever feel right again. Without Joan, he might as well be dead.

Waving away his attendants, he climbed the stair that led up to her rooms. And there she was, looking more fair than he had ever seen her. She leapt up when she saw him and hastened to him – but stopped short when she saw his face.

'What's wrong, Tom?'

'Everything,' he said, when he could speak.

'The King has dismissed you?'

'No. I wish he had. Oh, my darling, I do not know how to tell you—'

'What is it? Speak!' she cried. 'Is it Thomas? Or Dorothy?'

'No. It is the King. He will not have me called a hypocrite. He has commanded me... Oh, God, I cannot do this to you!' He broke down, weeping on her shoulder, his body heaving. He could feel her own desperation in her rigid stance.

'Tom, you must tell me what the King has asked of you!' She was frantic.

'He has commanded me to find you a husband to avoid a scandal.'

Joan pulled away. She was white with shock. 'And you said yes.'

'I challenged him, for your sake. I said I could not do it. But he was adamant.'

She sank down on a bench, shaking her head.

Tom knelt beside her, his silk robes billowing around him. 'Darling, words cannot describe how sorry I am, how terrible I feel. I tried to save us, to resist him. But the trouble is, he is right. In living with you, I *am* inviting scandal – scandal he is determined to avert.'

Tears were pouring down Joan's cheeks. 'And what if I say to you – and to him, and I would, God help me – that I do not want a husband and that I will not leave you? I am not a chattel to be passed from hand to hand!'

'He would not listen. Once his mind is made up, an angel from Heaven would not be able to persuade him to change it. Joan, darling, if I thought there was any hope of that, I would still be at court, arguing with him.'

'That it should end like this,' she sobbed. 'It sounds like petty revenge.'

'I am sure there is an element of that in it,' he said bitterly. 'He is sour with me for marrying off Bessie Blount and insisting that she leave court. Oh, my darling, I cannot bear to lose you! I cannot imagine my life without you, or yours without me.' His arms tightened around her. 'If I thought I could keep you here hidden away, I would do it. But we would be found out. I am convinced that some of my servants are in the pay of Buckingham or Norfolk. It's not worth the risk. If the King discovered that I'd defied him, there's no predicting what he would do.'

'And there's the rub.' Joan drew back, pushing him away. Her tone was flat, her eyes filled with pain. 'It's your career at stake, your wealth and your palaces – and your power.'

'You're more important than all that,' he assured her, frantic.

'Am I? If so, you would have resigned your high offices and we'd be talking about going off to live in obscurity in one of your parishes. No, Tom.' She stilled him with a gesture. 'A wise woman knows that she is not the whole of her lover's life and that he cannot live by love alone. I have always known that your career comes first with you. And I knew from the start that I was letting myself in for a life of subterfuge. I must ask myself, am I being selfish in wanting us to stay together? Would it not be better if I set you free so that you can live your life the way the King expects you to?'

Tom gripped her arms. 'No, it would not be better! And it isn't a matter of you setting me free, because you have no choice in the matter – and neither do I! Unless, of course, I go to the King now and resign.'

'Would you really do that for me?' Her voice trembled.

He knew, deep in his heart, that he did not want to, that he could not give up the power, the glory, the wealth. He saw why his enemies accused him of having overweening pride. Could he go back to being plain Father Wolsey and live a narrow existence in some country parish? But he had been born for greater things, and it would be wrong to waste the talents God had given him. Even if he did opt for such a life, he would still have to hide Joan away.

He had stayed silent too long, long enough for Joan to sense his reluctance. 'But you don't want to resign, do you?' she said gently.

'It would kill me, but I would do it for you,' he said, not sure if he meant it.

'Then it would be wrong of me to ask it of you.' She stood up. 'We have no choice, then, but to bow to the King's will. It is the right thing, the only thing, to do.' She turned to him. 'I will always love you,

Thomas Wolsey, and I will always hold you in my prayers. Never forget that. I ask only that you find me a husband who is kind and will understand that my heart is with you and our children.'

Tom closed his eyes, unable to bear the sight of her being so brave and so noble in her selflessness. 'My heart fails when I think of what I must do,' he said. 'How do we go about this? Do we lead separate lives until you wed? May I hold you one more time at least?'

She shook her head sadly. 'We should not. It would only make things more painful for us. We must start now as we mean to go on. It will be hard, but we will support each other. And one thing is certain. We will stay friends.'

'But I want so much more!' Tom burst out, burying his head in her lap.

'The choice is made,' she said, quietly disengaging from his embrace, rising and moving towards the door. There was no reproof in her voice, only profound sadness.

He wanted to die. He thought he might faint, so great was the feeling of devastation that overwhelmed him. He hated himself for bringing this upon Joan, and for rewarding her years of uncomplaining sacrifice with his crass selfishness. Yet still he could not bring himself to give up everything for her.

The next days felt like Purgatory. To be living under the same roof as Joan yet not be able to touch her was torture. Several times he found her in tears; several times he thought of defying the King and facing the consequences. But she would not hear of it. Her strength humbled him.

Somehow, he stumbled through his myriad duties. His chief thought was to find a man who would be a kind husband to Joan and give her a good life. Surely, though, once it was all settled, she would come round and love him again? And for that reason, she must be found a man who would be sufficiently grateful and complaisant to turn a blind eye to their continuing intimacy. For their love could not be quenched; it must go on. He had promised himself that and had tried to convince Joan that her marriage would make no difference.

But she had just given him a sad smile that had struck chill into his heart. He feared she was punishing him for not putting her before all else.

It went against everything sacred to him to find her a husband. He could not bear the thought of another man touching her, loving her, *owning* her. Yet he had to do it. He wrote to Thomas Larke, unburdening himself and asking for his advice. Thomas replied that his patron's kinsman, Master George Legh of Adlington, Cheshire, was looking for a wife. He was twenty-two, a rich man with a fine estate, and came from a distinguished family.

His heart almost failing him, Tom showed the letter to Joan. It pounded frighteningly when she laid it down and nodded. 'Yes, Tom, I will do as Thomas suggests, if Master Legh is willing.' She walked away. He feared she was weeping. He felt like weeping himself. This could not be happening.

He wrote to Master Legh, man to man, making no secret of the circumstances and implying that he intended to continue seeing Joan after her marriage. In compensation, he offered a generous dowry and a fine house at Cheshunt, a dozen miles from London. He could easily visit Joan there.

Legh was agreeable. His letter made no reference to the situation, but he professed himself honoured to accept Joan with such a generous settlement.

There was no reason to delay the wedding, and in truth, Tom could not suffer the torture of these terrible days any longer. It was anathema to him to see Joan packing her chests and winding up their life together. He became aware of her visiting Thomas almost daily and feared that it was because she could not bear to be under the same roof as himself. He could not express his anguish, only watch mutely, knowing that nothing he said could change things.

On the day she left, he caught her at her bedchamber door and pulled her to him, desperate to hold her for one final time before their parting.

'I will see you again soon,' he breathed.

'If God wills,' she whispered.

'I will never cease praying for it.'

Gently, she disengaged herself from his arms with that same fatalism she had shown when giving up her children, and picked up Cocksparrow, who she was taking with her.

'God keep you, Thomas Wolsey,' she said, and hurried down the stairs. Tom chased after her, unable to process what was happening, but she was already getting into the litter that was to carry her to Adlington Hall, and the whole household was watching. Remembering his dignity, he stood in the porch and raised a sad hand in farewell. When the litter had disappeared from sight, he hurried to his study, sank down with his head in his hands and cried like a baby, knowing that from now on, he would never be whole again.

When news came that the Infante Charles had been elected the new Holy Roman Emperor, Harry was struck speechless with disappointment – and Tom with deep concern. For Charles, at barely nineteen, was now not only emperor, but also king of Spain and master of a substantial swathe of Christendom. No ruler had held dominion over such vast territories since the days of Charlemagne. Harry was livid with envy, pacing Tom's study like a caged lion, almost sending a precious clock crashing to the floor.

Setting aside his own misery and resentment, and trying to regain some of his former love for his master, Tom attempted to soothe him. 'Sit down, Sir, I pray you,' he said, indicating the chair by the fire. 'If you are angry, the King of France must be even angrier, for he invested enormous sums in bribing the electors to make him emperor. He hates the war with Charles, and the feeling is mutual, but they seem bent on fighting to the bitter end. Both of them have sent appeals to you for support. This, Sir, is to your advantage. You will be seen by the whole world to be a peacemaker, which can only enhance your greatness.'

Harry ceased his glowering. He plainly liked the image of himself that Tom had evoked. 'Hmm. That is a role I would take on with the utmost satisfaction.'

'Your Grace should not envy the new Emperor,' Tom said. 'I have been giving much thought to this since I heard the news, because, aside from the prestige and power the office confers, it will bring its problems. The Empire has long been at loggerheads with the Papacy, and there is this new threat from Germany.'

'Martin Luther,' Harry said grimly. 'He is a heretic and should be burned. I wonder that he is allowed to live and go on spouting subversion.'

'Well, he will be the Emperor's problem now. I thought, when he nailed his ninety-five theses to that church door in Wittenberg, that the world would see him as a harmless fool. But his ideas are taking hold, especially in Germany.'

'They'd better not take root here!' Harry barked. 'He claims he is attacking abuses within the Church, but it's an attack on its very foundations – and on the Sacraments!' His voice rose. 'He claims there are only two, not seven, and it sticks in my craw. If only I could get my hands on him. I would love nothing better than to crush him in a public debate.' He clenched his fists as if he was crushing Luther himself by the neck.

'Which your Grace would do very ably,' Tom said, with sincerity. Harry was superb at debating; none could best him. 'And I wish you could, for I can foresee a schism ahead.'

'Charles would never allow it. He knows what is at stake. The Christian republic of Europe must be preserved at all costs.'

'Indeed it must, before this heresy spreads further. And the unity of princes.' Tom swallowed. The peace last year had been his finest moment, but he could see it crumbling before his eyes.

Long weeks passed before Tom heard from Joan. And then, at last, a letter came. She was married, she wrote, and her husband was a kind man. Cheshunt was a fine residence, but George had exchanged it for a grander house near London and the court. He and Joan would be living at Thames Ditton, a stone's throw from Hampton Court.

Tom's heart leapt. That could mean only one thing: that Joan was ready to rekindle their love, and that Legh was willing to facilitate it.

His beloved would be just a mile away. According to her letter, she would be moving into the new house within a month. Legh would be there, of course, but clearly he had heeded Tom's letter.

He waited in a fever of anticipation. Soon, Joan would be in his arms again. How he longed for her. But the weeks dragged slowly. He was grateful for the many distractions that work afforded him.

Three months passed before he received another letter from Joan, inviting him to come and see the new house.

No man had ever leapt on his horse so eagerly. Tom was aware of astonished servants gawking at him as he cantered through the great gatehouse of Hampton Court and turned left to catch the ferry across the River Thames. He had deliberately cast off his red robes and donned a black velvet gown that was kind to his portly figure. He was aware that he had little by way of looks to please a woman, but Joan had loved him in spite of that.

The house was imposing, built of brick and timber, but it could not hold a candle to Hampton Court or even St Bride's Inn. Yet when he was shown into the parlour, he was impressed by the expensive furnishings and the good taste shown in fabrics and plate. His dowry, he conjectured, had been used well. It was fitting that his beloved be housed in comfort and luxury.

And here she was, looking sleek and as beautiful as ever in her damask gown and gable hood. The gown was unlaced over her stomach. He could not believe his eyes.

'You are with child!' was the first thing he said to her, as she came towards him with one hand extended in greeting, when he had expected her to run into his arms.

'Welcome, Tom,' she said reprovingly. 'Yes, I am with child.'

'Is it mine?' He was desperate to know.

'I think not.'

He was reeling with shock at what he could not help but see as Joan's betrayal, but there was no time to probe further, for a young man had entered the room, a very handsome young man with a proud mien and showy clothes.

'My lord Cardinal,' he said in a cultured voice, bowing. 'Welcome to my house. This is a great honour.'

'Master Legh,' Tom managed to say. 'It's a splendid house you have here.'

'Your Grace's munificence enabled me to lease it,' Legh said smoothly. 'Joan, will you send for wine for our guest?'

Joan rang a bell, summoning the steward. The wine came promptly. Not a word was said as they waited for it to be poured. Tom was too shaken to conjure up any pleasantries. Joan was either lying about her child's paternity – or she had slept with her husband, which hadn't been his plan at all.

The conversation was stilted as they sat there drinking the wine. Tom was torn between love and anger, and dared not look at Joan lest she see the hunger and fury in his eyes. But he had no need to worry, for all her attention was focused on her husband, who was ostentatiously attentive. Didn't the young fool realise that Tom had the power to bring him down as quickly as he had enriched him? He burned with jealousy.

This was not how things were meant to be! He was longing to have a moment alone with Joan.

Fortune favoured him. After an excruciating quarter of an hour, the steward entered and murmured something in Legh's ear. Legh rose.

'Please accept my apologies, my lord. My lawyer has just arrived and I have business to attend to with him.'

He bowed and withdrew, leaving Tom and Joan alone.

'Is the child really his?' Tom asked.

'Yes,' she replied. He thought she was lying, but now that he felt calmer, he understood why. She could not bear to give up another child. To him, the alternative was worse. He could not tolerate the thought of another man making love to her.

'This was not what was arranged,' he protested. 'When am I going to see you?'

She turned cold eyes on him. 'What do you mean?'

He stared at her, incredulous. What had happened to the affectionate, devoted woman he had so loved? 'I mean, when are we to be together, as before?'

'We are not,' she said bluntly. 'We can be friends, of course, but in choosing to sell me into marriage, Tom, you have liberated me. With George, I can openly live as mistress of my own house. I do not have to be hidden away, waiting on your pleasure. I can bring up my own children. I run no risk of being the object of scandal. I am a wife, not a mistress.'

It was like a body blow. 'This isn't the old Joan talking,' Tom stuttered. 'You always said you didn't care for the conventions. You said that love conquered all.'

'I have been shown another way,' she told him. 'I will do nothing to betray my husband, who has been good to me, given the circumstances.'

'And yet you have betrayed me – and our love!' Tom cried.

'There can be no love between us now,' she said, rising. 'Only friendship, for old times' sake.'

Sorrow welled up in him. Joan, his lovely Joan, was rejecting him! Here he sat, the mighty Cardinal who ruled all, and he could do nothing to prevent it. He saw in a flash that this was his fault alone. He had not cherished her enough. He had put his career and his ambitions before his love for her – and he had not stopped to think how she was faring in the impossible situation in which he had placed her. And thus he had lost her.

He looked at her, feeling utterly deflated and sad. 'I should go,' he said, desperate to be away before he broke down in front of her.

'It is best this way, Tom,' she said, laying a hand on his sleeve. 'But let us stay friends. Come and visit whenever you want. And bring me news of Thomas.'

'Yes,' he said, picking up his bonnet and heading for the door. 'I am sure you are right.'

He would not go again, he vowed to himself as he rode back to Hampton Court. He would be done with her. How could he endure to see her looking happy with that self-satisfied husband of hers? But the tears were streaming down his face, and he knew that he might not be able to stay away.

For the first time ever, Tom was not happy to find the King waiting for him in his closet – a very angry King, who was waving a sheaf of papers.

'There you are!' he growled. 'Where have you been?'

'I was carrying out your Grace's bidding,' Tom almost snapped, then remembered whom he was addressing. 'I went to make sure that my mistress is settled with her new husband.'

'Oh.' Harry had the grace to look a little sheepish. 'I trust that she is.'

'Indeed, Sir.' Tom could hardly contain his resentment.

'It is for the best,' the King said complacently. 'Now, I want you to look at this.' He slapped the papers down on the table.

'This' was a morality play by John Skelton, entitled *Magnificence*. Tom was in no mood for an intellectual discussion, but as he scanned the pages, he could see why his master was angry, for Skelton had portrayed a king who took immoderate indulgence in pleasure and was urged to seek a compromise between showy display and parsimony. He had depicted him as failing because he had dismissed his wise ministers and given too much power to an extravagant one, and it was clear whom he meant. Tom bristled with anger. Would Skelton never shut up? Even shut up in the abbey, his malice was unbridled.

'What should I do?' Harry was asking.

'Nothing,' Tom said. 'It is not an overt libel. I myself have been parodied in several plays, but I have thought it best not to stir up controversy. Besides, Master Skelton would revel in the publicity.'

'Why can't he stick to traditional themes, like that goodly comedy by Plautus that I watched the other week?'

'Because he likes to be provocative, and I don't think that your Grace should indulge him. He is best ignored. And talking of Plautus, Sir, I intend to stage his *Menaechmi* at York Place next month, and I would be honoured if you would attend.'

'Is it a satire?' Harry asked warily.

'No, it is a comedy. A comedy of errors.'

'Then I will come.'

Mollified, Harry went on to speak of the fabulous tomb he wanted the Italian sculptor, Master Torrigiano, to build for him at Windsor. 'It must reflect my magnificence and my achievements,' he was saying, but Tom was barely listening. All he could think of was how bleak his life was without Joan in it. How would he watch the Plautus play knowing that he would not be tumbling into bed with her afterwards? How would he concentrate on the manifold tasks the King sent his way? How would he live without his beloved?

'Can I leave that with you?' Harry concluded, and Tom had not the faintest idea what had been asked of him.

'Of course,' he said, resolving to see Torrigiano and find out what was requisite.

'I'm going out hunting,' Harry told him, hastening to depart.

It was ever the same with him, Tom reflected. He was twenty-eight, yet still he devoted himself to sport and amusements day and night, being intent on nothing else. It was lucky, he thought resentfully, that he himself was here to deal with the important business of government. People might say he ruled everything, but by God, he had to, or the kingdom would grind to a halt.

Wearily, and desperately lonely, he resumed his daily round, fighting the depression that threatened to engulf him. He sought solace in his faith. He rose early and heard two Masses in his privy closet, then said his daily service with his chaplain. He made it his rule never to go to bed with any part of his divine service unsaid. After Mass, he donned his cardinal's robes and sat in his privy chamber, giving audience to the crowds of petitioners waiting without, among them peers and gentlemen.

Whenever he went abroad through the streets of London to Westminster or elsewhere, he made a resplendent show in his scarlet robes of satin, taffeta or damask, the best that money could buy. Borne before him was the great seal of England, followed by his cardinal's hat, held aloft by a bare-headed nobleman, as well as his two great silver crosses, preceded by his pursuivant-at-arms carrying a huge mace of silver gilt.

Hitherto, he had gloried in all the pomp, but now it meant nothing.

As he rode through the City, bowing to left and right at the people, his hand raised in blessing, he entertained wild thoughts about throwing it all off and reclaiming Joan – and be damned to her marriage! But as time went by, and he had no word from her, he began to believe it would be fruitless. He knew, deep down, that he could not bear to renounce the power he wielded, power that had enabled him to build up a fabulous fortune and indulge his passions for art, building and luxurious living. Yet it was not all about himself. He had promoted education and brought about reforms in the realms of finance, taxation and justice. He prided himself on having made a difference to the lives of ordinary people.

Could he give all this up for a woman who probably no longer wanted him, and to whom he could never offer the security and respectability of marriage? No, he could not. It would be foolhardy – or so said his head. His heart offered a very different argument. He just longed for anything to put an end to this misery.

He visited Thomas whenever he could: Thomas, his precious link with Joan. The boy seemed miserable too, and soon Tom found out why.

'My mother has not been to see me,' he said, sitting on a form, fidgeting with his hands. Tom suspected that Joan had not told her husband that she had a son, or that Legh had forbidden her to see him. God only knew what the separation was costing her, but he felt he could see how it was affecting Thomas to be parted from Joan. The boy was confused.

'I'm sure she'll come to see you soon,' he said, resolving to raise the matter with her. But how? He did not want to face Joan just now. In the end, he wrote to her.

Archbishop Warham had strongly resisted all Tom's attempts to exercise control over the Church in England. Tom had pressed him to reform the bishoprics, but he had proved obstructive. But Tom would brook no opposition. Today, in Council, he raised the thorny subject of the monasteries.

'They are sorely in need of reform,' he argued.

'And what makes you say that?' challenged the Primate.

'Some are corrupt, some are not financially viable and some are riddled with vices,' Tom countered. 'There has been a decline over the past hundred years, with only two new foundations being established.'

'Are you saying we should close down the monasteries?' Warham snapped.

'No, I am saying we should reform them.'

'Well, I disagree, my lord Cardinal. The last visitations I heard of were satisfactory. The Church must stand for stability. We cannot have change for change's sake.'

Tom bristled. 'And while you do nothing, my lord, the Church will become corrupt to the core.'

'Who do you think you are, to pass judgement on me?' flared Warham.

'One who cares about the Church!' Tom retorted, raising his voice.

'Now then, my lords, let us not get too heated,' intervened Norfolk.

Tom subsided, fuming. He knew that Warham would do nothing. It was in issues like this that his own lack of popularity worked against him. Many of the men sitting with him on the board deemed him an upstart and resented his rise to power; others, he knew, simply disliked him monopolising the King and the court and acting independently of the Council. They opposed his policies and blocked his attempts at reform almost on principle.

To add to the pressures, his triumph over the minions proved to be brief. By the autumn, Harry – by sheer force of will – had overridden his protests and invited most of them back to the Privy Chamber, insisting that they serve him side by side with Tom's protégés. Tom had the wisdom to know when he had lost a battle; he had to accept that the minions were too firmly entrenched in the King's favour to be ousted from court.

He was gradually acclimatising himself to his loneliness, but still feeling demoralised and depressed. In happier days, he would have unburdened himself to Joan, and she would have calmed him and soothed his stress. It was at times like these that he missed her the most. Yet she was only up the road from Hampton Court, and she had invited him to visit her. Why not? Why had he stayed away?

In not wishing to see her with young Legh, he had denied himself the sight of her and the pleasure of her company. Surely, he could still enjoy some vestige of what they had shared? It was not as if he would be asking to resume their intimacy – although his silly heart was hoping that one day they would come together again.

He sent ahead this time, to inform the Leghs that he was would be visiting. On a crisp November day, with leaves crunching beneath his horse's hooves, he rode south to Thames Ditton, feeling as nervous as a green lad going a-courting. If only he was!

Joan and her husband welcomed him courteously. He saw that she was slim again and wondered if her child had lived – and if it were indeed his. He sat in the parlour and drank wine, exchanging pleasantries. You would never have known, from Joan's demeanour, that they had ever meant anything to each other. Soon, it became obvious that Legh was not going to leave him alone with her and that there would be no opportunity to discuss Thomas, though Joan must have received his letter. He sighed inwardly and made himself be civil to his rival. It was essential that they remained on cordial terms for Joan's sake.

At length, Joan stood up. 'My lord, you must come to the nursery and see little Ellen.'

'Our daughter.' Legh beamed.

He followed them up the handsome staircase to a spacious panelled room, where the nursemaid bobbed him a curtsey. Joan lifted the swaddled babe from the cradle and Tom raised a hand in blessing. But his voice failed him as he saw that the infant was himself to the life. His eyes met Joan's and she nodded ever so slightly.

He rode home far more miserable than when he had set out. He had not had a moment alone with his beloved. He had another child to whom he could never be a father. And he felt as if he carried the weight of the world on his shoulders.

Part Four

'The pains that I have had to do him service'

Chapter 21

1520–21

Harry was all fired up when, in the New Year, Tom suggested a summit meeting with King Francis. He wanted to meet his rival, show off his superiority in every aspect of kingship and establish himself as the greater prince. Tom's concern, though, was to foster an amicable working friendship between the two monarchs, which would be infinitely preferable to war. He was already immersed in negotiations with the French. It was taking his mind off his troubles. The meeting was set for May.

By February, he was hard at work making the arrangements, drawing up protocols for the visit, instructing master craftsmen and overseeing every detail involved in transporting five thousand people across the English Channel to Calais, England's last remaining possession in France. For Harry was bent on taking his whole court and almost the entire English nobility with him. His overarching priority was to impress the French.

One morning, Tom sat down in the King's closet and spread out a rough map of Calais and northern France, drawn by the helpful Cromwell, on the table.

'Now, Sir, it has been agreed that the meeting will take place six miles from Calais in the open countryside between your Grace's town of Guisnes, where you will be based, and Ardres, where King Francis will stay. I fear, however, that Guisnes Castle is too small for a sufficient display of magnificence. Might I suggest, therefore, that we build a temporary palace at the meeting place?'

He laid a set of elaborate designs before Harry, who stared at them, impressed.

'It will be a palace of illusions,' Tom explained. 'Not even Leonardo da Vinci could have improved upon it. It will be built of timber on stone and brick foundations and covered with canvas painted to look like brickwork or masonry. The hall is to have a ceiling of green silk studded with gold roses, and a floor covering of patterned taffeta. There will be a King's Side, a Queen's Side, a suite for your Grace's sister, the French Queen, and one for my humble self. Senior courtiers will be accommodated in Guisnes Castle; the rest can stay in tents. I have ordered two thousand eight hundred of them. Now, these pavilions . . .' He unrolled a large page covered with colourful designs for tents of green and white, blue and gold, and red and gold, all adorned with the King's badges, beasts and mottoes. 'They will serve for entertainments and banquets. Your Grace will have your own dining tent of cloth of gold.'

'You have done marvellously, Thomas.' Harry beamed.

Tom smiled. 'The camp will be laid out according to your Grace's wishes. I have ordered in great quantities of livestock and foodstuffs. We must spare no effort or cost to impress the French.'

Harry nodded. 'It is a mighty enterprise,' he observed.

'Everything is under control, Sir. Many other items are being shipped abroad, including tapestries, furnishings and everything needful for tournaments. We have fifteen hundred spears from the Tower arsenal, one thousand Milanese swords and a great number of horses. I am moving the armourers' steel mill at Greenwich in its entirety to Guisnes for the repair of armour and weapons.'

Harry looked pleased.

Tom resumed. 'I gather that the French are jealously tracking our preparations. My agents tell me that they have no wish to outlay as much money. There will be no prefabricated palace for King Francis. Instead, the French court will be housed near Ardres in a little town of tents of cloth of gold and silver. Already they are calling it the Field of Cloth of Gold.'

The King's eyes gleamed. 'Then we shall outshine them!'

'Indeed, Sir, but we must consider the question of etiquette. I have taken it upon myself to resolve the numerous disputes that have arisen, and laid down rules governing precedence. It has been agreed that, in order to preserve the honour of both nations, neither your Grace nor King Francis will take part in any joust or combat against the other.'

Harry frowned. Tom knew he had envisaged himself vanquishing Francis in the lists, even unhorsing him, and winning all the prizes.

'It would not be politic, Sir. All things must appear equal, for your purpose is to forge a lasting peace. The very terrain is being flattened so as not to give either side any advantage.'

Harry looked mutinous for a moment. 'I suppose you are right,' he said grudgingly. 'We don't want a diplomatic incident.'

Tom returned to his lists. He had authorised the purchase of enormous quantities of livestock and foodstuffs at eye-watering cost. The food bill alone came to nearly £9,000. Extra kitchen staff had been hired, and numerous pots, pans and spits borrowed – at a high price – from London cooks. As well as provisions, many other items would have to be shipped abroad, including a great number of highly strung horses – not to mention highly strung nobles. While some were eagerly anticipating the venture, those with lower incomes did not hide their resentment at the ruinous outlay required of them, which only served to fuel hostility towards Tom, whom many believed to be the architect of the visit.

Tom was just ticking off the last of his to-do list for today, and feeling a deep sense of satisfaction at keeping on top of everything, when the King's usher summoned him back to the royal closet. Harry was still seated at his desk, but he was frowning.

'Thomas, I have to tell you that I am having second thoughts about this French venture. I'm not sure that an alliance with France is a good idea.'

Tom was staggered. 'Your Grace, at this late stage, I beg you not to pull out. Think of the consequences.' He was actually thinking of all his weeks of hard work going to waste.

'It is not so late in the day,' Harry countered. 'I am beginning to find the prospect of friendship with the Emperor more appealing. Charles is eager to bind himself in friendship with England, and I have invited him to visit me in May.'

Tom's anger rose. 'Sir, it is too late to cancel the French summit. The plans are far advanced, much expenditure has been outlaid, and it would be an unforgivable insult to King Francis, who will be rightly offended, especially if you are seen to be courting the Emperor, his enemy.'

Harry sat there, considering. 'Very well, I will go to France. Your hard work will not be wasted. But I am not sure that I will go ahead with the French alliance.'

Tom felt like shouting at him, and took a deep breath, trying to control himself. 'Sir, with respect, there is no point in all this extravagant outlay if you are thinking of breaking faith with King Francis.'

'I did not say I was. There is no harm in my wife's nephew visiting England.'

'The French might not see it that way.' Tom could not hide his displeasure.

'Then we will disabuse them of any doubts when we arrive,' Harry said breezily.

In May, leaving Norfolk and Bishop Foxe in charge of state affairs, and the little Princess Mary keeping royal state at Richmond, the King and his vast entourage left Greenwich and proceeded through Kent towards Dover, where they would embark for France. Tom was with them, riding on his mule beside his master's great charger. They stayed overnight at Charing, Otford and Leeds Castle, before arriving at Canterbury in readiness for the Emperor's coming. The King and Queen lodged in Archbishop Warham's palace, which had been specially refurbished for the occasion.

Katherine was so obviously looking forward to meeting her nephew. There was no doubting which alliance she favoured, and Tom was concerned that she would persuade Harry to do her bidding. But, he reasoned, her power was not what it had been. Her failure to bear a son had much to do with that, and Bessie Blount, who – he suspected – was still sharing the King's bed, despite her recent marriage. The King, he thought resentfully, was a lucky bastard.

Tom rode on to Dover and watched from the quayside as the

Emperor's ships approached in stately fashion. When they docked, the English fleet waiting in the Straits of Dover let off a thunderous salute. Charles walked ashore beneath a canopy of cloth of gold emblazoned with his black eagle emblem, and Tom bowed, welcoming him on behalf of the King. It struck him that Charles looked younger than twenty. His lugubrious Habsburg features were distorted by a jaw so overlong that he could not close his mouth. He was serious and reserved, with a natural dignity. As Tom conducted him to Dover Castle, where he would stay the night, and the two conversed, he gained the impression that here, for all his youth, was a statesman to be reckoned with.

Before supper, he sent to inform the King of the Emperor's arrival. Harry arrived in haste the next morning, in time to greet Charles as he came downstairs. Then he escorted him to Canterbury, where the citizens, who hated the French, gave him a warm welcome.

The Emperor set himself to charm everybody, and made a point of seeking out Tom.

'I understand,' he said, speaking in French, 'that you are highly influential with your master. I hope that you will do me good service in extolling to him the merits of an alliance with Spain and the Empire.'

The smile remained on Tom's face. 'Whatever my humble opinion, your Majesty, my master makes up his own mind in such matters.'

'But surely he heeds the wisdom and statesmanship for which you are universally renowned?'

'I like to think so, Sir,' Tom replied.

'Then I believe we can help each other. I am bestowing on you a handsome pension in return for your kind welcome.'

Tom maintained his composure. He was being bought. 'That is most generous of your Majesty,' he murmured.

'And I believe that you look for greater preferment in the Church. I wonder what higher rank a cardinal can aspire to? The Papal throne itself?'

Tom could not suppress a thrill. He had no ties now, no lover to keep him in England. Only Harry – Harry, who had deprived him of the most precious thing in his life. Harry, whom he still loved like a son, in spite of it.

'I have never dared look so high,' he said.

'With your talents and reputation, you should,' Charles urged. 'I myself would wish it. And when, God forfend, our present pontiff departs this life, I assure you that I will help you to secure the Papacy.'

'Your Majesty is too generous,' Tom replied, conscious that such support would come at a high price.

They talked a while, and when Charles went off to speak to the Queen, Harry drew Tom into a window embrasure. 'What make you of our guest?'

'I am impressed with him, Sir.'

'As am I. Look, Thomas, I mean to keep all my options open, so I have agreed to meet with him again, on Imperial territory at Gravelines, after my meeting with King Francis.'

'As your Grace pleases.' Tom was anything but pleased. The Emperor was friendly anyway. It was the French, England's traditional enemies, who needed to be wooed.

After Charles had departed, the King and his vast train of five thousand persons rode on to Dover and embarked for France in a fleet of twenty-seven ships. The sea was calm, and they arrived at Calais at noon that day, then began the march to Guisnes, which lay within the English Pale of Calais. Outside Guisnes were the open fields where the summit was to take place. The English camp had been transformed into a forest of tents, overshadowed by the magnificent royal pavilions.

Harry stared in wonder at the gateway to the temporary palace Tom had had erected. Built of wood and canvas, it was decorated with a scallop-shell pediment, the royal arms, two large Tudor roses and a golden statue of Cupid. On the lawn in front stood a gilded pillar topped with a statue of Bacchus, the god of wine, and a fountain in the ancient Roman style, from which flowed white wine, Malmsey and claret, which were free to all comers, day and night. Chained to the fountain were silver drinking cups.

Harry dismounted and stood back to allow Tom to escort him inside. Tom was eager to show him the spacious chambers decorated with gilt cornices and furnished with gorgeous tapestries, hangings of cloth of gold, Turkey carpets, carved furniture, buffets laden with gold plate, glass windows with diamond-shaped panes, and stone chimneys. He led the King into an exquisite chapel painted blue and gold and hung with cloth of gold and green velvet; on the altar had been placed a great gold crucifix, ten candlesticks, gilded statues of the twelve Apostles and many holy relics.

'This palace is a marvel!' Harry exclaimed. 'The French have nothing like it. You have done well, my lord Cardinal.'

Much gratified, Tom showed him the King's Side, then escorted Katherine to the Queen's Side before retiring to his own suite to wash.

It seemed as if the whole world was here, crammed into the English camp. Everyone was wearing their richest attire and most sumptuous jewels. Surveying the throng with Tom, Harry reckoned that the outlay must have ruined some of his courtiers.

'Everyone was ordered to attend in their best clothes,' Tom reminded him.

John Fisher, Bishop of Rochester, standing with them, was disapproving. 'Never have we seen in England such an excess of apparel.'

Tom wished Fisher would shut up. He had put so much work into making this summit a success, and it was imperative that it was, at least in Harry's eyes.

But Harry was frowning at the Bishop. He was his usual peacock self and had brought with him a wardrobe of increasingly spectacular costumes. For months now, he had been importing great quantities of rich fabrics for himself and the Queen. He had not been best pleased when she had hers made up into dresses in the Spanish style, but he had let it go in the interests of domestic harmony.

On the Feast of Corpus Christi, as cannons boomed simultaneously from Guisnes and Ardres, where the French encampment lay, the two kings, followed by a host of courtiers, rode to meet each other, decked out in battle array. Harry wore cloth of gold and silver, heavily bejewelled, with a feathered black bonnet and his Garter collar; his bay horse was hung with gold bells that jangled as it moved, and he was attended by the Yeomen of his Guard. King Francis, in cloth of gold and silver encrusted with gems, was flanked by his Swiss Guards. At the edge of the field, the kings paused, then, to the sound of trumpets and sackbuts, they galloped alone towards each other, doffed their bonnets and embraced. After dismounting, they linked arms and entered Francis's pavilion of gold damask lined with blue velvet embroidered with fleurs-de-lys and guarded by a statue of St Michael. Within, Tom looked on approvingly as the monarchs greeted each other warmly and talked together in friendly fashion for the whole afternoon, sipping spiced wine. Outside, their respective retinues were drinking toasts to each other.

For two weeks, the extravagant festivities continued. Jousts, sports, feasts and dances followed in quick succession. All seemed to be going well, and Tom allowed himself to relax.

Two incidents stood out in his mind. The first occurred after they had watched a wrestling match between the English Yeomen of the Guard and some Frenchmen. Forgetting that he was not supposed to be entering into any contest with Francis, Harry challenged him to a fight. Tom saw the gleam in Francis's eye. So the French King was as keen as his brother monarch to show off his prowess! Mouths agape, the courtiers looked on avidly. Queen Katherine and Queen Claude clasped each other's hands, dismay in their faces.

Harry did not look Tom's way as he stripped to his shirt and breeches, then faced Francis. For seconds, they grappled with each other, but it was plain from the first that they were unequally matched. Strong Harry might be, but Francis was leaner and more agile. Tom was horrified to see Harry thrown heavily to the floor, to a collective gasp from the spectators.

His cheeks burning, he scrambled to his feet, red-faced. 'Again!' he said.

'I think not,' Francis replied.

Harry was shaking with mortification. He made to lunge at his rival, but the two queens quickly stepped forward and pulled them apart. Furious at being deprived of the chance to avenge himself, Harry only calmed down when he won an archery contest later that day.

The second incident seemed trivial at the time, but in later years, Tom would recall it vividly. He was standing outside one of the tents talking to Norfolk and the latter's son-in-law, Sir Thomas Boleyn. They were discussing a marriage between one of Boleyn's daughters and the son of the Earl of Ormond, a title Boleyn claimed. A young woman joined them, a slender girl with dark hair and eyes and sallow skin.

Boleyn smiled at her. 'Come forward, Anne. My lord Cardinal, may I present my daughter, the one whose future we have been discussing.'

Anne curtseyed. She looked furious – and that was probably why she made an impression on Tom.

'Delightful, delightful,' he said, although to his mind she was no great beauty.

'We were speaking of you – and here you are,' Norfolk said to Anne. 'Come and kiss your old grandsire, child.'

'I gathered that you were discussing my marriage with James Butler,' Anne told him. She glared at her father.

'You may have cause to rejoice, Mistress Anne,' Tom said. 'If the King agrees, this will be a good match for you and for your family.'

'And will the King consent, my lord?' she asked.

'I shall advise him on the matter. He is, shall we say, well disposed.'

Father and grandfather beamed. Anne looked mutinous, but she must have known that she had no choice. If the King decreed it, she would marry Ormond's son.

For the final public event, Tom took centre stage. The tiltyard had been converted into a temporary chapel, and there, at noon, assisted by five other cardinals and twenty bishops, he celebrated a solemn Mass before both courts. The choir of the Chapel Royal sang alternately with its French equivalent, La Chapelle du Musique du Roi; then Richard Pace gave a Latin oration on peace. There was a momentary disruption to the service when a firework in the shape of a salamander, Francis's personal emblem, was accidentally set off, causing a brief panic.

Afterwards, everybody was saying that the summit had been a great success. But Tom was uneasy. Had it all been worth it? Would Harry and Francis ever forget their rivalry and be at peace? And was an alliance with France so desirable after all?

He was still entertaining doubts when he laid the foundation stone of a chapel dedicated to Our Lady of Peace, which the two kings had agreed to found on the site of their meeting. The ceremony was followed by an open-air feast, a final round of jousts and a spectacular firework display. Some were already calling the summit the eighth wonder of the world.

After taking leave of Francis and Claude, and exchanging many costly gifts, Harry moved his court to Calais.

'Well, that was a triumph,' he observed to Tom, who was riding on his mule beside him. 'I am as pleased with this meeting as if I had gained a great realm.'

'Indeed, your Grace. It will bear abundant fruit, I am certain.'

'It occurs to me,' Harry said, 'that with France and Spain vying for my allegiance, I can choose the ally who best suits my policies. Who would you choose, Thomas?'

Tom had given the matter much thought since the summit, and weighed all the pros and cons. In the end, he had surprised himself. 'If I had to choose, Sir, I would favour the Emperor.' Charles, who was paying him that handsome pension. 'Yes, peace with France is desirable, but England's economy will suffer from the loss of the lucrative cloth trade between England and the Netherlands if you make an alliance with King Francis.'

'Hmm.' Harry was thoughtful.

'Yet there is another way you might consider,' Tom said carefully. 'What if Europe's chief states united to seek to outlaw war among Christian nations? What if England became a neutral power whose arbitration and judgements were generally accepted as impartial justice?'

Harry thought for a while. 'It's an attractive and noble idea, but unworkable, I think, given the nature of princes. I too am inclined towards the Emperor, if only because I trust him more than I do Francis; and an Imperial alliance will leave me free to pursue my ambitions in France.'

Tom sighed inwardly. When would his master wake up to the fact that he was unlikely ever to conquer France?

'I will think more on the matter,' Harry said.

Tom returned to Hampton Court, which, for all its size and magnificence and many servants, seemed an empty place without Joan. Her rooms had been kept as she had left them, but all her personal possessions had gone. Tom could not bear to enter, and ordered that the apartment be locked.

Preparing for the Field of Cloth of Gold had filled his days, providing a welcome distraction from his loneliness, but now there was only routine business to attend to. He needed another project.

He became aware of speculation that, with the King lacking a male heir, Buckingham might be named his successor, and his spies reported rumours that the Duke might even attempt to seize the crown for himself. Given his wealth, vast estates and large following of clients and tenants, he had the potential to pose a very real threat to Harry. Determined to bring the Duke down, Tom made Harry aware of this, and the King looked at him uneasily.

'Be vigilant, Thomas!' he commanded.

'You can rely on me,' Tom replied. 'I do not trust Buckingham. The man is a fool, and fools do rash things.'

For the rest of that year, he kept a close watch on the Duke.

He placed his agents among the servants in Buckingham's household. They reported that the Duke was making ill-advised remarks about his proximity to the throne, and had predicted that Harry would never have sons and that he himself would be king one day. Tom felt that his suspicions were justified. It could have been pure hopeful speculation, but the Duke's intentions might also be sinister. Even if they were not, he had certainly behaved with a dangerous lack of discretion.

In October, Buckingham suddenly left court for the new castle he was building for himself at Thornbury in Gloucestershire. That set alarums ringing in Tom's head. It was time to act.

'I believe we have good reason to be concerned about the Duke of Buckingham,' he said, when Harry returned to Windsor after his late-summer progress.

'What has he done now?' Harry asked. They were sitting in his closet, catching up on business.

'I have reason to fear that my lord of Buckingham has designs on your throne. I am certain that he does indeed mean to be named your successor.'

'Never! I wouldn't inflict that on England.'

'Very wise! I have taken the precaution of making discreet enquiries among his servants.' He told Harry what the Duke's servants had said.

'How dare he!' Harry was seething.

Tom knew he had pressed a raw nerve. 'Do not fear, Sir. I have him under observation,' he said, smiling reassuringly.

He was secretly pleased that the Duke had been indiscreet. Given the great enmity between them, who could blame him if he wanted Buckingham brought down? But he would do what was best for his master, and for England; and if that happened to coincide with his own inclinations, so be it!

At New Year, Harry was surprised to receive the gift of a golden goblet from Buckingham, engraved *With humble, true heart.*

'I am inclined to think that I have misjudged my lord Duke,' he said, but Tom was not fooled. Soon, very soon, he hoped, Buckingham would play into his hands.

One day in March, having received a letter from Thornbury that both worried and gratified him intensely, he hastened to find the King, and found him waiting to take his turn at the archery butts in Windsor Great Park, his breath steaming in the cold air.

He bent to Harry's ear. 'Buckingham is mobilising troops,' he murmured.

Harry stared at him in alarm. 'Carry on,' he told his gentlemen, and led Tom a little way off. 'What is he up to?'

'Ostensibly, he needs them to protect him when he tours his estates in Wales, where he is not popular.'

'But he might use them against me!'

'We cannot discount it,' Tom said. 'I truly fear that he is plotting treason. One of my agents states that the Duke has sworn to assassinate your Grace and means to gain audience with a knife secreted about his person, so that, when kneeling before you, he will rise and stab you.'

Harry looked as if he could already feel the fatal thrust.

'His servants say he has purchased a large amount of cloth of gold and silver and will use it to bribe your Yeomen of the Guard to gain access to you.'

'Enough!' Harry barked. 'He must be stopped.'

Tom understood the need for caution. 'Sir, until we have more substantial evidence than malicious gossip, I advise you not to proceed against him.'

'No! I've heard enough. Have him arrested. I will bring down this overmighty subject. He might be stupid, but he is dangerous. My lord Cardinal, I will brook no more arguments!'

Tom did not hesitate. Here was his chance finally to rid himself of his old enemy. Setting niceties aside, he summoned Buckingham to Windsor and had him apprehended on the way.

'He has been taken to the Tower and charged with imagining and compassing the death of our lord the King,' he informed the Council, as Harry sat there gripping the arms of his chair, doubtless reflecting on what a lucky escape he had had.

The sentence of the peers who tried Buckingham – and who had been hand-picked by Tom – was death.

'The chief evidence against him was the testimony of his own officers,' Tom told Harry after the trial. 'But your Grace may rest assured that justice has been properly served.'

Four days later, the Duke was beheaded. Not for a long time had such a prominent noble – and one with royal blood, at that – been sent to the scaffold, and there was a great stir in London and at court. People believed that Tom, out of pure malice, had brought him down. It was being whispered that a butcher's dog had killed the finest buck in England. Let them all point! It had been the King who had pressed for Buckingham's arrest. Tom had merely been the catalyst.

Harry was left so shaken by Buckingham's treachery that he deliberately shunned those members of the older nobility who had blood ties to the Duke, lest they be tainted by his treason. The virtuous Lady Salisbury, who had Plantagenet blood, had recently been appointed governess to the Princess Mary, but, ignoring the Queen's protests and his daughter's tears, the King dismissed her, for her daughter was married to Buckingham's son and she was herself too close to the throne for comfort; then he sent her eldest son, Lord Montagu, to the Tower for a brief spell, as a warning to the family not to dabble in treason.

Meanwhile, despite feeling sick and feverish with malaria, Harry was busy dividing up Buckingham's extensive landed property, which had been forfeited to the Crown. He reserved the choicest properties for himself and distributed the rest among those lords and courtiers whose loyalty he felt he could depend on. As they scrambled for the spoils, the rumblings of discontent at Buckingham's fate died a quick death.

Not even Harry's illness could dampen his pleasure in the seven great houses he had seized from the Duke, among them Penshurst Place, Kimbolton Castle and Bletchingley Manor. But the greatest prize was the palatial Thornbury Castle, which was only partially completed. He could use it when he was on progress in Gloucestershire. Tom felt vindicated when Harry tried fully to express his gratitude.

'You have rid me of a traitor and munificently enriched me,' he declared.

Tom bowed his head. Such praise was sufficient to quell the twinges of conscience he felt at having brought down Buckingham. Yet why should he feel such pangs? The Duke had probably been guilty anyway. Suppressing his doubts, Tom could only feel relief that his great enemy was no more.

Chapter 22

1521

Soon after Buckingham's fall, and still feeling the need to flex his power against those who would bring him down, Tom heard that his old adversary Sir Amyas Paulet had been appointed treasurer of the Middle Temple. He had neither forgotten nor forgiven Paulet for clapping him in the stocks twenty-odd years ago, and he was damned if he was going to allow him to reap the benefits of his new office, so he sent for him.

'Who would have thought, when you punished a poor scholar, that he would one day be Lord Chancellor of England?' he asked him.

'I but did my duty as sheriff,' Paulet countered. 'And your Grace was drunk.'

'I tripped on a stone,' Tom growled.

'You were drunk!'

'You exceeded your authority! And I will not have you lording it over the Middle Temple. You are to attend upon the Council.'

'I will do no such thing. You have no jurisdiction over the Inns of Law.'

'I think you will find that I do!'

Tom dismissed him, in a fury. How dare the man speak to him so disrespectfully?

To his surprise, Paulet did present himself before the council board the next morning.

'I have discussed the merits of your appointment with my colleagues, Sir Amyas,' Tom told him. 'We are agreed that you should be dismissed and that you may not leave London without my permission, on pain of forfeiture of your possessions. You will remain in the Middle Temple, in the gatehouse.'

Paulet's look could have felled an army, but Tom ignored it. 'You may go,' he said.

The next he heard was that Paulet had had Tom's arms gloriously displayed on the Middle Temple gateway. It was an obvious attempt to appease his tormentor, and Tom relented, releasing him and allowing him to resume his office.

In truth, he was feeling guilty for having been so vengeful. If Joan had been here, doubtless he would have shown more leniency, or not taken revenge at all. But Joan was not here. She was at Thames Ditton with another baby, and his infrequent visits to her had become tortuous, since he could not quell his feelings for her – and he dared not show them. He could feel his frustration seeping into his work, finding himself irritable even with his most helpful servants. (Not with Cromwell, though, whose industry had given Tom great pride and satisfaction.)

He had continued to visit young Thomas at the house of Master Birchinshaw. Thomas was eleven now, but sullen in mood and not making much headway in his studies.

He remonstrated with his son. 'You must try harder, if you are to get on in life,' he told him, standing him at his knee in the otherwise empty form room.

'I do try, Uncle,' the child protested. 'The lessons are hard, though.'

Tom spoke to Master Birchinshaw. 'I have to say that I am dissatisfied with the boy's progress. He seems behind in most subjects, especially Latin.'

The tutor bridled a little. 'I am sorry that your nephew speaks less Latin than your Eminence might wish, but I am bound to say that the fault lies in the curriculum the boys here are required to follow. It is very demanding, and not entirely suitable for pupils who are a little slow.'

Tom was shocked. 'Are you saying my son is slow?' Too late, he realised what he had said, but it did not matter. The tutor did not look surprised; he wasn't a fool. 'What do you mean?'

'Exactly that. He does not assimilate knowledge as rapidly as his peers. In fact, he is not interested in learning. I suspect that he expects to fail. And, of course, the fact that his aunt no longer visits must have something to do with it. Tell me, my lord, why does she not come?'

Tom found he was sweating. This was all too much.

'She has married,' he said, 'and that is why she has ceased to visit Thomas. I should tell you that her husband knows nothing of his existence. But she will come, I am sure, when the time is right. I know that the present state of affairs grieves her greatly.' In fact, they had never discussed it.

Master Birchinshaw's expression managed to convey that he was thinking about the wages of sin. 'I pray she will visit soon, then, for young Thomas's sake. In the meantime, I will continue to do my best for him.'

'Thank you,' Tom said. 'I am indebted to you. And I trust that I can rely on your discretion. But tell me, before I go. Is there anything truly amiss with the boy?'

'Nothing specific,' Birchinshaw replied. 'It's hard to put a finger on it. But we are all as God made us, and he is young yet.'

Tom left, deeply troubled in his mind. He could not bear to think that there was something wrong with his beloved son.

'The Church,' Harry declared, 'is under threat. It seems that heresy is spreading.'

He and Tom were enjoying the warm May weather and sharing a ewer of wine in one of the little banqueting houses Tom had erected at Hampton Court.

'Indeed.' Tom frowned. 'Four years ago, when that damnable monk Martin Luther nailed his list of abuses to the church door in Wittenberg, we thought the storm he whipped up would blow over. Alas, it has not.'

'If he had stopped short at attacking corruption, I might have applauded him,' Harry said. 'I too heartily disapprove of the sale of indulgences. No one can buy their way into Heaven. The Vatican is corrupt, everyone knows that. But rejecting Papal authority, holy relics, pilgrimages, penances and clerical celibacy? Doing away with most of the Sacraments? Denying the miracle of the Mass? No. That is all heresy.'

'For which the Pope has excommunicated him.'

'And justly. But he stood before the Emperor at Worms last month and defended his views. And his following is growing in Europe. It's very worrying. Thomas, I see it as one of the most serious threats to the Church, and to the unity of Christendom. By one man's disobedience, many are made sinners!'

Tom drained his goblet. He had cast off his red robes and was sitting there in his shirtsleeves and breeches. 'It worries me too. Luther wants men to pray directly to God rather than through Our Lady, the saints and the priests. He is trying to render many priestly functions redundant.'

'He acknowledges only two Sacraments, baptism and communion,' Harry spluttered, almost beside himself with indignation. 'Even then, he claims that the consecrated Host is not transformed into the actual body and blood of Christ, but merely symbolises it. He sees faith alone as the basis of religion. It's intolerable that one man can cause so much havoc. If he were my subject, I'd have him burned. Thankfully, his heresy has not yet spread to England.'

Tom hesitated. 'Unfortunately, Sir, it has. This very morning, I received reports that it is being debated at Oxford and Cambridge, and that some have boasted of their conversions. Two heretical pamphlets and three Lutheran tracts have arrived on my desk.'

Harry was staring at him, appalled. 'I will not have it! This is a godly realm and I will not allow it to be corrupted by this canker. Cut it out, Thomas, and deal with it severely. We must set an example and a deterrent.'

'Wholeheartedly, Sir,' Tom concurred. 'I will install my agents in the universities. That is where the greatest danger lies. I am told that some who favour the new learning are the heartiest followers of Luther.'

'The new learning?' Harry growled. 'Why, I am a devotee of that myself, but it is all about the study of the ancients.'

'Alas, Sir, it seems that some see hints of Lutheranism in ancient philosophies.'

'Well, they shall not appropriate them to that purpose! Religious doctrine is a matter for those qualified to understand and interpret it, not the common man.'

Tom understood why his master was so exercised. Kings could not afford to let such heresies take root because they encouraged social division, sedition and even revolt, undermining the body politic made up of Church and state. These new ideas robbed princes and churchmen of power and authority. For Harry, they represented a threat to the order and hierarchy desirable in a Christian society.

'Thomas, I have been thinking,' he said. 'The Emperor and the King of France have had special titles bestowed on them by the Pope. Charles is "the Most Catholic King" and "Protector of the Holy See", and Francis is "the Most Christian King". For years now, I've been dropping hints to various Papal nuncios that I would like a title too. Now, with Lutheranism undermining true religion, would this not be the right time to do something to make me worthy of winning one?'

'Indeed, it would, Sir.' Tom rested his chin on his steepled fingers, thinking. As usual, his thought processes were quick and efficient. 'It occurs to me that your Grace is outstandingly learned and eloquent. Might I suggest that you put that excellent scholarship to good use and write a book defending the Church against Luther's heresies? No one is better placed to do it, no one more influential. There is no prince to equal you in learning.'

Harry's face had lit up. 'By St George, once again you have the sow by the right ear, Thomas! I'll start work on it tonight! I will discredit this Luther, this weed, this dilapidated, sick and evil-minded sheep!'

He called his book *A Defence of the Seven Sacraments against Martin Luther*. It was short and scathing and invested with all his outrage and passion. Richard Pace helped with advice, and Thomas More assisted in collating Harry's random arguments into a cohesive narrative. Otherwise, the book was, from first to last, Harry's own. He gave it priority over state affairs and even hunting expeditions, to everyone's astonishment.

Tom was present when the King read out a passage to Thomas More.

'"What serpent so venomously possessed this man who called the Most Holy See of Rome 'Babylon' and the Pope's authority 'Tyranny' and turns the name of the Most Holy Bishop of Rome into 'Anti-Christ'?"' he thundered.

'Sir, might I suggest you tone down that passage,' More urged. 'The Pope is a prince as you are, and there may one day be some conflict between you. I think it best therefore that his authority should be more slenderly touched upon.'

'No, it shall not,' Harry argued. 'I am so much bound to the See of Rome that I cannot do too much honour to it.'

'Very well, Sir.' More retreated.

'I am defending the Church!' Harry reminded him. 'I want everyone to see how ready I am to do so, not only with my armies, if need be, but with all the resources of my mind.'

The book was completed by the end of the month, when Tom proudly exhibited a manuscript copy at Paul's Cross to cheering citizens. That same day, he presided over the burning of Luther's books. Standing in the shadow of St Paul's Cathedral, he watched the pyre grow higher and higher as more volumes were thrown onto it. Crowds looked on as the fire took hold and the flames leapt skywards, crackling fiercely.

'Good people, if you would avoid a similar fate,' his voice rang out, 'stay faithful to the true Catholic religion!'

Some fell to their knees, crossing themselves. Tom raised his hand in blessing.

The King's book was printed, and thirty presentation copies were sent to Rome; one, beautifully bound in cloth of gold, was intended for his Holiness, and had been dedicated to him by the King's own hand. Harry was delighted to receive a warm letter of thanks, which he showed off to Tom and everyone else within sight. In it, his Holiness thanked God for raising up such a prince to be the champion of the Church, and expressed astonishment that Harry had found time to write a book, which was a very unusual thing for a king to do.

'He has offered me a title and asked which one I would like!' the King announced proudly to his Council. 'What shall I choose?'

The lords entered into a long discussion.

'"Most Orthodox"?' suggested Bishop Fisher.

'"Angelic"?' That was Suffolk, with a twinkle in his eye. Harry gave him a withering glance. In the end, he chose "Defender of the Faith", which had been put forward by Tom. There was a chorus of approval.

The book was selling faster than the presses could print it when Pope Leo died in December. When the news reached England, Tom felt an upsurge of excitement that he found hard to conceal. He had not forgotten the Emperor's promise, and he felt certain that Charles would not have done either, for Tom had enthusiastically steered Harry towards an alliance with the Empire while contriving to maintain friendly relations with France.

'The loss of his Holiness is a tragedy for Christendom,' he announced to the Council. 'He was a man who strove for peace. But now we must look to the future – and a new Pope.' The Emperor, he kept reminding himself, had great influence in the Vatican.

Chapter 23

1522

When the news came that Charles had backed another candidate, his former tutor, who had been elected as Pope Adrian VI, Tom could not contain his fury. He felt betrayed, tricked, slighted.

'My envoys report that Charles preferred him because he is hot against Luther,' Harry said at supper that evening, making little attempt to hide how pleased he was that his dear friend and chief minister would not be packing his bags and leaving for Rome.

The smile remained frozen on Tom's face. 'I had hoped that his Imperial Majesty would favour me. There would have been so much I could have done, as pope, for your Majesty.'

Henry toyed with his wine goblet and frowned. 'It wasn't for lack of pressure,' he said. 'I myself sent a hundred thousand ducats to buy you votes. I urged the Emperor to support you, Thomas. I am sorry that it was all for nothing. Still, the King of France is hopping with rage because the Emperor's subject has been elected.' He smiled wickedly. 'Maybe it wasn't all a wasted effort!'

On a bright January morning, Tom visited his son at St Paul's School and was overjoyed to see a great improvement in his work. Thomas's writings were accomplished, his Latin far better than it had been. Master Birchinshaw had finally instilled studious habits in him.

As the two men sat talking, while Thomas shot at the butts outside with his friends, Tom raised a matter he had been pondering for a while. 'I have a friend, Thomas Lupset, at Cambridge, where he is reader in humanities at Corpus Christi College. He is a great humanist scholar, and it has been my privilege to be his patron. He has a strong desire to visit the great universities of Europe, and it occurred to me that, as Thomas is now twelve, it would benefit him to go with him.'

'That is an excellent idea, my lord Cardinal,' Birchinshaw said eagerly – a touch too eagerly, Tom thought. 'The experience will broaden his mind immeasurably. And he could have no greater pedagogue than Dr Lupset, whose reputation goes before him.'

'The plan is to spend time at the universities of Padua, Louvain, Ferrara and Poissy,' Tom told him. 'Thomas will complete this academic year with you, and they will depart in the summer.'

'Excellent, excellent!' enthused the master.

Thomas was called indoors, and Tom explained what was going to happen. The boy looked doubtful.

'You will have a marvellous time,' Tom said. 'You are a lucky fellow to be offered the advantage of studying in such prestigious schools of learning. And you will be able to enjoy yourself at the same time, for I am bestowing on you several church offices; the stipends and tithes will afford you a comfortable income.' It was against the rules, of course, for a boy of Thomas's age to be given benefices, but Tom cared little for that, especially when he saw his son's face brighten.

'You will love travel. It offers so many new experiences,' he went on. 'I wish that I could see the glories of Italy!'

'You could come with me, Uncle,' the boy urged.

'Alas, my duties keep me here. But we will write to each other, and you can tell me all about your adventures.'

As he rode back to York Place, Tom realised that he ought to tell Joan what he had in mind for their son. He had not been to visit her for some time, since her husband had made it clear that he did not welcome it, and seeing her only reopened the wound he carried in his heart. But this matter concerned her. However, he would have to go delicately. For all he knew, Legh was still unaware that she had borne Tom two children.

He knew he could rely on the discretion of Master Cavendish, his new gentleman usher. George Cavendish had come highly recommended by his own father, a respected officer of the Court of Exchequer, whose judgement Tom valued, and he had not been disappointed, for the twenty-five-year-old Cavendish was a young man of great charm and trustworthiness whose only aim in life was clearly to please his master. Tom suspected that he rather hero-worshipped him.

He summoned Cavendish. 'I have a confidential mission for you,' he told him. 'There is a lady in whom I take a fatherly interest, and I fear she is oppressed by an unkind husband, a Master Legh. I would like to visit her to offer some comfort and advice, but not when he is there. I want you to ride to her house at Thames Ditton to find out Legh's movements.'

Cavendish nodded eagerly. 'My lord, you can rely on me.' He sped off.

Tom was gratified to learn that Legh was departing for Cheshunt on the morrow. Immediately, he set to work to clear his desk so that he would be free in the morning.

As he left Hampton Court, he felt a sense of anticipation. This would be the first time that he and Joan had been alone together in a long while. God willing, she would act differently towards him without her husband watching her.

She welcomed him courteously as he was shown into the parlour, and called for wine, then bade him be seated in the high-backed chair by the fireside, herself taking the smaller chair opposite – just as in the old days.

'To what do I owe the pleasure?' she asked.

'I wanted to speak to you about Thomas,' he said, and told her what he had arranged. 'I wanted your blessing, for he is your son too.'

'I think it's a wonderful plan,' she said. 'A career in the Church could do wonders for him, as it has for you.' Her face clouded over. 'I do miss him, dreadfully. George knows nothing of his existence. It's made me feel like Judas, having to deny my own son, who I love so much, but my husband is jealous. He does not like you visiting me.'

Tom was gripped by guilt. This he had done to her, the woman he should have cherished. 'I would not make things more difficult for you, Joan. I will not come, if that would help. But if Sir George is still away tomorrow, I will take you to see Thomas.'

'Would you?' Tears shone in her eyes.

'Why not? I am his benefactor. Why should I not take you to see him? Master Birchinshaw would be pleased, and I believe he understands our situation.'

'Then I shall go! Thank you!' She looked so full of gratitude that Tom thought she would kiss him, but she kept her distance.

'I miss you,' he said.

'I miss you too,' she whispered. There were tears in her eyes.

He fell to his knees before her, looking at her intently, and grasped her hands. 'We could rekindle our love!'

'No! I dare not.' She pulled her hands away.

'But I want you, Joan,' he pleaded. 'I need you. I find it hard to carry all the burdens I shoulder without you. I feel as if I'm half alive. I've tried to quell my love for you, but it's always there. And I hate myself for what I've done to you.'

She looked down at him sadly, as if to remind him that he had not loved her enough to choose her over his career. 'I wish I could say yes and be yours again. But I really do not want to complicate my life further. I feel as if I am walking on eggshells as it is. And you should not be risking scandal.'

He sighed and heaved himself to his feet, aware that he was growing stiffer in his joints and putting on weight. He was fifty, too old to play the gallant lover, and not getting any younger. A lonely old age beckoned.

'I will not make life difficult for you, Joan,' he said. 'But if ever you need me, or if ever I can do anything for you, then do not hesitate to send for me.'

'Thank you, Tom.' She wiped away her tears. 'Know this, that if I were free and you were not the King's chief minister, I would come running to you.'

Tom could not speak; he felt so emotional.

Joan rose. 'Take care, dear heart. I think it best if I go alone to see Thomas tomorrow.'

'I will send a litter to convey you,' he managed to say, then bent and kissed her hand and hastened to depart.

* * *

In February, a Papal legation arrived in England and the King's new title was formally proclaimed at Greenwich. He then went in procession to High Mass as trumpets sounded a joyous fanfare.

'It seems,' he said afterwards, when he and Tom were alone in his closet, 'that Luther has been stung by my criticisms. He has sent me a fierce response in which he accuses me of raving like a strumpet in a tantrum. He even claims that I did not write my book. Well, I'll put him right on that, but I will not stoop to answer his other scurrilous assertions. More can do it. I'll knight him for it.'

Tom was becoming aware that Harry's love and admiration for More had grown deeper. He could not do enough for the man, as evidenced by the lucrative offices he had bestowed on him. But Tom knew that Sir Thomas was under no illusions. One day, he emerged from his closet to find More giving advice to Thomas Cromwell, whom Tom had promoted to the post of collector of the revenues of the archdiocese of York and was now entrusting with confidential and sensitive tasks. 'I urge you to handle him with caution,' More was saying, 'for if the lion knew his strength, it would be hard to rule him.'

At first Tom thought More was referring to him, but then it dawned on him that he was talking about the King. More bowed and moved away, but Cromwell stood there impassively. 'Sound advice, my lord,' he said.

Although different in many ways, Tom and Cromwell had become good friends and colleagues in the past eight years, in which time Cromwell had unfailingly proved himself to be efficient and astute. Now he was working with Tom to suppress several minor religious houses in order to raise funds for a new college that Tom intended to found at Oxford. He was pragmatic, knowledgeable and often ruthless, a hard-working businessman with a talent for management.

'He is formidable,' Tom told the King, as they watched the bullheaded Cromwell carousing with a group of clerks at a feast. 'He gets things done with the minimum of fuss. And he is ready to assist in all things, evil or good.'

Harry's eyebrows shot up at that.

'Yes,' Tom said. 'If I want anything difficult or secret done, he's my man.'

Early in March, Tom sat shivering in a gallery watching the King take part in a tournament held in honour of the Imperial ambassadors, who were seated beside him. Harry's doublet was embroidered with the motto *She has wounded my heart*. No doubt he was pursuing another lady. Tom was aware that his love for Bessie Blount had burned itself out, but he had no idea who this new inamorata might be. For all he knew, the motto could just be part of some elaborate charade, the sort of chivalric game Harry loved to play. Tom very much doubted that a woman had actually rejected his advances. He was the King, handsome, athletic and powerful – and irresistible to the ladies.

Two days later, on Shrove Tuesday, Tom hosted a great feast for the King, the Queen and the ambassadors at York Place. After dinner, the hall was cleared and a large green castle on a wide stage was wheeled in. From its three towers hung banners: one depicted three broken hearts, the second a lady's hand holding a man's heart, and the third a lady's hand turning a man's heart. There were shouts of appreciation.

Tom rose from his seat next to the King. 'Le Chateau Vert,' he announced, as he had been instructed by the Master of the Revels.

Suddenly eight ladies sprang from the castle, all clad in gowns of white satin embroidered with lace and gold thread, wearing on their heads Milanese bonnets of gold encrusted with jewels and embroidered with the name of the wearer's character. Leading the troupe was the French Queen, still as lovely as ever at twenty-six, in the very apt role of Beauty. Constancy was personified by Lord Morley's daughter, Jane Parker, who was affianced to Sir Thomas Boleyn's heir, George, a handsome, unruly young page about the court. There too was Boleyn's married daughter, Mistress Carey, as Kindness, and her dark-haired sister Anne, the girl Tom had met briefly in France, who now served the Queen. She was Perseverance. He had to admit that, although she was not beautiful, she had a vivacious charm, and she danced superbly. Her prettier sister paled beside her.

Eight splendidly dressed masked lords entered the hall, their hats of cloth of gold, their voluminous cloaks of blue satin. They were named Love, Nobleness, Youth, Devotion, Loyalty, Pleasure, Gentleness and Liberty, and despite the disguise, it was obvious that the imposing figure of Love was the King himself. The lords gleefully rushed the fortress to an explosion of gunfire, yet the ladies defended it vigorously, throwing comfits at the besiegers, or sprinkling them with rose water. The men retaliated by assaulting the castle with dates and oranges, and predictably, in the end, the defenders were forced to surrender. The lords took their prisoners by the hand and led them down to the floor, where they danced with them most elegantly. There was much applause when they all unmasked, then the King, flushed with pleasure, led the Queen to a chamber Tom had made ready for her, where she hosted a lavish banquet for the ambassadors.

As he circulated among the guests, he saw his master enjoying the many tempting treats on offer and chatting animatedly to Thomas Boleyn's married daughter, Mary Carey, who was by far the prettiest lady in the room. Tom felt certain that she was the one.

His gaze fell on Mary's younger sister, Anne. She should be married by now. He sidled over to her father. 'I was wondering when you and the Earl of Ormond were going to set a date for the wedding of your daughter to his son. His Grace would like to see the dispute over the title settled.'

Sir Thomas Boleyn looked uncomfortable. 'So would I, my lord Cardinal, but there has been much haggling over the finer points in the contract.'

'If I may be of assistance, I am at your disposal,' Tom offered. 'It's about time Mistress Anne was wed. James Butler is an active, discreet and wise young man. He will make her a fitting husband.'

'I agree, my lord, and I thank you for your support. I am keen to see my daughter become countess of Ormond. As you know, I had wanted the earldom for myself, but I am content to settle the dispute this way.'

'I will speak to the Earl,' Tom promised.

It did little good. The sticking points remained seemingly insurmountable, beyond even Tom's intervention. When he told Boleyn, he could see the distrust in his face.

'I was sure that *you* could have found a way, my lord Cardinal,' he said. 'But maybe you favour Ormond in this matter.'

Tom restrained his anger. 'I have done my best, my lord,' he snapped.

Tom was doing his best also to tie up the hoped-for new alliance with the Emperor. Charles had finally weaned Harry away from Francis with promises of a joint invasion of France, the partition of any territory conquered and the recognition of Harry as king of France.

'Francis will never offer me that,' Harry grinned, as he sat by the fire with Tom on a chilly March morning, going over the terms. 'And Mary will be empress!'

Tom smiled. 'Yes, but alas, not for some time.' Mary was six, Charles twenty-two. They could not be wed for six years. But they would be betrothed.

The Queen, sitting at her embroidery and ecstatic at this new friendship between her husband and her nephew, looked up. 'My lord Cardinal, I was betrothed to Prince Arthur when I was just two. The Imperial crown is a prize worth waiting for.'

Watching her, it struck Tom that she had aged, almost without his noticing it. She was thirty-six now, well into her middle years, whereas the King, at thirty, was in the prime of his manhood. Tom knew he still visited her bed, and that it was mainly duty that called him there, but she had not conceived in more than three years, and no one now believed that she ever would again. Which meant that the King's only trueborn heir was a six-year-old girl.

Tom had quietly arranged the breaking of the Princess's betrothal to the Dauphin, to the Queen's undisguised relief and joy. She had been delighted when Charles asked for Mary's hand in marriage, saying she had always hoped for a Spanish match for her child. The Emperor was the greatest matrimonial prize in Europe, and Mary was assured of a brilliant future.

* * *

There was great pageantry when, towards the end of May, the Emperor arrived in England on a state visit to mark the signing of the new treaty and his betrothal to the Princess Mary. Once again, Tom met him at Dover and conducted him to the castle, where, soon afterwards, Harry again turned up as if by chance. He had wanted Charles to think that he had come on the spur of the moment, from affection. In fact, he could not wait to show off his new warship, the *Henry Grâce à Dieu*, and other great vessels, and rushed Charles away at the first opportunity. Tom watched from the quayside as the two monarchs were rowed around the harbour in a little boat, the Emperor clearly admiring the well-armed English fleet.

The royal retinues then travelled to Gravesend, whence they embarked in thirty barges for Greenwich. As they passed, all the ships in the Thames, which were decked out with streamers and banners, fired a salute to the Emperor.

At Greenwich, Tom was present when Charles met his intended bride. At the hall door, the Queen, the Princess and all the ladies received and welcomed him, as he knelt for Katherine's blessing.

'It is a great joy to me to see you, dear Aunt, and especially to meet my cousin Mary,' he declared, rising.

During the dancing that evening, he led the little Princess out to the floor. Watching them, the tall, ungainly man and the tiny girl, Tom wondered if Mary really understood what this marriage would mean for her. Harry understood only too well, for it meant that if he died, Charles would rule England in Mary's name, and England – inevitably – would be subsumed into the Empire. He had confessed to Tom that the prospect kept him awake at night.

After Charles had made a state entry into London, Tom entertained him to a feast at Hampton Court. At Windsor, days later, the marriage treaty was signed, and Mary and Charles were formally betrothed before the entire English court. When his guest left, Harry rode with him to Southampton to say farewell. It had all gone very well, Tom reflected.

Soon afterwards, Tom saw his son off to Padua. He felt very emotional, not knowing when he would see Thomas again, but both the boy and Dr Lupset had promised to write to him regularly. He watched as the litter carrying them to Dover was borne through the gatehouse of Hampton Court and out of sight, then he hurried to his closet, not wanting his servants to see him weeping.

In April, England had declared war on France. Tom had sighed to think of how little had been achieved by that expensive charade, the Field of Cloth of Gold. The chapel to Our Lady of Peace had never been built, and his dream of world unity now seemed like a fantasy.

But now, in August, he was to cross the English Channel on an embassy to the Emperor. No one, Harry assured him, would handle it better. To that end, he was to go accoutred like a great prince, for the honour of his master, accompanied by many gentlemen clothed in crimson velvet liveries with chains of gold about their necks; and his yeomen and other officers in coats of fine scarlet, guarded with black velvet. They would make a fine sight.

Charles was staying at Bruges. Admiring the magnificent brick buildings of this prosperous city, Tom was received with great solemnity, as befitted so mighty a pillar of Christ's church, and was saluted almost as a king. The Emperor entertained him royally. Every night, the Imperial officers went in procession through the town to the fine houses that had been placed at the disposal of Tom and his entourage, delivering manchet bread, two great silver pots of wine, gold drinking bowls, sugar, candles and torches. Each morning, they would return and ask for an account of his expenses, defraying them all and ensuring that he and his train lacked for nothing.

In August, on the King's behalf, Tom signed a secret treaty with the Emperor, promising that England would join Spain in an invasion of France if France refused to sign a peace. It was agreed that Harry would keep the Channel clear to allow Charles free passage between England and Spain. Charles, in turn, guaranteed the safe crossing of English ships between Dover and Calais. They made a pact jointly to invade France by May 1523 if Francis proved uncooperative.

Soon afterwards, Tom was seated at table enjoying a hearty Flemish stew when his usher handed him a letter bearing the royal seal. Harry had written: *The Queen my wife has desired me to send her most hearty recommendations to you, for she loves you well; and both she and I would like to know when you will return to us.*

He no longer felt so resentful towards Harry for forcing him to part from Joan. He was learning to live with the wound he carried in his heart for his lost love. He visited her occasionally, braving Legh's disapproval, and sometimes left wondering if she was happy in her marriage, which no longer seemed as comfortable as she had once led him to believe. But he never had an opportunity to ask her. He took comfort in the knowledge that the King loved him, this King he had come to regard almost as a son, and whom he loved like his own flesh and blood. When he returned home in great triumph, he was overjoyed to find himself held in even greater estimation by his master than he had ever been before.

He felt apprehensive when he learned that Thomas was studying in Louvain. He prayed that his son would apply himself and do well. He wondered if the lad was writing to Joan. It was unlikely, of course – she would have forbidden it, lest Legh find out that she had a son. Tom felt sad that she was cut off from the boy. When Thomas came home – although God alone knew when that would be – he would try, somehow, to arrange a meeting.

Each Sunday, as Yuletide approached, he took himself off to the court at Greenwich, appearing with his usual pomp and estate. Always, he was nobly received by the lords and chief officers of the royal household and conveyed to the King's chamber. After dining with Harry, and consulting with the councillors, he returned home with all his train. Despite the great sadness in his life, he was beginning to bask once more in the honour and the glory. Ambassadors, nobles and officers of state thronged York Place and Hampton Court, where his feasts and entertainments were legendary. Harry often visited him, for Tom was adept at finding ways to provide him with opportunities for recreation and relaxation. Such pleasures he devised! There were banquets, pageants, masks and mummeries, all graced with beautiful women so that the King and his lords could enjoy dancing (and no doubt less innocent pleasures). There was music of all kinds, and the bell-like voices of Tom's own choir united in heavenly harmonies that left Harry in raptures.

'Truly, Thomas, I have the best times of all when you entertain me,' he declared, his eyes shining. He rewarded his right-hand man with more than praise. Not long before Christmas, Tom's wealth was handsomely augmented when the King appointed him abbot of St Albans, the richest abbey in England. It brought him two fine residences in Hertfordshire, The More and Tittenhanger, both of which he immediately set about refurbishing. The More, he promised himself, would be even more splendid than Hampton Court.

Chapter 24

1523

In February, Tom learned that the Bishop of Durham had died. It occurred to Tom that, having already showered young Thomas with church offices and benefices, he could put his son forward to fill the vacancy. Of course, at thirteen, the boy was far too young to be ordained and rule that important bishopric, but had not Pope Alexander VI's bastard, Cesare Borgia, been made a cardinal and an archbishop at just sixteen? Durham could easily be administered for Thomas until he was of an age to exercise episcopal power himself. Why, he himself could hold it as patron!

He brought up the matter with Harry at dinner one evening and was dismayed to see him frown.

'He's too young,' he said. 'There would be a scandal. This is not Italy!' Then he grinned. 'But I'm willing to make you prince-bishop of Durham instead.'

Tom saw the wisdom in this, saw that the office would give him extensive political power in the north.

'As usual, your Grace has made the right decision,' he said. There would be another bishopric for Thomas, by and by.

Alongside his manifold other duties, he immersed himself in preparing his new foundation in Oxford. It was to be called Cardinal College, and he was touched when Queen Katherine showed an interest in it. He supposed she was well disposed towards him on account of his having brokered the alliance with the Emperor. As she stood with him and the King looking at the plans, her prematurely aged face lit up.

'Great good will come of this project, Madam,' Tom told her.

'Thanks to the example and teachings of Erasmus and others, my college will be a cradle of the new learning. And you yourself will be particularly prayed for in its chapel.'

'I am so glad to hear that,' she said. 'It will be a joy to me to see the college flourish, as I am sure it will. When do you think it will be ready, my lord Cardinal?'

'Next year, Madam.' Work was progressing well. When finished, his foundation would be the largest and grandest of all the Oxford colleges.

It was a glorious summer and life was good. There came a day when Harry asked Tom to walk with him in his garden. He liked to discuss state affairs out in the open air, when no one was nearby. Today, he looked troubled.

'Is there anything amiss, Sir?' Tom asked.

Harry flushed. 'Yes, I fear there is. Very much amiss. It is a delicate matter.' He hesitated. 'The Queen's physicians tell me that she is past the ways of women.'

It took Tom a moment to work out what he meant. Then the import of his words sank in. 'That is a great tragedy, Sir. I feel for you both.'

'There will be no more children,' Harry said sadly. 'Thomas, what am I going to do? This kingdom needs an heir! When I betrothed Mary to the Emperor last year, I thought there was some hope of Katherine conceiving again. I did not fail in my duty, but her courses have ceased, and she now has a disease in her womanly parts that precludes us doing that act.' The King's face was bright red. He was prudish in such matters. 'And when I die, England will be ruled by Charles. I cannot bear the thought. I don't know what I have done to offend God, that he would deny me sons.'

Tom was thinking fast.

'Your Grace has a son. A fine boy.'

'Yes, but he is baseborn.'

'As I once told you, Parliament can declare him legitimate. You could name him your successor. I am sure that the people of England would prefer that to foreign rule or civil war.'

Harry was pensive. He stood by the riverbank, the breeze whipping his hair, frowning. 'Could I, Thomas?'

'Parliament will understand the terrible dilemma in which your Grace finds yourself.'

'My Yorkist relations wouldn't stand for it. I'm sure some of them think they have a better claim to the throne than I do.'

'That is why I have them closely watched, Sir. But I think that they and others could be made to see the wisdom in naming Master Fitzroy your successor. Let him win their love – it will be easy, for he is a delightful child. Make your intentions clear. What the people love is peace, and stability, which you have given them these thirteen years. In Fitzroy, they will see your line continuing.'

Harry was nodding. 'Yes, Thomas. I like the idea. I believe it could work. But I think we should wait a year or two, until the boy is of greater understanding. He is only four.'

'I agree,' Tom concurred.

'I knew I could rely on you to come up with a solution.' Harry walked on.

'Sir, I wish to raise another matter. I have in my service Lord Henry Percy, the Earl of Northumberland's heir.'

'Indeed,' Harry replied. 'I have seen him serve you at table.'

'You ought to know that he has taken to resorting for his pastime to the Queen's chamber, where he dallies with her maids. It has come to my attention that he is courting Mistress Anne Boleyn, and that they mean to marry.'

Harry swung round. 'That is quite out of the question. He is to be betrothed to the Earl of Shrewsbury's daughter, a match to which I have just given my hearty approval.' He was bristling with annoyance. 'Boleyn's daughter is no fit mate for a Percy. We can't have sprigs of the nobility marrying where they please, without my consent.'

Tom nodded, striving to keep up with his master's brisk pace. 'I'll summon his father to court and talk some sense into the young fool.'

'Thank you. It's a shame the Butler match fell through.'

'It is,' Tom sighed. 'And that Sir Thomas Boleyn decided that the title should be his after all. The wrangling is still going on.'

'Mistress Anne is a strange girl,' Harry observed. 'All those French airs and graces, and the fashions she affects. She's no beauty, yet the Queen says the young gallants make much of her, and clearly Percy is smitten.'

'I can't see the attraction myself,' Tom said. 'I will speak with her too, and teach her a lesson.'

'Make sure they haven't entered into a precontract,' Harry instructed. 'If they have, it'll need to be broken.'

Tom smiled. 'Do not concern yourself with that, Sir. I have the means to do it.'

Back at York Place, he sat in a window seat in his picture gallery, gathered some of his household officers around him, with Cromwell poised to take notes, and summoned Henry Percy. When the young man presented himself, all swagger and affectation, he stared him down until Percy began to look frightened.

'I marvel not a little, Lord Henry,' Tom said, 'that, through your folly, you have entangled yourself with a foolish girl; I mean Anne Boleyn. Tell me, are you precontracted to her?'

Percy looked alarmed. 'Yes. We have agreed to wed.'

Tom glared at him. 'Did you not consider the estate to which God has called you? Are you not aware that, after the death of your noble father, you will inherit and possess one of the greatest earldoms in this realm? If you were contemplating marriage, did it not occur to you to ask for your father's consent – and, more importantly, consult the King's Highness, since your marriage requires his princely sanction?' His voice rose. 'You should have submitted the whole matter to his Highness, who wishes to make a match for you that is appropriate to your estate and honour. But now, behold what you have done through your wilfulness! You have not only offended your father, but also your most gracious sovereign lord, and matched yourself with one whom neither the King nor your father can approve.'

Percy looked truly terrified now. He was trembling and kept putting his hand to his neck, as if it might be at risk of a close encounter with the headsman's axe.

Tom was relentless, guiltily aware that he should have known what was going on and stopped it before things became this serious, and angry that not one of his spies had sniffed out the affair earlier. 'I have sent for your father, and when he comes, he will either break this unadvised contract or else disinherit you. Make no doubt, the King's Majesty himself will complain to your father about your conduct and require no less than I have said.'

Just to make sure that Percy understood there could be no further dalliance with Anne Boleyn, he told him that the King had chosen a husband for her. It was untrue, but the fool swallowed it. In fact, he broke down and wept, and could say nothing for a time, such was his distress.

When Percy could speak, he was still sobbing. 'Sir, I knew nothing of the King's pleasure, and I am very sorry for it. I considered that I was old enough to choose a wife, especially one I could love, and I did not doubt that my father would have been persuaded to agree to my choice. Though Mistress Anne is a simple maid, and her father is but a knight, she is of noble lineage. Her mother is the Duke of Norfolk's daughter, and her father is descended from the earls of Ormond. What cause had I, Sir, to think her no fit match for me? Her estate is equal to mine!' He fell to his knees, still weeping. 'Your Grace, I most humbly require your favour, that you will entreat the King's Majesty on my behalf for his princely benevolence in this matter, for I cannot deny or forsake Mistress Anne. I love her! I would die for her!'

Tom turned to his officers. 'Sirs, you can see what wisdom is in this wilful boy's head! I thought, Lord Henry, that when you heard me declare to you the King's anger, you would have wholly submitted yourself to his will and pleasure, to be directed and ordered by his Grace in whatever way seems best to him.'

'Sir, I would,' cried Percy, 'but in this matter I have gone so far, and before witnesses, that I do not know how to extricate myself or to discharge my conscience.'

Tom permitted himself a grim smile. 'Why, do you think that the King and I know not what we have to do in as weighty a matter as this? Yes, we do, I warrant you. But I can see in you no submission to the King's will.'

Percy was now shaking with fear. 'My lord, if it pleases your Grace, I will submit myself wholly to the King's Majesty and your Grace in this matter, if my conscience can be discharged of the weighty burden of my precontract.'

So much for undying love, Tom thought. 'Well then,' he said, 'I will await your father's coming, and he and the King and I shall devise a remedy for your hasty folly. In the meantime, I charge you, and in the King's name command you, not once to resort to Mistress Anne Boleyn's company, if you hope to avoid his Majesty's high indignation.'

He rose and went into his chamber, leaving Percy on his knees, snivelling.

The next day, when Tom opened his door to order Master Cavendish to summon Anne Boleyn, he was astonished to see Anne herself standing in the outer chamber with a young man he recognised as Percy's friend James Melton. Melton hastily knelt to kiss his ring, but Tom's eyes were on Anne, who was regarding him boldly – and balefully.

'Master Melton,' he said, 'you are a gentleman of great prescience, for you have brought me the young lady I was about to summon. I wonder how that could be.'

Melton stood up, visibly trembling, but it was Anne who spoke. 'My lord Cardinal, I insisted on coming to see you, and this gentleman reluctantly agreed to escort me.'

'Indeed? How very fortunate that he was at hand. James, I will speak with you later.'

James flushed and bowed himself away.

'Your Eminence,' Anne said, 'I do hope you will not think amiss of Master Melton for his goodness to me. He but brought me a letter from Lord Henry Percy. He was puzzled as to what it was about. It was I who, having read the letter, insisted on coming here.'

'I understand,' Tom said. 'No doubt you have guessed that I am aware of your pretended precontract to Harry Percy.'

'There was nothing pretended about it, Sir!' Anne bridled.

'Then you are clearly unaware that Lord Percy is betrothed to Lady Mary Talbot, the Earl of Shrewsbury's daughter.'

'I do not believe it,' she said defiantly.

'Mistress, you are deluding yourself. The King and I approved the betrothal. It was a most satisfactory arrangement, the parties being of equal rank.'

He could see that the barb had gone home. Her eyes flashed with fury – and contempt.

'In the circumstances,' Tom went on, 'it was rash of Lord Percy to promise himself to you. He must have known that his father would not approve.'

'Harry is an honest man!' Anne cried. 'I do not believe he would have gone so far if he was betrothed to another.'

'You should know, Mistress Anne, that I have discussed the matter with the King, and he is very angry at your presumption. It is his prerogative to consent to the marriages of his nobility.'

Anne said nothing. She suddenly looked crestfallen.

'I spoke to Lord Henry,' Tom told her. 'I conveyed the King's displeasure. It is coming to something, Mistress Anne, when the heir to a great earldom thinks he can with impunity betroth himself to some foolish girl at court, and so I told the young fool.'

Anne was seething, but he ignored her. 'I told him I marvelled at his folly in offending his Grace, and I have sent for his father, the Earl, who will naturally be scandalised. I am sure that he will warn the wilful boy that if he does not break this unadvised contract, he will disinherit him for ever. Are you listening to me, girl? You should know that the King's Majesty will complain to your father of you and require him to ensure that you behave yourself in future.'

'How have I misbehaved myself?' she asked. 'I have conducted myself with propriety. I knew of no betrothal! I had no doubt that my father would approve such a match.'

'Oh, indeed he would!' Tom laughed mirthlessly.

She threw him a filthy look. 'But I gave my promise to Harry!'

Tom frowned. 'Rest assured, you will not see Lord Henry again.

He has been commanded in the King's name not to have anything more to do with you, on pain of his Grace's high indignation, and he is to be married to Lady Mary Talbot as soon as it can be arranged. Now be a sensible girl and accept it.'

'But the Queen approved it! She encouraged us!' Anne was frantic.

'The Queen has no power in such matters,' Tom sighed. 'Mistress Anne, you are proving tiresome, and I have pressing business to attend to. It is the King's command that you leave the court and go home.'

'No!' Anne protested. 'That is grossly unfair!'

'Are you criticising his Grace's judgement?' Tom fixed a steely gaze on her. 'Now go.'

'You have not heard the last of me, my lord Cardinal!' Anne cried as she flounced out to the gallery, caution abandoned in her fury, and a hundred faces turned and gaped.

When the Earl of Northumberland arrived at court, having ridden all the way down from the north, he demanded at once to see Tom.

'What is going on?' he asked, when Tom received him alone in his gallery.

'My lord, calm yourself. The matter is all but resolved. Your son rashly precontracted himself to a girl who is most unsuitable for him, but his Grace feels that some paternal admonition is in order.'

'By God, I'll disown him, the young fool!' roared the Earl. 'He was about to be betrothed. What was he thinking of?'

Tom rose and poured some wine for them both.

'It was the folly of youth,' he said. 'Rest assured that I have dissolved the precontract and banished the girl from court. The King and I now wish to see Lord Henry married to Shrewsbury's daughter without delay.'

'I'll speak to the boy now,' Northumberland growled. 'I'll give him a piece of my mind!'

'He is waiting without.' Tom rose and summoned the young man, who looked petrified, then withdrew into his closet. He could hear the Earl shouting, calling his son a proud, presumptuous wastrel and much more besides, then assuring him that if he did not do as he was told, he would disinherit him. Percy's panicked replies were indistinct, but there was no doubt that he was much chastened. When, later that day, father and son left court, it had been arranged that the young man would be married without delay.

Anne Boleyn left court at the same time. One of Tom's spies reported that she had been incandescent with rage and proclaimed that if it ever lay in her power, she would work the Cardinal as much displeasure as he had done to her.

Absurd! he thought. What could that chit of a girl do to him?

In October, there was portentous news from Rome. Pope Adrian had died after a tragically short reign, and there was to be another election. There were reports that Tom had been put forward as a candidate, and he began to believe that this time the Emperor would help him to achieve his greatest ambition. He braced himself for a long, suspenseful wait and prayed for good news.

In November, he knew crushing disappointment. The Papal election had taken place and not a single cardinal had voted for him. Charles had put his weight behind an Italian, Giulio de' Medici, who had been elected Pope Clement VII. Clement was in his prime and might live for many years. Tom had to face the fact that he might never be pope now.

Of course, he did not voice his anger at what he saw as another betrayal on the part of the Emperor, for Charles was Harry's friend, and although he was probably aware of it, Harry said nothing. Struggling with bitter thoughts of what might have been, Tom could not help feeling antagonistic towards Spain and the Empire, and sometimes found himself wishing that Harry had made a treaty with France after all.

Chapter 25

1524–5

Despite the March wind, Tom made his way to the tournament ground to watch the King take on Suffolk in the joust. Harry had asked him to be there, for he wanted his old friend to see him accoutred in a new suit of armour he had himself designed, and was eager to try it out. He looked quite splendid as he rode into the lists, but when he and the Duke charged against each other, lances couched, Tom shot to his feet with the rest of the spectators, for Harry had forgotten to lower his visor.

'Hold! Hold!' the crowd screamed, for Suffolk's lance was pointed at the King's exposed face. But the Duke was wearing a heavy helmet and evidently could not see or hear much. He crashed into Harry, and his lance struck him on the brow, right under the guard of the headpiece; as his spear broke into splinters, it pushed the King's visor to the back of his head. Tom's heart was in his mouth.

Miraculously, Harry righted himself in the saddle and waved at those watching. Suffolk, however, was badly shaken. Tom could hear him apologising heartily and swearing never to run against his sovereign again.

'No one was to blame but myself.' Harry cried, then proceeded to run six more courses just to prove that he had taken no hurt, much to Tom's joy and the evident relief of the courtiers. But in Council later that day, the lords voiced their concerns.

'Your Grace came literally within an inch of losing your life.' Norfolk shuddered, shaking his head.

'And England came perilously near to civil war,' Tom chimed in.

'To be plain, Sir, there are those who might dispute the right of the

Princess, a little girl, to be queen.' That was Surrey, who would surely soon succeed his ailing father as duke of Norfolk. He was a martinet, tough and blunt, and lacked the geniality of his sire, but he had a point.

Harry sat at the head of the board, looking troubled. 'I agree. The problem of the succession must be settled, and soon. I will be candid with you, my lords. It is five years since the Queen's last pregnancy. She is thirty-eight now and past the ways of women. I fear that, for all my prayers, there will be no more children – and no son to inherit the throne.' He raised dejected eyes to them.

The lords looked uncomfortable, glancing at Tom, doubtless looking to him for a solution.

'I know that I speak for us all, Sir, when I say that should anything befall your Grace, we will ensure the smooth succession of the Princess,' he said reassuringly. Now was not the time to raise the matter of Fitzroy. It was best to wait until the boy was a little older. Besides, he needed to look at the legal position.

'Thank you, Thomas,' Harry said, rising abruptly and leaving them.

In May, Tom rode back from Thames Ditton feeling dejected. His visits to Joan had become few and far between, for Legh always seemed to be at home these days, and there was rarely an opportunity for him to see her. And when he did, she would never open up to him about herself and her life. She listened readily to his news, offered wise advice when he asked it, and spoke wistfully of Thomas, yet Tom could sense that she was unhappy and that being parted from their son was not the only reason.

'What's wrong, Joan?' he had asked her this afternoon.

'Nothing,' she had replied. He'd pressed her, but she kept repeating it.

'You can talk to me,' he said.

'I know, but there is no need.' He knew she was lying.

He returned to Hampton Court to the news that Norfolk, that doughty old warrior, had ceded his last battle and died. Hurriedly, he called for his barge and hastened to the King at Greenwich, for while he could feel no personal grief for his old adversary, he knew that Harry would be mourning a faithful friend who had served him well,

He found his master already dressed in black. 'We will not see his like again,' he said, staring out of the window of his closet. 'His son is a good soldier, but he has none of his father's greatness. I saw him this morning to express my condolences, and he betrayed no emotion at the old Duke's passing. He has no heart.'

Tom did not like the new Duke very much either. Norfolk was fifty-two. A martyr to rheumatism and indigestion, he was constantly grumbling or sighing, but he was an efficient, often ruthless, military commander, and an able and polished courtier. Like his brother-in-law, Sir Thomas Boleyn, the guiding factor of his life was self-interest.

'With Buckingham gone, Norfolk will regard himself as the foremost of the older nobility,' Tom observed later, as he and Harry were inspecting the new building works at Greenwich. 'He has no time for new men.'

Harry grunted, sidestepping to avoid a bucket of plaster. 'You men, continue with your tasks and stop gawping!' he ordered, and turned to Tom. 'When I made Suffolk a duke, Norfolk told me that a prince may make a nobleman, but not a gentleman. He was most put out.' He grinned at the memory.

'He has no love for the clergy either,' Tom said, 'and he hates me. In that, at least, he is at one with Suffolk.' Norfolk, he feared, might prove as vicious an adversary as Buckingham.

Harry bent to inspect some brickwork. 'For all his faults, he is useful to me. You must work with him.' He beckoned to the foreman. 'That pointing needs seeing to. Have the men work late to repair it, under canvas if it rains. My lord Cardinal, see that ale, bread and cheese are brought to them.' He led Tom away from the site. 'Ah, see who comes! Talk of the devil.'

It was Norfolk himself, with his handsome dark-haired nephew George Boleyn in tow, carrying bows and arrows and clearly on their way to the archery butts. They bowed when they saw Harry, but ignored Tom.

'Good day to you once more, my lord Duke,' the King said, 'and to you, Master Boleyn. I see you are making the most of this fine weather.' It was a remark made pointedly.

'I seek solace in distraction, Sir,' Norfolk said, a touch shamefacedly. 'An hour at the butts, and then we'll be off hunting. Anything to get this lad's nose out of a book. I never did hold with all this learning.'

'I doubt his Grace would agree with you, Uncle.' George Boleyn smiled. 'We should all profit from the example of a learned king.'

Harry smiled thinly, acknowledging the compliment.

'Work is coming on apace over there.' Norfolk nodded in the direction of the palace.

'More slowly than I would have liked,' Harry said. 'I hear that you are rebuilding Kenninghall. I must come and visit you in Norfolk when it is finished.'

'I would be honoured,' the Duke said proudly. 'I'm having it done in the antick style. It will be a showpiece when it's finished.'

'It's strange,' Tom observed, as they parted company, 'how a man with such old-fashioned views can favour modern architecture.'

'Like most of my nobles, he is keen to emulate me,' Harry said. 'At least it keeps them all out of mischief.'

'Young Boleyn is a promising chip off the old block,' Tom commented. 'One to watch, Sir.'

'He is to be married soon. I gave permission for him to wed Lord Morley's daughter, Jane. I'm giving them a manor in Norfolk as a bridal gift. I wish her joy of him. He's promiscuous, I hear.'

Tom lowered his voice. 'My gentleman usher, Cavendish, keeps his ear to the ground at court, and he told me that Master Boleyn is a beast who deflowers widows and virgins whether they be willing or no.'

'Is that so?' Harry's expression darkened. He would not brook blatant immorality at his court.

'It may be pure malicious gossip,' Tom said. 'He's as proud as the rest of his family. But for that, he'd be more popular, for he is intelligent and witty, and something of a poet. And he may be useful to you, for he speaks fluent French.'

'I will bear that in mind,' Harry said.

Some good news at last! Pope Clement had confirmed Tom as Papal legate in England for life, making him his special representative, which gave him far-reaching powers. He had also approved the founding of Cardinal College and sent his blessing. Of course, he needed Tom's support, and England's. King Francis had just invaded Milan, and Clement had every reason to fear the French King's territorial ambitions in Italy.

Tom braced himself for the extra burdens of work and responsibility that had been laid upon him. He knew he was equal to them. He might be fifty-three but he felt as vigorous as a man in his thirties. He was blessed with an army of officers and clerks to do his bidding and had long been expert in organising and delegating his duties. He did not feel daunted by his duties as Papal legate; after all, he had sought and wanted the office. It did not matter that he would now be in demand from dawn until dusk; he had no private life to speak of anyway. As long as he could get away from time to time to see Joan, he would be content – or as content as he would ever be in the circumstances.

Tom used his new powers as Papal legate to dissolve thirty decayed religious houses where monastic life had virtually ceased in practice, most of them in Oxford and his home town of Ipswich. He appointed the capable Cromwell to arrange the sale of monastic lands and goods, intending to use the proceeds to found a grammar school in Ipswich and enrich Cardinal College. At the same time, again in his legatine capacity, he set about reforming the monastic orders, which he feared had become lax. It did not win him any popularity and he met with some resistance. Yet he persisted, undeterred. Never let it be said that the abbeys in England had fallen into decay on his watch.

In a buoyant mood, he turned his thoughts to the splendid tomb in which he would one day lie; Harry had given permission for his burial in Westminster Abbey, and Tom had commissioned a renowned Italian sculptor, Benedetto da Rovezzano, to build a splendid monument of white marble and black touchstone, with eight bronze statues of angels standing on pillars, and a lifelike effigy of himself lying recumbent. That was how he wanted the world to remember him, as a munificent and magnificent prince of the Church.

* * *

March 1525 found Tom looking at the royal accounts and thinking that Harry had been making spasmodic war on France for three years now, with little success. He was wondering whether it was worth pouring more money and men into the conflict when, on an unseasonably mild day, the Emperor's messenger, with the Imperial eagle blazoned on his livery, arrived at court and informed him that Charles had defeated the King of France in battle at Pavia in Italy and taken him prisoner. Tom was so jubilant he could have kissed the man. As he hurried off to see the King, he reflected that the aid England had sent to the Emperor had been money well spent.

Harry had heard the good news already and was ecstatic. 'By St George, that man was as welcome as the Archangel Gabriel was to the Virgin Mary! I want him well rewarded for his pains. Have the news proclaimed, and order that bonfires be lit in the streets of London and free wine distributed to the citizens. My great enemy is a captive. God has smiled upon me!'

That month, the King went in state to St Paul's to give thanks for the Emperor's victory. Then he commissioned a painting of the Battle of Pavia to remind him of that great triumph.

'This is the perfect opportunity for me to invade France again and seize the French crown,' he told Tom. 'I'm asking Parliament to raise a new tax to pay for it.'

Harry was still gloating over the capture of King Francis and the disarray in which France now found herself when Master Fermour, a merchant of Calais, brought a jester called Will Somers to Greenwich and had him perform for Tom. Tom would have employed him, but he already had a fool, his devoted Patch, who had often diverted him when he was downcast; but this Somers fellow was good enough to be recommended to the King.

'You should receive him,' Tom urged Harry. 'I've never seen a funnier fool.'

He himself presented the lean, hollow-eyed, stooped Somers to him. Somers soon had both monarch and courtiers in fits of laughter as he thrust his comical face through a gap in the arras, then emerged with a monkey on his shoulder and minced around the room, rolling his eyes. The monkey performed some tricks, and Somers told jokes, laughing uncontrollably at his own punchlines, or mercilessly impersonating those who were the butt of his jests. Harry was immediately won over by his wicked sense of humour and, without hesitation, offered him a place at court. Tom witnessed an instant rapport between the two men.

Soon, however, he was beginning to regret introducing the fool to his master, for people had begun to say that few men at court were more beloved than Somers, and that he ruled the King with his merry prattle. Certainly, he seemed to have become the constant companion of Harry's leisure hours.

Tom could not suppress his jealousy. He did not want a rival for the King's affections.

It was April, and Anne Boleyn was back at court. Tom saw her walking behind the Queen with other ladies and maids on their way to the Chapel Royal. Doubtless Harry had sanctioned her return. Tom shrugged and forgot about her. Before long, however, he kept seeing her at feasts, at dances and frolicking in the gardens, surrounded by a group of admiring gallants. He heard her laugh ringing out. How quickly this strange young woman had become one of the stars of the court. It was extraordinary. Tom supposed it was her French manners and becoming apparel that made her stand out.

They rarely crossed paths, yet once when they did, he saw her eyes flash and knew she had not forgiven him for banishing her two years ago. And her father, Boleyn, was distinctly less friendly these days. Well, it was no loss to Tom.

That spring, he accompanied the King on progress. While they were staying at Knebworth, he was astonished to see Harry crashing into the hall covered in mud.

'I nearly died while hunting near Hitchin today,' he said breathlessly, looking shaken. 'My horse tumbled me into a stream and my head got stuck in the mud. I couldn't get out and I couldn't breathe, as my face was under water. But some fellow came and rescued me. Had he not, you might have had a new queen by now.'

'By God, you should take greater care, Hal!' cried Will Somers, who had been idling by the hearth. But Harry ignored him; he was looking at Tom.

'I am utterly relieved that he did,' Tom said, shocked at how close England had again come to disaster, but secretly pleased that his master had turned to him rather than to the fool, which showed that Somers wasn't perhaps such a threat after all.

Later, when Harry had washed and changed his clothes, and he and Tom were alone, he knew he must express his concerns. 'Given that your Grace has now suffered two brushes with death, I would urge you to think about acclimatising the people to Master Fitzroy. He is a fine boy, one you should be proud of.'

Harry locked eyes with him. 'Can I really make him my heir?'

Tom smiled. 'Indeed, you can. I have been busy at the law books. Baseborn children can be legitimated in certain circumstances. Yet before your Grace embarks on such a course, the first step would be to bring the boy to court, where he will be in the public eye. Then you will be able to judge whether he would be acceptable to your subjects.'

Harry got up and began pacing the floor. 'He is six. His tutors say he is wayward and doesn't concentrate. They fear his mother has spoiled him.'

'A firm hand is all he needs, Sir,' Tom soothed, thinking of his own wayward son. 'It is time for him to be given into the care of men. But he is a charming boy and will win hearts. A little boisterousness is only natural in one so young.'

'I will take your advice,' Harry declared.

Henry Fitzroy was duly brought to Windsor in time for the chapter meeting on St George's Day, when he was made a Knight of the Garter. The Queen showed no rancour towards him. She even came to watch the ceremony from her closet above the high altar in St George's Chapel. Tom was impressed, for Fitzroy was a living reproach to her for her failure to bear an heir, and a reminder of her husband's infidelity; accepting him could not be easy for her. But where she led, others would follow. And the boy conducted himself well; Harry had had a stern word with him beforehand. He looked proud with his son sitting beside him in the second stall on the sovereign's side of the chapel. Tom was watching the lords and clergy in the congregation. There was not a hint of disapproval to be seen in any face; in fact, many were smiling indulgently at the boy.

Vastly encouraged, Harry was full of plans. 'I mean to make my intention plain,' he told Tom as they sat up late sharing a ewer of wine. 'I am going to create Fitzroy a duke. In fact, I am giving him two royal dukedoms, those of Richmond and Somerset. My father held the earldom of Richmond before his accession, and he made my brother Edmund duke of Somerset, a title that was borne by my Beaufort ancestors. These titles will proclaim to the world my son's high status and royal blood. And look, I have designed a coat of arms for him.' He pushed a parchment across the table.

'I have been taking soundings,' Tom said, nodding approvingly. 'Many fear a disputed succession; they would like to see the matter settled. I think they will accept Master Fitzroy as your heir.'

'We shall see how his ennoblement is received,' Harry murmured.

The investiture of those chosen to be ennobled took place in June in the presence chamber at Bridewell Palace. It was intolerably hot, and Tom, standing behind the King under the cloth of estate with the dukes of Norfolk and Suffolk and the earls of Arundel and Oxford, was sweltering in his cardinal's robes. The room was packed with courtiers and stank of sweat.

A fanfare sounded and Henry Fitzroy entered the chamber. Tom smiled at his little godson, who looked very regal in his fine attire, and nodded encouragingly as he knelt before his father. Tenderly, Harry clothed him in a crimson and blue mantle, then handed him the sword, the cap of estate and the coronet of a duke, as the patent of creation was read aloud. Thus invested, the child took his place beside his father on the dais, taking precedence over every other peer in the room, despite looking very small beside them. The message was loud and clear: he was now next in rank to his Majesty and might, by the King's means, easily be exalted to higher things.

Next came forward Harry's nephew, Henry Brandon, who was

created earl of Lincoln; his cousins, Henry Courtenay, Earl of Devon, who was made marquess of Exeter, and Thomas Manners, who became earl of Rutland; and lastly Sir Thomas Boleyn, bursting with self-importance at being elevated to the peerage as Lord Rochford. The others were men Tom respected, but he was liking Boleyn less and less these days, for the man's pride had become overweening and no one displayed more self-interest. The animosity was clearly mutual: as Boleyn rose, he looked at Tom with a sneer on his lips.

When Tom saw Harry later that afternoon, he expected him to be in high good humour, but he found him in a grumpy mood.

'I've just come from the Queen,' he growled. 'She has taken great exception to my son's ennoblement. She says it is a threat to the Princess.'

'One can understand her position,' Tom said, 'but the needs of England must come first.'

Harry was not mollified. 'And then I ran into Boleyn. He's not happy either, for he has just been told that he is to resign his office of Lord Treasurer to Sir William Fitzwilliam, and he's furious because he's not going to receive any financial compensation. For this, he blames you, Thomas.'

'Well, it was my idea, Sir. Fear not, I will find some compensation for him.'

He did not want another run-in with the Boleyns. He could not afford to make more enemies. His dominance was still unchallenged, yet his opponents were growing ever more powerful, which left him little choice but to take account of their opinions. Harry, of course, still relied heavily on him, yet he was no longer the untried young King whom Tom had mentored, but a mature man in his thirties, experienced in statecraft and aware of his own exalted status. Not until now had Harry ever shown any overt jealousy of Tom's vast possessions, but recently, Tom had gained the impression that he was at last growing resentful and jealous of his Cardinal's wealth and power. He was beginning to fear that his enemies had been busily at work.

* * *

When Hampton Court was finally completed in August, Harry came to see it. Tom escorted him through the main courtyards, proudly pointing out the new terracotta medallions of Roman emperors carved by the Florentine sculptor Giovanni di Maiano on the west front, then led him through many of the palace's thousand rooms. Standing in the lofty great hall, Harry exclaimed, 'Thomas, you are more magnificent than your sovereign!'

Tom leapt to respond. 'It is only fitting that your Majesty's servant should reflect the greater magnificence of his King!'

'Is that so?' Harry's eyes narrowed. 'You know, Thomas, people tell me that my palaces are nowhere near as splendid as yours.' He waved his arm to indicate the fine tapestries, the carved and gilded plaster frieze of gambolling cherubs, the glowing glass in the soaring oriel window and the abundance of gold plate on the buffet. 'All of this belongs to a subject. Not that you do not deserve to be well rewarded for your labours.'

Tom guessed that his enemies had been pouring vitriol in the King's ear. He was quick to take the hint. It was politic to make a grand gesture, one that might be crucial to his future prosperity. 'Your Grace, without your favour, I am nothing,' he said, his hand to his heart. 'All I have is yours. It would give me the greatest pleasure to present Hampton Court and all its contents to you.'

Harry looked astonished. Clearly, he had not expected such a munificent response. He clapped Tom on the back. 'Was ever king so beholden to a subject? Thomas, I did right to raise you high, and you have rewarded me a thousandfold. Thank you for your gift. But I cannot take it without giving something in return.' He thought for a moment, but his eyes were on the treasures he had just acquired. 'I will give you in exchange Richmond Palace,' he said. It was nowhere near as big or magnificent as Hampton Court. 'But, my friend, you are welcome to make use of Hampton Court whenever you wish, especially for official entertaining.'

Tom bowed his head in gratitude, resolutely suppressing his consternation at having made that impulsive gesture.

At supper that evening, he made an effort to be scintillating company, enthusing about Cardinal College and the fine tomb he was having built for himself. And Harry was bursting with approval, showing himself as loving a master as ever. Soon, Tom was glad he had made his magnificent gesture. The gift of Hampton Court had shown Harry how devoted he was to him, and it seemed to have increased his love a hundredfold.

'Was ever king so blessed in a servant?' he kept saying. Tom could do no wrong, it seemed. He had silenced his critics and was in high hopes of reaping great benefits in the future.

He was wrong. For once, he had badly miscalculated. Parliament had refused to vote for a tax to fund Harry's invasion of France, so Tom had to try to raise money independently. He imposed what he had been pleased to call an 'Amicable Grant', a levy of a tenth on the goods of ordinary people and a sixth on those of the clergy. It had provoked an outcry, and in Suffolk the people had risen in protest.

The problem was that Parliament had not approved the levy, so there was no legal machinery in place to enforce it. And with so little money raised, there was no war chest. Harry was furious, not just with those who had revolted, but with Tom too.

'You've left me no choice!' he thundered. 'I'll now have to denounce your Amicable Grant, and distance myself from it. By St George, Thomas, you've made me look a fool.'

Tom quailed before his wrath, thankful that they were alone in his closet with no one to witness his humiliation. 'But your Grace was in agreement with the policy,' he protested.

'I relied on your wisdom! It seems I can do so no longer.'

Tom felt as if he had been pushed to the edge of an abyss. He fell to his knees. 'I acknowledge my fault. I beg your forgiveness, Sir. But, in mitigation, I must declare that I imposed the grant in your interests – and England's.'

Harry was still seething. 'Next time, consult Parliament!' He stamped out, leaving Tom kneeling there, quaking. Slowly, he pulled himself to his feet. Heaven forfend that his beloved master should ever lose faith in him. Without Harry's love and favour, his life would not be worth living. How could he retrieve the situation?

Harry sulked for a day, then reverted to his usual genial self. Gradually, Tom relaxed. The danger was past. Everything would be all right.

But the Queen was another matter. When Tom encountered her, her manner was frosty.

'I fear that her Grace blames me for the advancement of my lord of Richmond,' he ventured to Harry as they sat updating the King's privy purse accounts. 'Three of her Spanish ladies have apparently been encouraging her to make a fuss about his recent elevation. I immediately had them dismissed.'

'I know,' Harry muttered. 'She has asked me to rescind the order, but I refused and told her to submit and have patience.'

'I am sorry to have caused trouble for her Grace,' Tom said.

Harry frowned. 'If reports from abroad are anything to go by, she will soon have real cause for concern. For I can feel a distinct draught blowing from Spain.'

'I am aware of that. The Emperor is offended because you keep refusing to send him his bride.'

'The Princess is too young to leave us. She's nine! We'll see how well grown she is when she reaches marriageable age in three years.'

'A wise decision, Sir. And one with which the Emperor should surely concur.'

'He wants her brought up to Spanish ways. I am in no doubt that her mother will do an excellent job of that, and I have told his ambassador that it would be cruel to separate her from her child when she is so young.'

Tom winced inwardly. Had Harry forgotten that he had forced Joan to part from her children when they were babes in arms? He must be aware of the pain she had suffered, being reluctant to be apart from his own child. Or did he only think of himself? Was it fair to expect the Lord's Anointed to have normal human feelings?

Tom fought down the bitterness that was threatening to engulf him and reminded himself that Harry had had his reasons for wanting to avoid a scandal that could have rebounded on him – and on Tom too. But that did not alter the fact that Dorothy was lost to him irrevocably – and Joan. He missed her still; sometimes, his longing for her was unbearable, even after all this time.

Yet there was comfort to be found in the letter that had arrived this morning. Thomas was on his way back to England.

Chapter 26

1525

Tom felt compelled to go to Thames Ditton and tell Joan the good news. As before, he sent the faithful Cavendish ahead to ascertain when Sir George Legh would be away. Assured that Joan was at home alone, he rode off to see her at once.

He found her in the parlour, a baby at her breast and the two little girls playing at her feet.

'No, don't get up,' he said, taking the stool opposite, drinking in the sight of her. Maturity suited her, and motherhood; she looked more beautiful than ever, and the sight of her exposed breast made him catch his breath. What would he not give to know her again in the biblical sense. Just once! Although that would never be enough.

'How are you, Joan?' he asked gently.

'These three keep me busy.' She smiled. 'Ellen, curtsey to my lord Cardinal.'

The elder of the two girls got up and made a pretty obeisance. There was no doubting whose daughter she was. Tom felt a lump rise in his throat.

'Thomas is coming home,' he said briskly. 'I thought you would want to know.'

'Oh, that is good news!' she cried, covering her breast and laying the baby in the cradle. 'I have missed him.'

'Maybe you will be able to see more of him,' he ventured.

She shook her head. 'George still does not know he exists. I dare not say anything. Shh.' She indicated the little girls, then called for the nurse, who took them off to have their dinner.

She looked at Tom sadly. 'I did not want to say anything they might repeat. George reproaches me as it is for my past life.'

Tom's anger flared. 'That is unfair of him.'

She shrugged. 'It's only what most men would say. And I must bear the consequences of my sin.'

'It was no sin,' he growled. 'How can love as beautiful as that be a sin?'

'It was against all the tenets of the church you serve, my lord Cardinal,' she countered. 'You were in holy orders, and we were unwed.'

'Cannot love rise above such things? Isn't that what you used to say?'

'I am not the young woman I once was, Tom.'

'But I still love you,' he blurted out. For a long moment, their eyes met.

'Alas, it cannot be,' Joan said. 'I could not endure the subterfuge – and you should not risk the King's good opinion. Think of your career.'

He heard the reproach in her voice and knew himself bested.

'Please don't come here again, Tom,' she whispered. 'It is finished between us.'

'No!' he groaned. 'I must see you. My life is empty and meaningless without you. All I want is to behold your face from time to time. Is that too much to ask?'

She rose and took his hands. Her touch sent his senses reeling. 'Goodbye, my dear friend. It is time for you to leave – and may God go with you.'

'No, Joan,' he protested.

'Go!' she urged. 'Before I lose my resolve. It is for the best.'

He kissed her hands, her dear hands, and walked away, feeling as if he was dying inside.

As ever when he felt depressed, Tom threw himself into work. And there was plenty to distract him. Cardinal College had just opened its doors to students, and he decided to make an official visit to Oxford to see how it was prospering. Admiring the splendid buildings, the glorious chapel and the excellence of the staff, he experienced a sense of elation, even though he still felt empty inside. His parting from Joan had been so horribly final, and he feared there would be no way back.

On his return to court, he visited Queen Katherine, who had been pleased to take an interest in his college, and told her how it was thriving, but again he sensed a coolness in her. Of course, she still blamed him for the advancement of Henry Fitzroy. But afterwards, Harry told him that he had decided to send the Princess Mary to Ludlow Castle on the Welsh Marches to learn something of the art of government and of Wales, of which she was nominally princess. He had not had the heart to bestow the title formally. He was still saving it for a son.

'The Queen is unhappy about it,' he confessed. 'She says the Princess is too young to be parted from her. But, as I reminded her, Lady Salisbury will be going with her as governess.' That good woman had not remained out of favour for long, for the Princess had pined for her and she had quickly been reinstated. 'And,' the King was saying, 'it is the tradition in England that the heir to the throne resides at Ludlow. My uncle, that was King Edward V, was sent there, and my brother Arthur.'

Tom was remembering what Harry had said not so long ago about it being cruel to part Mary from her mother when she was still so young. But evidently it was not so cruel when it conformed to his own desires.

He suppressed his irritation. 'I am sure the Queen will come around to the idea. She must know how important it is for the Princess to go. Would your Grace like me to talk to her?'

Harry nodded wearily. 'See if you can do better than I did! But be subtle. Say I have asked you to consult her in drawing up guidelines for Lady Salisbury as to the regime to be followed by the Princess at Ludlow. Make her feel better about it.'

Tom stood before the Queen, explaining why he had come to see her. Uninvited, he sat down at the table and produced paper, pen and ink from the bulging leather scrip he always carried.

Katherine glared at him, clearly resenting what she no doubt viewed as interference. 'As to that, my Lord Cardinal, I myself have asked Lady Salisbury to have the most tender regard for the Princess's honourable education and her training in virtuous behaviour. Lady Salisbury and I are of one mind about these aspects, and I will tell you about the regimen that we have drawn up, which is what you will implement.'

Tom was thrown. 'If I may advise—'

'There is no need,' she interrupted. 'It is all decided. The Princess is to enjoy plenty of fresh air and take walks in the gardens for her health and comfort. She is to practise her music, but not too much, for fear of tiring her; and she must continue to learn Latin and French, but her studies are not to be wearisome. She enjoys dancing, so she must have time for that.'

Tom had begun taking down her instructions. She waited until his nib had ceased its scratching.

'As to her diet, let it be pure, well prepared, dressed and served with merry conversation, in an honourable manner. Her lodgings, her clothes and everything about her must be kept clean and wholesome, as is proper for so great a princess. There must be no dirt or evil smells, and her servants are to behave wisely, virtuously and discreetly, and treat the Princess with humility and reverence.'

She had covered everything. He could not have done better himself. He noted that she did not ask for his opinion of her orders; she had made it clear that this was her business, and that he was here to relay her instructions, no more.

'That will be all, my lord Cardinal,' she said.

After the humiliating failure of the Amicable Grant, Tom had spent the summer negotiating a peace with France, treating with Louise of Savoy, who was acting as regent for her imprisoned son, King Francis. The peace was signed later that month at Tom's own house, The More, and it put an end to the war.

Harry was not pleased at being forced to abandon his dream of a coronation at Rheims, but given that relations with the Emperor were cooling and Charles had shown himself reluctant to support his dynastic ambitions, he had had to accept that he had no choice but to make peace.

Tom felt he had somehow failed his master, but his uneasiness was overlaid by joy at seeing his son again. When Thomas returned towards the end of the year, Tom's heart filled with joy as he embraced him by the great gatehouse of Hampton Court. As they walked towards Thomas's lodging, he could not take his eyes off the boy. He was now fifteen, and had grown tall during his absence, and there was about him a polish that travel and a fine education had conferred. Tom was delighted with him. In the week after his son's return, he rewarded him with more church offices, which made him a very wealthy young man. He was now a canon of Lincoln Cathedral as well as archdeacon of York, chancellor of Sarum, Norfolk and Richmond, dean of Wells and much else besides.

'I would like you to visit these places,' Tom said, as they walked in the park beneath skeletal trees, wrapped up well against the cold. 'Even if others are administering them for you, you should be aware of what that entails.'

'Can it wait until the spring?' Thomas asked. 'The weather will be better then.'

'I suppose so,' Tom replied, disappointed, for he himself had never let weather interfere with his plans, and he had expected the lad to be fired up with enthusiasm for his new offices. 'I hope you are sensible of the honours conferred on you. Many would kill for them.' He thought of the hordes of petitions that littered his desk every week.

'Oh, I am, Sir,' Thomas protested, watching wistfully as a deer disappeared into the trees. 'Can we go hunting?'

Tom felt a touch exasperated. 'We could, but I wouldn't want the weather to put you off.'

Thomas looked at him sharply. The barb had gone home.

Tom sighed. He hadn't expected their reunion to be like this. If only the boy would show some spark of interest. He could not expect to enjoy the fruits of his new offices without doing something to earn it. But he did not say this to him. He feared to cause a rift; that he could not bear. Pursing his lips, he resigned himself to having Thomas idling around the house for the winter, and cast about in his mind for ways to keep him occupied. A little clerking would do him no harm. But Thomas quickly became bored, and again, Tom feared to provoke a quarrel, telling himself that it was enough to have his son home, and that he would be gainfully occupied in the spring.

He was infuriated when he heard that an irritating cleric, Dr Robert Barnes, had preached a contentious sermon on Christmas Eve in Cambridge, declaring that, by the law of God, no man could be a bishop of two or three sees. It was, in effect, an attack on Tom for holding so many high offices in the Church – and for conferring numerous others on his 'nephew', although doubtless most people had guessed by now who Thomas really was.

He summoned Barnes to answer for his provocative remarks and received him in his gallery. There, he read aloud to him the offending sermon.

'This touches me, Dr Barnes,' he said, glowering at him. 'Do you indeed think it wrong that one bishop should have so many sees under him?'

Barnes hesitated. 'I know of no ordinance of the Church concerning this, only what St Paul said, which was that in the Apostles' time, there were many sees, and over each was there set but one bishop. I thought this far-fetched, but I cannot deny it.'

'It is far-fetched,' Tom snapped, 'and clearly you have misunderstood Scripture.'

He dismissed Barnes, but he knew the cleric was not the only person to criticise him for holding multiple bishoprics. That was why he had singled Barnes out, as a warning to anyone who might seek to undermine his credit with the King. Under no circumstances could Harry be given cause to regret his munificence towards his old friend.

Chapter 27

1526

After Christmas, Tom joined Harry at Eltham Palace, unwilling to be absent from him for too long. Somers was always in attendance these days, and although he had so far proved no threat to Tom, it was important to keep making it plain to the fool who really had the King's ear.

Taking advantage of the failure of the Amicable Grant, the minions – Carew and Sir William Compton in particular, overgrown schoolboys the pair of them – were again doing their best to undermine Tom. This time, he was determined to trounce them, and he had the perfect pretext. The court was extravagant, wasteful and inefficient. That gave him the ideal opportunity to counter the threat to his authority from the Privy Chamber, the one centre of power at court over which he lacked influence.

Choosing his moment well, he raised his concerns.

'I can't allow this situation to continue,' Harry declared. 'We must draw up a list of ordinances for the reform of my household.'

Tom had come prepared. 'My aim, Sir, is to save money and eliminate waste.' He laid the list of his proposed reforms on the table.

The King read them and nodded. 'I have long felt the need for these changes. They are necessary. The war with France has drained my treasury.' All that gold inherited from his father had disappeared, spent on palaces, entertainments, kingly display and petty wars. Harry had been overgenerous in granting positions to his favourites and their clients.

Tom assumed his most paternal, solicitous manner. 'Your Grace, those who surround you should lead by example as your courtiers.

They should be eloquent, learned and well informed, and thus able to influence their master in a beneficial way. They ought to be perfect examples of chivalry and courtesy, lovers of the arts and expert in martial exercises and sports. But these virtues are not apparent in the Privy Chamber. It is full of pride, envy, indignation, mocking and derision. There is more malice than moderation, and there are too many young men of a martial bent with time on their hands.'

Harry opened his mouth to protest, but evidently thought better of it. How could he argue when Tom was right? Those who surrounded him *were* greedy to feather their own nests, and averse to giving place to anyone else. 'But I provide them with outlets for their energy and aggression,' he said. 'There are many opportunities for sport and feats of arms and entertaining diversions. I've built tiltyards, houses of pleasure for playing at chess, backgammon, dice, cards and billiards, and bowling alleys, archery butts and tennis plays.'

'Might I suggest that, in the interests of economy and concord, your Grace's gentlemen be reduced from twelve to six? And maybe Master Pace should be dismissed?' Tom had become convinced that Harry's secretary was one of those who were working against him. 'Perhaps he could be sent abroad on a useful diplomatic mission?'

Harry agreed. The reforms were implemented. Several people left court burning with resentment, chief among them Tom's enemies Sir William Compton, Sir Francis Bryan, Sir Nicholas Carew, Lord Rochford and George Boleyn. Doubtless they were all vowing revenge upon him and scheming to recover their former positions.

It was obvious that Harry missed his friends. He had insisted on retaining as chief nobleman of the Privy Chamber his cousin the Marquess of Exeter, who was no friend to Tom. To counter his influence, Tom quickly brought in his own adherent, the one-eyed Sir John Russell, an ambitious courtier, soldier and diplomat. He saw that the charming and polished Henry Norris replaced Compton as Groom of the Stool and head of the Privy Chamber; he was close to Harry and eminently fitted for this most confidential of court offices.

Tom also implemented many reforms at court, with the King's full approval. Servants surplus to requirements were pensioned off, hangers-on ejected; the Yeomen of the Guard were reduced to one hundred, and their court duties shared with the Gentlemen Pensioners, who were provided with ceremonial battleaxes. He imposed tighter controls over expenditure on food and other provisions and introduced stricter codes of discipline and curbs on absenteeism. Food was rationed, although fairly generously. Henceforth, all members of the household were to be appointed on merit, and those who gave good service would benefit from new channels of promotion. The King's servants were to wear the Tudor livery of green and white at all times. The result was a far more efficiently run household and a saving of both money and resources.

On Shrove Tuesday, Harry hosted a tournament at Greenwich. Tom was horrified when he entered the stand and saw the banished minions clustering around their master below, looking smug and defiant.

He raced down the steps and pursued the King to his tent, where his armourer was waiting for him. 'Sir, we agreed that those gentlemen—'

Harry did not let him finish. 'I have need of them,' he said. 'I will brook no arguments.'

He had clearly felt the need to assert his authority. Tom swallowed and bowed his head, telling himself that he was there to advise, not to enforce, and wondering if his influence was on the wane. He stood shaking, watching the King ride into the lists, his jousting dress bearing the mysterious motto 'Declare I dare not'.

Another secret amour. Tom sighed and made his way back to his desk.

In April, Harry was enraged to hear that the Emperor had repudiated his betrothal to the Princess Mary and married Isabella of Portugal, who had brought a huge dowry and was of an age to bear him children. He stormed and shouted, and was in a foul mood for days. The news drove him into the open arms of King Francis, who had recently been released from his Madrid prison. Tom was happy to steer him in that direction, and leapt at his suggestion that he undertake the negotiations personally. This new alliance was Tom's project from start to finish; he had not forgiven or forgotten being ousted from the contest for the Papacy. Now it was agreed that neither England nor France would have dealings with Charles without the approval of the other.

Tom was busy elsewhere on the European stage, helping to organise the League of Cognac, an alliance between France, the Papacy and some Italian states against the Emperor.

Working under intense pressure, he grew tired of his son lazing in idleness at home. It was an aimless existence for one who held at least twenty ecclesiastical offices – in none of which he showed any interest, save for the income they brought him. All the boy wanted to do was eat, play music and meet up with his friends to go carousing in the local taverns. Occasionally, he bestirred himself to play some sport. Tom found it galling to realise that it was as difficult to impose his will at home as at work.

One evening, he caught the lad sneaking out of Hampton Court by a secret stair that he himself had made available for his spies.

'Where are you going?' he asked.

'Out,' said the lad, with a touch of bravado.

'Carousing again, no doubt,' Tom said drily. 'Thomas, you are wasting your life. I've paid for a fine education for you and paved the way for a great career in the Church, and yet you show no interest. You've said nothing about going to visit your benefices. You have every advantage, and that is not something given to many. It's time you looked to the future. You're sixteen this year – not a child any more.'

Thomas turned a mutinous look on him. 'No, I'm not a child. I can choose how to spend my own time – *Uncle*.' Tom was taken aback by the emphasis on the word. Could it be that the boy had guessed the truth?

He decided to ignore that. 'You should be attending to your offices. Those deputising for you will expect you to do so one day, and soon.'

'But I do not want to go into the Church,' Thomas protested. 'I don't want to take holy orders. I want to get married!'

'Married?' Tom was astonished. That had been the furthest thing from his own mind when he was fifteen. He had been too preoccupied with defying his father over entering the priesthood. His adolescent self had thought of women only in physical terms. 'And what do you think you can offer a wife? Without your church offices, you have nothing.'

'I'm sure you could help me,' the boy said complacently.

'Do not presume on my generosity!' Tom retorted. 'I have done everything in my power to pave the way for your advancement in the Church. It is the only path to prosperity for a lad without a fortune.'

'Or I could marry an heiress,' Thomas said, surprising Tom again. 'Master Cavendish told me that my lord of Essex has an only daughter who will inherit his earldom and his fortune one day.'

'And you think he will consider, even for one moment, a penniless fellow like you?' Tom said, laughing mirthlessly, and inwardly cursing Cavendish.

'He might think it an advantage to marry his daughter to the son of the mighty Cardinal of York,' Thomas said, eyeing him closely. 'Do you deny that you are my father?'

Tom started trembling. It had come, the moment he had both dreaded and longed for – when he must admit his sin to his son in order to call him his own.

'I do not deny it,' he said. 'And I have loved you like a son, and showered every advantage on you.'

'But you sent me away.' The hurt was there in the boy's eyes.

'I had no choice. And most men of rank send their sons to be brought up in another noble household. I sent you to the best school in London. You have attended some of the finest universities in Christendom. You even bear your own coat of arms, thanks to me. Thomas, you must know that I love you above all earthly things.'

Thomas nodded. 'Yes. And if you love me, will you please arrange this marriage for me?'

Tom shook his head. 'I will not give in to emotional blackmail, Thomas. Even if I could enrich you with a secular income, I doubt that would satisfy my lord of Essex. He will want someone of noble blood to carry on his line. I am an innkeeper's son. I made good in life through my own efforts, as must you. The Church is your way forward. If you wish it, I can procure a dispensation for you to become ordained as a priest, for you are too young without one. I may even be able to get a bishopric for you.'

Thomas looked mutinous. 'Father – if I may call you that – I do not want to enter the Church.'

Tom shrugged. 'Look, I understand that. I did not want to either when I was your age and my father was pressing me to do so, but I know now it was the right decision. Look at the benefits it has brought me.' He saw Thomas open his mouth to make a further protest, but held up his hand. 'We will discuss this later. I am tired, and you are eager to be out. Go along with you, and think carefully on what I have said.'

He went to bed shaking, conscious that the dreaded moment had come and gone without drama – and, sadly, without the happy recognition he had long hoped would ensue.

Tom considered Thomas's future for a long while, until at length he came up with the idea of sending him to the university of Paris, far away from his drinking mates. Let him spend time at that excellent institution, for it would do him a power of good, and when he came home, God willing, he would be older and wiser.

Thomas was enthusiastic at the prospect, especially when Tom told him that he would be going unchaperoned.

'You are old enough now to be responsible for yourself,' he said, wondering if he was doing the right thing. Yet he himself had friends and colleagues in Paris who were willing to keep an eye on Thomas and report how he was faring. 'You will have a train of servants and stay in comfortable lodgings, but I expect to hear that you have attended lectures and done the work expected of you.'

'Yes, Father.' Thomas was barely listening. Already, it was plain, he had gone from here. Freedom was beckoning.

All through that summer, Tom sensed that Harry was preoccupied. It worried him a little, being concerned that the King might be growing cool in his friendship – but Harry soon gave proof that that was not the case. He was as genial as ever, clapping Tom on the back and praising his work. It seemed that the Amicable Grant had been forgotten. Tom devoutly hoped so. Yet he could not work out why Harry's attention often seemed to be elsewhere.

He didn't have much time to brood on it, because he was disturbed by reports from his acquaintances in Paris. Thomas was living extravagantly. He had suspected as much, given the boy's constant requests for money. He was also using his connection to his 'uncle' to associate with the highest in the land. It was heartening to read that doors opened for him because he was related to the great Cardinal Wolsey, but Tom was more concerned about his being such a spendthrift, and by hints that he wasn't working as hard as he should be. He took to asking anyone who was travelling to Paris to look out for the lad.

He knew that Thomas would not be writing to Joan. Aware that she would want to know how the lad was faring, he had told him to send letters to her via himself, which he would give Cavendish to pass to her in secret. He longed to see her, but dared not defy her ban on his visits. He missed her, missed being able to share his worries with her. What a comfort that would be to him now. Dare he go against her wishes?

Yes! he told himself. Thomas was their son, which alone justified a visit. Joan couldn't argue with that.

He called one evening when Legh was in London, and found her alone, with the children in bed. As the steward showed him into the parlour, she rose, looking disconcerted to see him. He was almost certain that she had been weeping. Nevertheless, she greeted him courteously and bade him be seated.

'I asked you not to come, but I am glad you are here,' she said, as soon as the door had closed behind the steward.

Tom's heart leapt, yet he was concerned to see her in evident distress.

'What's the matter, Joan?' he asked.

She wrung her hands. 'George has a mistress.' Suddenly, she was in tears. 'It's not that,' she sobbed. 'I'm glad he has her, if it takes him away from me. He has never loved me, and he is forever reproaching me for my past. He says I am unworthy of him. In truth, he makes me feel like a fallen woman.' She was crying harder now. 'I'm sorry to burden you with this, Tom, but he was vile to me today before he left for London. It worries me that our daughters will pick up on it and come to despise me as he does.'

Tom rose and bent stiffly to his knees beside her, taking her hand. 'I will speak to him. He shall not treat you like that. You should be cherished, my dearest. You are wasted on a man like him.'

'You must say nothing!' she cried. 'He hates you. It would only make things worse.'

'Then I will take you away from here.' He was longing to do it.

'And what will the King say about that?'

'He will not know! I have many houses.'

'Where I can live in subterfuge again?'

'Is that worse than what you now endure? And we could be together, as we were always meant to be!'

'But what of my girls? Legally, they are my husband's. I have no right to them. If I took them away, he would hunt them down.'

'He will never find them. I will make sure of that! Joan, come away with me tonight. I will take you to The More. It's a big house and you can hide there. Oh, darling, come with me!' He would do anything for her, anything she asked.

'I dare not,' she wept, and clung to him.

'Then go home to your family for a time,' he urged, feeling desire well up in him. 'Take the children to visit them. Give yourself a respite from him.'

'I cannot,' she sobbed. 'He has forbidden it. He says I am not worthy of being with such respectable people.'

He burned with anger. 'How dare he treat you thus? I will not have it!'

'Oh, Tom, it is hopeless!' His robes were wet with her tears.

'Never say that, darling,' he said, and then suddenly he was kissing her, and she was kissing him back, and it was as if all the pent-up emotions of years were exploding at once. In seconds, they were on the carpet, grabbing at each other's clothing, and soon Tom was inside her, lost in his need for her. It was the most glorious feeling he had ever had.

When it was over, they lay quietly for a time, and then Joan tidied herself and got to her feet. Tom followed suit.

'Forgive me. I should not have taken advantage of you,' he murmured, thinking how beautiful she looked with the flush of love still on her.

'I'm glad you did,' she said fervently. 'You have no idea what you have done for me, Tom. You've made me feel human again – and loved.'

'And that is how you should feel,' he told her, clasping her tightly and kissing her lips again and again. 'Would that I could keep on loving you like that!'

'But we cannot,' she said.

'Think about what I have said, I beg of you,' he urged, mad to have her away from her appalling husband.

'I will think on it, but I do not know what my answer will be,' she said sadly. 'It is a huge step and there would be no going back. But the thought of staying is terrible to me.'

'Come now. The Joan I knew would not have stood any nonsense from Sir George Legh. Show him that he cannot get away with treating you badly. Or leave him and come to me. Then we can be together and know the joy of loving again.'

'I will think on it, I promise,' she said again, and smiled at him.

He rode away, taking heart from that, and only when he arrived at Hampton Court did he remember that he had not mentioned Thomas at all.

Part Five

'Now fickle Fortune hath turned her wheel'

Chapter 28

1526–7

In December, Don Íñigo López de Mendoza, the new Imperial ambassador, arrived at court. The Spaniard was a swarthy, attractive man with a shock of dark hair and a very correct manner. Tom knew that he was here to try to prevent England from making a new alliance with France, and that Harry, for all his blustering about Charles's perfidy, was anxious to preserve England's trade with the Empire, even though he and the Emperor remained at odds.

Tom waited for Mendoza to emerge from his first audience with the King, ready to take him to see Queen Katherine. He was impressed to see that the ambassador was remarkably composed, considering that Harry was still furious with the Emperor. He had expected to feel a certain antipathy towards the Spaniard, but the superb diplomacy of the man made him warm to him.

He took Mendoza to meet the Queen. 'She will be pleased to see her countryman,' he told him. But he had an ulterior motive for accompanying the ambassador. He was aware that the rift between Harry and Charles, and the breaking of her daughter's betrothal, had caused the Queen much grief, and that the prospect of her daughter marrying the King of France or his son would be anathema to her. He was here to ensure that she did not try to meddle with Mendoza to revive the Imperial alliance.

As a groom admitted them to the antechamber, Anne Boleyn suddenly swept past them, all dark eyes and swishing skirts. She turned and bobbed a brief curtsey. 'My lord Cardinal, I will tell her Grace that you and the ambassador are here,' she said. Her expression was cold.

Tom presented Mendoza to the Queen. The ambassador bowed and kissed her hand.

'Highness, his Imperial Majesty wishes me to convey his most sincere love for you and enquires after your health.'

Katherine was restrained in her welcome, clearly conscious of Tom's presence. 'I am gratified to hear it, for I have been hurt by his Majesty's neglect. For more than two years I have had no letters from Spain, and yet such are my affection and readiness for his service that I deserve better treatment.'

Mendoza looked uncomfortable. 'Highness, there has been a coolness, shall we say, between his Majesty and the King your husband. His Majesty has not felt able to be in contact with you, and he wishes you to know that he is very sorry about that. But now I hope that matters will improve.'

The audience was a short one. Tom saw to that. 'There are many important matters that the King wishes me to discuss with you,' he said to Mendoza, after a mere five minutes of courtesies. 'Her Highness will surely excuse us if we take our leave and depart. You shall have an audience at another time.'

Christmas at Greenwich was a splendid affair, with banquets, masques, dancing and tournaments. On 3 January, Tom was back at York Place, hosting a lavish banquet for the Privy Council when he heard a sudden roll of drums and a blast of cannon fire outside. There was a commotion below, and then his chamberlain appeared, looking flustered, followed by a procession of torchbearers and drummers, who marched into the hall.

The guests were astonished, but Tom had his suspicions as to who might be behind this, and they were confirmed when a dozen masked men appeared, dressed in cloth of gold and fine crimson satin, with wigs and beards of gold or silver wire. He thanked God that his kitchens had prepared sufficient food for extra guests, and welcomed them with his usual urbanity, as if he had been expecting them, smiling indulgently, certain that the King was among them. Even at thirty-five, Harry still loved dressing in disguises and surprising everyone.

The chamberlain stepped forward. 'My lord Cardinal, these gentlemen are shepherds from another land and can speak no English, so they have desired me to declare to your Grace that, learning of this triumphant banquet, where you have assembled so many fair dames, they could do no less than repair hither to view their incomparable beauty and accompany them in dancing and card games. Therefore, they humbly ask your Grace's leave to join the company.'

'I am very well contented that they should so do,' Tom replied, trying to work out where Harry was standing. He had his steward set places for them at table and gave orders that the choicest food be served to them. Then he took his seat beneath the cloth of estate bearing his cardinal's arms.

It was a wonderful evening. The maskers saluted the ladies and produced a cup full of gold crowns, and the dicing began. When the game was over, they emptied all the crowns they had won back into the cup and gave it to Tom. He still could not determine which masked man was Harry.

Mischievously, he addressed his chamberlain. 'It seems to me that there is among these shepherds some nobleman whom I suppose to be much more worthy to occupy this seat than I; to whom I would most gladly, if I knew him, surrender my place, according to my duty. I think the gentleman with the black beard is he.' He rose and offered his chair to the tall man standing with his cap in his hand. But when he took off his mask, Tom saw he had been mistaken, for it was Sir Edward Neville, who closely resembled the King.

A loud guffaw could be heard, as another tall fellow ripped off his visor, revealing Harry's laughing face. There was much merriment as Tom bade him sit in his chair.

'I will go and change first, Thomas,' he replied, and Tom escorted him to his own bedchamber, where he had a great fire made up, before which the King's gentlemen dressed him in princely garments. Then they all rejoined the company and tucked into two hundred dishes of choice fare. Thus passed the whole night with banqueting, dancing and other pleasures, to Harry's evident delight.

It gave Tom deep pleasure to see his sovereign so nobly entertained and beaming, no matter the cost. He wished only that Joan could be here, celebrating the festive season with him, and could not help wondering what life would be like if she left Legh, although that seemed a vain hope now – and he would still have to keep her hidden away.

At the beginning of March, Harry and Tom welcomed to London a French embassy headed by the Bishop of Tarbes, come to discuss terms for a treaty of eternal peace, which was to be sealed by the marriage of the Princess Mary to the Duke of Orléans, second son of King Francis. Since Harry had no son, Orléans, it was anticipated, would one day rule England as Mary's consort. This, for Harry, was not a satisfactory solution to the problem of the succession, but it was the best he had in the circumstances, for he had still not taken the momentous step of legitimising young Richmond.

He laid on a magnificent programme of entertainments for the envoys. There was a great tournament, in which he himself ran many courses for their edification, and afterwards, he hosted a costly banquet in the Queen's chamber – a great privilege for the Frenchmen.

The next day, Tom and Harry sat down with them to discuss the finer points of the treaty. As Tom shuffled his papers, he felt confident that they were close to finalising the formalities. All was proceeding well, but soon he became aware that the Bishop of Tarbes seemed ill at ease. He and the King exchanged glances.

'Something is troubling you, my lord Bishop,' Harry said.

The lean-faced cleric hesitated. 'There is one rather delicate matter on which King Francis will need some reassurance from your Majesty.'

Harry frowned. 'What reassurance?'

Tom raised his eyebrows. 'I thought we had covered all bases, my lord.'

'Yes, my lord Cardinal, but I have received further instructions. I fear that doubts have been raised about the Princess's legitimacy.'

'Doubts?' Harry echoed sharply.

The Bishop looked embarrassed. 'My master has learned that the legality of your Grace's marriage was queried at the time. I would refer you to the Book of Leviticus in Scripture.'

Harry's smile did not reach his eyes. 'Let me reassure you that Pope Julius issued a dispensation for my marriage, which he pronounced entirely lawful. The injunction in Leviticus did not apply.'

'There can be no doubt that the Princess was born in lawful wedlock,' Tom chimed in.

'I thank your Graces for confirming that. King Francis will be delighted to hear it.'

Harry nodded graciously. 'Well, gentlemen, are we finished? If so, then we have another pageant for you.'

That afternoon, Tom was not surprised to receive an urgent summons to Harry's closet. It was a hot day, and he found himself sweating in his robes despite the breeze coming through the open lattice window by the King's desk.

'Thomas,' Harry said, 'I need your wise opinion in a delicate matter.'

'Your Grace can always unburden yourself to me,' Tom assured him.

Harry cleared his throat. 'I have to tell you that my conscience is troubling me in regard to the validity of my marriage. I cannot banish from my head what the Bishop said. I have always tried to be a good son of the Church, but I fear that I have sinned in marrying my brother's wife, and that my lack of a son is proof of Almighty God's displeasure.'

Tom was stunned. 'But the Pope issued a dispensation.'

'Yes, but was it sufficient? The Book of Leviticus warns of the severe penalty God inflicts on one who marries his brother's widow: "And if a man shall take his brother's wife, it is an unclean thing: he hath uncovered his brother's nakedness; they shall be childless." Thomas, I am as good as childless, lacking a male heir. God does not smile on this marriage!'

Tom felt shaken to the core. 'Sir, the law as laid down in Leviticus only applies where there are children of the first marriage, and clearly there were not; indeed, Prince Arthur left her Grace a virgin, as was established at the time. And the Book of Deuteronomy enjoins a man to marry his brother's widow and raise up children in his name.'

'Deuteronomy is ambiguous! Thomas, I know it in my bones, and I think I have known it for some time. My marriage is unlawful, and it should be dissolved so that I can take a wife who can give me sons!'

The enormity of this was so great that Tom could not comprehend it at once. Horrified, he fell to his knees in a swish of silks. 'Sir, I beg you, consider well before you take this matter further. To call into question Pope Julius's dispensation would be to undermine the authority of the Church at a time when she is under attack from the heretics. It would injure a most gracious queen and will surely arouse the wrath of the Emperor. And it could call into question the legitimacy of the Princess, your only heir, although if you both entered into the marriage in good faith, believing it was lawful, then she might still be deemed legitimate. Even so, there is the French alliance to consider; King Francis will not marry his son to a princess of doubtful birth. Sir, I urge you to take this no further. The consequences could be grave and far-reaching.'

'No, Thomas,' Harry said. 'My mind is already made up. I decided today. I want an annulment. Will you approach Rome for me?'

Tom had to sit down. He heaved himself to his feet and sank into his chair, at a loss for words. 'You know you can rely on me to do your bidding,' he said at length, feeling a little sick at the prospect of working to annul a marriage that was probably valid, and all the ramifications that would ensue. But he could deny his beloved King nothing. He was also aware of the need to retain Harry's love.

As so often, he suddenly saw things more clearly. Something good might come of this. 'If your Grace's union is deemed invalid, then the French alliance can be cemented with *your* marriage to a French princess. I am sure King Francis will see the advantage in that, and it will hopefully provide you with a solution to the problem of the succession.'

Harry opened his mouth as if he was going to say something, then closed it again.

'As Papal legate, I will convene a secret ecclesiastical court at York Place,' Tom continued. 'Archbishop Warham can preside with me.'

'Can you, as legate, yourself pronounce on the validity of my marriage?' Harry asked eagerly.

'If the bishops agree, I may be able to. Your Grace must understand that this is a very difficult, sensitive matter. But I will consider the evidence formally and hopefully we will be able to reach a decision favourable to your Grace.'

He began by searching for evidence to bolster the King's case. His first line of enquiry centred on whether Arthur and Katherine had consummated their marriage, although that was really immaterial. He also tried to find evidence that Harry had been pushed into marriage with Katherine; if he had entered into it unwillingly, the Pope might take a liberal view.

He found nothing. Nor did Cromwell, who had been helping him to search through the dense legal tomes. There could be no doubt that the Queen's first marriage had remained unconsummated, and all the evidence showed that Harry had been eager to wed her. Tom himself could testify to that. He remembered it well.

Nevertheless, he issued a summons, charging the King with cohabiting with his brother's widow and requiring him to present himself before an ecclesiastical court. At worst, it could order him to separate from Katherine until the Pope had ruled on whether their marriage was valid. But he hoped that he himself would be able to give a ruling when the court sat.

He was immersed in the paperwork when an usher delivered a letter bearing a plain seal. It was from Joan. She had borne a son whom she had named Thomas.

He knew at once, without counting back the months, what she was telling him. She had not thought to inform him of the births of her daughters, not even that of Ellen, whom he was certain was his. A son was of greater importance, of course, but the choice of name was telling.

He was seized with the urge to leave York Place and ride hotfoot to Thames Ditton. His head was teeming with questions. How was George Legh treating the mother of his legal heir, who surely deserved some respect now? At the same time, Tom was consumed with jealousy at the thought of a creature like Legh playing the father to his son.

But he could not get away. The King's business must always take precedence, and in truth, Tom was overwhelmed by it just now. All he could do was write to the Leghs, congratulate them and send his priestly blessings. He enclosed a silver-gilt cup for little Thomas, hoping it struck the right note. The gold cup he would have liked to send might arouse suspicions.

The new Treaty of Perpetual Peace with France was signed at Westminster at the end of April. Under its terms, the King agreed to give up his claim to the French throne in return for a yearly payment from Francis. Tom had done his work well. He had brought together two great rivals and left the Emperor out in the cold.

Now the celebrations could begin. When the French and English envoys arrived at Greenwich early in May, they were conducted to a new banqueting house, which was hung with tapestries depicting the story of David and had a ceiling covered with red buckram embroidered with roses and pomegranates. The room was illuminated by iron sconces and antick-style candelabra and dominated by a massive buffet seven stages high and thirteen feet long, and another cupboard nine stages high, both with wonderful displays of gold and gem-studded plate. At the far end of the room was an antick triumphal arch designed by a German painter, Hans Holbein, who had been recommended to Harry by Thomas More. Above the arch was a large painting by him of the King's victory over the French at Thérouanne, a somewhat tactless choice of decoration, Tom had thought, but Harry had overruled him.

'I'd have had a painting of Agincourt as well, if there was space for it,' he'd added, grinning.

As Tom had feared, when Harry pointed out the picture to his French guests, they were somewhat offended. But he made up for it by entertaining them more sumptuously than he had ever entertained guests in the past. Tom could take little pleasure in it all, worried as he was about managing Harry's desire for a divorce, and hoping that the outcome of the treaty would justify the huge cost of the festivities. Harry, on the other hand, was revelling in them. The next day, he appeared at a tournament wearing a jousting costume of purple Florentine velvet trimmed with gold that must have cost a fortune. Yet he was unable to participate this time, having injured his foot playing tennis. Tom was vexed to see the Master of the Horse, the aggravating Sir Nicholas Carew, triumphing that day in the lists. Afterwards, Harry hosted a lavish feast in the banqueting house, at which sixty huge silver-gilt plates of costly spices were handed around. This was followed by a recital by the Chapel Royal in a new theatre that had tiered seating around three of its walls and a vast proscenium arch adorned with terracotta busts and statuary. The floor was carpeted with silk embroidered with gold lilies, in honour of the French, and above was a ceiling painted by Holbein, which depicted the earth surrounded by the seven seas, like a map; beneath it hung a transparent cloth, painted and gilded with the signs of the Zodiac and glittering with stars, planets and constellations. Everyone marvelled at it.

The recital was followed by masques. In one, Harry led out his daughter, who had just returned from Ludlow and now appeared decked out in what looked like all the gems of the eighth sphere. Tom smiled when he saw the King pull off her netted caul, letting her abundant red-gold tresses cascade about her shoulders, to the evident delight of the French ambassadors.

The dancing went on until sunrise, then the celebrations continued for several days. Tom staged a play celebrating the alliance, which was performed by the Chapel Royal, and gave a feast for the envoys at Hampton Court; among the many fantastic subtleties served was one fashioned like a chess set. Tom magnanimously presented it to a Frenchman who had admired it.

Summoned to appear before the secret ecclesiastical court convened at Westminster, Harry seated himself before Tom and Archbishop Warham, with ranks of senior clergy on either side of the stone-aisled room with its tall Gothic windows.

Tom took a deep breath. He was aware that the process he was about to initiate would have far-reaching consequences for Harry, for England and maybe even for Christendom at large, and he was still wishing with all his heart that he wasn't playing a part in it.

'Your Grace,' he began, 'you have been asked here to account, for the tranquillity of your conscience and the health of your soul, for having knowingly taken to wife your brother's widow.'

Harry bowed his head. 'I admit the charge. I confess I have had doubts of conscience about my marriage for a while.' He explained his concerns, pleading the ban in Leviticus. 'I ask, in all humility, for a decision to be given on my case.'

'We thank your Grace,' Tom said briskly. 'Now we will confer and debate the matter.'

Harry withdrew and left them to it.

They could not reach a decision, despite Tom's best efforts. He wanted a unanimous response, affording him the leeway to dissolve the King's marriage. But John Fisher, Bishop of Rochester, pointed out that any ruling they made could be overturned by the Pope, so it was best to refer the case to Rome.

'So there is a case to answer?' Tom wanted to know.

'I would not say so,' said Fisher. 'As far as I can see, the marriage is valid.'

'And what do the rest of you say?'

There were murmurs of dissent. The bishops looked unhappy. In the end, a vote was taken, and it was concluded that there was a case to answer. Tom felt a little relieved – he didn't want to think about Harry's reaction if they had decided against referring the case to Rome – but his heart was sinking. The Papal court moved slowly at the best of times, and who knew how sympathetic his Holiness would prove?

'As Papal legate, I will refer the case to Rome,' he pronounced, and a letter to the Pope was written and sealed.

Tom found Harry engaged in a vigorous game of tennis. When he saw Tom approaching, he flung down his racquet and hurried over to the net that divided the tennis play from the spectators' gallery.

Tom leaned in and spoke in a low voice. 'Your Grace, we find that there is a case to answer, but the matter has had to be referred to Rome for judgement. The messenger has just left.'

Harry scowled, picked up his towel and his doublet and walked to the door, motioning to Tom to follow him. 'I thought you could give a ruling.'

'The bishops fear, Sir, that any ruling I give might be overturned by Rome. Considering that the succession could be impugned, it is best that the case be determined by his Holiness.'

'Who is in the pocket of the Emperor, who is Katherine's nephew,' Harry growled. 'Some chance I have of an annulment now!'

'I have laid out most potent arguments and authorities in my submission,' Tom said, feeling anything but optimistic. 'The Pope has but to validate them.'

'I pray God he sees sense!' Harry did not sound hopeful. 'What happens now?' he asked, as they emerged into the sunlight. 'What shall I do about the Queen?'

'There must be no open rift between you.'

'I have no personal quarrel with her,' Harry said, striding along the gravelled path to the privy garden. 'She has been a good wife, loyal and devoted.'

'And that is how your Grace must play it. You love the Queen; it will pain you to leave her, but you must do what is right and have a care to the salvation of your soul. While awaiting his Holiness's decision, you should appear together in public, dine and be of company in private, and show each other every courtesy. But on no account can you bed with her Grace.'

'It is rare for me to do so these days, and then I do it only for form's sake,' Harry confided, reddening. 'Nothing passes between us.'

Tom nodded. 'Above all, her Grace must not be allowed to confide in Mendoza. I will block any attempt she makes to see him in private. We do not want any hint of this matter reaching the ears of the Emperor at this stage. I have impressed on his Holiness the need for discretion until a decision is given.'

Harry beckoned Tom through the wicket gate that led into the sanctum of his privy garden and found a seat in an arbour shaded from the sun.

'The Queen must be watched,' he said.

'Sir, several of her women are already in my pay. They keep me informed of her activities in return for gifts and financial inducements.'

Harry gave Tom a strange look, but Tom ignored it. 'I will ensure that every letter her Grace sends or receives is scrutinised before it is sent,' he said.

One evening, when the festivities to celebrate the treaty were still in full swing, Cavendish tapped Tom on the shoulder and beckoned him outside. In the antechamber, where the buzz of conversation and music was muted, he gave him a letter. As Tom read it, he crossed himself, shuddering.

'I must tell the King,' he said. Emerging from the arras, he hastened over to Harry. 'Your Grace, there is dreadful news,' he announced in a loud voice. 'Rome has been sacked by mercenary troops of the Emperor.'

'What?' Harry looked shocked; the Queen began weeping. The envoys were looking at each other in horror, and all conversation in the hall had ceased. 'Tell us what has happened, my lord Cardinal.'

Tom himself was trembling. 'The mercenaries were out of control. This report relates the terrible atrocities that have been committed. Nuns have been raped, men murdered in cold blood, churches desecrated. The entire Papal guard was massacred on the steps of St Peter's itself. I will spare the ladies further details, but the carnage is appalling. It is thought that half the city may have perished.'

'What of his Holiness?' Harry cried, his face ashen.

'He fled, but was taken and is now a prisoner in Castel Sant'Angelo.'

'And the Emperor himself? Could he not control his troops?'

'He was not there. It is said he too is appalled by the violence, and by the way his forces have made the Pope captive.'

'No doubt he sees it is to his advantage to have his Holiness in his power, for he may now wrest the territory he covets with impunity, and obtain other advantages from him,' the Bishop of Tarbes observed. 'It strikes me that his Imperial Majesty has got the Pope exactly where he wants him.'

As Tom was surrounded by people wanting to know more, he noticed Harry sitting silently, frowning. He knew what his master must be thinking. What hope was there now that Clement would grant him an annulment? Katherine was the Emperor's aunt, and Charles was unlikely to allow him to dissolve her marriage.

The King collected himself and stood up. 'My lords and ladies, in the circumstances, all festivity must now cease. Please return to your lodgings.' He took the Queen's hand and led her out of the hall.

Everyone was in shock. The French envoys quietly returned home.

Tom tried to reassure Harry. 'I am sure that his Holiness will soon be free and that all is not lost. In time, your Grace, you may win your case. But you may have a battle on your hands. It would be politic to obtain the Queen's co-operation. If she supports the nullity suit, then it has a better chance of succeeding, for even the Emperor cannot complain if she herself wants any doubts resolved.'

'You mean I should break it to her?' Harry looked terrified.

'I do, Sir. Somehow, it has become public knowledge that you are seeking an annulment. The matter will soon be infamous. Better that she hears about it from your Grace.' He hoped that the King would do it quickly – and kindly.

Tom was making sure that each attempt the Queen made to see Mendoza in private was frustrated. Judging by her tenacity in the matter, he suspected she had some inkling that something was afoot, and no wonder, for three weeks into June, the 'Great Matter' was as notorious as if it had been proclaimed by the town crier, which irritated Harry, who commanded the Lord Mayor of London to ensure that the people ceased their gossip on pain of his high displeasure. This achieved absolutely nothing, and the rumours spread like flames running amok. Reluctantly, Tom was obliged to inform all the English ambassadors abroad of the King's suit.

And still Harry had said nothing to the Queen. Whenever Tom urged him to tell Katherine face to face what was happening, Harry baulked.

'Could *you* tell her?' he asked.

'It would be better coming from your Grace,' Tom insisted. Harry left, looking as if he was about to face the lions in the arena.

He was back within the hour, distraught. 'I told her that I was much troubled in my conscience and that we must separate until my doubts have been resolved. I asked her to choose a house to live in. She took it most displeasantly and cried a lot. I said I intended only to establish the truth, given the doubts expressed by the Bishop of Tarbes, and that all would be done for the best. I ordered her not to speak of the matter to anyone. But she would not stop weeping, so I left her.'

Privately, Tom thought that Harry had handled things badly. He wished now that he had been able to put the right words in his mouth, or even been there himself. But the deed was done. No doubt Katherine was already scheming to get a message to Mendoza or the Emperor.

Soon, one of the ladies who spied for him in her household came hurrying to see him on soft-slippered feet and breathlessly informed him that the Queen blamed him for what was happening, and that it was inconceivable to her that Harry himself could have instigated these proceedings. She was convinced that he had led the King astray and planted doubts in his mind, and she saw it as her sacred duty to rectify the situation and persuade her husband that he was in error.

Tom warned Harry to handle Katherine gently. She could prove a dangerous obstacle to his case. Harry concurred.

'She is quite capable of inciting the Emperor to war, or my subjects to rebel. Have her watched closely, Thomas.'

Tom tightened the net of spies around her, but he could not silence the people. When the Queen appeared in public, crowds would gather, some crying, 'Victory over your enemies!' Women, in particular, spoke out in her favour, being convinced that the King sought to be rid of her purely for his own pleasure. Tom knew that if the matter were to be decided by women, Harry would lose the battle.

Tom did not think that Katherine would go as far as to incite the Emperor to declare war on England, but he did fear that she might prove a formidable adversary in Rome. And he was proved right when one of her servants was arrested in Calais and found to have on him a secret message from her to Charles, asking him to intercede with the Pope for her. If Harry were in any doubt, he now knew that his wife was not going to submit meekly to having her marriage annulled.

From his spies, Tom learned that most people at court, especially those who looked for preferment, tended to support the King. But there were dissenters. Both Bishop Fisher and Thomas More, men well respected for their opinions, told Harry that they believed his marriage to be lawful. Even Warham was unsure of his position. He had been one of those who had long ago advised his master not to marry Katherine, and the Pope's dispensation had not entirely set his mind at rest, as now became clear. He was sufficiently the King's man to endorse Harry seeking to have the validity of his marriage established.

'However displeasantly the Queen might take it, the truth and judgement of the law must be followed,' he told Tom.

To Harry's dismay, his sister Mary supported the Queen, of whom she was very fond. Her husband, Suffolk, supported the King, which probably did not make for marital harmony. And although Suffolk owed much to Tom, who had intervened to save his neck in the wake of his ill-advised marriage, he now showed himself more hostile than ever towards him, evidently believing – as so many seemed to do – that he was the one who had instilled these doubts in Harry's mind. It grieved Tom to see the Duke ingratiating himself with Norfolk and the Boleyns.

Tom had become aware of the increasing hostility of Norfolk and his brother-in-law, Lord Rochford. The Howards had never liked him, but the attempts to undermine him in Council, verbally or strategically, were growing ever more vicious. It concerned him deeply because Norfolk was hugely influential, being considered by his colleagues as a man of the utmost wisdom, solid worth and loyalty to his sovereign.

Tom found it hard to believe that this granite-faced martinet had such qualities. He saw in the Duke only ruthless antagonism and overweening ambition.

Norfolk made no secret of his belief that Tom was preventing him and other peers of the older nobility from enjoying the power that should be theirs by right of birth. He was supported in this by Rochford, a new man if ever there was one, yet linked to the Howards by marriage and therefore a strong ally. Rochford was still bitter at having been forced to resign his post of treasurer without any financial compensation, and at being briefly ousted from the Privy Chamber. For these things, he blamed Tom, with some justification.

Of late, however, Tom had become aware that there was a third prominent person in the Howard faction. He had seen Anne Boleyn with Norfolk and Rochford, noted the hostile stares as he passed, and heard her strident voice ringing out behind him, leaving him in no doubt that, given the slight he had dealt her over the Percy affair, she was no friend to him. But what ill could a mere girl like that do to him, the mighty Cardinal of York?

And then, by chance, gazing out of his closet window, pondering some knotty problem, he saw her with the King in the garden below. Harry was trying to kiss her, but she was pulling away, laughing.

Tom smiled grimly. So that was how it was. The young lady was playing hard to get. But she would give in in the end, like the others. And she would go the way of Harry's other mistresses. If she thought to use her brief burst of influence against him, the King's chief minister, she must think again, for Harry never allowed his women to dabble in politics. In fact, he kept them very much in the background. So if Mistress Anne thought to plot against him with her father and her uncle of Norfolk, she must have an inflated sense of her own importance.

When he was closeted together with Harry the next morning, he was aware that Harry was preoccupied. They were discussing the terrible situation in Rome and its implications when he suddenly said, 'Thomas, I need your advice on a personal matter.'

Tom leaned back in his chair. 'What can I do for your Grace?'

The King flushed. 'I have spoken with a young lady who has the soul of an angel and a spirit worthy of a crown – but she will not look kindly on me.'

Tom knew what that meant. She would not sleep with him. He assumed the young lady was Anne Boleyn, whose sister had not been so angelic. Tom suspected that the daughter Mary Boleyn had borne her husband was actually the King's. She was Harry to the life.

'I take it that your Grace has offered to honour her with your love?'

Harry nodded.

'Well then, if she is worthy of a king's love, becoming your mistress should be sufficient honour for her.'

'She is not of ordinary clay,' sighed Harry, 'and I fear she will never condescend in that way.'

Tom smiled knowingly. 'Great princes, if they choose to play the lover, have means of softening hearts of steel. I think your Grace does not need me to give advice on that. Write her love letters, songs and poetry, give her gifts. She will come around.'

And then, he thought, Harry would tire of her. It was the thrill of the chase that captivated him. In the meantime, reasoning that it was prudent to keep your enemies close, he decided that he would do his best to be a friend to Mistress Anne; in so doing, he would please as well the King as her.

'Maybe your Grace would like to bring her to a banquet or a feast at York Place?' he suggested.

Harry's face lit up. 'That's a capital idea, Thomas! But a private banquet, I think. I don't want this affair becoming common knowledge. Anne would not stand for that.'

So that was how it was, Tom thought uneasily.

She sat queening it at the high table, in the place of honour on the King's right. Tom, seated to his left, had to admit that she looked very becoming in her green gown with its hanging sleeves. And she had been cordiality itself since she had arrived. Yet he was not deceived; there was no warmth there. She was dissimulating; he had caught the knowing glances between her, Norfolk and Rochford, whom he had invited too. He was glad that they could all see how openly affectionate Harry was being towards him and hear him warmly expressing his gratitude for the evening's lavish hospitality. Let them all know how important his friend was to the King, and that there was no chance of that solid rapport between them being undermined.

Chapter 29

1527

Tom was for France. He and Harry were confident that King Francis would be willing to join them in pressing for Pope Clement's liberation, and to support Harry's bid for an annulment, especially – Tom said – if it freed Harry to marry a French princess and enabled him to break his ties to Spain.

He had not planned to visit Francis in person – he would have preferred to stay in England at the hub of affairs – but the lords of the Council insisted, and in this he could perceive the malice of Norfolk and his allies. 'No one is more fit to take upon him the King's commission and travel beyond the seas in this matter,' the Duke said, 'and it is a mission that needs your Eminence's high discretion, wit and authority to bring to pass a perfect outcome.'

Tom was no fool. It was a ruse devised to remove him from daily contact with the King and get him out of the realm, so that they could complain of him to Harry in his absence and oust him from favour. And they had already got at Harry, clearly.

'It is the King's command that you go,' Suffolk said, 'so you must prepare for the journey.'

Tom obeyed, with a heavy heart. His outward purpose was to discuss arrangements for the marriage of the Princess Mary with the Duke of Orléans, and suggest a marriage for the King with Renée of Valois, daughter of the late King Louis.

He summoned Cromwell to his closet and told him that he was going away. 'Master Cromwell, you know how matters stand between me and Mistress Anne's faction. While I am in France, can I depend on you to look after my interests here and inform me at once if there are any adverse developments?'

'You can rely on me,' the lawyer said, and laid a reassuring hand on Tom's shoulder. He had never made such a gesture before, and Tom suddenly felt comforted. He knew he had a true friend in this den of wolves that was the court.

At the beginning of July, he left York Place and rode through the City of London, resplendent in his sumptuous scarlet robes, his mule trapped with crimson velvet, his stirrups of copper and gilt. He was preceded by a great number of gentlemen riding three abreast, all garbed in black velvet coats with great chains of gold about their necks. Among them was the faithful Cavendish, on whom he was beginning to rely in so many ways. Behind him followed his yeomen and servants, wearing French-style tawny livery, with a cardinal's hat and the initials T. and C. for 'Thomas Cardinalis' embroidered on both back and breast, ahead of twelve hundred mounted lords and gentlemen. The procession was guarded by a veritable regiment carrying longbows and spears. It crossed London Bridge and proceeded towards Dartford, where Tom and his train were to lodge that night in the house of Sir Richard Wiltshire.

The next day, he rode to Rochester, and stayed in the Bishop's Palace. He was entertained to dinner by Bishop Fisher, who told him that the Queen had asked for his counsel. They discussed the Great Matter at length, as Harry had instructed, hoping that Tom would change the Bishop's opinion.

'You should know that the Queen is acting very suspiciously and casting further doubts than his Grace ever meant or intended,' he said to the Bishop. 'And she has, by her behaviour, her words and the messages she has sent to several people, made the matter more public.'

'Well, I greatly blame the Queen for that,' Fisher said, surprising him. 'I will expostulate with her for her wilfulness and disobedience. You may rest assured that I will do nothing but what stands with the King's pleasure.'

'I rather thought you supported her Grace's view,' Tom said.

Fisher frowned. 'Yes, but I do not like the publicity she is courting.'

Tom smiled to himself. *I think he will change his opinion*, he wrote to Harry that night.

He made several stops along the road to Dover, and at each he was received splendidly. At Canterbury, on the feast day of St Thomas Becket, he joined a solemn procession, wearing his legatine regalia and his cardinal's hat. At his command, the monks sang a litany praying for the Virgin Mary to liberate Pope Clement, during which Tom knelt at the entrance to the choir, weeping for the plight of the Holy Father — and, inwardly, at the thought of what mischief his enemies might be making in his absence.

Despite the blessing of a swift, smooth crossing from Dover to Calais, he suffered from seasickness and was feeling rather queasy when he was received in procession by the town fathers of Calais. Gratefully, he knelt by the Lantern Gate and offered up prayers before making his entry into the town. Steeling himself against the rising tide of nausea, he rose and walked on, with everyone going before him, singing songs of praise, to St Mary's church, where he stood at the high altar facing the people, gave them his benediction and absolved them from their sins. Afterwards, he was conducted to the Checker, the royal residence where he was to stay. Thankfully, he closed the door of the sumptuous bedchamber, stripped off all his clothes and crawled into bed, still feeling sick.

An hour or so later, Cavendish woke him.

'My lord, Monsieur du Biez, the Captain of Boulogne, is here with a number of gallant gentlemen. I have arranged for them to dine with you.'

Tom groaned, but after he had arisen and washed, he felt better, well enough to play the congenial host to the Frenchmen. Over the next few days, he received regular visits from French nobles and was able to establish a friendly rapport with them, which he knew would stand him in good stead when he met with their master. Already, King Francis had conferred on him several honours and the great privilege of pardoning and releasing prisoners and delinquents confined in the towns through which he was to pass, as if he were the King himself. The only wretches to be excluded from this amnesty were those guilty of capital crimes.

The next morning, Tom rode out of Calais with his vast train, all the spearmen of Calais escorting him. They rode in driving rain to Sangatte, then pressed on through Picardy. King Francis had ordered the Captain of Picardy, with a great number of men-at-arms, to accompany him on his journey, for both he and Tom feared that the Emperor might have laid some kind of ambush. But Tom reached the town of Boulogne without incident and was warmly received. The next morning, after Mass, he pressed on to Montreuil, where he was welcomed with speeches and pageants.

'*Le Cardinal pacifique!*' the people cried. It was the same in Abbeville. There, for the next eight days, he was lodged in the stately brick house where King Louis had married Harry's sister. He spent much of his time entertaining local lords and dignitaries.

He had heard nothing of concern from Cromwell, yet as the days flew by and he passed further into France, staying at abbeys, noble chateaux and inns, his fears about what might be happening in his absence deepened. Who knew what Mistress Anne and her acolytes were saying to Harry in private? He wrote to his friends in England, asking what the King was doing and who was with him, and was dismayed when Cromwell reported that Harry was on progress, hunting by day and supping with Norfolk, Suffolk and Rochford every evening. It was hardly reassuring. A year ago, Tom would have relished his mission; now, he could not wait to get back to England to repair whatever damage had been done.

To his consternation, the King's Great Matter was common knowledge in France. He heard the rumours with dismay, deploring the fact that such a delicate subject was being bandied about in taverns and churches. It was widely anticipated that the King of England would be marrying a French princess, a prospect that raised much excitement. It was what Tom was hoping for himself, so he was disconcerted to be given, on arrival at his night's lodging, a letter from Harry forbidding him to raise any question of remarriage when he spoke with King Francis.

He stood there shaking in the rustic bedchamber, hurt that Harry had not told him as much before he left court. He had thought that the King was interested in a nuptial alliance; it had been one of the main reasons for this embassy. Somehow, he sensed that this about-turn boded no good to himself. Had Harry changed his mind about taking a second wife? Surely, he had not decided to abandon his nullity suit? He would have said so and summoned Tom home. So clearly, he still wanted King Francis's support. And he needed a son to succeed him. Who, therefore, was he thinking of marrying?

No, Tom said to himself, dropping the letter. It could not be Anne Boleyn! Even Harry would not be so blinded by love – or lust – as to think that she would make a suitable queen. A mere knight's daughter! He would have laughed if he had not been so distressed. But he recalled that Harry's grandfather, Edward IV, had married a commoner, and caused a great scandal, for it was then unheard of for a king to wed for love. Monarchs married for policy, to make alliances and gain prestige. Why would Harry throw away such an advantage?

Well, he wouldn't – of course he wouldn't! A thousand voices would be raised in protest. And there was another matter, a serious impediment to such a marriage. Had the King not realised that marrying Anne would place him in exactly the same situation as he was now with Katherine? He would be asking the Pope to dispense with the same impediment! Any union with Anne could never be valid, for her sister had borne him a child.

Yet Tom knew Harry. When the King wanted something, he went the whole way. And if he wanted Anne Boleyn . . .

Intuition told Tom that his master might well contemplate such an act of folly, and the prospect turned his veins to ice. Marrying Anne would be a disaster, not only for Harry and England, but also for him, Tom. She was his enemy. If he carried on working his guts out to obtain an annulment for the King, he might well be bringing about his own downfall.

But he had no choice. His loyalty to Harry and his sense of self-preservation were such that, even though he knew the King's case to be based on spurious arguments, he would continue to spare no efforts to secure the desired annulment, whatever the consequences, if only to please his beloved master.

Quivering with stress, he sat down and wrote a letter telling the King that he was occupied with solving his problems as if it were his only means of obtaining Heaven. Harry replied that he trusted, by Tom's diligence, shortly to be eased out of his present trouble. There was something of a command in the tone of the letter. It gave Tom further cause for anxiety.

His consternation deepened the following night when, arriving at a priory guest house, saddle-sore and tired after a long day's journey, he received a letter from Cromwell informing him that Anne and her supporters were constantly with the King. It seemed they were dripping poison into his ear. They had made no secret of their belief that Tom, far from working to secure an annulment, was secretly doing his utmost to prevent the Pope from granting one.

Tom prayed that Harry would not credit such nonsense. But Harry, he knew, was very suggestible. Once a doubt was planted in his mind, it could easily take root. But surely their long friendship counted for something?

At Picquigny Castle, above the waters of the Somme, Tom learned that the French King was approaching Amiens, six miles away. Two days later, he rode there on his mule.

Informed that Francis was nearby, he alighted at an old chapel by the road and had his gentlemen dress him in his finest robes, then, with a quarter of an hour to spare, he mounted a fresh mule trapped with crimson velvet and a deep fringe of gold. He dug in his stirrups and rode forward to greet the King, drawing to a halt within a few yards of him.

Francis, royally garbed in purple, nodded courteously in his direction and sent a nobleman, who dismounted and made reverence to Tom, asking the cause of his visit.

'To discuss our peace,' Tom replied, whereupon the young man rode back to the King, who then advanced forward. They came together, embracing each other on horseback, smiling warmly.

'Come, my friend,' Francis said. 'Ride with me to Amiens!'

The members of both retinues raced to greet each other as if they were old friends. The press was so thick that some had their legs crushed by horses and had to be rescued by their fellows and hauled away, yelling for help. It was a miracle that no one was killed. But the French were unheeding.

'*Marche, marche, devant, allez devant!*' the King's officers cried, and Francis, with Tom on his right hand, spurred his mount. Behind them, every uninjured English gentleman was riding next to a gentleman of France; the train, Tom heard later, stretched for two long miles. At Amiens, they were nobly received with a gun salute and costly pageants, after which Francis escorted Tom to his lodging in the Bishop's Palace and left him to rest after his journey.

The next day after dinner, accompanied by his retinue, Tom rode to the King's residence, but was disconcerted to be told that he was ill in bed. Nevertheless, Francis received Tom in his bedchamber, where he was attended by his mother, Madame Louise, the Cardinal of Lorraine and many French noblemen. Only pleasantries were exchanged, and after drinking a cup of wine with Louise, Tom returned to his lodging.

They got down to business the next day, and continued their discussions over the following fortnight, with time off for feasting and entertainments.

'I am most desirous to have the Princess Mary wed my son, and to have her delivered into my hands as soon as possible,' Francis said. They were sitting on a balcony overlooking the lists, where the champions of France were showing off their prowess.

'My master is as eager for the marriage as your Majesty,' Tom said. 'But I pray you, let us leave the final arrangements until another day. I have a weightier matter to discuss, if I may crave your indulgence. A most sensitive matter.'

'So sensitive that it is bruited about the whole kingdom.' Francis smiled that foxy smile of his. 'We shall discuss it in greater privacy at Compiègne, where I ride tomorrow. You are to be lodged in the castle, where I myself will be staying.'

Tom was flattered, and even more pleased when he found that his apartments were connected to the King's by a gallery, in the middle of which was a wall with a door and a window. There, he and Francis met many times and secretly conversed together, and soon they were visiting each other's chambers, deep in discussion – and not always amicably. But, for all Tom's efforts, the French King would not commit to writing to the Pope in support of Harry's nullity suit.

'You must understand that, having been awarded the title of "Most Christian King" by his Holiness, I have my position to consider,' he had said, when Tom first broached the subject.

'May I remind your Majesty that my master also has a title, "Defender of the Faith", and that it sits ill with that for him to be bound in an invalid marriage. All he is asking is that Rome resolves his doubts. A word from your Majesty would work wonders, and counteract the prejudiced arguments of our mutual enemy, the Emperor.'

'Who has the Pope in thrall,' Francis said drily. 'I am not sure we can do much to rescue him, short of making war on Charles.'

'I am in no doubt that his Holiness is terrified of his Imperial Majesty,' Tom declared.

'I am considering how best to secure his release,' the King said.

'Your Majesty's support will be a great comfort to him – as it would be to my master if you could see your way to backing him.'

'I will think on it,' Francis promised. So far, he had gone no further.

Again, there was laid on for Tom an endless round of festivities and feasts, even a boar hunt, which Harry would have loved.

'I shall have a boar sent to your King so that he can hunt it,' Francis said, after Tom told him that boars were extinct in England.

As they were riding back to the castle, he leaned over in his saddle. 'I have received a certain book, in which it is written that your Eminence has come here to conclude the marriage between the Princess Mary and my son, and propose another between your King and my kinswoman Madame Renée. I know not where this book came from. It is written in French and was found in my chapel. It seems strange that you have said nothing about your master marrying Madame Renée. Or is it just gossip?'

Tom was wondering who had given the book to Francis and where it had come from. Was someone trying to undermine him in Harry's eyes? He wished he had more spies in France; in England, he could quickly have learned who the culprit was. But this was like punching in the dark. Renée had indeed been the princess Tom had had in mind for Harry, but only a few people had been privy to his plan. Had one of them leaked the information?

He knew better now than to tell Francis what his intentions had been. 'It is a fantasy, Sire.'

He wished it wasn't. He had seen Madame Renée and knew she would have made an excellent queen, born royal as she was, unlike Anne. As he returned to his rooms, he was telling himself yet again that Harry would never contemplate making Anne queen. The idea was absurd! But even if his thoughts did not tend that far, she still had a strong hold over him. And she hated Tom. He wished that Harry would hurry up and bed her and get her out of his system, like he had the women before her. It was demeaning, a king being led by the loins like that.

Yet the tone of Harry's letters had been as loving as ever, and Tom tried again to persuade himself that his passion for the woman would soon subside, and that he himself had got carried away by an overactive imagination. No doubt Harry had thought of another advantageous marriage alliance and wanted to discuss it with him on his return.

He was feeling more positive – until the day he entered his bedchamber and found that some lewd person had engraved on the window a cardinal's hat and a gallows, with something written beneath it that did not bear repetition. It chilled him to the bone. Was it a threat? Or evidence that someone was aware that his mission to elicit Francis's support had failed?

He called urgently for Cavendish. 'Have you seen this, George?'

The usher stared at the window. 'By St Mary, my lord, who did that?'

'I wish I knew.' Tom's mouth set in a grim line. Someone in his train was in the pay of the Boleyns, he was sure.

* * *

The farewells had been said, and now it was time to go home. Riding northwards to Calais, Tom's thoughts turned to Joan, as they had often done lately. He had heard nothing more from her. Did she know he was abroad? Would there be a letter waiting when he returned. Miracles did happen. But did she not want him to help her? The thought tortured him. He was beginning to doubt that she would ever leave Legh and that they would ever be reunited.

He had wondered if he could make time to go to Paris to see Thomas, but when he was told that it was ninety miles away, he knew he could not fit it into his busy schedule. Maybe it was as well, since he might not be able to restrain himself from criticising the lad's extravagance. But, oh, how he wished he could see him and hold him in his arms.

After docking at Dover, Tom made straight for Richmond Palace, his heart pounding at the thought of the reception that awaited him.

When he arrived, as was his usual custom, he sent Cavendish to Harry with a message requesting a private audience to discuss his mission. Where would his master be pleased to receive him?

Cavendish was back in the antechamber within minutes, looking disconcerted. 'My lord, I delivered your message, but Mistress Anne Boleyn was with the King, and she said to tell you that you must come to him.'

Tom clenched his fists. 'But my business necessitates a private audience. Did his Grace not gainsay her?'

'No, my lord.' Cavendish looked distressed – but nowhere near as distressed as Tom felt. Anne had put him in his place and made him look like a petitioner; she had challenged his power, and she had done it very publicly. His heart plummeting, he sensed that this was the beginning of a bitter power struggle, and feared that, given her evident hold upon Harry, he would be the loser.

As he walked towards the hall, the buzz of chatter and music grew louder. When the doors opened for him, silence descended, and he was aware of a hundred pairs of eyes on him as he bowed, walked towards the dais and bowed again. It was humiliating to be received like any other courtier, with his enemies looking on triumphantly, but

Harry received him genially, as the smile froze on Anne's face. She was seated next to him at the high table – not in the empty Queen's chair, thankfully – looking alluring in costly black velvet and pearls. Harry could not keep his hands off her. While he was greeting Tom, his fingers were caressing her fingers or her cheek.

'The treaty is concluded, your Grace,' Tom said.

'I am gratified to hear it.' Harry beamed. 'And the other matter?'

'If your Grace would care to discuss that in private . . .'

'Of course. Attend me in my closet,' Harry said amiably. Anne's eyes shot daggers at him, but he ignored her, rose and left, with Tom at his heels.

The amiable mask lifted when Tom, quailing, admitted that his mission had failed.

'I fear that support from King Francis in your Grace's matter will not be forthcoming.' All grist to Anne's mill, no doubt. 'I could not break his resolve to remain neutral.'

'That is perhaps as well,' Harry said slowly. 'For I have resolved to marry Mistress Anne Boleyn as soon as I am free.'

Tom gaped at him. His worst fears had been realised. 'Your Grace, you cannot!' His chest felt so tight that he feared he might have a seizure.

'No one tells me what I can or cannot do,' Harry said sternly. 'Kings are answerable only to God.'

Tom was frantic. 'But kings do not marry their mistresses – they marry for policy! And they marry those of royal blood. Mistress Anne, whatever her virtues, is a commoner.'

Harry clenched his fists. 'She is not my mistress. And my grandfather, King Edward IV of happy memory, married a commoner, who proved an excellent and fruitful queen.'

'Nevertheless, Sir, I beg of you to reconsider. You have not asked her yet, I trust?'

'I have, and she has accepted. And that is an end to the matter, my lord Cardinal. Do not offend me by trying to dissuade me. My mind is made up.'

Tom could not speak. It wasn't just because of this terrible news; it was the way Harry was looking at him, as if he was a stranger who had crossed him.

'You will continue to support me in this matter?' the King barked.

'I am your Grace's humble servant,' Tom replied, mustering a weak smile. 'You can rely on me.' Inside, his heart was pounding.

That night, he called upon Cromwell to confer with him, and they seated themselves on a window seat in his private gallery at York Place, with the light from the candles reflecting in the diamond window panes.

'The King means to marry Anne Boleyn,' Tom said. 'Did you know of this?'

'I had a suspicion,' Cromwell declared, his thickset brows beetling. 'But I reported to you what I knew, that she and her family were spending a lot of time with him. I did not know he had gone that far.'

'He can't marry her,' Tom said agitatedly. 'It would be a disaster for him and for the kingdom. He would be throwing away a great political advantage – and all for lust!'

'I fear there is more to it than lust,' Cromwell opined. 'I have been watching them together. He is mad with love for her, like a man obsessed.'

'And she's still saying no, I imagine.'

Cromwell paused. 'That's the thing. I'm sure that she did say no, but the word is that he is now holding off because he can't risk an illicit pregnancy. Of course, his Queen must be virtuous.'

Tom snorted with contempt. 'Are we supposed to believe that Anne Boleyn is virtuous when she spent seven years at the court of France? It's said that no maiden ever leaves that court unravished.' He sighed. 'But no doubt our sovereign lord believes it. Love, Master Cromwell, is blind – and dangerous in this case.'

'But while his Grace is so besotted, your Eminence cannot counteract her influence.'

'No – and she hates me. She made it plain today that she means to oust me from my place as the King's chief counsellor and confidant. Well, she has met her match.'

* * *

He knew he must do something to re-establish his supremacy at court. So many had witnessed his humiliation, and he had to disabuse them of any notions that his power was waning. So he summoned all the noblemen, judges and justices of the peace who were present at Westminster to an assembly in the Star Chamber, and addressed them, aware of Norfolk and Rochford standing at the front, not bothering to hide their hostility.

He rose from his chair on the dais. 'My lords and masters, I have called you here today to inform you of the outcome of my embassy into France, where the King of France showed himself to be heartily bound with this realm in our new alliance, which is enshrined in the new Treaty of Perpetual Peace. Now there shall be such friendship between England and France, and trade, that it shall seem to all men that the two kingdoms are but one monarchy. Gentlemen, you may now travel quietly from one country to another for your recreation and pastime; and merchants can travel about their affairs in peace and tranquillity, so that this realm shall prosper for ever.'

He was watching them keenly to judge their reactions and was grateful when most of them applauded. He saw Norfolk and Rochford look at each other and shrug. Dismissing everyone graciously, he departed into the dining chamber to eat with the lords of the Council.

In October, a great French embassy came to England, more than eighty of the noblest and worthiest gentlemen of France. The peace treaty was signed in St Paul's Cathedral. Tom, the King and all the Frenchmen, accompanied by many lords of England, proceeded to the high altar, where Tom, as Papal legate, celebrated a solemn Mass, assisted by twenty-four mitred bishops and abbots. In that moment, he felt invincible once again. He was the arbiter of peace, an international statesman. Surely no one, even Mistress Anne Boleyn, could touch him.

After the last Agnus Dei, the King rose and knelt on a cushion before the high altar; and the Grand Master of France, the chief French ambassador, fell to his knees beside him. Tom divided the sacrament between them, and they received it with firm oaths and assurances that they would observe this perpetual peace. After Mass, Tom read out the terms of the treaty, in both English and French, and the King subscribed his signature, while the Grand Master did likewise for King Francis. Then the treaty was sealed, to resounding applause that echoed to the four corners of the mighty cathedral.

Afterwards, Harry and the ambassadors dined with Tom at York Place, and there was much talk of weighty matters concerning the new peace, with many toasts offered. Then Harry took his barge back to Greenwich, having invited his guests to go hunting in Richmond Park.

'You must all come to Hampton Court too,' Tom said. 'It will be my pleasure to entertain you to supper.' Already he was planning how to impress on them – and his enemies – his importance, with a lavish display of wealth and abundance, and the resources he had to produce a great feast at a moment's notice. How he loved being at the centre of affairs! It was the breath of life to him.

Tom hoped that the envoys had not heard the bruits that were raging around London. The King's love affair with Anne Boleyn was now common knowledge and the subject of furious speculation, and there was nothing he or Tom could do to stop the rumour mill. Tom deplored the fact that Harry was so amorously affectionate, that he had lost all sense of discretion. He seemed to be gripped by a kind of madness. He could not stop speaking of his darling, could not bear to be apart from her, and she knew it, for she was always shooting back to Hever Castle, her family home in Kent, leaving him in anguish.

Some conjectured that she had succumbed to his advances, but Tom knew differently. Harry was too worried about getting her with child, which would be a disaster, given that he was ready to proclaim her virtue as loudly as he could to the Pope and anyone else who would listen. But, of course, people preferred a scandal – as if the case was not scandalous enough already.

There came a day when Harry looked up from the report he was reading, laid it down and looked shiftily at Tom. His fair face had flushed a deep red.

'Thomas, I am in a dilemma. I once dallied briefly with Mistress

Anne's sister, and I fear it has created the same barrier to my marriage to her as that which impeded my union with the Queen. Would it be possible to obtain a dispensation from the Pope?'

Tom took a deep breath. 'There is no harm in asking,' he said smoothly, eager to show Harry that he was always ready to do him a service and trying not to dwell on the staggering implications. 'We can send an envoy on a secret mission to Rome to obtain such a dispensation.'

'My new secretary, Dr Knight, could go,' Harry suggested. 'He is reliable and discreet.'

'A good choice, Sir. And while he is there, he could apply to the Pope for a general commission that would give me, as Papal legate, the authority to examine your Great Matter. My findings could then be submitted to his Holiness, who would hopefully act upon them, and the Queen would have no right of appeal.'

Harry grinned. 'That sounds perfect, Thomas! I knew I could rely on you.'

'I will write to the Pope today,' Tom said.

He wrote an impassioned letter asking for Clement to dispense with the awkward matter of Mary Carey, and urging him to grant an annulment. He made every effort to convince him that his predecessor's dispensation was void as the marriage clearly disobeyed the injunction in Leviticus, and begged that, as Papal legate, he be allowed to judge the case.

What am I doing? he asked himself, as he laid down his pen. He knew the King's case to be weak; the marriage was valid, and Leviticus had no bearing on it. But he loved Harry like a son and could deny him nothing, even to the point of compromising his own integrity and honesty. And, in truth, he dared not do anything else, because the King would brook no refusal from anyone, and Tom had too much to lose.

But it was wrong, wrong! Clement would surely know that too and wonder why Cardinal Wolsey was pressing him to overturn the just dispensation of his predecessor and authorise the King to marry within the forbidden degrees of consanguinity.

Tom's conscience drove him to his chapel, where he knelt before the crucifix and began praying for forgiveness. God would surely understand why he was doing this, and his fear of the consequences if he failed his master. And he was not the one who would be ruling on the King's case. The responsibility was Pope Clement's. If Clement did as Harry wished, all would be well, and Tom would be safe, for even Mistress Anne would surely be overwhelmed with gratitude for the crown he had brought her. He knew he was putting self-interest before moral duty, but he had no choice! God must know that.

Dr Knight was going to Italy with Gregory Casale, an Italian who had become an English diplomat. Before they left, Tom summoned them to his chamber and impressed upon them the delicacy and import of their mission. 'You are to say that the King is absolutely resolved to satisfy his conscience, and that he had never wished to wed the Lady Katherine.' An outright lie. 'The King's friendship is of the utmost necessity to the Pope, so I hope that his Holiness will find a way to ease his conscience. I urge you to stress to him the vehement desire of the whole nation and the nobility that the King should have an heir. And pray tell the Holy Father that, if he grants what the King is asking for, his Grace is ready to declare war against the Emperor to procure his freedom from bondage.'

He picked up two documents. 'To make things easier for his Holiness and bring the whole business to a speedy resolution, I have drafted two dispensations, one annulling the marriage, the other authorising a second, to which he need only affix his signature and seal.'

When the envoys had gone, he sank down by the hearth, his head in his hands. Cavendish, who had become such a support to him of late, laid a hand on his shoulder. 'Are you feeling unwell, my lord?'

Tom looked up at him. 'You heard what was said just now. If the Pope is not compliant, my life will only get worse.'

'I wish I could ease your Eminence's mind,' Cavendish murmured. 'Alas, I have not the power, but I will fetch you a heartening goblet of ale.'

If only there *was* someone who could help him. Tom sat there, praying that Knight and Casale were forceful enough in their arguments.

A month later, he was dismayed to hear from Casale that the Pope wanted Harry to take matters into his own hands, have Tom pronounce a divorce, and remarry; then Clement would confirm the second marriage, and so judgement would have been passed to the satisfaction of all – as long as no one guessed that the idea came from Clement himself.

Harry was furious. 'If he's happy to do that, why doesn't he do it himself? If you pronounce my marriage invalid and the Emperor doesn't like it, he could put pressure on the Pope to revoke your judgement. Tell Casale I won't agree to this. I have the future stability of the succession to consider!'

Tom informed Knight and Casale of the King's response, then instructed them to ask Clement if he would appoint a fellow legate with power to pronounce judgement on the King's case and send him to England to try it jointly with Tom. He suggested Cardinal Campeggio. 'He is one of the best and most learned men alive.'

He was disappointed to hear that Clement had said he could not spare Campeggio, and that, despite all that Harry had said, his Holiness had again hinted that Tom should pronounce the divorce himself and seek Papal confirmation afterwards. It seemed that the Holy Father was determined to frustrate the King at every turn.

In December, Tom invited the King to dine in private and was surprised when Harry said that he was bringing Queen Katherine with him. He rarely dined with her these days, and Tom suspected that he was anticipating a confrontation and wanted moral support.

As he donned his robes, he sighed. Outwardly, Katherine had shown a patient face to the world and remained as affectionate as ever towards Harry, and courteous beyond belief to Anne Boleyn. But behind the scenes, his spies kept telling him, she was active in opposing the nullity suit, and Tom was hard put to it to keep her in isolation. She was a tenacious woman, convinced that she had right on her side, and she had made it very clear that she was not going to submit patiently to being put away.

The worst thing was that she was right. Tom was aware that, in pressing for an annulment, he was doing her a great injury, whereas Harry really was suffering a crisis of conscience and could not accept that his marriage was valid. Of course, he was blinded by love for Anne, but his doubts were sincere, Tom was sure of it.

The atmosphere in the dining chamber was tense. Katherine had greeted Tom civilly enough, but he guessed that she would have preferred to see Harry alone.

It was late, dinner was over and the candles were burning low. So far, they had kept only to pleasantries and innocuous subjects of conversation. Tom was warming his hands at the fire when Katherine finally opened her mind.

'I hear that you have sent an embassy to Rome,' she said.

'It is no secret,' Harry replied stiffly. 'I have sent again to enquire as to whether the dispensation issued by Pope Julius is sufficient, for I believe it was founded on certain false suggestions.'

'What false suggestions?'

Tom hastened to intervene. 'Madam, the King is absolutely resolved to satisfy his conscience. He never wished for this marriage.'

'That is a lie!' she cried, rounding on Harry. 'My lord, surely you will refute that?'

Harry looked uncomfortable. 'All I hope for, Madam, is that the Pope will ease my conscience.'

'The Pope will never consent to our marriage being annulled,' Katherine insisted.

'If Your Grace is thinking that the Emperor's will holds sway in Rome, you are mistaken,' Tom said. 'I have assured his Holiness that, if he grants what the King asks, his Grace is ready to declare war on the Emperor to procure the freedom of the Holy Father.'

Her eyes flashed. 'You are the cause of all this trouble, my lord

Cardinal!' she cried. Before he could answer, she rose, made a curtsey to the King and swept from the room, leaving the two of them gaping at each other.

'I must disabuse her of that, by your leave,' Tom said, and hurried after her. He caught up with her in the moonlit gallery. 'Madam, I beg of you to hear me,' he pleaded breathlessly. 'I did not seek this divorce. It is the King's will. I have no choice but to do as he bids me. If the Pope is not compliant, my very life will be at stake, and I dread to anticipate the consequences.'

She looked at him uncertainly. She must have detected the desperation in his voice.

'I am not your enemy, Madam,' he went on, knowing how much he had wronged her. 'You have my sympathy, and your daughter. If it were up to me, I would not be putting his Holiness in this impossible position. Disrespect for the Papacy is growing daily, and it worries me that this Great Matter will only make things worse. And if the King declares war on the Emperor – believe me, it will happen in the next few weeks, if his Imperial Majesty puts pressure on his Holiness – your position will be even more precarious. I would not add wood to the fire. But Mistress Anne and her friends have undermined my influence with the King. He does not always listen to me these days, yet he needs me, for he knows that if anyone can get him what he wants, I can. So my hands are tied.'

'We all do as we must,' Katherine said, 'and you have much to lose if you forfeit his favour.'

'As do we all, Madam. I am aware of that. And now I must go, for I cannot risk being seen talking privily with you at length. The King will be coming to find out where I am. I wish you a good night.'

He wished he had bitten his tongue and said nothing. There was a chance that, in a heated argument with Harry, the Queen might betray his confidences, which could spell disaster. With Anne and her faction doing their utmost to undermine his influence with the King, the last thing he wanted was for Harry to think he was working against him. He kept reassuring himself that Harry still needed him, that he knew him to be the most able of his ministers and the only man capable of securing an annulment.

As the winter days dragged on with no further news from Rome, Tom took himself down to Hampton Court. He toyed with the idea of visiting Joan at Thames Ditton, for he needed to unburden himself to her, but Cavendish reported that the house was shut up and the steward had said that the master and mistress were away visiting family in Lancashire.

In a fever of anxiety, Tom took to bombarding the envoys in Rome with instructions, promises, threats and inducements.

When, oh, when would Clement speak?

Chapter 30

1528

The news that came from Rome in the new year was not good. Full of dread, Tom sought a meeting with the King. When he stood before him in his closet, he was shaking – he, who had always showed to the world an effortlessly confident, urbane manner.

'I have received a report from our envoys,' he said. 'The good news is that the Pope has negotiated his freedom with the Emperor, but it appears that he is still in fear of him, and reluctant to provoke him by furthering your Grace's suit.' He took a deep breath. 'I fear he has said that he feels unable to annul your marriage at this time.'

Harry looked like a lion ready to pounce. 'Then *when* will he feel able to do so?'

'Sir, I think he wants me to give a ruling, for he is sending me a general commission.'

The lion subsided. 'Surely that's excellent news?'

'Sir, I still fear that his Holiness could overturn any decision I might give.'

'He's hardly likely to do that if he's armed you with a commission,' Harry pointed out.

'He might if the Emperor puts pressure on him. So, with your consent, I am going to ask again for Cardinal Campeggio to be sent as legate to England to give judgement with me. Then I can never be accused of bias.'

'You think the Holy Father will agree?'

'I am assured that he is eager to please your Grace. Indeed, we have proof of that, for he has issued a dispensation enabling you to remarry within the prohibited degrees should your first marriage be declared unlawful.'

'That's something, I suppose,' Harry said dejectedly. 'Of course, it's worthless if I am denied an annulment. Oh, Thomas, I grow sick of all these delays. When is this matter going to be resolved?'

'Very soon, I hope,' Tom assured him, praying that it would be. 'I will do all in my power to help your Grace.'

'I know that, Thomas.' Harry clapped him on the back. 'No one could be working harder on my behalf.'

Tom felt guilty, knowing he could have agreed to take a risk and give judgement himself. It was the first time he had denied his master anything.

'In reward,' Harry was saying, 'I am granting you a licence to establish a college in Ipswich. I know you have long desired that.'

'I thank your Grace!' Tom said, feeling even more guilty, and relieved too, because of late he had wondered if Harry's munificent generosity to him was drying up.

In late January, England and France declared war on the Emperor, in accordance with the terms of their treaty. It was an unpopular move in England because it threatened lucrative trade links with the Low Countries, and the London merchants were in a fury.

Harry made no preparations for war. The gauntlet had been thrown down merely as a warning to Charles not to interfere with the Papacy. Anyway, the King was too preoccupied with his Great Matter, which had continued to polarise opinions at court. Many of Tom's friends and allies openly supported the King. The older nobility and those with Plantagenet blood discreetly backed the Queen and would certainly relish the backlash if Tom failed Harry. And the Boleyn faction, which was now the most influential, seemed determined to break his monopoly on power. Tom believed that Norfolk and Suffolk, having long plotted his downfall, saw in Anne a means of achieving it. Norfolk was motivated by self-interest; Anne's advancement could only benefit the Howards. And she, as Tom was painfully aware, was agreeable to the aims of her supporters because she herself wanted to bring him down.

He still could not fully understand why. Surely it was not because of the Percy affair? Had he stung her pride that deeply? Did she mean to avenge her father's removal from two very lucrative and prestigious offices? Or was it simply that she wanted to rule the King herself and was determined to have no rival for power?

Tom was beginning to fear that he no longer enjoyed Harry's fullest confidence, and that Harry was making more decisions without his knowledge. He had of late had a distinct feeling that he was no longer being received at court as graciously as before.

He longed for the King to do something to disabuse him of these dismal notions.

Thomas returned from Paris. As Tom hastened downstairs to greet his son in the Base Court at Hampton Court, he was longing to see him. And there Thomas was, dismounting from his horse and looking tall and debonair, a young man now, with a young man's swagger.

'My lord.' He knelt for Tom's blessing.

Tom raised him. 'My son,' he murmured in his ear, 'I rejoice to have you back.'

He knew, from those he had set to watch over Thomas, that the lad had idled away his time in Paris and failed to get a degree. The matter of his future was pressing. At supper that evening, Tom felt he had to raise it, as tactfully as possible, for he wanted no falling-out. When the meats had been cleared, he dabbed at his mouth and laid down his napkin.

'Now that you have finished your education, Thomas, what are your plans?'

'I haven't made any,' Thomas said, downing yet another goblet of wine.

Tom felt a sense of despair. The boy needed motivating. 'I might be able to help you,' he said, as genially as he could. 'I hold the bishopric of Durham, which is one of the wealthiest sees in the kingdom and brings in far greater revenues than all your benefices put together. I would be happy to ask the King to confer it on you.' He was convinced that were this munificent opportunity to be dangled like the proverbial carrot before Thomas's nose, he would willingly take it.

'No,' said the young fool. 'I don't want to be ordained or go into the Church.'

'You don't know what you're turning down,' Tom retorted, with some acerbity.

'I'm sorry, Sir, but I do not want it.'

Tom let the matter rest there, for the sake of family harmony, but he was thinking that the King might be able to help. It was frustrating not being able to make Thomas see sense about his future, as worrying as his fear that Harry was starting to distance himself from him.

He took his barge to Richmond Palace the next day, glad to find the King in a good mood.

'Your Grace, I crave a favour,' he said, as soon as they were seated in the King's study. 'Might I ask again that the see of Durham be granted to my poor nephew Winter, if I resign it?'

Harry frowned. 'He is under age, if I remember aright.'

'He is eighteen, Sir, but he holds many other church offices and I am sure that I can obtain the necessary dispensations – you know, for age, pluralism and non-residence – and on account of his illegitimacy, which is a bar to the priesthood.'

Harry gave him a searching look. 'I know he's your son, Thomas. The world knows it, I believe. It is natural for a father to want the best for his son. I only wish I had a son too. If this Great Matter drags on for much longer, I will have lost the potency to sire one!' It was a jest, but Harry's mouth was set in a grim line. 'By all means get the necessary dispensations – and pray you meet no opposition – for they will stand the lad in good stead in the future. But for now, Thomas, even you must see that he is too young to be a bishop, and that I cannot bring the Church in England into disrepute by allowing it.'

Deeply disappointed – not least at the prospect of Thomas lazing away his aimless days at Hampton Court, but also because he believed that at one time, not so long ago, Harry would have granted his request – Tom sought by stealth to undermine his enemies, counteracting their influence with the King by securing the appointment of his own clients to the Privy Chamber. He did his best to sweeten Mistress Anne with gifts and entertainments. Relations between them were always outwardly cordial, but he was not deceived. There came a day when, hurrying down a gallery at Greenwich, he met her coming in the opposite direction with her brother in tow, and was taken aback to see the hatred flashing in her eyes. It left him in no doubt that her elevation to the consort's throne would mean his own downfall, yet still he hoped to mitigate that disaster by doing her as much good service as he could. Surely, she would not compass the ruin of one who had worked so tirelessly to bring her a crown?

He sought to please her by resolving the feud with the Butlers over the earldom of Ormond in favour of her father, and received from her a most gracious letter of thanks. *Think of what thing in the world I can imagine to do you pleasure, and you shall find me the gladdest woman in the world to do it*, she assured him.

Yes, he thought; just go away. But that, he knew, would never happen.

In February, Tom assembled a committee of lawyers at Hampton Court, and it was agreed that the King should press the Pope to grant a commission empowering him and Cardinal Campeggio to try the Great Matter in England and pronounce a definitive sentence.

Immediately, Harry dispatched to Rome two canon lawyers: his chaplain, Dr Foxe, and Dr Gardiner. Both could be relied upon to present their arguments with conviction.

'Repeat without ceasing that his Majesty cannot do otherwise than separate from the Queen,' Tom enjoined them. 'If all else fails, let the vehemence of your words excite a wholesome fear in the Pope.' If Clement could be intimidated by the Emperor, he could be intimidated by Harry too!

Harry was chafing at yet another delay.

'I'm not feeling myself,' he complained to Tom when they were out riding in Windsor Great Park on a chilly March morning. 'I keep getting these feverish headaches and aches and pains. I fear I must be getting older. I'm thirty-seven in June, you know. And since I fell from my horse the other week, I've had a sore on my leg that won't heal.'

'The leg will get better. Give it time, Sir,' Tom soothed. 'And

I'm sure that all the stresses of the past months are to blame for the headaches.'

'That's as may be,' Harry said, calming his horse, which had shied at the sound of a dog barking. 'It worries me, encroaching age. What if I die leaving no son? My Great Matter *must* be resolved soon, for the sake of the succession and the continuing peace of the realm. Surely his Holiness can understand the urgency!'

'I am confident that it will be resolved,' Tom said, 'and that the Pope will agree to send Cardinal Campeggio to England.'

'Let us hope so!' Harry muttered, his prim mouth set in a defiant line.

They were closeted together a week later, discussing the King's case yet again, when Harry suddenly changed the subject.

'I believe you have in your possession a book, William Tyndale's *The Obedience of a Christian Man*,' he said. 'One of those you banned.'

'I do indeed,' Tom replied. 'A young gentleman was brought before me only two days ago, having been found reading it. He said he had taken it from one of Mistress Anne's maids. He was justly terrified when I told him that I would report the matter to your Grace.' He was wondering why Harry was interested in the book.

'Mistress Anne showed it to me,' Harry told him.

Tom bridled. Who was she to think she could read a proscribed book with impunity?

'She received it from abroad,' Harry explained. 'She fell to her knees before me and confessed she had read it. She said she was struck by the arguments it contained. I read it that night in bed, but then she lent it to one of her maids, and the girl's betrothed snatched it from her. Mistress Anne would like her book back.'

'Sir, it is subversive!' Tom protested. 'She ought not to be reading it.'

Harry scowled at him. 'Thomas, I am at a loss to understand why. I have to say I was impressed by Tyndale's criticisms of the Papacy and his emphasis on the authority of monarchs. By St George, it is a book for me and all kings to read!'

Tom knew himself bested. 'Then I bow to your Grace's greater judgement.'

Harry nodded, satisfied. 'I have given Mistress Anne the freedom of the royal library.'

Tom's heart sank, because he knew that it contained, for Harry's personal reference, other heretical books that had been banned in England. Heaven only knew how Anne would use them to her advantage.

'However,' Harry was saying, 'I do not want Tyndale's book removed from the banned list. It is not suitable for my subjects to read.'

At least, Tom thought, he had not lost all his senses.

The next day, George Heneage, one of Tom's servants, informed him that Mistress Anne had spoken to him. 'She said she was afraid that your Grace had forgotten her because you sent her no gift by your last messenger to the King, but I explained that you had sent the man in great haste. Now her lady mother has asked that your Grace send her some tuna fish, and some of your good carp, shrimps and other delicacies. I beseech your Grace to pardon my boldness in passing on her request; it is but the conceit of a woman.'

Tom smiled to himself. Anne would have a gift from him, and Lady Rochford her fish, if that was what it took to keep them sweet. Heneage's observation on women led him to ruminate on the sex in general, which of course led his thoughts to Joan. If he could unburden himself of his troubles to anyone, it would be her. It was a long time since he had seen her, yet she had never been far from his mind, neither her nor the young son he could never acknowledge. He longed to see them both, but it had proved impossible. He had sent Cavendish several times to report on Legh's presence at Thames Ditton, but it seemed that the fellow was always at home. Presumably he had given up his mistress.

He wondered if Joan still thought of him. Dare he write to her? She would want to know that Thomas had returned. No, he must resist the urge. There would be hell to pay if her husband found out. Realistically, the best thing he could do for her would be to leave her alone. But he missed her. How he missed her.

With the spring came news from Rome. Gardiner and Foxe had seen his Holiness, who unfortunately had heard that the King wanted an annulment only because of his vain affection for a lady far from worthy of him. Gardiner had sprung to his master's defence, pointing out that he was in dire need of a male heir and declaring that Anne Boleyn was a lady of the noblest sentiments, and that he, and the Cardinal of York and all England paid homage to her virtues. Tom laughed out loud at that.

After reading on, he gave a shout of exultation and hastened to find Harry, who was with Anne in his privy garden.

'Forgive the intrusion, your Grace, Mistress Anne,' he said, bowing, 'but I have good news.'

Harry sprang up. 'Tell me!'

'His Holiness has granted me and Cardinal Campeggio a commission to try your nullity suit in England.'

'Praise God!' Harry exclaimed. 'And you can pass judgement?'

Tom hesitated. As usual in this matter, nothing was straightforward. 'No, Sir, it's not that kind of commission; it allows us to examine the evidence and make a recommendation to Rome. But the Holy Father has promised to send a general commission soon, which will indeed permit us to make a ruling, and it should arrive in time for the hearing.'

'You mean, my lord,' Anne said, rising, 'that the Holy Father is stalling again. Why didn't he grant a general commission in the first place?'

'Dear lady,' Tom said reassuringly, 'these are complex matters, but do not worry. I feel optimistic about the outcome. And so do our envoys, who have spoken with the Pope at length.'

Anne shot him a look that told him she was not convinced.

'Darling, be reasonable,' Harry pleaded. 'Our good friend Thomas here, like so many others, is doing his best to obtain our hearts' desire. Just be patient a little longer.'

Anne assumed a tragic mien. 'I know. It's just that I can't rid myself of the feeling that I am wasting my time and my youth to no purpose.'

Harry put an arm around her, instantly frantic. 'Don't say such things, sweetheart, I beg of you. Time spent together is never wasted.'

She turned to him, which Tom felt was the signal for him to withdraw.

'With your Grace's leave, I will get back to work,' he said. Harry waved him away impatiently.

Late in April, Tom learned that the Abbess of Wilton had died. The nunnery at Wilton was an ancient and rich foundation, fashionable and aristocratic, and its Abbess enjoyed great prestige and standing, so it was important that a suitable replacement, a nun of spotless reputation and learning, be elected soon. Most of the convent favoured the Prioress, Dame Isabel Jordan, and Tom approved, having heard of her piety and business acumen.

What he had not known was that two sisters of Anne Boleyn's brother-in-law, William Carey, were nuns at Wilton, and it transpired that the Boleyns wanted one of them, Eleanor, to be abbess. *Great pressure is being put on the nuns*, one of Tom's agents reported. Influence being brought to bear in such matters was not unusual, although in this case Tom thought Dame Isabel the better choice and believed that the community would elect her anyway. However much he needed to ingratiate himself with Anne, he was determined that she would not have her way.

But Anne had got at Harry. 'Mistress Anne has asked me to urge the convent to have Dame Eleanor elected abbess,' he announced one morning in May.

Tom nodded. 'Please reassure Mistress Anne and her family that if she is not elected abbess, I will push for her election as prioress. But the election cannot take place yet. A prescribed interval has to be observed between the death of the Abbess and the election of her successor.'

'More waiting!' Harry smiled grimly. 'Is there any news of Cardinal Campeggio's coming?'

'Not yet,' Tom replied, feeling a little anxious. Surely the legate had set off by now?

When he was hard at work later that day, he was informed that the King was coming to see him, and was astonished when Harry burst into his closet, holding Anne Boleyn by the hand. In their wake came Foxe and Gardiner, newly returned to Greenwich from Rome. From the joyful looks on Harry's and Anne's faces, they had brought good news.

Ecstatic, Harry made them recount what had passed during their embassy and beamed as they stressed the goodwill the Pope bore towards him and his eagerness to have the King's case resolved.

'The outcome is certain!' Harry cried, kissing Anne heartily. 'We will soon be wed, my love!'

'Excellent, excellent!' Tom said. Watching them, his heart filled with dread. He was still sceptical about the Pope's intentions, even doubting whether the promised commission would ever be sent. He would have obtained it with his own blood if he could. Yet he dared not betray his fears to Harry. 'I am glad for your Grace!' he declared. 'And I am more than satisfied with the commission granted to me and Cardinal Campeggio.'

Fox was looking embarrassed. 'There is just one cause for concern, your Grace. His Holiness has heard rumours that Mistress Anne – forgive me, Mistress – is with child, and he feels she may not be worthy to be queen.'

'That's a lie!' Anne protested.

Harry's expression was thunderous. 'Darling, I won't have you slandered so! My lord Cardinal, you will write to the Pope and inform him that he has been labouring under some misapprehension. You will emphasise Mistress Anne's excellent virtue, her constant virginity, her chastity, her wisdom, her descent from right noble and regal blood, her good manners, her youth and her apparent aptness to procreate children. You will tell him that these are the grounds on which my desire is founded, and the qualities for which Mistress Anne is held in esteem here.'

'I will write immediately, Sir,' Tom promised. 'The world shall know the truth about Mistress Anne.' He bowed to her.

Harry thanked him, but Anne just smiled tightly. The dispatch was sent that evening.

* * *

In late May, the dreaded sweating sickness broke out in London and quickly spread. It was the worst outbreak Tom could remember. Forty thousand cases were reported in the capital alone, and Harry, horrified to learn that members of his household had succumbed to the disease, fled with the Queen, Anne and a small retinue to Waltham Abbey in Essex, which he deemed far enough from the contagion – for now.

On the day he left, he summoned Tom to his closet.

'Thomas,' he began, looking terrified, 'I am deeply troubled in my mind. I cannot stop wondering if this plague is a visitation from God because I am trying to divorce the Queen.'

The same thought had occurred to Tom. It seemed more than coincidence that the sweat had broken out as the hearing was within sight. He trembled, thinking of the plagues God had visited upon Egypt. Harry must be deterred.

'I fear that your Grace may be right,' he said firmly. 'It could well be the manifestation of God's wrath, and it may be intended as a warning.'

'Do you truly think so?' He could see the fear in the King's eyes.

'I do! And I beg of you, Sir, to abandon all thoughts of divorce!'

'Never!' Harry erupted. 'God knows that my doubts of conscience about the validity of my marriage are sincere. Surely, He would not punish me for seeking to have them resolved by His vicar on Earth?'

'Sir, you are taking a dreadful risk. Think of your people—'

'I *am* thinking of them, you fool. I need a son! I am living in sin. It's more likely that God is punishing me for allowing the situation to continue.'

He had never spoken thus to Tom, but Tom was undeterred. He fell to his knees. 'Sir, I beseech you. So many have died. And God sees that you are already resolved to make Mistress Anne your wife, even before your case has been heard. It may be that which has angered Him. Again, I urge you, abandon this Great Matter!'

'By St George, I now see your malice!' Harry spat. 'This is your way of getting rid of Mistress Anne. You've never liked her, never wanted her as queen. I've seen the way you look at her. I tell you, Thomas, heads have rolled for less. Well, know that I would give a thousand Wolseys for one Anne Boleyn! No other than God shall take her from me!' He was beside himself.

Tom was reeling, consumed by fear. Never had Harry shouted at him in anger. He wrung his hands in supplication. 'Your Grace, I beg you to believe me when I say that I bear no enmity towards Mistress Anne, only love and goodwill. No one has worked harder than I to secure your annulment, but if it is offensive to God, as you yourself have wondered, then I have only sought to find a remedy.'

Harry's rage was subsiding. He stood there red-faced, not meeting Tom's eye. 'Thomas, forgive me. I should not have spoken thus. It is dread of the sweat that makes me edgy.'

'There is nothing to forgive,' Tom said, clambering to his feet. 'I understand perfectly your Grace's fears. We are all on edge.'

'You're all right – you've had the sweat and recovered. But I haven't, and the thought of what might happen to England if I died torments me.' Harry was calmer now, but Tom could not still his pounding heart. 'I didn't mean what I said about your misliking Mistress Anne. You've been a true friend to us.'

Truer than you know, Tom thought.

They parted amicably, yet he felt that something had broken between them.

From Waltham, and a succession of other houses where he kept fleeing to escape the sweat, Harry sent a stream of letters, wanting to know how matters stood in London, but mostly bombarding Tom with good advice. He was to avoid any places where there was a risk of infection; if anyone in his household fell ill, he was to remove himself speedily; he was to keep out of the open air, have only a small, clean household, sup with as few guests as possible, drink little wine, and take special pills once a week. If he did fall ill, Harry had devised a posset of herbs that would bring out the sweat; the recipe was enclosed. Above all, he was to look to his soul. The King's anxiety – and his hypochondria – was plain in every line.

Tom understood why his master was so afraid. He was concerned himself about his loved ones and kept sending Cavendish to Hampton Court to ensure that Thomas was all right, and to Thames Ditton to discreetly find out how Joan was faring. He always sagged with relief when the usher returned and told him that they were both well.

'I realise you have put yourself at risk travelling abroad on this mission,' he told him, 'but would you go back next week and check again?'

Cavendish invariably agreed without hesitation. Had ever master had such a loyal servant?

In the third week of June, Tom had to inform the King that William Carey, Anne's brother-in-law, had died of the sweat, as had Sir William Compton, one of the minions Tom had once dismissed. Tom was told that Carey had expressed a dying wish that he would use his influence to make Eleanor Carey abbess of Wilton.

He shelved the matter. The epidemic would delay the election, and God Himself might intervene. Then he would press for the election of Dame Isabel Jordan.

He thanked God daily for sparing him from the sweat, and for sparing the King. He prayed that Harry would see his way clear to dropping his nullity suit and taking back the Queen. Then England might be spared further mortality.

God's displeasure could not have manifested itself more plainly, he realised, when he learned that Anne and her father had fallen victim to the sweating sickness and taken to their beds at Hever Castle. In evident panic, Henry wrote to say that he had sent his own physician to attend them. Again, his heart in his mouth, Tom begged him to abandon all thoughts of his Great Matter. Now it appeared that Harry had been badly frightened, for he told Tom he had returned to the Queen's company.

When Anne recovered, however, he resumed pursuing his case as vigorously as ever. In late June, clearly at his behest, Anne sent Tom a flattering letter expressing her gratitude for his good work on their behalf. He was not deceived. Doubtless she and her faction were still zealously compassing his destruction, and her malice was all the more deadly because it was concealed under a cloak of friendship.

As the sweat abated, Tom rode to Wilton Abbey to ensure discreetly that Dame Isabel was elected. This was one battle that Anne was not going to win. He summoned the nuns before him, one by one, and asked them for their honest opinions of the two candidates for the abbacy.

When it was Dame Eleanor's turn, she stood tall and slender, beautiful even in her habit, but visibly quaking.

'I understand, Dame Eleanor, that you are a candidate for the office,' he began.

'Yes, my lord.' He could hardly hear her.

He spoke gently. 'Is something troubling you? Do you not want to be abbess?'

She hung her head. 'My family want it, but I fear I am not worthy.'

'And why is that, my daughter?'

She would not look at him. 'I confess that I have had two children by two different priests, and that I am now the mistress of a servant of Lord Brooke.' She began weeping.

Tom was not shocked. Things like this happened all the time in religious houses, especially when parents offered a child with no vocation to God, to store up treasure in Heaven for themselves. He was thinking that the Almighty moved in mysterious ways, and was thankful that He had moved Dame Eleanor to confess her sins to him.

'You know there can be no question of your election now,' he told her. 'And I say to you, as our Lord said to the woman taken in adultery, go away and sin no more.'

He wrote at once to Harry, informing him why he was now going to cast his weight behind Dame Isabel Jordan. A reply came by fast messenger. Harry had backed down, clearly fearful of offending God. He wrote that he would not, for all the gold in the world, clog his conscience to make the ungodly Dame Eleanor ruler of a religious house, and he knew that Mistress Anne would never want him to compromise his honour by doing so. But Tom was to desist from championing Dame Isabel, for Mistress Anne had just uncovered some secret immorality in her past, and Harry wanted him to question her about it. It was probably malicious gossip – Tom would know what nunneries were like for that – but there had been talk of an illicit affair two years ago.

Tom had a very good idea of where this malicious gossip had originated.

He summoned Dame Isabel, and was surprised to see a frail old lady who carried about her an air of sanctity. He could not credit that she had ever indulged in love affairs, certainly not two years ago, and that conviction strengthened when he talked to her. And so he informed the King.

Harry wrote back: *To do you pleasure, I have ordered that the abbacy shall go to some other good and well-disposed nun who will reform the house, so that there will be no more scandals.*

Tom smiled. For once, he had a chance to best Anne. He could always plead that the King's letter had arrived too late.

He called for the election to take place. Under his guidance, the nuns voted for Dame Isabel, who was duly enthroned as abbess.

Harry was furious. When Tom returned to court, he found himself quaking to his marrow as the King ranted at him. 'How dare you contravene my order? Who do you think you are to defy me? You've gone out of your way to offend Mistress Anne, and I must say I'm beginning to agree with her that you are secretly doing your best to prevent the divorce.'

Tom waited, trembling, for his master's rage to spend itself. Then he threw himself to his knees.

'Sir, I beg you to hear me in my defence. I had not received your letter when the Abbess was elected. When I did, the deed was done. I assure you that I never intended to offend Mistress Anne. I was merely satisfied that the malicious gossip was unfounded. As for preventing the divorce, I have no idea where that calumny springs from, and I assure you again that I have done everything in my power to bring it about. I am heartily sorry for my hasty action at Wilton, and I crave your Grace's forgiveness. I will send Mistress Anne a kind letter and a rich present to show that I bear her no ill will.'

Harry fixed narrowed eyes on him. 'Well then, consider yourself forgiven.' It was grudgingly said, but Tom was deeply relieved. He wondered whether it had been worth besting Anne in this matter. Of all things, he could not bear to lose Harry's love.

Chapter 31

1528

On a hot August morning, the Queen's almoner, Dr Shorton, asked to see Tom in private.

After kissing Tom's ring, he rose. 'Your Eminence, I felt bound to come to you because her Grace wishes me to assure you that her marriage to Prince Arthur was never consummated. He was too ill with consumption to make her his wife. She has sworn this on the salvation of her soul.'

'Thank you for informing me,' Tom said, refraining from saying that this had no bearing on the case, because he did not wish to afford Katherine an advantage. It was imperative now that he secure an annulment; his future depended on it. 'Might I suggest that, to save herself any more distress, her Grace retires to a convent, leaving the King free to remarry?'

'I fear she will never agree to that,' Dr Shorton said. 'She sees her vocation as being queen of England. Besides, she has in her possession a copy of a brief of dispensation issued by Pope Julius II in 1503 at the request of her mother, Queen Isabella. This brief differs from the original bull of dispensation in that it omits the word "perhaps" in regard to whether or not the first marriage had been consummated.'

Alarums were ringing in Tom's head. If genuine, this brief could demolish the King's already weak case, since Pope Julius had permitted him to wed Katherine regardless of whether her first marriage had been consummated or not.

He appeared in a rush in the Privy Chamber. Harry took one look at his face and hastened him out, ignoring the startled looks of his gentlemen. Not until they were in the chapel did he turn to him. 'What now, Thomas?'

Tom told him about the brief.

'I've never heard of it,' Harry said.

'I certainly haven't,' Tom concurred, 'and I doubt that anyone in England has.'

'It must be a forgery.'

Tom nodded. 'It may have been given to the Queen by Mendoza.'

Harry was glowering. 'She must be censured for not having informed us of its existence before.'

Together, they made for Katherine's apartments. Harry was seething, and Tom privately pitied the Queen as they entered her chamber unannounced and the King waved away her women.

'Where is it?' he demanded, as she sank into a bewildered curtsey.

'Where is what, Sir?' Her voice faltered.

'The brief you claim to have!'

Standing up, she went to her writing desk, unlocked it and handed a document to him. He read it and frowned, then passed it to Tom without comment.

Tom studied it. 'Madam, it seems very strange that no one in England has ever heard of the existence of this dispensation,' he said, 'and I'm afraid that leads me to conclude that it must be a forgery.'

'Are you accusing the Emperor of being a liar?' Katherine demanded of him.

'Of course not, but there may be those in his service who are not so scrupulous.'

'I hope you are not suggesting that Mendoza is one!' she flared.

'I did not say that, Madam.'

'You should have informed me of the existence of this dispensation before,' Harry reproved her.

'I did not have it – or know of it. It arrived only today. The Emperor writes that the dispensation was found when a search was made among the papers of Dr de Puebla, who was my father's ambassador then, and that this is a true copy.'

'It may be so,' Harry grunted, 'but it is only a copy, and cannot be submitted in evidence. We need to see the original.'

'His Grace is right,' Tom interjected, 'and as your Grace looks for the continuance of his love, you will send to Spain for it, as the lack of it might ruin your case and endanger your child's inheritance.'

Katherine flushed. 'Very well,' she said stiffly. 'I will send my chaplain.'

Mendoza, when questioned by the Council, insisted that he had given the Queen a true copy of the brief, and that the original, which remained in the possession of the Emperor, was genuine. When he had gone, the Council decided that it must be removed, by fair means or foul, from the Imperial archives, and destroyed. The Queen was again instructed to send to Spain for it.

Harry was growing ever more impatient for news of Campeggio's coming, so he was infuriated to learn later that month that the Cardinal had not left Rome until the end of July. The delay was due to his having suffered agonising attacks of gout.

'By St George, it will be weeks before he reaches England,' Harry complained. 'This gout will slow him down.'

Tom privately suspected that Clement had taken this into account when appointing Campeggio legate, and that it was another stalling tactic. He feared that Clement was hoping that the King would tire of Anne and forget all about an annulment. But he said nothing to Harry. After all, his fears might be unfounded, for he himself had asked for Campeggio. As for Harry tiring of Anne, that would never happen. He was so infatuated with her that God alone could abate his madness.

But her influence could be mitigated.

She no longer served the Queen; Harry had installed her in a luxurious apartment off the tiltyard at Greenwich. But her anomalous position, as both an unmarried woman with a reputation to protect and the King's intended consort, presented a problem, especially now that the legate was coming.

'I am neither maid-of-honour nor wife,' she complained to Harry one evening, on one of the rare occasions when they dined privately with Tom. 'There is no real place for me at court.'

'It would be more in keeping with propriety, Mistress Anne, for you to have an establishment of your own,' Tom said. Those who did not know better would have thought, these days, that they were best friends, so effectively had she feigned affection for him, and gratitude for all he was supposedly doing to push forward the Great Matter.

'That would be best,' Harry said. 'I could visit you there, darling. We must find a house for you.'

Anne considered for a moment. 'Since your Grace is so often here at Greenwich, I should very much like one nearby.'

'Perhaps, Sir, I could investigate what is available,' Tom suggested.

'Excellent!' declared Harry. 'The sooner we can arrange this, the better it will be for everyone.'

'Thank you, both,' Anne smiled, 'but you will not object, Sir, if I go home to Hever until my house is ready?'

Harry groaned. 'Not again! I swear I'll raze that place to the ground.'

'If you do, I will just have to go to my father's house at Norwich, which is much further away,' Anne said sweetly.

'No!' Harry cried. 'I cannot bear to be that far apart from you.'

The next day, Tom put all his efforts into finding a suitable house. Nothing could be found close to Greenwich Palace, but there was a property available not too far away.

Harry was delighted. 'You never fail me, Thomas! Anne will be so pleased. To tell the truth, it will be a relief not to have her and the Queen under the same roof. Anne hates it, and has been pressing me to send Katherine away, but I've told her I cannot do that until our marriage has been dissolved. It would not look good with the legate due to arrive soon.'

But Campeggio was taking his time.

'He should have been here by now,' Harry fumed, almost dancing with impatience. 'All this delay has given the Queen leisure to marshal support. Bishop Fisher is foremost in her defence, and that chaplain of hers, Thomas Abell. Even Warham thinks my marriage valid.'

'Yes, but he will support you.' Tom felt unusually weary; he longed for this matter to be resolved. When he looked in his mirror, he could see that the strain was telling on him in veined cheeks, a pasty countenance and sagging jowls. He was fifty-seven and growing old. He prayed that Harry had not noticed. He could not have him thinking that his chief minister was losing his touch. These days, with the Boleyns and their supporters riding high, he often felt as if he was teetering on the edge of a precipice.

In the middle of September, they learned that Campeggio was in Paris and had been welcomed by Suffolk, whom Harry had sent to France to escort him to England. The legate had had talks with King Francis. When Suffolk relayed Francis's warning that Campeggio's mission to England would be mere mockery, Harry did not believe it.

Having been delayed by storms and heavy rainfall, Campeggio finally arrived at Dover at the end of September. Now he was resting there. More delay!

'It seems he is minded to go slowly and make the case drag on as long as possible,' Harry grumbled.

Privately, Tom was beginning to wonder if the legate's prime mission was to persuade Harry to withdraw his suit. But he did not voice his concern to Harry. He would wait to see what Campeggio had to say.

Harry was all for laying on a lavish welcome at Blackheath, something that was normally afforded to visiting royalty, but Campeggio politely declined, saying that he was not only sore vexed with the gout, but also that his humility precluded his being entertained with any such pomp or vainglory – which Tom felt was a pointed barb aimed at himself. When he finally arrived in London on 8 October, he came by barge to Bath Place, the London house of the bishops of Salisbury just outside Temple Bar, which Harry had placed at his disposal. Tom had furnished it with every comfort their visitor could possibly desire, and an abundance of provisions.

The next day, Tom hastened to visit Campeggio, to see if he could determine whether his co-legate had a hidden agenda. He found him lying in bed, but the Italian pressed him to stay so that they could discuss the Great Matter.

Campeggio wasted no time. 'In my opinion, the best solution would be a reconciliation between the King and Queen.'

'That is never going to happen!' Tom declared, panicking.

'One never knows in these cases,' Campeggio said smoothly, 'and I intend to do my best to reconcile their Majesties before we proceed to hearing the case.'

'It will not work!' Tom objected. 'Others have tried and failed. The King's conscience tells him that he is living in sin, and he wants a remedy! I urge that we expedite the business with all possible dispatch, for the affairs of the kingdom are at a standstill.'

But Campeggio was immovable. Tom visited him three or four times after that and argued with him for hours, but he might have saved his breath.

Campeggio was not well enough to see the King until 22 October, when they met, with Tom present, in Harry's privy closet. Harry greeted him as warmly as if he had been the Saviour Himself.

'Let us not waste time, my lord Cardinals,' he said. 'I am keen to have my doubts resolved and a decision given on my nullity suit.' He looked at Campeggio, eagerly expectant.

Tom tried to suppress his frustration as the older man took his time in answering. 'Your Grace, this is a difficult matter, one to which his Holiness has devoted much thought and prayer. But he has asked me to assure you that your doubts are unfounded, and to bring about a reconciliation between you and the Queen.'

Tom dared not look at Harry. He knew his master had staked his hopes on Campeggio bringing instructions from Pope Clement to annul his marriage. The last thing he wanted was to have him push for a reconciliation.

'Am I hearing correctly?' Harry asked. 'His Holiness knows I have long been tormented by doubts of conscience. Doctors and scholars have assured me I have a case to answer. It's there in the Bible itself, man!' He was beside himself now. 'Yet you come all this way to tell me, glibly, that my doubts are unfounded? Or is it that his Holiness is afraid to provoke the Emperor?'

Campeggio raised his hands defensively, looking pained. 'Your Majesty, rest assured that his Holiness has not allowed worldly considerations to influence his position. The truth is that the law of Leviticus only applies when a child has been born of the first marriage. The Queen and Prince Arthur had no children, so there was no bar to your union.' Tom restrained himself from nodding in agreement.

'Not so!' Harry retorted, impassioned. 'Leviticus warns that if a man marries his brother's widow, he has uncovered his brother's nakedness, and they will be childless. There's nothing ambivalent about that.'

Campeggio shifted on his bench and held up his hand again. 'Before we enter into further debate, his Holiness did suggest another way out of your predicament. He asked me to persuade the Queen to enter a convent, which would free your Grace to remarry.'

Harry brightened. 'By St George, that would solve everything!' Tom agreed. It was the perfect solution, and if the suggestion came from the Pope himself, Katherine might just agree, as it was to her advantage. She could enjoy a comfortable retirement, Mary's legitimacy would not be challenged and Harry would be free to remarry. If only the matter could be resolved that simply.

'It would,' the legate agreed.

'I should point out,' Tom said, 'that I have already made such a suggestion to her Grace's almoner, and he was very clear that she sees her vocation as being queen.'

'Go to her, both of you,' Harry urged. 'Tell her I'll have her made an abbess; she can keep great state, like a queen, see the Princess whenever she wishes and be free to come and go as she pleases. What has she got to lose? I no longer share her bed or play the husband. But I am more than willing to treat her most honourably as my sister-in-law. And Mary can keep her place in the succession after any sons I have with a future wife.'

'His Grace is being most generous,' Tom said.

'I see that,' Campeggio replied, a touch drily.

'Admit it, the marriage is invalid,' Tom persisted. 'That would solve the problem once and for all.'

The legate looked distressed. 'Alas, I have explained that the matter is a difficult one, with serious implications for the Church.'

'That would appear to contradict his Holiness's objective view of the case,' Tom challenged. 'Clearly, he will not admit that his predecessor was not infallible!'

'Your Eminence should try to understand my position, but I feel I am speaking to a rock,' Campeggio said plaintively. 'Remember, I am trying to help.' He turned to Harry, who had been listening in increasingly evident dismay. 'Sir, there is a third way. To settle the problem of the succession, his Holiness is ready to grant a dispensation for a marriage between the Princess Mary and the Duke of Richmond.'

Both Tom and Harry stared at him aghast. 'But they are half-brother and half-sister,' Harry expostulated. 'It would be incest! How could the Pope sanction it? And you worry about the Church being brought into disrepute!'

'I do!' Campeggio countered. 'And so does his Holiness. Pope Julius's dispensation was sound; challenging it could indeed compromise the integrity of the Holy See. It's as simple as that.'

Harry looked ready to explode with rage. 'The integrity of the Holy See is not best served by one Pope granting a dispensation on dubious grounds and another encouraging incest! If this divorce is not granted, the authority of the Holy See in this kingdom will be annihilated.' He was red with fury.

The legate was equally angry. 'I trust you are not threatening his Holiness. Because he says your marriage is valid, and I came only to set your Grace's mind at rest. Yet you are not listening. You want only one ruling, and if an angel were to descend from Heaven, I fear even he would not be able to persuade you to the contrary. For it is obvious to me, and to his Holiness, what impels your Grace to seek this annulment. We are aware that there is a certain young lady whom you wish to marry. We are assured that you have not proceeded to any ultimate conjunction, but Pope Clement fears that this passion has clouded your judgement.'

Tom winced. Even he had never dared speak so plainly to Harry, who seemed to be momentarily speechless. 'My intentions towards Mistress Anne Boleyn are entirely honourable,' the King growled at length, 'and the matter of the succession is pressing, whether or not I intend to marry her. I cannot live any longer under God's displeasure! I looked to his Holiness for a remedy, but he has failed me abysmally.' Tears filled his eyes.

Tom was feeling desperate. 'Sir, I too have legatine powers, and I promise you that I will work with Cardinal Campeggio to reach a solution.'

Campeggio stared down his long, thin nose at him. 'Let us all pray that God shows us the right path to take. I am authorised by his Holiness to let you see this.' He produced a document from his scrip. 'It is a Papal bull granting me alone the power to judge your Majesty's case. The Holy Father wishes its existence to be kept secret, but he desires to demonstrate the goodwill he bears towards you.'

Tom was immediately suspicious. Why should such a commission be kept secret? And why had he not been granted the power to judge the case with Campeggio? No, he thought, this was a sop to keep the King happy while avoiding provoking the Emperor. He hoped that Harry would not place too much reliance on it.

But Harry appeared mollified. 'Your Eminence, I am gratified to hear that.' He eyed the bull hungrily. 'I trust you will both now visit the Queen?'

'We will,' Campeggio assured him. Tom was praying that she would prove amenable.

He left the meeting quite despondent.

Warned of their coming, Katherine had donned her regal robes, her velvets, furs and jewels, and one of her costliest gable hoods, but she looked old beyond her years, and haggard, and Tom could not help feeling sorry for her. This was what all the grief and strain had done to her.

Campeggio too seemed to be having a bad day, for he hobbled into her chamber, leaning heavily on a stick, his florid face strained and severe. He looked as if he would rather be anywhere else. Tom was feeling tense. He kept reminding himself that he was the King's man first and foremost, and must not let sympathy for Katherine – or guilt over his betrayal of her – cloud his judgement.

She kept them standing, as if to remind them that she was still the Queen.

Campeggio seemed to think it his right to act as spokesman. 'Madam, we have been appointed as indifferent judges in the King's case. His Holiness cannot refuse justice to anyone who demands it, but this Great Matter is full of difficulties, and he counsels you that, rather than face a trial, you should take some other course, one that would be satisfactory to God and your conscience, and would be to the glory and fame of your name.'

'And what is that?' she asked.

'It would greatly please his Holiness if you would enter a convent,' Campeggio said.

'No,' she replied, to Tom's exasperation.

'But Madam, there is an honourable precedent. You will have heard of Queen Jeanne de Valois, the first wife of the late King Louis of France. She could not bear him children, so she agreed to a divorce and became a nun. She founded a holy order and is now popularly reputed a saint. Could any woman ask for more?'

'I have no vocation,' Katherine said, 'and I have my daughter to consider.'

'Your Grace should think of your position,' Tom intervened. He was perspiring, despite the autumnal chill.

'His Majesty believes your marriage to be invalid,' Campeggio said. 'I do not think it possible for anyone to persuade him to change his view.'

'He has been unduly influenced,' Katherine said sharply.

Campeggio gave her a smile of rare sweetness. 'There are the strongest arguments in favour of your Grace entering a nunnery. Your piety is renowned. Your daughter's rights would be preserved, and you could see her regularly. If you took this course, the Pope could issue a dispensation allowing the King to remarry, and the Emperor could not possibly object. His Majesty could then take another wife and have sons to secure the succession. You would still keep your honours and your worldly possessions. Most important of all, the peace of Europe and the spiritual authority of the Holy See would no longer be under threat.' He paused, looking at her hopefully. Tom felt like applauding him.

'How can it be under threat?' Katherine asked. 'Is not the Pope Christ's representative on earth?'

'Madam, the King warned me only today that if this divorce is not granted, the authority of the Holy See in this kingdom will be annihilated. Yes, I see you are shocked by that, as am I. So you must see that it is in your best interests to retire gracefully and save everyone a lot of trouble. This solution will be extremely pleasing to the King, who is prepared to be very generous. You stand to lose only the use of his person by entering religion; and some comfortable house can be found where you can still enjoy any worldly comforts you desire.'

'No,' said Katherine again.

Campeggio and Tom exchanged irritated glances.

'Madam,' Campeggio went on, 'it pains me to say this, but I am sure that his Grace will not return to you, however things fall out.'

Katherine stood up. 'My lords, you speak of practical solutions, but you are forgetting the most importance issue at stake, which is whether my marriage is valid, and whether Pope Julius's dispensation be good or not. If the Pope finds it good – as surely he must – then my husband must return to me.'

Tom felt the sweat run down his face. He could feel both admiration and fury for this dogged, stubborn woman.

Campeggio looked pained. 'Madam, it is not easy to reason with the King. Evidently, he is so blindly in love with a certain lady that he cannot see his way clearly and is determined upon this divorce.'

'He has to have grounds for it first!' Katherine snapped. 'My lords, I can affirm to you, on my conscience, that I did not sleep with Prince Arthur more than six or seven nights, and that I remained as virginal as when I came from my mother's womb. I bore him no children. So how can my marriage to the King be invalid?'

'His Majesty insists that the marriage was consummated,' Tom said, hating himself.

'Does he call me a liar? He knows the truth, in his heart. I intend to live and die in the estate of matrimony to which God called me.

I assure you, I will always remain of that opinion and will never change it.'

Campeggio spoke. 'It would be better to yield to the King's displeasure rather than risk the danger of a sentence given in court. Think of the scandal!'

Katherine flared. 'I will not yield when I know I am in the right!' She turned to Tom. 'And for this trouble, I have only you to thank, my lord Cardinal of York! Because I have always marvelled at your pride and vainglory, hated your voluptuous life and cared little for your presumption, you have maliciously kindled this fire – and mainly on account of the great grudge you bear to my nephew the Emperor because he would not gratify your ambition by making you Pope!'

'Madam,' Tom protested, trembling with the injustice of her accusations, 'I am not the beginner or the mover of the King's doubts, and it was against my will that your marriage ever came into question. I give you my solemn promise that, as legate, I will be impartial. Believe me, I would obtain a happy solution with my own blood, if I could!'

'I do not believe you,' Katherine said.

'Believe it or not, I wish you nothing but good.' Tom was annoyed that she was not being more objective about her situation.

'Then there is nothing for us to discuss,' Katherine declared.

'Then we must leave you for now,' he said, his voice strained.

'Will you hear my confession?' she asked.

Tom felt stricken. He knew what she would say, and that he and Campeggio would have no choice but to believe it.

'I will come again tomorrow,' Campeggio told her.

'I always thought her to be a prudent lady, and now more than ever,' Tom observed as they descended the stairs.

'Prudent, but perhaps misguided,' Campeggio said. 'I wish she could be a little more pragmatic.'

'So do I!' Tom agreed.

Harry insisted that they both return on the morrow to put more pressure on Katherine to enter religion. Tom waited in the antechamber while Campeggio heard her confession. When he returned, he looked grave. 'She has authorised me to tell you that, under the seal of the confessional, she affirmed, upon the salvation of her soul, that she had never been carnally known by Prince Arthur.'

Tom's heart sank. 'This sets the King's arguments at naught.'

'Perhaps he will now accept that basing his case on Leviticus is unsafe.'

Tom shook his head. 'I fear he is immovable. Shall we go in?'

'Yes. Her Majesty is waiting.'

'We have returned at the King's request,' Campeggio informed the Queen. 'He asks again if you will enter a nunnery, and we urge you – nay, we beg you – to comply, lest some dire punishment befall you.'

'I will do nothing to my soul's damnation or against God's law,' Katherine declared fiercely. 'I will abide by no sentence save that of the Pope himself. I do not recognise the authority of the legatine commission to try the case in England, since I believe it to be biased in my husband's favour.'

'Madam, the King's wrath can be terrible,' Tom warned her.

Katherine hesitated, but not for long. 'Neither the whole kingdom nor any great punishment, even though I be torn limb from limb, can make me alter my opinion,' she insisted, her voice impassioned. 'And if, after death, I should return to life, I would prefer to die all over again rather than change my opinion.'

Tom and Campeggio retired. Tom dreaded to think of Harry's reaction.

Campeggio was furious with the Queen. 'She should retire to a convent! She is undermining my position here, and that of the Pope. The peace of Europe and the spiritual authority of the Holy See are under threat as it is, without this Great Matter making things worse.'

Tom was shaking. 'I fear what the King might do if he is thwarted. He is so determined that I fear he may resort to extreme measures. And if he marries Anne Boleyn, I foresee trouble, because Katherine is popular and Anne is not, and the possibility of a disputed succession may arise.'

'*If* he marries Anne Boleyn,' Campeggio said.

When Tom saw Harry alone and relayed what Katherine had said, the King exploded.

'That cursed woman! What has she got to lose?'

Tom could have mentioned a crown and a husband, but didn't dare.

'You've got to get that Papal bull,' Harry insisted. 'Wrest it from Campeggio and let's see what it says, because I suspect that it may give *you* the authority to dissolve my marriage, and that's why he's keeping it close.'

'But why would he do that?'

Harry glared at him. 'I don't know, but I fear there's some skulduggery going on. Just go and demand to see it. Now!'

Tom hastened away, bruised at being treated like a lackey by the master he revered. Anne had brought about this change in Harry, there was no doubt about it. His heart burned with hatred.

'I can only do what his Holiness has instructed,' Campeggio said, when pressed. 'And he has ordered that the bull is for my eyes only – for now.'

Tom could have screamed with frustration. Dreading Harry's reaction, he retreated to his closet and wrote to Gregory Casale in Rome, urging him to persuade the Pope to order Campeggio to show the bull to him. *The King feels his honour touched by this, especially considering what a benefactor he has been to the Church. Without the Pope's compliance I cannot bear up against the storm,* he ended desperately.

Then he returned to Campeggio, his mind in turmoil. 'I think we should put more pressure on the Queen to enter a nunnery,' the legate said. 'It is in her best interests to do so as soon as possible, so that she can avoid the embarrassments that might arise if the King's case goes to trial, for the intimate details of her married life will surely be exposed to public scrutiny.'

Tom was just about to send an usher to the Queen to crave another audience when one of her household officers presented himself. 'Her

Grace has sent me to inform your Eminences that the Emperor has refused to send the Papal brief to England for fear it will be destroyed.'

'That would not be consistent with the King's honour!' Tom snapped. 'He would never contemplate such a thing.'

Campeggio merely raised his eyebrows.

Nearly weeping with vexation, Tom wrote again to Casale, ordering him to make a search for the copy of the brief that should have been filed in the Vatican archives. To show that he meant business, he dispatched five clerks to Rome to assist him. If they found the brief and ascertained that it was authentic, they were to ask the Pope if the King could follow Old Testament precedents and have two wives, the issue of both being deemed legitimate. Desperate causes called for desperate measures!

He also dashed off a note to the Queen, telling her that the version of the brief she had in her possession was useless, since no court would recognise a copy. He ordered her to write to Spain again and demand that the original be sent to England for the court to see.

When he reported back to the King, Harry was incandescent, calling down curses on the Emperor, the Pope, Campeggio and Katherine. But not, thank God, on Tom.

'I will have this divorce, I swear it!' he ranted.

'And your Grace will, if I have anything to do with it,' Tom assured him. 'It is useless for Campeggio to think of reviving your marriage.'

'If he persists, there will be consequences,' Harry growled.

The Queen had obeyed Tom's order to ask the Emperor again to send the brief, but what arrived in December was merely a copy.

'This other document attests to it being genuine, and it has been signed in his Imperial Majesty's presence by the most eminent Spanish bishops,' Mendoza declared loftily, laying the papers before Harry and Tom.

Harry's expression darkened as he read the brief, then he passed it to Tom, who saw at once that it contained a statement that Katherine and Arthur had consummated their marriage, and that Pope Julius had still sanctioned Katherine marrying Arthur's brother without impediment.

'I suspect trickery,' Harry barked when Mendoza had been dismissed. 'Write to Rome. Ask Clement to declare the brief a forgery. Without it, the Queen's case will founder.'

Tom duly wrote, praying that Casale and his clerks would not find any copy in the Vatican archives. He also sent two more clerks to Spain to see the original brief and report back on its authenticity.

When Tom next left York Place to go to the Court of Chancery at Westminster Hall, the streets were crowded, and he could see a small procession ahead, fighting its way through. Then he heard angry shouts. 'Nan Bullen shall not be our Queen! We'll have no Nan Bullen!'

As the closed litter passed him, he saw outriders wearing Anne's livery before he himself was caught up in a raging mob, extricating his horse only with difficulty as his men pushed the people back. It was a frightening experience, and it brought home to him the strength of feeling among the King's subjects. He wished for the thousandth time that Harry had never embarked on his Great Matter.

It was with relief that he escaped that evening to the tranquillity of Hampton Court. Thomas was out, God knew where, so Tom could put off worrying about how to motivate him until another time. Ensconced in the luxury of his great bedchamber, wrapped in a furred robe, he settled down by the fire with a steaming goblet of heartening aleberry and Boccaccio's bawdy *Decameron*, and felt the tension begin to ease.

He was just dozing off when Cavendish was at his elbow. 'My lord, Lady Legh is without, asking to see you.'

Joan! Tom was instantly awake.

'Send her in,' he said, getting up and smoothing his hair.

And there she was, wrapped in a hooded cloak of finest wool, her dark eyes regarding him almost yearningly. He reached out his hands and took hers. They were cold, for it was a bitter night.

'Joan!' he said. 'What a wonderful surprise. What brings you here?' He ushered her towards the hearth.

'I had to come, Tom,' she said, taking the chair he offered. 'I am worried about you.'

'Me?' He was taken aback. 'I am all right.'

'I fear not,' she said. 'I hear things. George knows people at court, and the word is that you are falling from favour.' She looked at him and he could see tears in her eyes. 'They say too that your enemies have united to bring you down.'

The chill he felt was not due to the winter night. 'I know that, but as for falling from favour, no.' He wished he could say it with conviction. 'The King knows that I am working hard to resolve his Great Matter; he appreciates my efforts on his behalf, and when everything is brought to a successful conclusion, he will be undyingly grateful.' He wished he could believe it.

Joan was looking at him with dismay in her face. 'But will Mistress Anne Boleyn?'

'If she attains a crown because of me, she will have every reason to feel gratitude.'

'More likely, George believes, that she will use her power to oust you from the King's counsels.'

It was no less than he feared, of course, but still he could not bear to hear it put into words.

'Tom.' She spoke urgently. 'I have asked little of you in the years that I have known you. I have loved you without making demands. But this one thing I now beg of you: that you will resign from the King's service before your enemies destroy you.' A tear trickled down her cheek. 'The legatine court will sit soon, and if the decision goes against the King, I fear he will throw you to the wolves.'

Tom could not credit what she was asking of him. 'I cannot do that if I want to keep his favour. No one else has the means or the influence to bring a happy outcome to pass.'

'Tom!' she cried. 'That influence is dwindling. Anne Boleyn is seeing to that. What use will all your pomp and vainglory be if you fall from favour? Or rather *when* you fall from favour! You would not give it all up for me, and I understand that, but give it up for yourself, for your own safety! Go north and be a proper archbishop of York! I cannot tell you how much I fear for you. I've barely slept these past nights.'

'Joan, stop!' Tom cried. 'You are tormenting yourself for nothing. All will be well, you'll see.' He realised that he was reassuring himself as much as her, for all might not turn out well.

'I wish I could believe it,' she said. 'I couldn't bear to see you brought low.'

'I will be watchful,' he promised. 'Please don't worry.'

He stood there gazing into her eyes, then knelt by her chair. 'I perceive that you still have feelings for me.'

'I will always have feelings for you,' she whispered.

'I am deeply touched,' he said, feeling like crying. He reached for her hand. 'Stay with me.'

She shook her head. 'I would like to. You'll never know how much I would like to. But I daren't. George thinks I am unwell in bed with a megrim and cannot be disturbed. I slipped down the back stairs. I cannot stay any longer.'

They both stood up, and Tom could not resist putting his arms around her. 'I still love you,' he murmured.

'Don't!' she reproved tearfully, pulling away and hurrying to the door. 'Remember what I said!'

Tom could not sleep. Her words kept echoing in his head. Of course, he could never give it all up. His success and all that had followed meant everything to him. If he had not given it up for Joan, he would hardly do so now. And yet, he had to admit that he was weary of the relentless pressure and backbiting, and that the prospect of stepping off the treadwheel and escaping from duties that now seemed onerous was enticing.

But he wasn't ready to do that yet. He had a battle to fight, and he intended to win it.

He thought he had made the right decision when Harry invited him and Campeggio to be his guests of honour at Christmas. Thomas was going to spend the season with his drinking friends in London, so Tom was pleased to be at Greenwich, where there were jousts, feasts, banquets, masques and disguisings.

The Queen was present, sitting beside Harry, who seemed restless and ill at ease.

'Her Grace looks like the proverbial spectre at the feast,' Cromwell muttered in Tom's ear, as they sat covertly eyeing the royal couple.

'And he would rather be sitting with Mistress Anne,' Tom murmured grimly. 'But of course, she cannot show herself while Cardinal Campeggio is here.' He had been relieved to find her absent.

He felt sorry for the Queen. Her eyes only lit up when she looked upon the Princess Mary, who had been brought to court for Christmas.

'All this lavish outlay is meant to sweeten Campeggio,' Cromwell observed, biting into a piece of gilded marchpane.

It was certainly not for himself, Tom knew. Harry's welcome had been less gracious than usual, and once, when there was a friendly argument at table, he'd rounded on Tom angrily. A tense atmosphere pervaded the festivities. More than once, Tom saw Mary's small, serious face regarding the King warily. Of course, the child – she was twelve now – must by now have heard something of the Great Matter. He felt for her. This case had touched so many lives already, not least his own, and he wished that he was going into the new year with optimism, rather than with the sense of dread he seemed to carry all the time now.

Chapter 32

1529

Once Christmas was over, Tom and Campeggio began preparing to hear the nullity suit. Anne had returned to court, and one day, coming upon Tom in a gallery, she cornered him.

'My lord Cardinal, why are we having to endure such a long delay until the court sits?'

'Alas, Mistress Anne, this is a complex matter—'

'Don't give me that, my lord!' Her eyes flashed. 'You're stringing it out, hoping that the King will give up his suit – and me! In fact, he suspects that you are opposing his case.'

'Madam, nothing could be further from the truth!' Tom protested, breaking out in a cold sweat. 'No one has worked harder for its success.'

'With very little to show for it! And all the while, the years pass and I am getting no younger. It's a shame you didn't stay in Ipswich, butchering cows!'

She swished away, leaving him reeling at the insult. It was rich, coming from her, whose forebears had been in trade! But he swallowed his pride and resolved to ignore it.

'The Queen has lodged an appeal in Rome against the authority of the legatine court,' Campeggio said. 'I doubt it will be heard soon, for his Holiness is sick.'

More delays. Tom's heart felt like a lead weight as he walked with the legate to his closet. There, he found a letter from Casale, stating that he had found no record of the brief at the Vatican. There was also one from Spain, where Tom's clerks had inspected the original. *It is undoubtedly a forgery*, they had written.

Jubilant, he turned to Campeggio. 'The Queen must be informed of these developments.'

He himself went to see her. 'My envoys have found no trace of the Emperor's brief in Rome,' he declared.

'That does not surprise me, my lord!' she replied drily.

He ignored her tone. 'More envoys were dispatched to Spain to see his Imperial Majesty's copy. It is clearly a forgery, so there is no point in your Grace producing your copy as evidence in court.'

Katherine gave him a withering look. 'It is unlikely that the case will be heard here anyway, my lord, not now that I have appealed for it to be heard in Rome. And then we will see the truth come out.'

'I think you will find that it will go ahead here,' Tom countered. 'Cardinal Campeggio and I have his Holiness's commission. The Holy Father is not likely to revoke that.'

Pray God he did not, he thought as he hastened away. If that happened, Tom would be in the greatest trouble that he had ever been.

The following weeks and months flew by, as Tom made arrangements for the legatine court, on top of all his other duties. He worked long hours, hardly taking time out to eat or even relieve himself. But that was as well. He needed distractions, when so much was hanging on the outcome of the case and Thomas was still idling about at Hampton Court, taking advantage of his besotted generosity.

Now, it was May, and everything was finally ready for the hearing. At the end of the month, the King formally licensed the legates to convene their court. It was to sit in the great hall of the monastery of the Blackfriars in London, where Parliament sometimes met. Bridewell Palace, where the King and Queen would stay for the duration of the case, was nearby.

Tom had left no stone unturned to make the King's case watertight, and he was hoping against hope for a happy outcome. There was enormous public interest in the proceedings because never before in England had a king and queen been summoned to appear in court.

He was feeling a touch optimistic as he went over the final arrangements with Harry. After all, the Queen's trump card had been disqualified. 'We will win,' he assured his master, as he showed him how the great hall of the priory of the Blackfriars had been turned into a legatine court.

'Do you think the Queen will obey the summons?' Harry wondered.

'It would be in her interests to do so,' Tom replied severely. 'Let us hope there are no demonstrations in her favour.'

'That's a vain hope,' Harry said, gazing around the hall. 'Opinions are running high.'

'There is indeed great interest in the proceedings. But set your mind at rest, Sir. I think Cardinal Campeggio will deliver the verdict you desire.'

'I pray so!' Harry said, with feeling. No doubt he was missing Anne, whom he had sent home to Hever, thinking it politic while the court was sitting.

It was officially opened on 31 May, but because workmen were still busy preparing the hall, the actual proceedings could not yet commence, much to Harry's annoyance – and Tom's.

Tom was conferring with Cromwell at York Place when a letter arrived from Joan. He was shocked to read that her husband had got into debt and been thrown into the Fleet prison.

'I must go,' he said. 'A private matter.'

Immediately, he took his barge from York Place to Hampton Court and rode from there to Thames Ditton.

She was pleased to see him, but deeply worried. 'I had no idea that he had money worries. It seems he borrowed beyond his means to sustain this lifestyle.' She waved a hand around the handsome hall with its vivid tapestries and elegant furnishings. 'Someone called in a debt, and he couldn't pay.'

'Who was it?'

'One of his creditors. A man called Urian Brereton.'

Tom knew him. He was a member of the Privy Chamber and close to the King – and to Anne Boleyn and her friends. Suspicion mounted. Had Legh just been profligate in his financial dealings and called upon one he thought a friend to help him? Or could Tom's enemies possibly be targeting him through the man who had married Joan, sending a subtle message that they could ruin him too?

He did not confide his fears to Joan. She was distressed enough.

She took him to the steward's room, where papers were piled up on a desk. 'There is no money to pay the debts, and very little to live on.'

'What of Cheshunt?'

'Mortgaged, and likely to be repossessed. And that will be the fate of this house if the money is not repaid.' She rubbed her hands distractedly. 'In truth, Tom, I don't know what I'm going to do. I have four children to consider. George can't help, as he has to remain in prison until the debts are cleared. How in God's name am I supposed to find the money?'

At that moment, the door opened and a little boy ran into the room, an angelic child with a halo of blonde curls. 'Mama, Ellen won't give me back my hobby horse!' he complained.

Over his head, Joan's eyes met Tom's. He stared at the boy. Flesh of his flesh. His son. A deep wave of emotion gripped him. 'Joan—'

'Mama!' the child insisted.

'Tell her I said to give it back, Tommy,' she said. Tommy ran off.

'Yes, he is yours,' she said to Tom. 'As is Ellen.'

'He's an engaging little fellow,' he observed, his voice hoarse. 'He has spirit.'

'And a strong will!' She smiled, but the smile soon faded. 'Tom, I'm sorry to have burdened you with my troubles, but I did not know where else to turn. Of course, I could ask my father for help—'

'I'm glad you came to me,' Tom said. 'You must not worry. I will settle the debts. How much do you owe?'

She showed him a page of figures. He blenched. But he had given his word. 'I will have the money sent to Brereton tomorrow, privily, through an intermediary. He won't know where it came from.' He would not give his enemies more ammunition against him.

'Tom, I don't know how to thank you.' Joan was weeping.

'I'm doing this for you, and our children,' he said, folding her in his arms. 'I cannot see you distressed like this, and you and the little ones need to keep a roof over your heads.'

There was a knock on the door, and Joan hurriedly pushed him away. It was the steward.

'Beg pardon, my Lady Legh, but Sir George's man has come back from London and wants to see you urgently.'

'Bring him in here,' she said. 'Tom, please stay.'

A young man in the Legh livery hurried in. He looked stricken.

'My lady, I fear I bring bad news. Sir George is dead of gaol fever.'

Joan's hands flew to her mouth. 'No! It cannot be!'

'He was ill for just two days, my lady. The gaoler said they're dying like flies in this heat. The whole place is stinking.'

Joan had gone deathly pale.

'Sit down,' Tom urged, then turned to the steward. 'Some wine for my lady, please.'

The steward hurried away.

'Do you want me to go?' Tom asked. 'I can come back whenever you wish, and I will still pay the debt, as I promised.'

'I . . . I don't know,' Joan said, flustered. 'I can't take it in. I can't believe George is dead.'

'You need time to think, my dear.' He rested a hand on her shoulder, then quickly removed it, as he noticed the young messenger watching them. 'I will see you soon,' he told her, and left.

All he could think of was that Joan was free. Free of that bounder, free, with his help, from money worries, free to make her own choices. Was she free to be his once more? She lived in her own house – well, it was little Thomas's now, but it would be years before he was of age – and in theory it would be easy for Tom to visit her without causing scandal, which was the last thing he wanted, but he needed her so badly that he was prepared to take the risk.

But the still, small voice of reason was cautioning him. Would such visits really go unnoticed? If he could spy on his enemies, he could be sure that they were spying on him, intent on finding ways to discredit him. And if they had been the cause of Legh's arrest – and, in truth, his death – then they would not hesitate to move against Tom himself. No, he would not give them the satisfaction.

The hall of the Blackfriars was packed and stank of sweat, for the weather was warm and everyone was wearing heavy robes or their best clothing. Tom sat sweltering in his red silks, surveying the scene. Great care had been taken in preparing the court. Two chairs upholstered in cloth of gold were placed ready for the legates on the railed dais at the end of the hall; before them stood a table covered with a Turkey carpet for their papers. To the right, in the body of the court, the King sat on a throne beneath a cloth of estate, and to the left, the Queen occupied a rich chair. The rest of the hall was laid out like a courtroom with tables, benches and a bar. Directly in front of the King's throne and the two cardinals sat Archbishop Warham and all the other bishops, with counsel for both parties at each side. Tom frowned when he saw Bishop Fisher, who was defending the Queen against Harry's team of bishops.

'Pray silence!' The crier's voice rang out. Then the legates' commission was read aloud, after which the crier called: 'King Henry of England, come into the court!'

'Here, my lords!' Harry said in a firm voice.

'Katherine, Queen of England, come into the court!'

To Tom's consternation, she rose, made her way around the room and knelt before the King. There was absolute silence, as if the court was holding its collective breath.

'Sir,' she said, 'I beseech you, for all the love that has been between us, and for the love of God, let me have justice and right, take pity and compassion on me, for I am a poor woman and a stranger born out of your dominion.' She was looking directly at Harry as she spoke, but he was staring straight ahead, unheeding, an ominous flush rising from his collar. Undeterred, Katherine pressed on, making an impassioned plea that should have moved the stoniest heart. Tom cringed for her; she might have saved herself the effort, for she was only succeeding in embarrassing Harry, and that would do her cause no good at all.

'I have here,' she was saying, 'no assured friend, and only indifferent counsel; one of my judges was the prime mover in this matter and he is a man of pride and voluptuousness.' Her face turned towards Tom as he sat in his high seat, feeling himself flush. He could not believe his ears. It was him to whom she was referring publicly in such disparaging terms – and it was not true that he had instigated the King's nullity suit. He burned with the injustice of the accusation.

But Katherine was not looking at him now. She had eyes only for Harry. Tom was so mortified that he could not take in the rest of her words. He only heard her say at the end that if the King would not spare her the court hearing, she would commit her cause to God.

Harry did not flinch. He remained silent. After a few terrible moments, Katherine rose, made a low curtsy to him and walked slowly towards the doors at the far end of the hall, leaning on the arm of one of her officers.

'Call the Queen back, crier,' Harry ordered.

'Katherine, Queen of England, come into the court!' The words rang out, but she ignored them and departed.

Harry rose. 'My lords and masters, since the Queen has gone, I will, in her absence, declare to you all that she has been to me as true and obedient a wife as I could wish or desire. She has all the virtuous qualities that ought to be in a woman of her dignity. She is a noble woman.'

Tom could contain himself no longer. He rose and bowed to the King. 'Sir, I most humbly beseech your Highness to declare before this audience whether I have been the prime mover of this matter to your Majesty; for I am greatly suspected of that by the Queen and, it seems, many others.'

'My lord Cardinal,' Harry replied, 'I can well excuse you of that charge. Indeed, you were rather against my pushing the matter forward. And to resolve any doubts, I will declare to you the special cause that moved me to do it. My conscience was pricked when the Bishop of Tarbes, the French King's ambassador, raised the question of my daughter Mary's legitimacy. His words bred a doubt in my breast, which so vexed and troubled my mind, and so disquieted me, that I became in great fear of God's indignation, which seemed manifest, since He has not sent me any male issue; all my sons by the Queen died immediately after they were born. So I cannot doubt that God has punished me.'

He was speaking from the heart and everyone present was hanging on his words.

'It was partly my conscience, and partly my despair of ever having any sons with the Queen, that drove me at last to consider the danger in which this realm stands for lack of a male heir to succeed me in this

Imperial dignity. I thought it good, therefore, to relieve the weighty burden of my scrupulous conscience, and for the quiet estate of this noble realm, to have the case examined and to find out whether I might take another wife in the event of my marriage being found unlawful. And this I intend not for any carnal reason, or because I am displeased with the Queen's person or her age, for I could be content to live with her if our marriage may stand with God's laws. It is those doubts that will now be tried by the learned wisdom and judgement of you, our prelates of this realm here assembled for that purpose; to whose conscience and judgement I have committed the charge according, and to which I will be right well contented to submit myself.'

He sat down, looking pensive, as if he was pained to find himself in such a situation. Tom could almost believe that a pair of dark eyes had never led him astray.

When the court reconvened, the King's counsel put it to the cardinals that his marriage had been invalid from the beginning because Prince Arthur had known Katherine carnally. Tom could sense Campeggio stirring next to him. Both were aware that this was not a valid pretext for an annulment.

'No man could know the truth of that,' Campeggio said.

A tall, gaunt figure stood up. 'I know the truth.' It was Fisher.

'How do you know you the truth?' Tom asked him, exasperated.

'I know that God is truth itself, and forasmuch as this marriage was made and joined by God, I say that I know the truth; for it cannot be broken or loosed by the power of man.'

'All faithful men know as much, as well as you,' Tom replied. 'Yet this reasoning is not sufficient in this case, for the King's counsel argue that the marriage was not lawfully joined by God at the beginning. And it cannot be doubted but that their arguments must be true, as it plainly appears; therefore, to say that the matrimony was joined by God, you must prove it and avoid making presumptions.'

Fisher subsided, but he was no doubt marshalling his arguments. Tom feared they had not heard the last from him.

* * *

Harry did not attend the court during the days that followed. He relied on Tom to keep him informed of its proceedings. The weather stayed hot, and Tom often arrived home perspiring and uncomfortable after long hours of sitting on his high seat.

'Another day of interminable depositions and heated discussions,' he reported to Harry, after a month had gone by and the King's temper was becoming so frayed that he was like a lion at bay with all who approached him.

'We are getting nowhere,' growled Harry.

'I fear so,' Tom agreed, feeling drained. 'Much of the evidence relates to whether Prince Arthur consummated his marriage. We've had a whole host of lords lining up to boast that they were capable of it at his age, which really is immaterial – and quite distasteful.'

'But the case *is* going my way?' Harry could not disguise his anxiety.

'I think so. Much of the evidence is heavily weighted in your Grace's favour.'

'What about Campeggio?'

'He gives nothing away, but I sense he is sympathetic. I do not think your Grace should be concerned.'

But Tom was deeply concerned, because he had the unnerving sense that the Italian Cardinal was keeping something up his sleeve. He redoubled his efforts to gain possession of Campeggio's bull, only to have his co-legate round on him. 'It is of no import, my lord! His Holiness has written expressly to forbid its use.'

Tom felt faint. 'That will be my ruin!' he lamented, dreading to contemplate Harry's reaction.

'I am sorry, but the matter is out of my hands,' said Campeggio.

Tom did not dare tell Harry the truth.

The hearing continued, as did the endless arguments. By the end of June, Tom and Campeggio were no nearer a conclusion than when the court first sat, and Tom was wondering if he himself would have any say in the matter. Then the King came into court, with the Queen.

'I beg of your Eminences,' Harry said, 'pray reach a final end to this matter, as I am so troubled in spirits that I cannot attend to anything that should be profitable for my realm and my people.' He looked distraught. Katherine said nothing; the court had declared her contumacious, as she had appealed to Rome against it.

After that, the daily sessions continued without the principal parties. To Tom's dismay, the consensus of opinion was that the King and Queen's marriage could only be lawful if Katherine had been left *virgo intacta* by Prince Arthur. The problem was that while she had sworn on the Blessed Sacrament, and in open court, that she had, Harry – the only other person who knew the truth of the matter – was alleging otherwise, and he had made Tom go to great lengths to seek out witnesses to that first wedding night. At the end of June, nineteen of them gave evidence, much of it deeply embarrassing to the Queen, and all of it inconclusive.

Fisher's insistence that the marriage was lawful clearly carried a lot of weight.

'The King can no longer persist in dissolving the marriage,' Campeggio told Tom. 'This one man's aversion to it has persuaded many, and I believe that the kingdom will not permit the Queen to suffer wrong.'

'I cannot agree!' Tom said hotly. 'The case must stand on its own merits, and the King insists that the Queen was no virgin on their wedding night.' But Campeggio just gave him a disbelieving look.

Tom's spirits plummeted further when he learned that the Pope had finally made a formal peace with the Emperor, which meant it was highly unlikely that he would support an annulment. The outlook was dismal. And all the time, Tom was worrying about Joan and how she was faring. He had sent the money to clear the debts, but had found it impossible to get away to visit her, so had had to content himself with writing letters, although he found it difficult to express in them the things he wanted to say. And Joan rarely replied, beyond the odd brief thank-you for his kind words. Poor soul, she had enough to contend with just now. He couldn't even cheer her with good news of their son, because Thomas was often out carousing with his friends and was prone to snarling when Tom took him to task for doing nothing with his life. And Tom felt so drained that he had not the mettle to reprove him for it.

* * *

One morning, as the court was breaking up for dinner, Harry sent for him. In great trepidation, Tom crossed the bridge that led over the River Fleet from the monastery to Bridewell Palace.

As he had feared, Harry was in a foul mood. 'Why haven't you given judgement yet? You've had weeks to deliberate.'

'Sir, this is a highly complicated matter,' Tom protested, but before he could elaborate, the King interrupted.

'It boils down to one thing: was Katherine's marriage to Arthur consummated? If it was, then her marriage to me is invalid. And I have told you, on the word of a king, that she was no virgin when I had her at the first. Many in there believe me. What's the problem?'

Tom was sweating, and not just from the heat of noonday. 'Sir, Cardinal Campeggio has heard the Queen's confession – and heard her swear an oath that she came to you a virgin. She publicly avowed it in court. The matter is still being debated.'

'Tell them I'll brook no more delays!' Harry was in no mood for compromising. 'I'll have this annulment if it's the last thing I do!'

It might be the last thing *I* do, Tom thought, as he hastened down to Blackfriars stairs, where his barge was waiting, greeting the waiting Bishop of Carlisle, who was to dine with him.

'York Place!' he instructed the boatmen, mopping his brow.

'It is a very hot day,' the Bishop observed.

'Yes,' Tom said with feeling, 'and if you had been as well chafed as I have been within this hour, you would say it was very hot.'

The Bishop gave him a sympathetic look. 'This is all putting a terrible strain on you, my lord.'

'Indeed,' Tom sighed. 'If it was down to me, I would have passed judgement long since. But I am hampered by the other legate's views and the Pope's dictates. My legatine authority is as nothing.'

The Bishop looked uncomfortable. 'Well, hopefully, you will soon be able to put this all behind you.'

'I am longing for the day,' Tom told him.

One afternoon in the middle of July, it was sweltering, and Tom was so exhausted that when he arrived back at York Place after a gruelling session of the court, he stripped off all his clothes and lay down on the bed, leaving the windows open. Despite the stifling heat, he was asleep within minutes.

He had not slept two hours, as he saw by his clock, when Cavendish came to wake him.

'My lord, Lord Rochford is here. He says he has a message from the King.'

Tom forced himself to come to his senses. Pulling the sheet over his nakedness, he sat up. 'Bring him in here.'

Rochford sailed in, his manner disdainful, and knelt by the bedside. 'My lord, his Grace wants you and Cardinal Campeggio to go immediately to see the Queen at Bridewell, and use your wisdoms to urge her to surrender to the King's pleasure in this Great Matter. You are to say that this will do more for her honour than enduring this trial of law, in which she may be condemned for perjury, which would be much to her slander and defamation.'

Tom was furious at being treated so peremptorily by Anne's father, of all people. 'I am ready to fulfil the King's pleasure, and will get up and go to Bridewell, but I must say this, my lord, that you and others who are close to the King are not a little to blame for this situation in which we all find ourselves, for you have put such fantasies into his head, whereby you have brought great trouble to all the realm. And for this, I assure you, you will get small thanks either from God or from the world.'

Rochford gave Tom a filthy look as he got up and left.

Tom rose, feeling disorientated and fatigued, and made ready. Then he went by barge to Bath Place, where he collected Cardinal Campeggio, and they went together to the Queen's lodging at Bridewell. In her deserted presence chamber, they informed a gentleman usher that they wished to speak to her. Presently, she emerged from her privy chamber with a skein of white thread about her neck and several of her attendants behind her.

'You see my employment,' she said. 'In this way I pass the time with my maids, who are not the ablest counsellors, yet I have no other in England, while Spain, where there are those on whom I could rely, is,

God knows, far off.' She gave them a sad smile. 'My lords, I am very sorry to cause you to attend upon me. What is your pleasure with me?'

Tom spoke first. 'If it pleases your Grace to go into your privy chamber, we will tell you why we are here.'

'My lord,' she said, 'if you have anything to say, speak it openly before all these people here, for I fear nothing that you can say or allege against me, but I would rather that all the world should hear it; therefore, I pray you, speak your minds openly.'

Tom felt flustered. This was not for her maidens' ears. He began to speak to her in Latin.

'No, my lord,' Katherine protested. 'Speak to me in English, I beseech you.'

He took a deep breath. 'Well then, Madam, we come to find out where you stand in this matter between the King and you, and also to declare secretly our opinions and our counsel to you, out of zeal for your Grace.'

'My lords, I thank you for your goodwill, but I cannot give you an immediate answer, for you found me sitting among my maids at work, thinking little of any such matter, which needs longer deliberation and a better head than mine. I have need of good counsel in this case, which touches me so nearly; and I fear there is no impartial counsel or friendship in England. Think you, my lords, will any Englishmen counsel me against the King's pleasure, being his subjects? Bear with me, for I am a simple woman, destitute of friendship in a foreign land. So I will not refuse your counsel, but will be glad to hear it.'

A simple woman? Tom knew from bitter experience that she was a formidable adversary who had been soundly advised, not least by Bishop Fisher. But he was touched when she took him by the hand and led him into her privy chamber, with Campeggio following.

'I thank you for your kindness, Madam,' Tom said, sinking heavily into the chair she indicated. 'It has been a somewhat trying day.' He mopped his brow. 'It is the King's wish that you surrender this whole matter into his hands. He fears that if the case goes against you, some judicial condemnation might follow, and then shame and slander might accrue to you. His Grace wishes to avoid all occasion for that. He asks you, as his wife, to remit your cause to him.'

'But he is trying to prove that I am not his wife,' Katherine protested. 'He cannot have it both ways. As for this judicial condemnation with which you threaten me, no one could say I have not been a true wife to his Grace. There is no crime with which he can charge me. And anyway, if, as he says, I am not his wife, then I am not his subject and therefore exempt from his laws.'

'Perhaps I should have said censure, rather than condemnation. If the case goes against you, and you persist in an adulterous marriage, we, the legates, and perhaps even his Holiness, may feel that some admonishment is in order.'

'Are you threatening me?' Katherine snapped. 'God knows, and you know, that my marriage is not adulterous! I am the King's true wife, and I will remain so until my dying day!'

Tom and Campeggio looked at each other in despair.

'Madam, we will report your answer to the King,' Tom said, rising creakily to his feet; and with that, they took their leave.

Harry was almost stamping with rage. 'Will that woman never cease to confound me?'

'Sir, we have tried our utmost—' Tom began.

'She's cozened you with fair words! You should have threatened her, been firmer with her. Until our marriage is dissolved, she's my subject and she'll obey me! Sometimes, my lord, I wonder at your competence.'

Before Tom could protest, Harry had turned to Campeggio. 'As for you, my lord, maybe you can tell me if you really intend to prorogue the court until October, after the summer recess of the Papal court, and if so, why I had to learn of it from a third party?'

Campeggio put his hand to his heart. 'Your Majesty's information is incorrect. I am hoping to give judgement soon.'

Harry thrust his face into the legate's. 'I hope so, my lord, I truly hope so!'

During the next session of the court, Norfolk, Suffolk and other lords stood up and said that the King had willed them to require the legates to make an end of the matter. 'Whatever judgement your Eminences give, he will gladly accept it for the quietness of his conscience,' Norfolk said.

He leaned across to Campeggio, ignoring Tom. 'The people will now expect a sentence within days,' he murmured.

Campeggio regarded him sternly. 'All in good time. I will not fail in my duty. When giving sentence, I will have only God before my eyes, and the Holy See.' With mounting dread, Tom realised that his co-legate was not going to commit himself to anything. It infuriated him, for were they not meant to be giving judgement together? Yet there was nothing he could do. Campeggio was receiving instructions from the Pope, and Tom had to abide by them.

Chapter 33

1529

With August only days away, Campeggio hinted that he was ready to come to a decision. In a jubilant mood, Tom sped to Harry to tell him the good news. Given how the discussions had gone over the past few days, he was hopeful that the verdict would be what the King wanted to hear.

That afternoon, Harry came to the Blackfriars and sat in a gallery overlooking the dais where Tom and Campeggio were sitting. Then his learned counsel at the bar called for judgement to be pronounced.

Campeggio rose slowly to his feet. 'I will give no judgement in this case until I have reported to the Holy Father all our proceedings. The case is too notable and famous for us to make any hasty judgement, considering the royal birth of the parties and the doubtful allegations that have been made.'

Tom feared he might faint, he was so shocked. To have waited so long, and to no purpose, was crushing. He had put his heart and soul into this business. He dared not look up at the King.

Campeggio was still speaking. 'I did not come so far to please any man, for fear or favour, be he king or any other potentate. I have no such respect to anyone that I will offend my conscience, and I will not do anything against the law of God. I am an old man, sick and impotent, looking daily for death. What should it then avail me to put my soul in danger of God's displeasure, to my utter damnation, for the favour of any prince or high estate in this world? My being here is only to see justice ministered according to my conscience.'

Tom could sense the King's anger; it seemed to emanate from

where he was sitting. He saw the fury in the faces of Norfolk, Suffolk and Rochford.

'The truth in this case is very doubtful and difficult to determine,' Campeggio went on, 'and matters are complicated by the fact that the Queen will make no answer, but has appealed to the Pope to have the case heard in Rome, for she thinks we cannot administer indifferent justice for fear of the King's displeasure. Therefore, to avoid all these ambiguities and obscure doubts, I will wade no farther in this matter unless I have the assent of the Pope. Wherefore I will adjourn this court to the court of Rome. I hereby declare it dissolved.'

There was a stunned silence as he sat down, and Tom tried to take in the import of his words. Ruin was staring him in the face. Adjourned to Rome . . . That could mean a delay of weeks, if not months. Harry would be devastated – no less devastated than Tom was feeling now.

A fist banged down hard on a table. It was Suffolk, his face red with anger. 'By the Mass, it was never merry in England while we had cardinals among us!' he shouted.

At last, Tom glanced up at the King, who gave him such a scathing look that he quailed, knowing he had failed his beloved master miserably. He turned to Suffolk.

'Of all men in this realm, my lord, you have least cause to be offended with cardinals. For if I, a simple cardinal, had not come to your aid when you married the King's sister, you would have no head upon your shoulders.'

The Duke glared at him, but Tom was undeterred. 'I wish you knew that I and my brother legate here intend the King and his realm only honour, wealth and quietness, and that we would gladly accomplish his lawful desire. But, my lord, I pray you, show me what you would do if you were the King's commissioner, having a weighty matter to treat upon, and the conclusion being doubtful. Therefore, banish your hasty malice and consider that we are but commissioners and may not proceed to judgement without the consent of the Pope. And if any man is offended with us for that, he is an unwise fellow.'

His words were not intended just for Suffolk, but for everyone in the courtroom. He hoped that Harry had been listening. But when he looked up, the King had gone.

The court gradually emptied. Tom stayed in his chair, reluctant to move, for once he had done so, he would have to go to the King and face his wrath. He was in no doubt that Harry would visit it on him and hold him to blame for what had happened. He could not take out his anger on Campeggio, for fear of alienating the Holy See, but here was Tom, his subject, at hand, and at his mercy.

'Are you not coming, my lord?' Campeggio asked kindly.

'Yes, I suppose so,' Tom said, getting up reluctantly. He gathered up his papers and took himself off to the room he had used as an office. There, he sank down with his head in his hands, feeling that it was the end. That was how the King's usher found him when he came with the summons.

He could hardly face Harry, whose expression was cold. Tom had never seen him like that. He had known that the King would take the decision badly, but this blatant antagonism was dreadful, especially after Tom had worked so long and so hard on his behalf.

'You realise what this means for me?' Harry barked. 'The Papal court will not sit again until October, but both you and I know that its proceedings progress infuriatingly slowly, so it will now be a matter of months, if not years, before the Pope reaches a decision – and the wait might be in vain. In the meantime, I will still be living in sin at the risk of God's further displeasure and England has no male heir to the throne.'

'I am well aware of all that, Sir,' Tom replied, 'and no man is more heavy-hearted about it than I.'

'So you should be!' Harry flung back. 'I was warned that you were working against me, and here is proof of it.'

'Never!' Tom cried, stung into retaliation. 'I did my best to get the marriage annulled. Your Grace knows the truth of that. My enemies have been telling you lies.'

'Your enemies have made me aware of the truth!' Harry shouted. 'What they warned me of has come to pass. With Clement hand-in-glove with the Emperor, judgement will no doubt be given in the

Queen's favour. But I will fight them. You can tell my ambassadors at the Vatican that my royal dignity will not admit to my being summoned to appear at the Papal court, nor, I am sure, will my nobles and subjects allow it. Tell them to tell Clement that if I go to Rome, it will be at the head of an army, and not as a supplicant for justice.'

'I will tell them, Sir,' Tom said miserably.

'Do it,' Harry muttered, and with an impatient wave of his hand, he dismissed him, leaving Tom in no doubt that he was in disgrace, and that Anne, Norfolk and the rest of their faction would now have an excuse to be rid of him for good.

He dragged himself back to his office and wrote to Rome as the King had instructed. Then, feeling in dire need of comfort, he resolved to go to the one person who could give it.

He arrived at Joan's house in the evening, hot, drained and feeling like a wreck. She looked shocked at the sight of him.

'What has happened?' she cried.

He told her. He ended up falling upon her neck, weeping as if he would never cease. To her credit, she never reminded him that she had begged him to resign, although he wished now that he had heeded her. But it hadn't only been the power and the wealth that had stopped him, but breaking away from Harry, who he regarded almost as a son – the other great love of his life. Harry, who now – it seemed – loved him no more. His grief was immense.

He poured out his heart to Joan, and she listened, holding him. And in the end, she led him to her bedchamber and gave him the greatest comfort that one human being could give to another. As he lay in her arms, he wept again, but he did feel better. Possessing her had made him feel of some worth again, that there was something beyond the life he had known that was precious and offered hope for the future.

He would return, he assured her late that evening, as they walked to where his horse was tethered. They would be together again. She smiled and said nothing.

Part Six

'Naked to my enemies'

Chapter 34

1529

He did not have to wait long for Anne Boleyn to show her hand. The very next day, Cavendish, looking nervous, brought him a letter. It struck dread into his heart.

My lord, although you are a man of great understanding, you cannot avoid being censured by everybody for having brought on yourself the hatred of a king who has raised you to the highest degree to which the greatest ambition of man can aspire. I cannot comprehend, and the King still less, how your reverend lordship, after having allured us by so many fine promises about divorce, can have done what you have in order to hinder it. Having given me the strongest tokens of your affection, you have abandoned my interests to embrace those of the Queen. I put my confidence in your promises, but I find myself deceived. For the future, I shall rely on nothing but the protection of Heaven and the love of my dear King, which alone can set right again those plans you have broken and spoiled, and can place me in that happy situation which God wills, the King so much wishes, and which will be entirely to the advantage of the kingdom. The wrong you have done me has caused me much sorrow, but I feel infinitely more in seeing myself betrayed by a man who pretended to look to my interests. I acknowledge that, believing you sincere, I have been too precipitate in my confidence. It is this which has induced, and still induces, me to stay moderate in avenging myself, not being able to forget that I have been your servant, Anne Boleyn.

There would be no more need for hypocrisy. Anne had declared her enmity openly. The night crow, as he privately thought of her now, was poised to swoop, like the bird whose cries, overheard in darkness, were a harbinger of doom. Tom knew himself bested.

Not knowing what to do, he withdrew to The More, his house in Rickmansworth, accompanied by Cavendish and a reduced household. It would be much further away from Joan and Thomas, but he hoped to be back at Hampton Court in a short while. He could rely on his army of officers, secretaries and clerks to attend to business in his absence, and kept in touch with them daily by fast messenger. Then he moved to Esher, to be nearer to his loved ones, and invited the King to entertainments there, as in the old days. The King declined.

Early in September, he was informed that Harry had been cited to appear at the Papal court to have his Great Matter determined. It had prompted an outburst of fury.

The calling of the case to Rome will not only completely alienate the King and his realm from the Holy See, but will ruin me utterly, Tom wrote to Casale. He felt he was in Purgatory. Harry and Anne were the only people with the power to rescue their affectionate servant from the gates of Hell. If they did not, he knew he would stand in the gravest danger. His spies had reported speculation that he would lose his head. But surely, he reasoned, the King would not go so far as to put to death a prince of the Church, not when he wanted the Pope's co-operation? Even so, Tom could end up impoverished or even imprisoned, cut off from everything that had mattered to him.

This very night I was as one that should have died, he confided in a letter to Thomas Cromwell, who had proved his loyalty over and over again, and was now often at court, testing the water. *I pray you to exert all possible means of attaining Mistress Anne's favour.*

Cromwell could do nothing. When the King and his sweetheart went away on progress, Tom was informed that he was not to join them. He consoled himself by pouring out his woes to Joan in a torrent of letters, to which she sent consoling replies. Each time he wrote, he hated himself, because Joan had enough to cope with without shouldering his burdens. Oh, but he longed to see her, longed to pour his heart out to her and know again the intimate comfort only she could give him, but she had now gone to visit her family in Yarmouth, so even that consolation was denied him.

* * *

Cardinal Campeggio was going home. To his surprise, Tom was summoned to accompany him to the royal hunting lodge at Grafton in Northamptonshire, so that he could take his leave of the King, who was still on progress. It was two months since the legatine court had risen, two months since Tom had seen his master. His spirits soared. Could this signal a thawing of Harry's anger? Had he at last realised that it was not Tom who had failed him?

But when they arrived, and Campeggio was escorted away to the lodging that had been prepared for him, Tom was left in the courtyard, sitting desolately on his mule, painfully aware that no accommodation appeared to have been made ready for him. As Cavendish scurried off to find someone in charge, passing servants and courtiers stared curiously. Tom could not have felt more wretched or mortified.

Then he saw someone hurrying towards him. It was Sir Henry Norris, Chief Gentleman of the Privy Chamber, one of the King's closest friends – and a partisan of the Boleyns. Tom's heart sank. But Norris was bowing to him.

'My lord Cardinal, have they abandoned you? I'm sure there has been a mistake. His Grace would not want you to be treated thus. Come to my chamber. You can change out of your riding clothes before you see the King. I will find a lodging for you.'

Tom was touched by the man's kindness and courtesy. He had heard both Harry and his own spies speak highly of him over the years. 'Thank you for your gentle offer,' he said.

Norris beckoned to a groom and had Tom's travelling chest carried upstairs. As they followed, Tom was feeling some trepidation. 'Am I to see the King?'

'Yes, my lord. His Grace sent me to summon you and Cardinal Campeggio to his presence chamber.'

Was it to be another public humiliation? Tom felt a rising sense of dread at the thought of the courtiers witnessing his first meeting with Harry after the rift. He wished they could have met in private.

He was tense as he entered the crowded presence chamber. He looked anxiously for Anne, who was nowhere to be seen, but he saw Norfolk, Suffolk, Rochford and their supporters waiting like birds of prey for the kill, and the curiosity in the faces of others who had come only to watch how the audience played out. He knelt before his master, not daring to look up. If only things could be as they had once been between them. Would Harry even speak to him? He feared he might burst into tears.

'My lord Cardinal!' the King cried. 'You are most welcome!' He actually stepped down from the dais and helped Tom up from his knees, then led him by the hand to a window embrasure, where they could talk without being overheard. He was as amiable and cheerful as ever. Tom's heart filled with joy; his knees felt as if they would give way. No matter that the courtiers were staring, or that his enemies were glowering at him! Harry still loved him. That was all that mattered.

'Your Grace, forgive me,' he murmured. 'I did everything I could to persuade the legate to grant your suit. I strongly suspect he had orders to adjourn the case before he even left Rome. If there is anything I can do to make amends, I shall not hesitate to do it.'

Harry placed an arm around his shoulder. 'I am sure there is a way through this impasse. Let us work together to find it. Now go to your dinner, and afterwards I will talk with you again.' Whereupon Norfolk and George Boleyn immediately left the room, no doubt to report back to the night crow.

As Tom left the chamber, he glimpsed the countenances of those who had clearly expected to see him utterly cast away, and suppressed a smile.

After dinner, he received a message that the King would see him in the morning as he was otherwise occupied. Tom wondered if Anne had got at him, and felt a twinge of unease. Later that evening, Cavendish came to him.

'My lord, I heard from those who waited upon the King and Mistress Anne at supper that she was much offended with his Grace because he had so warmly welcomed you. She said that if any nobleman had done but half as much as your Grace had done, he would have lost his head.'

Tom's anxiety deepened. Had Harry put off their meeting to

placate Anne? Would she now be even more zealous to bring him down? Worst of all, would Harry heed her? He could not wait for the morning to come, so that he could see the King and be reassured that all was indeed well again between them.

He got up early, ready for their meeting, but heard men and horses gathering below. When he emerged into the courtyard where Campeggio was waiting, he found his master dressed for riding, mounting his horse. Anne was with him.

'My lord Cardinals,' Harry called from the saddle, 'I fear I have no time to talk this morning. We are going to hunt in Hartwell Park and have dinner outdoors. I'll say farewell to you both now. I will be back late, so you had best return south, as I would not delay you. Fare you well!'

His heart plummeting, Tom had no choice but to bow and take his leave. Harry gave him an amiable smile and rode off with Anne, who threw a triumphant smile at Tom over her shoulder.

Tom clenched his fists in frustration. Harry's sudden departure, of course, had been arranged by the night crow, who must have been determined to ensure that he should not return until Tom had left. Well, he would best her. He had all the time in the world to wait.

The Queen did her best to entertain him and Campeggio. She was kind, no doubt aware that Tom was growing increasingly anxious as the evening approached. By then, Campeggio was restive. He wanted to be on his way before nightfall. Tom could delay no longer, having agreed to travel south with his fellow legate. At length, he rose reluctantly, utterly defeated, and took his leave of Katherine.

'I had hoped to see the King before I left,' he said.

'I am sure your Eminence will see him soon,' she replied.

'No, Madam,' he said. 'The night crow has got at him.' Too late, he realised what he had said, but he could barely bring himself to say her name. 'She seeks my ruin. He will not send for me again.'

Katherine was silent. She probably knew that he was right.

Tom and Campeggio parted company at The More, when Campeggio set off on his long journey towards Rome. The legal Michaelmas

Term was approaching, so Tom returned to York Place. When the term began on 8 October, he went to Westminster Hall as he had always done, as Lord Chancellor, and sat in the Court of Chancery all day, hearing pleas and adjudicating on disputes. But when he arrived the following morning, an official of the Court of King's Bench was waiting for him.

'My lord Cardinal, I am here to serve you a writ summoning you to present yourself before the Court of King's Bench to answer the charge of praemunire.' He thrust a scroll into Tom's hand. 'Come with me.'

Tom could not speak. He was shuddering with shock and felt faint. This was the night crow's work. Harry would not have done this to him of his own accord.

He followed the official across Westminster Hall to where the Court of King's Bench was located and was ordered to stand at the bar before a panel of judges, all of whom were familiar to him. Anxiously, he searched their faces for some sign of recognition and friendliness, but found none.

'Thomas Wolsey,' said one, 'the King's Grace has commanded that you be indicted under the Statute of Praemunire, which prohibits Papal interference in English affairs without his royal consent. You have received bulls from Rome and accepted the office of Papal legate. Both are offences under the Statute. What say you? Are you guilty or not guilty?'

His head swimming, Tom cast back frantically in his mind, trying to recall anything he had done to justify the charges, before realising that he could not deny them. There was no use in protesting that he had committed these offences in the King's interests, or that Harry had known about them, and approved them, at the time. The Statute of Praemunire was being used merely as an instrument to bring him to ruin.

'What say you?' the judge repeated.

'Guilty, my lord, but only of working to further the affairs of the King's Highness, and with his full knowledge.'

His words were ignored.

'Thomas Wolsey, you are found guilty, and the penalty is forfeiture of all your lands and goods.'

The blow had fallen so swiftly that he left the court reeling and could barely see the way to his barge. Was it his barge any more? He supposed not.

As he was rowed along the Thames, he tried to take in the fact that he was now a pauper, reliant on the King's generosity. They would all be seized, his great houses, the personal possessions he had so proudly amassed, the estates he had purchased, even the clothes he wore.

When he got to York Place, nothing was amiss. He wondered how long it would be before the King's men came and threw him out. But wait! This was not his house; it was the London residence of the archbishops of York, and he was entitled to live in it. Hampton Court belonged to the King anyway. Yet the Crown could still take his other houses and all his personal property. His chief concern was that Thomas would be ejected from Hampton Court. He wrote urgently, bidding his son attend him in London, but there was no response. He sent a messenger to his steward, only to be informed that Thomas had gone to visit his uncles at Yarmouth.

Tom was surprised, for the lad had shown little interest in his mother's family. Had Joan, fearful for the future, somehow arranged to send him there? If so, he wished he could have thanked her for lifting one burden of worry from his shoulders. And when he thought about it, it might remove another, for the hard-working Larkes would not tolerate idleness.

But what would become of himself? He hurried to his closet and wrote to Harry, begging for mercy.

For eight anxious days, he heard nothing, and then Norfolk and Suffolk came to see him, their faces cold.

'My lord Cardinal,' Norfolk said, 'his Grace has sent us to inform you that he has stripped you of the office of Lord Chancellor of England. He requires you to surrender the Great Seal to us and retire to your house at Esher. Before you depart, you are to take an inventory of every room in York Place.'

So Harry meant to have that too. The night crow had done her work well. There could be no doubting that she had turned Harry utterly against him. But he was not going to give in easily. He would insist that this was done according to the law.

'My lords, what commission do you have to give me such commands?'

'We are sufficient commissioners, having the King's commandment from his own mouth,' Norfolk growled.

'Yet that is not sufficient for me without a formal command from his Grace,' he protested. 'The Great Seal of England was delivered to me by the King's own hands to enjoy during my life, with the administration of the chancellorship of England. I have the King's letters patent to prove it.'

'And we have the King's command to the contrary,' Suffolk snapped. 'You must obey his orders.'

'I cannot surrender that which was entrusted to me without a proper warrant,' Tom insisted. Fuming, the two dukes went away, saying they would report his disobedience to the King.

The next day, they returned, and this time they had a commission that bore Harry's familiar signature. It gave Tom an agonising jolt to see it; he felt tears welling as he read the formal words, willing himself not to be unmanned in the presence of his enemies. 'I am now content to obey the King's commandment,' he said.

He opened a drawer, took out the Great Seal of England in its embroidered velvet burse and placed it in Norfolk's outstretched hand. Then he took off his gold chain of office and handed it to Suffolk. With it, he relinquished all his temporal power.

What next? he wondered. Where would the night crow's vindictiveness end?

He took great pains to have everything in order. He summoned all his officers and instructed them to make an inventory of everything in the vast, rambling palace. When they had finished, his gallery was crammed with tables bearing piles of silk, velvet, satin, damask, taffeta, grosgrain, sarcenet and other rich fabrics, as well as five hundred pieces of fine holland cloth. He had ordered that the hangings of cloth of gold and silver be left on the walls, and that his richest vestments and copes be hung on pegs. In the two chambers adjoining the gallery, there stood long trestle tables on which was laid out all his gold and silver plate, some set with pearls and precious stones. Beneath the tables were baskets containing old or broken plate. On each table was a book in which the items on it were listed. As he watched Cavendish hurrying about with the rest, but with tears streaming down his cheeks, and Cromwell, who had come from court to offer his support, looking on grim-faced, Tom tried not to think about the pleasure these possessions had given him, tried not to mourn the days when he had taken them for granted. He must be content now with what was spared to him.

He retreated to the study where he and Harry had discussed business so many times, and wrote to both Joan and Thomas, telling them what had happened and where he was to be found. He hoped that Thomas was still at the farm to receive the letter. Esher was less than three miles away from Thames Ditton. Although he could not go to her, Joan would easily be able to visit him. He prayed that she would. It would be the greatest comfort to see her.

When the King's officers arrived and demanded that he surrender the keys of York Place to them, he obeyed without a murmur, praying that his uncomplaining co-operation would placate his master. Then he prepared to leave for Esher, taking nothing but some provisions for his house. At the door to the landing stage, he commanded Sir William Gascoigne, his treasurer, to see everything delivered safely to the King.

Sir William looked distressed. 'I am sorry for your Grace, for I understand you are being taken straight to the Tower.'

Tom froze, horrified. It could not be true. No, of course it wasn't true. There were no guards here come to haul him off.

'Is that all the comfort you can give to your master in adversity?' he snapped, his nerves frayed. 'I would have you know, Sir William, and anyone else who spreads such lies, that there is nothing more false, for, thanks be to God, I never deserved to go there, even though it has pleased the King to take my houses for his pleasure at this time. Therefore, go on your way, and make sure that nothing is embezzled!'

With that, he walked down to the privy stairs, followed by a dozen of his gentlemen and yeomen and a few menials, and boarded his barge for Putney, where he had arranged for horses to be waiting. As he was rowed upstream, he found the Thames crowded with what looked like a thousand boats full of men and women, presumably come to see him being taken to the Tower. And they were rejoicing!

It chilled him to the bone. After all his years of service and sacrifice, all that he had done for his King and his country, he could not but feel bitter. But, he told himself, the natural disposition of Englishmen was to desire an alteration in the fortunes of those in power, for men in authority were always greatly disdained by the common people, especially those who ministered justice to all men indifferently, as Tom felt sure he had. He kept his gaze averted as he passed, trying to look as if he had not a care in the world.

At Putney, he took his mule, and his gentlemen mounted their horses. His fool, Patch, brought up the rear. As they set forth on the road to Esher, he saw a man riding down the hill towards him. It was Sir Henry Norris.

Norris saluted him. 'My lord, the King's Majesty bids you be of good cheer, and has asked me to tell you that you are as much in his favour as ever you were. And he bade me give you this ring in token of it.'

Tom's heart was racing. It was too much to take in. This morning, he had been wondering if he was to go to the Tower. Now, he was back in royal favour. His eyes filled with tears as he took the cameo ring, the privy token long used between him and his master whenever Harry wanted Tom to be sure that secret orders came from him. He put it to his lips and kissed it reverently.

'His Grace also said that you shall lack for nothing,' Norris went on. 'And although you may think he has dealt with you unkindly, he says it is not for any displeasure he bears you, but only to satisfy those whom he knows not to be your friends. You well know that he is able to recompense you with twice as much as your goods are worth, and this too he bade me say to you. Therefore, Sir, have patience. And for my part, I trust soon to see you in better circumstances than ever.'

Tom felt overwhelmed. The King still loved him! Tears streaming down his face, he slid off his mule and knelt down in the dirt, holding up his hands for joy. Norris stared at him in amazement, then he too dismounted and fell to his knees beside him, embracing him in his arms. 'Be of good cheer,' he said. 'Think on what the King has said.'

'Master Norris,' Tom wept, 'when I consider your heartening news, I can only rejoice, for the sudden joy I felt made me realise it was my bounden duty to give thanks to God, and to the King, who has sent me such comfort when I most needed it.'

Still on his knees in the mire, he tried to tug off his velvet skullcap, but he could not undo the knot under his chin, so he wrenched at the laces, pulled it from his head and prayed bare-headed. Then he covered his head again and arose. He would have mounted his mule, but found that he was stiff and could not do so with his customary agility, so he had to call upon his footmen to set him in his saddle. Then he rode on up the hill, talking with Norris. At Putney Heath, Norris took his leave and would have departed, but Tom detained him.

'Gentle Norris, if I were lord of a kingdom, one half of it would be insufficient reward for your coming here and your good news. But I have nothing left but the clothes on my back, so I desire you to take this small reward from my hands.' He took from his neck his cherished gold crucifix. 'It contains a tiny piece of the True Cross. When I was in prosperity, although it seemed of little value, I would not have parted from it for a thousand pounds. Therefore, I beseech you to take it and wear it about your neck for my sake, and when you look at it, remember me to the King's Majesty whenever opportunity serves you. Assure him that I will always pray to God for the preservation of his royal estate, and that he will long reign in honour, health and quiet life. Tell him I am his obedient subject and poor chaplain, and that I account myself of no estimation, but only by him, whom I love better than myself; him whom I have truly served to the best of my wits.'

'I will,' Norris promised.

Tom took him by the hand, bade him farewell and spurred his

mule. But he had only gone a short distance when he wheeled it around. 'Sir Henry,' he called, 'I am sorry that I have no token to send to the King. But if you would take with you Patch, my poor fool, I trust his Highness will accept him well, for surely he is worth a thousand pounds.'

Patch looked horrified. 'No, my lord, I will not go!' he protested. 'I want to serve *you*!'

'For my sake, go and make the King laugh,' Tom bade him.

'Not I!' The man was working himself up into a rage.

'Listen to me, Patch,' Tom urged. 'I may not be able to pay your wages for much longer. You will have much better prospects with the King.'

'No! I will not go!' shouted Patch.

Tom nodded at his six tall yeomen. 'Convey this fool to the court,' he ordered them. 'Do not heed his bleating. Go peacefully, Patch, and think on me sometimes. I shall miss you.' Patch went, swearing great oaths.

Tom journeyed on to Esher, hoping fervently that Harry meant what he had told Norris, and regretting having forced Patch to leave him, even though it was for the best. Hopefully, when Patch was going through his antics, Harry would be reminded of his faithful servant and think kindly on him.

It was fortunate that the house at Esher belonged to the diocese of Winchester – unless, of course, the King decided to take it too. When they arrived, Tom found that nothing had been made ready for him. There were no beds, sheets, tablecloths, cups or dishes. He realised that they had not brought nearly enough necessities with them.

'Well, my masters, we will have to make camp,' he said cheerfully. 'I have no doubt that the King will supply all that is needful. We have plenty of victuals, and sufficient beer and wine.' And, of course, he still had the revenues from the sees of York and Winchester. He was not destitute.

His optimism was ill-founded. After three weeks of making do, he was obliged to ask his friends the Bishop of Carlisle and Sir Thomas Arundell if he could borrow dishes, drinking vessels and linen.

He soon learned that the King had seized York Place, The More, Tittenhanger and Esher, although his Majesty was graciously pleased to allow him to remain at the latter. Harry had also taken full possession of Hampton Court. Everywhere, Tom's coats of arms had been torn down and replaced with the King's. He could hardly bear to think about it. Was this what it meant now to be in favour? What of Harry's fair words, relayed by Norris? They had been meaningless.

Late in October, he learned that Sir Thomas More had been chosen to replace him as chancellor. He knew More to be an upright and learned man, and that he had resolutely never meddled in the Great Matter. But now, Tom supposed, Harry would be putting pressure on him to support him in his quest for an annulment. Norfolk, he heard, had been made Lord President of the Council, with Suffolk as his deputy, but – as ever – above them all was the sinister night crow. Doubtless none of them had any influence except what it pleased her to allow them.

On the feast of All Hallows, he summoned the faithful Cavendish to help him prepare his closet for Mass.

Cavendish seemed upset. 'My lord, Master Cromwell is here. I found him in the great chamber saying Our Lady's Matins most earnestly. I bade him good morrow, and then I saw that he was weeping. I asked him why he was so sorrowful, and he said he feared he was likely to lose all for doing your Grace true and diligent service. He said he was held in disdain by most men for your sake, and without just cause.'

Tom could have wept himself. Loyal Cromwell, who had been such an able and faithful servant.

'Go and bring him to me,' he said.

Cavendish looked uncomfortable. 'Alas, I fear it would do no good, for he is in a hurry. He said that he intends to return to London and the court this afternoon, to ensure that no calumny attaches to him for supporting your Grace.'

'I will speak to him before he goes,' Tom said.

After Mass, he returned to his chamber, where he dined with his two chaplains and his steward. Cromwell joined them, but the talk was all of domestic matters.

When he had finished eating, Tom laid down his napkin. 'I should like to commend you all for so loyally serving me these past weeks,' he said, looking at Cromwell. 'I know that it has perhaps been at some cost to yourself.'

Cromwell spoke, as plainly as he always did. 'In all conscience, my lord, you ought to thank the rest of your servants, those who are not here with us at table, for their true and faithful service, for they too have never forsaken you in all your trouble. They deserve to be rewarded.'

'Alas, Thomas,' Tom replied, 'you know I have nothing to give them, and words without deeds are not often taken well. I am ashamed and sorry that I am not able to reward their loyalty.'

Cromwell gave him an odd look. 'Why, Sir, do you not employ a number of chaplains to whom you have liberally granted promotions? Some have gained a thousand marks per annum, some even more. They have done well at your hands, but your other servants have had nothing at all, yet they have taken far more pains for you in one day than all your idle chaplains have done in a year.'

Rarely had Cromwell spoken so frankly. Tom felt chastened. 'Thomas, I hear what you say. Call my servants and have them assemble in the great chamber after dinner.'

When they were all gathered together, Tom took his place in the window with his chaplains about him. He could not speak, for his heart was full of tenderness for them. He turned his face to the wall, dabbing his eyes discreetly. He would not let them see his tears. When he had composed himself, he addressed them. 'Most faithful and true-hearted yeomen, I very much lament my negligent ingratitude towards you all, that in my prosperity I did not do for you so much as I might have done. But then I did not realise what treasures I had in you. Now, experience has taught me better. I am sorry that I have not promoted or preferred you according to your merits.' He paused, struggling to control his emotion. 'But since it has pleased the King to take all I have into his possession, I most heartily require you to have patience for a little while, since I doubt not that he will shortly restore me again to my living, so that I will be able to reward you. And if he does not restore me, I will see you bestowed in other posts according to your own wishes, and write recommendations for you, either to the King or to any noble in this realm. Go home, take a month off, then come back to me, and I trust by that time that the King's Majesty will have extended his clemency to me.'

He looked up and was moved to see that several were weeping.

At Cromwell's behest, he gave them money for their keep. Many departed, but a few stayed behind, saying they would not leave him until they saw him restored to favour.

Tom returned to his chamber, sad about sending away his servants. Cromwell comforted him as well as he could.

'Give me leave to go to London now, where I can either make or mar your fortunes before I come back,' he urged. Tom sent him on his way.

'You shall hear shortly from me,' Cromwell said, 'and if all goes well, I will not fail to be here again within two days.'

Tom was preparing for bed that night when Cavendish knocked on the door and entered. 'My lord, Sir John Russell is come from the King and desires to speak with you.'

Was this good news at last? Tom pulled on his nightgown.

'He has had an awful journey,' Cavendish told him. 'He was soaked to the skin when he arrived, so I had the fire made up for him in the gatehouse, to warm him.'

'Send him in,' Tom said. 'I pray he brings glad tidings.'

Cavendish smiled. 'Yes! He bade me tell you that he has brought you such news as will make you greatly rejoice.'

'God be praised!' Tom breathed.

Sir John was brought before him and went down on one knee. Tom bent and raised him. 'You are most welcome!'

'Sir, the King commends himself to you. He has sent you this ring as a token and bids you to be of good cheer, for he loves you as well as ever he did, and he is concerned to hear of your troubles. Indeed, before he sat to supper last night, he called me to him and commanded me to come here secretly to visit you, to afford you comfort. Sadly, I have had the worst journey I can ever remember.'

Tom thanked him for his pains and his good news. 'Have you supped, Sir John?'

'No, my lord.'

'Master Cavendish,' Tom said, 'tell the cooks to provide some meat for our guest, and have a chamber with a good fire made ready for him, that he may rest awhile.'

Cavendish hurried away, and Tom chatted to Sir John while they waited for the food to be served. All the while, he was weighing up what the knight had said. It did seem that Harry himself bore him no ill will or grudge and would happily have received him fully back into favour, but that the night crow and her cohorts were preventing it. He could not escape the conclusion that the King – a man who inspired dread and terror in many – was frightened of the woman. Otherwise, why the need for secrecy? Did he fear the lash of her tongue, or that she would leave him? That, Tom was convinced, would be the best thing that could happen to Harry. But he doubted that Anne would ever give up her hopes of a crown.

After Sir John had rested, he sped away to Greenwich in the middle of the night, to ensure that no one knew of his visit.

Soon afterwards, Tom received a letter from the King's secretary, informing him that his Grace had placed him under his own personal protection, and was permitting him to retain the archbishopric of York. He was to move to his diocese and take up his duties there as soon as was convenient.

On the face of it, this was good news, yet to Tom it felt as if he was being sent into exile. His enemies had been at work on the King. Probably they had perceived that Harry was now kindly disposed to him and feared that he would reinstate him, so had manoeuvred to have him sent as far away from the court as possible, to prevent their meeting. York was two hundred miles away – two hundred miles from Joan, who had not yet come to see him.

He wrote again to her, warning her of his coming departure and sending his heartfelt blessings to her and the children. His tears blotched the page, spilling unheeded as he wondered if he would ever see her again.

He sent a messenger with the letter in the afternoon. That night, as he was at prayer, Cavendish tapped him on the shoulder.

'Lady Legh is here,' he murmured. 'I have put her in your closet.'

It was strange that in the midst of his sorrow, Tom could feel so suffused with joy. He rose stiffly to his feet and hastened from his bedchamber.

She was standing in the moonlight from the window, wrapped in a furred cloak, its hood about her shoulders. 'Forgive me, I had to come . . .' She paused, staring at him. 'Tom, what have they done to you?'

He knew what she meant. His mirror had shown him how he had aged of late.

'Alas, my dear, I cannot help getting older. I am nearly fifty-nine. But let us not think about that. What matters is that you are here.' He crossed the room in three strides and pulled her into his arms. 'Thank God you have come! I thought . . .' Then he was once more weeping on her shoulder. 'I'm sorry, I'm sorry,' he moaned.

'There is nothing to be sorry for,' she soothed, her hands working on his back, pressing him closer to her. 'You have had a terrible time – and you have not deserved it! I could kill them all – yes, even the King!'

'Hush,' he said, recovering himself and drawing back to look her in the eye. 'To speak of the King's death is treason! And he is not to blame. He's been entangled in the snares of a woman. He means me well.'

'It doesn't look like it from where I'm standing,' Joan retorted, her old feisty self again. 'He should have better sense than to let a woman rule him. The whole realm is in an uproar. His brain is in his breeches, so don't make excuses for him!'

'Oh, Joan.' Tom found he was smiling. 'Our great reunion, and we're bickering already. And we have so little time. I leave soon for Yorkshire. It seems like the end of the earth.'

'It's not so far from Yarmouth,' she said. 'Thomas is there with my people, and I shall take the children and join him. I could visit you.'

'You'll still be two hundred miles away,' Tom said sadly. 'Almost as far as York is from London. And it would be a difficult journey. I no longer have the means to make it comfortable for you.'

'I would travel a long way for you, Thomas Wolsey,' she declared, kissing him heartily on the mouth. Normally, his body would have responded, but to his dismay, nothing happened. He was too distressed, he reasoned.

'It has been enough to see you tonight,' he whispered. 'I shall live on the memory for months.'

'Let us love each other one more time before you go,' Joan murmured, twining her arms around his neck. 'Leave me something to remember too!'

Dare he risk taking her to bed and hoping that all would be well? Would the sight of her nakedness excite him? And could he bear the humiliation if it did not? No longer the omnipotent cardinal, was he about to fail as a man as well?

'Thomas?' She had sensed his hesitation.

'Believe me, I want to,' he muttered, 'but it is hard to think on carnal desire when your mind is filled with fear of the future – and the realisation of what is gone.'

'I understand.' She smiled, touching his cheek. 'It has been enough just to see you.'

He was making the final arrangements for the removal of his household when he heard from Master Cromwell, who had been busy on his behalf at court. Cromwell had even sought and obtained an audience with the King, which was encouraging in itself, because Harry knew how highly Tom esteemed the man. But further perusal of the letter left Tom startled, for Cromwell seemed to be more in the King's confidence than ever. He had not, it turned out, gone to plead for Tom's restoration, but had taken it upon himself to suggest a solution to the Great Matter, urging the King to overcome the difficulty of the Pope's opposition to his suit by taking the apostolic authority into his own hands and declaring himself head of the Church in his realm. Harry had been full of praise for Cromwell. It sounded like boasting and felt like betrayal. Tom had believed that Cromwell loved him and would have stayed in his service for as long as possible. But, as he knew from his own experience, what man could resist the lure of power and position? And could it be true that Cromwell had despaired of ever seeing Tom restored fully to favour? Had ambition triumphed over loyalty? It appeared so. Yet who would blame him for what he had done? A man had to make his way in the world.

Tom wrote to Cromwell, congratulating him, yet subtly implying that he was disappointed in him. Back came a letter, almost by return courier, to counter the implied reproof. *I am informed that your Grace believes I have dissembled with you or done something contrary to your profit and honour. I am surprised that you should think this, considering the pains I have taken on your behalf. Therefore, I wish you would speak without feigning, so that I may clear myself of whatever I have done wrong. Yet I shall bear your Grace no less goodwill. Let God judge between us! Truly, your Grace can overshoot yourself in some things.*

Tom was hurt, but he replied that he had no suspicions of Cromwell and would rely on no man's help or counsel but his. *Continue steadfast,* he ended. *Remember your old friend and give no credit to those who sow variance between us, for that would leave me destitute of all help.*

Suddenly, Cromwell was back at Esher, grinning broadly and looking much happier than he had when he departed – as well he might!

'I can't stay,' he said, as soon as they were seated together in the ornate, exquisitely panelled gallery, the feature at Esher in which Tom took the most pleasure. 'I must ride back this night to London so that I can be at the Parliament House in the morning. I have been diligent in your Grace's cause. I used my influence to get myself elected to Parliament. So now, never fear, if anyone speaks against you there, I will give sufficient answer to demolish their arguments, to the point where they can do you no harm. I will show them the truth!'

Tom felt tears welling in his breast. He cried so easily these days.

'For your honest behaviour in my cause, Thomas, you must be the most faithful servant a master could desire, and you deserve to be greatly commended by all men.' He should never have doubted Cromwell. He was truly a man of the highest worth.

'I will keep your Grace closely informed of what transpires in Parliament,' Cromwell said, and was gone, galloping away in a cloud of dust into the December twilight.

Tom waited anxiously to hear. but Cromwell was as good as his word. The first letter came within two days, by fast messenger.

The news was far worse than he could ever have anticipated. Parliament had presented the King with a list of forty-four charges against him. The Boleyns had been busy, no doubt. From what Cromwell could glean – and he appeared now to have friends in high places – Harry had agreed to consider the accusations, yet seemed reluctant to lift his hand against his old friend.

With each day that passed, Tom's anxiety deepened. He dreaded the arrival of visitors, expecting at any moment to see a detachment of guards come to carry him off to the Tower.

He wished he knew what the charges were. He feared this was a bid to have him condemned for treason. Cromwell would know, he told himself, and he himself might be able to help bolster Cromwell's arguments in his own defence. In his distress, he wrote to him: *My own entirely beloved Cromwell, I beseech you, as you love me and will do anything for me, come hither this day as soon as Parliament is broken up, for I need to talk to you. I pray you hasten your coming, for my comfort and quietness of mind. With the rude hand and sorrowful heart of your assured lover.*

Cromwell paid another flying visit the next evening to tell him that the charges were to be laid in the morning, and they talked long into the night before he had to leave, disappearing into the darkness.

Tom prayed that those charges would be disposed of quickly. This waiting was torture. If he knew his fate, he could face it manfully. It was the not knowing that was killing him.

Cromwell's messenger arrived two days later. Parliament had debated the charges, but Cromwell had inveighed against them so skilfully that the session had ended in stalemate. The King had thereupon refused to proceed against his old friend, and Parliament had had no choice but to acquit Tom.

Tom rejoiced to hear that the King had again been merciful, and that he would not find himself in the Tower after all. He was deeply grateful to Cromwell. Yet he reckoned that Cromwell must have known that Harry was reluctant to prosecute him, for surely he would not have dared to oppose Parliament if the King's pleasure had been otherwise?

Chapter 35

1529–30

Cavendish brought Tom a letter bearing Norfolk's seal. The Duke was coming to see him, on the King's business. He felt a churning in his bowels. What now?

Yet Cromwell had written to say that Anne had fallen out with her uncle of Norfolk, and that he had spoken kindly of Tom. Apparently, she had alienated others too with her strident tongue and her arrogance. Pity it was that she had not alienated the King!

To show Norfolk that he was not reduced to nothing, Tom summoned all his gentlemen and yeomen to wait upon him and, his head bare, led them to the gatehouse to receive his visitor. He was surprised when the Duke dismounted and embraced him, for he had expected hostility. Yet this new Norfolk was pleasingly civil as Tom led him by the arm through the great hall and into his chamber.

As the Duke passed the yeomen who were lined up in the hall, Tom was astonished when he stopped and spoke to them. 'Sirs, for your loving and faithful service to my lord in this time of his calamity, the King has commanded me to say that he will see you all prosper in the future.'

Tom could hardly believe his ears. He seized his moment. 'Sir, I am sorry that I am not able to do for them as my heart wishes. I therefore ask you to put in a good word for them, when you have the opportunity, to the King.'

'You need not doubt that I will be an earnest suitor for them to the King; and if need be, some I will retain in my own service,' Norfolk promised. He turned to the yeomen. 'God's blessing and mine be with you!'

They ascended to the great chamber for dinner. Tom felt that some gesture was called for to show Norfolk that his friendship would be valued.

'My lord, of all other noblemen, I have most cause to thank you for your noble heart and gentle nature, which you have showed me in my absence from court, as my servant, Thomas Cromwell, has reported to me. I am aware that, even though you helped to remove me from my high estate and brought me low, yet you have now extended your favour most charitably to me. My lord, you well deserve to bear on your arms the noble lion, whose natural inclination is, that when he has vanquished a beast and sees him lying prostrate at his feet, to show clemency and do him no more harm, nor suffer any other beast to do damage to him.'

Norfolk inclined his head in acknowledgement. 'I thank you for your courtesy, my lord. Sometimes in life, one is obliged to do things one later regrets.'

A bowl of water was brought so that they could wash their hands before eating. Tom bade Norfolk wash with him, but he refused courteously.

'It does not become me to presume to wash with your Grace any more now than it did before, when you were in your glory.'

'Yet,' Tom said sadly, 'my authority and legatine dignity, the founts of my honour, are gone.'

'I care not a straw for that!' the Duke declared. 'I regard the honour you have as archbishop of York and a cardinal, whose estate outranks that of any duke. Therefore, content yourself, for I will not presume to wash with you.'

Tom washed his hands alone, Norfolk following suit. Then Tom indicated that his guest sit in the high chair on the dais, but he humbly refused, so another chair was set for him, lower than Tom's.

After the tablecloth was removed, they repaired to Tom's bedchamber to continue their conversation over a ewer of warm spiced wine. Tom was still wondering why Norfolk had come, but his fears had been somewhat lulled by now.

While they were talking, Cavendish appeared to say that a Master Shelley, one of the King's judges, had arrived and was asking to see

Tom. Norfolk said he would retire to give them some privacy, but he collided with Master Shelley at the door.

'My lord of Norfolk!' said the judge. 'I am come with a message from the King to my lord Cardinal. I pray you, stay while I impart it to him.'

As Tom quailed inwardly, wondering why Harry would have sent a judge to him, Norfolk gave Shelley a withering look. 'I have nothing to do with your message, and I will not meddle in it,' he barked, and stalked off to his chamber.

Shelley stood before Tom, clearly not relishing his mission. 'My lord, the King's pleasure is to make York Place, your house at Westminster, a royal palace. He wants your Grace to recognise, before me, as a justice of this realm, that he has the right by law to take it.'

'Willingly I would do so,' Tom said, 'yet it is the property of the archdiocese of York and not mine to give.'

'Aye, but has he the right to sequester it?'

'Master Shelley, I know the King; he will not do anything unlawful.'

Shelley looked uncomfortable. 'There is some conscience in this case,' he conceded, 'but having regard to the King's high power, it might be best for him to make recompense to the archdiocese with double the value.'

'That sounds like an acceptable arrangement. Let me see your commission.'

The judge gave it him.

'Master Shelley,' Tom said at length, 'you may report to the King that I am his obedient subject, and faithful chaplain, and that I will not disobey his royal commandment, but will most gladly do his princely will and pleasure in all things, as long as *you* say that I may lawfully do it. Yet I pray you, tell his Majesty from me that I most humbly desire him to call to his most gracious remembrance that there is both Heaven and Hell.' He had not been able to resist this parting shot, yet he doubted that Shelley would dare to convey that part of his message to the King.

* * *

Norfolk had gone. It seemed that he had visited only to convey his own and the King's goodwill. Tom was pleased that he had come in person. Yet Harry, for all his assurances of love and favour, had not come himself.

However, there was good news in the next letter from Cromwell. The King, moved by compassion, had promised Tom a pardon in the most ample form. He caught his breath. What did that mean? Was his property to be given back to him? Was he to be restored to his former greatness?

He wished he could make some grand gesture or do something, anything, to help to achieve that. If only he could somehow procure the annulment Harry longed for, that would certainly do it. Yes, that was the best way forward. He was sure that he could bring about a workable solution. Even the night crow would surely be grateful to him.

He mustered all his eloquence in a letter to Pope Clement, begging him to restore his legatine authority so that he could take the burden of ruling on the case from the Holy Father's shoulders. He wrote to the Emperor too, asking him to look kindly on the granting of the King's suit, and to the Queen, urging her most eloquently to enter a nunnery for the sake of the kingdom. He sent the letters in the full knowledge that, if he failed in this new attempt to give Harry what he wanted, he would be finished, for he had dared once more to invoke the authority of a foreign power. But if he succeeded, the benefits would be manifold, and it would have been worth the risk.

He was now receiving daily messages from Cromwell, who warned him that his enemies were plotting new ways to disquiet and discredit him. *They fear your Grace more after your fall than they did when you were in prosperity, and they are terrified that you will be restored to your former eminence – because they know that the King still loves you. They fear that if that happens, you might take revenge on them for their cruelty and malice, and that they might themselves end up being dispossessed.*

Tom read Cromwell's words with mounting unease. What concerned his friend most was that, having failed to secure his condemnation for treason, the Boleyn faction now appeared to be waging a war of nerves. *They mean to give your Grace such cause to fret and worry that it will affect your health to the point where you might die.*

He felt sick when he read that. How evil could people be? He made himself read on. *They plan to do something against you every day. It will be something that will unsettle or distress you. Be warned.*

He stayed watchful, resolving not to let anything his enemies did upset him, and sure enough, a series of petty incidents followed – the King demanding to take some of his gentlemen and yeomen, his servants gossiping about new accusations against him, demotions given to those Tom had promoted. Well, it would take more than that, he thought grimly. Yet the situation was exacting its toll. He never knew what might happen next, or if their campaign would get more savage. Never a day went by without him going to his bed with chest or stomach pains.

Christmas was approaching. He had still not received the promised pardon. Was that another of their stabs at him? With a heavy heart, he wrote to Cromwell, and to his old friend Gardiner, begging them to make suit for it to the King. When he signed the letters, his hand was trembling.

It was a miserable Christmas, lacking the magnificence and cheer of earlier Yuletides. He was feeling low, not himself, and missing Joan and Thomas badly. She was still in Norfolk and written twice, surprised to hear that he was still at Esher. *If I had known, I would have come to see you*, she'd told him.

On St Stephen's Day, he fell ill with a fever and felt like death. Dr Agostini, his Venetian physician, who had occasionally acted for him as a spy during the six years he had worked for him, was in attendance. His swarthy, clever face bore a concerned expression. Tom wondered if he really was dying.

Then Dr Butts appeared at Esher. Harry, apprised by Cromwell, had sent his own personal physician. Tom was so moved by the gesture that he broke down and wept. In his weakened state, he let his tongue run away with him as Butts sat gravely by the bed.

'I feel so alone,' he confided. 'I keep being told that the King holds me in favour, but he has not recalled me or even written to me. And I fear that Mistress Anne hates me and wishes me ill because I could not obtain the annulment. She believes I am working against her. Dr Butts, I live in fear, and in longing.'

Butts nodded. 'There is no doubt that the King loves you. His anger has long since abated. He was very sorry to hear that you were sick and dispatched me at once, with orders to send him regular bulletins. My lord, you have a bad imbalance of the humours, which is causing you to feel so ill, but in my view, anguish of mind has contributed. I will report back to his Grace.'

'Don't tell him I criticised Mistress Anne!' Tom croaked.

'I won't.' Butts smiled. 'Actually, it's the Lady Anne now. Her father has just been created earl of Wiltshire and Ormond.'

God in Heaven! The Boleyns would be more powerful – and dangerous – than ever, Tom thought, but he felt so ill that he did not care. He drifted into sleep, and when he woke, Dr Butts had left for Greenwich.

He returned the next day. 'How are you feeling, my lord?'

Tom felt drained. He had barely the energy to get up to use the close stool. They had had to place it right by his bed. 'Poorly,' he said. 'I can't stop shaking.'

'Well, I have come to cheer you,' Butts told him. 'The King was distraught when I told him how ill you are. He said he would not lose you for twenty thousand pounds. And he drew this ring from his finger, saying that you gave it to him, and that now he gives it back to you. He said to say that he is not offended with you in his heart. He prayed God to send you life and bade you be of good cheer.'

Tom wept as Butts laid the ring in his hand.

'Then he summoned the Lady Anne and asked her to send you a token with some comfortable words. She took a gold tablet from her girdle and gave it to me to give to you with her very good wishes for your speedy recovery.'

Tom was sceptical, but took the tablet, which was surely valuable, for it opened as a book and contained several pages of prayers in minuscule writing. He kissed it with reverence, for his reaction would surely be reported at court. 'When you see them again, give them my hearty thanks, good Dr Butts.'

Cheered by Harry's signs of goodwill, he mended quickly. Within four days, he was out of danger, up on his feet and fancying food again. He found it hard to believe in Anne's display of concern, though, considering the hatred she had always borne him. No doubt she had done it just to please Harry. He could not forget that she was an accomplished mistress of the art of dissimulation.

Another month passed. Just before Candlemas, Tom was deeply touched to receive four cartloads of household stuff – vessels, plate, hangings and chapel furnishings. It had been sent by the King, he was informed, so that he could observe the feast in a proper and honourable manner. He hoped he could believe this was further proof of Harry's favour, and rendered his most humble thanks to him and to those who had brought the carts.

'It's not of the best quality,' his steward said, casting a dubious eye over the items.

'No, Sir,' Tom protested, not wishing to have his pleasure in the gift tainted. 'He who has nothing is glad of anything, though it be never so little.'

It augured well for the future, but on the day after Candlemas, Tom was startled to hear a loud, insistent knocking on the front door. When he hurried downstairs to the hall, he was appalled to see a party of guards in the King's livery demanding admittance.

They had come for him! It was what he had been dreading for months. Still weakened after his illness, he thought he might faint.

But no. They had come, inexplicably, for Dr Agostini.

'Why?' Tom demanded to know. But they would not tell him. He was dumbstruck, for the Venetian had served him well and never given cause for complaint. Agostini himself, when found, looked bewildered as they hauled him away.

Cromwell's next letter enlightened him. *He confessed, under interrogation, that your Grace had written to the Pope, asking him to excommunicate the King and lay an interdict on England if he did not dismiss the Lady Anne and treat Queen Katherine with proper respect.*

The page danced before Tom's disbelieving eyes. He had never done any such thing, would never have dreamed of doing it! What kind of interrogation had it been to make the physician say such a thing?

He made himself read on. *The Lady Anne flew into a rage when she heard, but most people think that Dr Agostini had been bribed by her faction to give false evidence. She has said quite openly that it would cost her a good 20,000 crowns in bribes before she has done with you. She and her party have not ceased to plot against you, and she never gives over weeping and lamenting her lost time and her honour, and keeps threatening the King that she will leave him. I assure you, he has gone to much trouble to pacify her. I was told that although he prayed her most affectionately, with tears in his eyes, not to speak of leaving him, she said that nothing would satisfy her but your Grace's arrest. But do not fear. The Council could find nothing to corroborate Agostini's story. The King has refused to heed the Lady Anne and he has issued your pardon and restored all your other church offices. The Lady was not pleased with his Grace, but they will make it up. As usual in such cases, their mutual love will be greater than before. I am convinced that reinstating your Grace in the King's favour would not be difficult, were it not for the Lady Anne. I fear she has made him promise not to see you, for she knows he could not help but pity you.*

The pardon was enclosed, but Tom let the document, long sought after, fall to the floor. It was a pretty pass when he could no longer trust members of his own household. It must have been a hefty bribe to make a man like Agostini sell his soul to the Devil. Who else might fall prey to the lure of money? Truly, he could trust no one now. At least he had Cromwell working on his behalf.

His thoughts turned to Joan. They had had another exchange of letters, but it was little compensation for her absence. He longed to see her and be comforted by her, but he doubted he would be allowed to leave Esher until he received orders to travel north.

He wished he could get away from Esher. He had grown weary of the house, and after months of continual use, it had become unsavoury and smelly, for the cesspits had not been emptied. He wrote to Cromwell, bidding him ask the King if he might move to another house where he might more speedily recover his health.

Before he could receive a reply, a team of workmen turned up at his front door.

'Saving your Grace's presence, we've come to take down the gallery,' the foreman said, doffing his cap.

Tom was aghast. He had only recently had it installed. 'On whose authority?' he snapped.

'The King's, of course. We're to take it away and reassemble it at York Place.'

Protest would be futile. Tom stood there and watched in horror as the men began work. His beautiful gallery, one of the finest in England – they were smashing it to bits, it seemed. It was a corrosive experience. His enemies had done this to torment him. He wanted more than ever to leave Esher, his vandalised house, and never come back.

Cromwell had not been idle. In his next letter, he reported that he had thought it best not to approach any of the King's Council, for some were Tom's mortal enemies and would either hinder his moving, or move him farther from the King. Instead, he had gone to Harry himself. *He heard my suit graciously and granted your request. You can remove to Richmond Palace.*

That was good news, for Richmond had once been his, given to him by Harry in exchange for Hampton Court. It was one of the most beautiful of the King's houses – and it was not far by boat from Thames Ditton. With a lighter heart, Tom had his servants pack everything up, and he and his household rode the short distance to their new abode. When its towers and pinnacles appeared in the distance, he felt a surge of optimism. Surely this move signalled a return to greater things?

When he arrived, however, the steward informed him that he was not to stay in the palace itself, which was closed up, but in a lodge in the great park. This was a disappointment, but the lodge was a very pretty, neat house, small, but with a large garden offering pleasant walks and alleys. Because of the lack of space, Tom could only keep a few servants, and was obliged to dismiss the rest on board wages. At least, he thought, there would be fewer people to betray him – and he had Cavendish with him, whose loyalty he could never doubt.

Despite his fears for the future, it was an unexpectedly pleasant existence, and it reminded him in some ways of his childhood, living in a small house crowded with people. As the spring evenings lightened, he took to walking in the garden, saying the divine offices. Once, at dusk, he saw Cavendish standing in an alley, staring at a row of wooden images of heraldic beasts on poles by the lodge wall.

'What are you looking at so attentively?' he asked, coming up behind him.

Cavendish jumped. 'Heavens! If it please your Grace, I am looking at these beasts, especially the dun cow, in which it seems to me that some workman has most expertly showed his craft.'

'Yes,' Tom agreed. 'It is one of the King's emblems. And it reminds me of a prophecy: "When the cow rides the bull, then, priest, beware thy skull."' He shivered as he said it. 'The shield of the Boleyns bears three bulls.'

Cavendish was, as ever, the soul of diplomacy. 'How dark and obscure riddles and prophecies are,' he observed.

The church of the Charterhouse at Sheen was adjacent to the lodge, and a gallery led to it from the house. Feeling in need of spiritual consolation, Tom attended services there every day, and in the afternoons he would visit the cell of one or other of the elderly monks and sit in contemplation with him. He discovered that he enjoyed conversing with these holy fathers and listening to their wisdom. It brought him a kind of peace, especially when they spoke of the vainglory of the world being as nothing compared to the love of God. They gave him a hair shirt, which he took to wearing next to his skin to chastise his flesh whenever he felt the need; it was a battle he feared he might never win, especially since he could not get Joan out of his head. And so he passed his days in holy contemplation and longing.

Chapter 36

1530

At Lent, the Council finally ordered him to move north to his diocese of York. Cromwell came to tell him; Cromwell, who remained convinced that Tom's enemies had colluded to send him far away to pre-empt his restoration. Tom agreed. But, of course, the order was couched in terms he could not challenge. It was necessary that he go where he could do much good – and a lot more in that vein. Harry would have taken the suggestion in good faith and been easily persuaded. Norfolk had told Cromwell that it was the King's pleasure that Tom should go with speed and look to his duty. And Tom had thought that Norfolk was looking kindly on him!

He dared a small defiance. 'Well then, Thomas,' he said, 'seeing there is no other remedy, I intend to go first to my diocese of Winchester. I pray you, inform my lord of Norfolk.'

But the councillors would have none of it. They would not, he knew, permit him to plant himself so near the King. They moved Harry to give him a pension of four thousand marks, a fraction of the revenues of Winchester, and to distribute the rest among the nobility; and they persuaded him to do the same with those of St Albans and Tom's colleges in Oxford and Ipswich, which Harry now took into his own hands. Cromwell was designated to receive the money and distribute it. And, as he told Tom, without vanity, he did it so justly that he was held in even greater esteem. It was plain that he was advancing ever higher in the King's favour. 'And by this means, I hope to do you some good, my lord,' he said.

But there was no time. When Cromwell next visited Tom, he brought bad news.

'My lord of Norfolk came to see me last night,' he said, his jowly face grave. 'He complained that you are making no plans to depart, and said I was to tell you that if you do not go north shortly – forgive me, my lord – he will tear you apart with his teeth. He advises you very strongly to prepare for the journey as soon as you can, or else you will be escorted to Yorkshire.'

Tom was shocked at Norfolk's venom – he could only suppose that the night crow was now friends with him again. Yet he was resigned. In York, he would have power and prestige as archbishop; he would have palaces and great houses at his disposal. He would not be burdened with a welter of affairs of state. It would be a simpler life, a more peaceful one, and to be truthful, he was quite looking forward to taking up his spiritual duties. Above all, it would be a relief to be far away from the hurly-burly of the court and the viciousness of his enemies. One he had gone out of their sights, he would surely be gone from their minds.

'Thomas, it is time to be going,' he said. 'Therefore, I pray you go to the King and say that I would, with all my heart, go to my benefice at York, but for want of money; and desire his Grace to assist me with the cost of my journey. You can also tell my lord of Norfolk and others on the Council that I would depart if I could afford it.'

'Sir, I will do my best,' said Cromwell, reaching for his bonnet.

The King wasted no time in sending funds. Bidding him be of good cheer, he assigned Tom a thousand marks and sent a message by Cromwell to say that he would forward a thousand pounds more.

Wondering mournfully if he would ever look on Harry's face again, Tom ordered his servants to prepare for the journey. He sent to London for livery clothes for those who were accompanying him. The rest he dismissed, giving them his hearty thanks for their service after his overthrow. As he and his retinue would be travelling for more than two hundred miles, he decided to be carried in a horse litter, for he was not able to ride long distances these days. He took a very repentant Dr Agostini back into his employ, for he feared he might need his expert services, and forgave him for his betrayal, but he knew he would never be able to bring himself to trust him again. Instead, he would be watching him.

He was just drawing up a list of instructions to be sent to the steward of Cawood Castle, where he was to take up residence in Yorkshire, when a letter arrived from Joan. At last! He seized it and broke the seal, waving away the usher who had brought it.

She was married. She had taken a second husband: George, the younger brother of Sir William Paulet, a member of the King's Privy Council. She was leaving Thames Ditton and going with her children to live with him at his house at Crandall in Hampshire. She wished Tom well and thanked him for all he had done for her.

Not a word of love – or any acknowledgement of what they had been to each other. Tom sat there, stunned. He wondered if his poor, thudding heart could take much more. To lose Joan, his beloved Joan, when he had foolishly hoped that, given the chance, they could rekindle their love, hair shirt or no hair shirt, was the cruellest blow – crueller still when he was forced to conclude that she believed he was finished and could no longer look to her interests. And who could blame her? He was being sent north, probably permanently. She must have thought that there could be no future for them.

When he had calmed down and staunched the too-ready tears, he reasoned that her decision was for the best. Marriage into the Paulet family would give her security, a comfortable life and a home for her children. His children. It was something he could never give them himself, for he dared not risk any scandal now, with his enemies poised to pounce. Thomas, twenty now, would have to bestir himself to take up his duties in one of the benefices he still held. It was about time, for the lad had been wasting his opportunities.

Tom sighed. At least he could now go to York with no strings to tug his heart south again. He was free of ties. It was a freedom he did not want. He would rather be chained.

At the beginning of Passion Week, before Easter, Tom left Richmond with a train of one hundred and sixty persons and rode north via Hendon, Royston, Huntingdon and Peterborough, arriving at the abbey there on Palm Sunday. He could not but compare his journey with that of Christ's to Jerusalem, could not shake off the sense of dread that something terrible awaited him at the end of it. But he did his best to ignore it, reminding himself that he was going to do God's work – work he should have done years ago.

On that Palm Sunday, he went in procession with the monks, bearing his palm, and took Mass. On Maundy Thursday, he went to Our Lady's Chapel in the abbey, where fifty-nine poor men – one for each year of his age – awaited him. Reverently, in imitation of Jesus, he washed, wiped and kissed their feet, and gave each twelvepence, three ells of canvas to make shirts, a pair of new shoes, a loaf of bread, three red herrings and three white herrings. Upon Easter Day, in the morning, he attended the ceremonies in the abbey church, then went in procession through the city in his cardinal's robes. Then he returned to the abbey and sang High Mass very devoutly.

From Peterborough, he rode to the house of Sir William Fitzwilliam, where he was warmly welcomed and entertained. He was much gratified, for he had once supported Fitzwilliam in a nasty dispute with the Lord Mayor of London, and had then taken him into his service, first as his treasurer and then as his high chamberlain, being impressed by the man's wisdom, gravity and eloquence. Fitzwilliam had risen to become a member of the King's Council. It was heartening to see him so eager to demonstrate his gratitude.

One day, after Evensong, Tom and his old friend were walking in the garden when they were joined by Cavendish, who had lately arrived from London with new liveries.

'What news is there?' Tom asked him. 'Did you hear people speak of me?'

Cavendish nodded slowly. 'Sir, if it please your Grace, I happened to be at a dinner in the City, where I met many old acquaintances who asked how you did and how well you accepted your adversity and the loss of your goods. I told them that you were in health, thanks be to God, and that you took all things in good part; and they lamented your ill fortune, saying it could not be good for the realm. For they realised that you always did much to advance the King's honour. They marvelled that, being so excellent in wits and discretion, you would simply confess yourself guilty of praemunire, when you might have stood trial. They said they understood from some of the King's learned counsel that you had been greatly wronged. To the which I said I doubted not that you acted upon some greater consideration than I could comprehend.'

Tom felt greatly cheered. 'It is not the King who has wronged me. You see, there has long been a serpent about him, who would, if I had opposed her will, have cried continually in his ear with such vehemency that I should have earned his indignation rather than his favour. I mean the night crow.' He would not name her. They knew who he meant. 'Therefore, I thought it better to keep his loving favour, even after the loss of my goods and dignities, than to win back all yet lose his love; to me, that would be a living death. That is why I pleaded guilty to the accusation of praemunire. Since then, I understand that the King has suffered a certain prick of conscience, and that he took the matter more grievously than people realised. For he alone knew whether I had truly offended.'

Fitzwilliam clapped a hand on his shoulder. 'You did for the best, my lord, and I am heartily sorry that it ended badly for you. But let us hope that all will, in time, be set right.'

'Let us hope so,' Tom said fervently.

He stayed with Sir William for a few more days, enjoying choice food and good wine, and being entertained royally. If only all men were as kind as his host!

He pressed on northwards via Stamford, Grantham and Newark. The Bishop's Palace at Southwell, eight miles further east, belonged to the see of York, so he was planning to lodge there next, but it was badly dilapidated – evidence, he realised, to his shame, of his long absence from his diocese – so he had to stay in a prebendary's house next door, having impressed a team of workmen to repair the palace. There he spent much of the summer. He kept a noble household once more and was gratified to be visited by many local lords and gentlemen. He revelled in being able to entertain again, sitting at the head of the table and taking care to ensure that his guests had the best cheer he could devise for them, and was repaid a thousandfold with their unfeigned affection and esteem. It was so different from being surrounded by the flatterers and self-seekers at court. These northerners liked him for himself, he realised – and they made plain their opinion that he had been wronged and misjudged.

He made sure that there was plenty of meat and drink for all his visitors, and much was given in alms at his gates. He showed charity and pity towards his poorer tenants and the destitute, visiting humble cottages with baskets of provisions, and distributing money to the beggars who clustered at his gate. He was so glad to be doing some good at last that he learned to be familiar with his inferiors and not to stand on ceremony. He acted as a mediator between members of his flock who had fallen out, and brought about many agreements and concords between them, sometimes settling feuds that had dragged on for years. It was heartening to have facilitated such peace and amity. Nor did he neglect his spiritual duties and private devotions. And all the while, he was winning love and friendship. He could not resist smiling to himself, thinking how displeased his enemies would be to hear of his successes in the place to which they had exiled him. The news would be no pleasant sound in their ears!

On Corpus Christi Eve, Tom retired early, for he was planning to sing High Mass in Southwell Minster the next day. He was kneeling by the bed in his nightgown, saying his prayers, when Cavendish appeared at the door.

'Sir, Master Brereton and Master Wriothesley, two gentlemen of the King's Privy Chamber, have come from his Highness to speak with you. They will not tarry, and are asking to speak with your Grace immediately. I have left them in the porter's lodge.'

'Well then,' Tom said, hauling himself to his feet, 'bid them come up into my dining chamber, while I prepare myself to see them.'

When he walked in, he was pleased to see them making a humble reverence to him. He took them by the hands.

'Good sirs, how is the King, my sovereign lord?'

'Right well, in health and merry, Sir, thanks be to our Lord,' Brereton said, eyeing Cavendish, who was hovering near the door. 'Sir, we desire to talk with you privately.'

Cavendish disappeared, and Tom drew the two men into a window alcove, where they placed on the stone seat a small coffer covered in green velvet and bound with bars of silver and gilt. They unlocked it and took out two skins of parchment, to which many seals were attached.

'This, my lord, is a petition to the Pope, beseeching his Holiness to decide the King's case in his favour,' Wriothesley said. 'It has been signed and sealed by all the lords spiritual and temporal of England. We have come to require you to add your signature.'

'Gladly will I do so.' Tom smiled, relishing the chance to give the lie to Anne's falsehoods about his working against the King, though privately thinking that they were all fools if they thought that Clement would heed their petition. He had never once deigned to reply to Tom's pleas.

They gave him wax for his seal and he subscribed his name.

'I hope this brings his Grace his desire,' he said. He was inordinately pleased to have been asked to do this one thing for Harry.

The clock chimed. 'Good sirs, it is after midnight. Will you not stay the night?'

They shook their heads 'Thank you, but no. We must ride with all speed to the Earl of Shrewsbury's.'

Tom called Cavendish back. 'Fetch these gentlemen some cold meats and a cup or two of wine,' he directed, ignoring their protests. When they had snatched a few mouthfuls, he gave each of them four gold sovereigns in reward for their trouble. 'Take them. If I had been of greater ability, your reward would have been more.' He got the impression that they had expected more.

He watched from the window as they rode away. He had not ceased to think of the Great Matter, but having heard nothing from the Pope or the Emperor, he had long since concluded that they thought him a spent force. It had been a vain hope anyway, he supposed. Realistically, if he had not been able to obtain an annulment when he was in power, he had not a hope in hell of securing one now. He went to bed thinking that he should keep trying, for Harry's sake.

There was one person who might be able to help: Eustace Chapuys, the new Imperial ambassador, whose opinions, Tom had heard from Cromwell, carried much weight with the Emperor. At the end of June, he wrote to Chapuys to ask how the Queen's case was progressing. *Sir, I urge strong and immediate action, for I think that, with the case settled, I have a good chance of returning to power.*

In July, he learned from Cromwell that the Emperor had demanded that the Pope order Harry to separate from Anne until judgement had been given on his case, on account of the scandal their relationship was causing. Tom wrote to the Pope, adding his plea. With Anne out of the way, Harry would act more rationally, he was sure, and there would be no obstacle to Tom's restoration. But the Pope, as usual, dithered, and nothing changed.

Tom felt crushed to hear that Harry had ordered the closure of his college in Ipswich. He wrote to protest, but it made no difference. When he learned that the beautiful buildings were being demolished, he wept.

He consoled himself with prayer and the love of the people of the north. He knew he had been hated there before he came to these parts, and deservedly so, for he had never once visited his diocese to administer to the spiritual needs of his flock. But he was making up for that now. It was a wonder to see how people's attitudes to him had changed, how those who might have been enemies had become his dear friends. He had done all he could to win men's hearts. On holy days, he now rode five or six miles from his house to celebrate Mass at different parish churches or help one of his priests with a sermon. He liked to sit among his flock, listening to their concerns, giving advice. He set about restoring their churches, many of which were falling into decay. He always brought his dinner with him and shared it with those he visited. Sometimes he gave it away. He asked men if there was any debate or grudge between them, and if there was, he summoned both parties to the church and made them reconcile.

* * *

He remained at Southwell until the hunting season was under way, when he arranged to move his household north to Scroby, another residence of the archbishops of York. So many local people gathered to lament his departure that he felt moved almost to tears. On the day before he left, many knights and gentlemen descended on him, intending to accompany him on his journey. Tom was worried about how the King would view his being so honoured, fearful that his enemies would make capital out of it and use it to turn his master against him. Yet he did not want to offend these well-meaning gentlemen. He had to think of a way to put them off.

That night, he summoned Cavendish in secret and commanded him to have his mule and six horses saddled by dawn. In the morning, immediately after Mass, he left early for Welbeck Abbey, sixteen miles away, taking only Cavendish and a few of his gentlemen. His well-wishers were still in their beds at Southwell, unaware of his departure.

As he had anticipated, when they got up and realised that he had gone, they came galloping after him. But when they arrived at Welbeck, he was in his bed, having left orders that they were to be provided with a good dinner. When he joined them at table, he made a jest of his escapade, prompting much laughter, and all was well.

When he arrived at Scroby, he was overcome with emotion to find himself greeted by joyful, cheering crowds. Humbly, he dismounted, knelt in the road and thanked the people. During his stay, he continued to carry out his many deeds of charity.

At Michaelmas, he embarked on the last leg of his journey, which would end at Cawood Castle, his episcopal residence, which lay seven miles from York. On the way, he paused at St Oswald's Abbey, where he stood in the church from eight o'clock in the morning until noon, confirming children. After snatching some dinner, he returned and confirmed more children until four o'clock struck, when, utterly weary, he had to sit down in a chair. But he recovered enough to take Evensong before gratefully going to sup with the brethren in their refectory.

The next morning, he made ready to depart for Cawood, but before he could do so, crowds of parents arrived with more children, and he confirmed almost a hundred of the little ones before he could get away. Word of his deeds had gone ahead of him, and hordes of people were waiting for him by a stone cross standing on a green near Ferrybridge. He alighted and, raising his hand in blessing, proceeded to confirm another two hundred children. Then he remounted his mule and rode to Cawood, where once more the crowds had gathered. He was deeply touched to find himself greatly honoured and loved by rich and poor. Dismounting before the castle gatehouse, he knelt in the dust and gave thanks to God for his safe arrival.

When the steward showed him around the house, he was pleased to find that it was clean, well heated and comfortable, but noted that it was in a poor state of repair, since he had never lived there in the fifteen years he had been archbishop.

'I will have this place refurbished,' he promised, eyeing a bucket that had been placed in the chapel to catch drops of rainwater from a leaking ceiling.

There proved to be no shortage of offers of assistance. At least three hundred artificers and labourers hastened to help, to whom Tom gratefully paid daily wages. Soon, he was able to keep an honourable and plentiful house for all comers.

The clergy of York visited him often, as their father and patron. To a man, they had welcomed him joyously.

'It is no small comfort to see you among us, my lord,' the Dean said, speaking for them all, as Tom entertained them to a fine dinner with the October wind rattling the diamond panes of the dining-parlour windows. 'It is a great consolation to see our Archbishop, who has been absent from us for so long, taking services, dispensing charity and settling disagreements. We have been like fatherless children, comfortless and longing to see you in your own church.'

It was a gentle rebuke, well meant. Tom bowed his head. 'That is why I have travelled to these parts, not to be among you for a time, but to spend my life with you as a true father and a mutual brother.' He was coming to terms with the fact that he might never return south.

They conversed for a while about how the archdiocese was administered and how the canons could assist Tom and guide him in his responsibilities, and he made it clear to them that he intended to take full charge in due course.

'Sir,' the Dean said, 'let us acquaint you with the ancient customs of the cathedral of York. Traditionally, the Archbishop ought not to occupy any stall in the choir until he is installed in his office. If you should happen to die before your installation, you cannot be buried in the choir, but in the body of the church. Therefore, we ask your Grace that you will promise to do as your noble predecessors have done, and that you will not infringe or violate any of our ordinances.'

They showed him the records confirming their customs, and he consented, and appointed the day for his enthronement as archbishop. Preparations were set in motion, but he decreed that the ceremony was not to be as sumptuous as those of his predecessors; he did not want anything said of him to his great slander, or to attract charges of extravagance.

On All Hallows Day, the Dean came again to dine with Tom at Cawood to discuss the final order for his installation. 'Your Grace will walk on a cloth runner from St James's chapel, which stands outside the city gates, to the minster. Then the cloth can be cut up and distributed among the poor.'

Tom remembered hearing that a newly elected pope had once put off his hose and shoes before entering Rome barefoot and bare-legged, and so passed through the streets towards his palace, with such humility that all the people held him in great reverence. 'Although my predecessors walked on cloth, and sumptuously, I do not intend, God willing, to go on foot in my hose; I will go barefoot, for I would not presume to enter the minster in triumph or vainglory, but only to fulfil my duty to the Church. Therefore, be contented with my simplicity,' he said.

The Dean nodded his approval. 'It shall be as you wish, my lord.'

'I mean to go to York the night before and lodge there in your house, if I may. After my installation, I will host a dinner for you and all the clergy of the cathedral close. Next day, I shall dine with the mayor, and return to Cawood that night.'

After dinner, he said farewell to the Dean and sat down again with his chaplains and officers, feeling at peace with himself and the world. His coming installation, with its simple ceremony, would be all the glory he would ever need now.

It was 4 November, and he was to go to York that evening. When the dinner table was cleared and his companions were about to disperse, Dr Agostini rushed in. The sight of him, wild-eyed and apparently out of control, struck fear into Tom, and he stared appalled as the physician pulled off his black velvet gown and threw it over the great silver cross of York, which was always carried in procession before Tom when he went abroad, and was now propped up in a corner of the dining chamber, leaning against a wall hanging.

As the cross fell to the floor, making a jarring crash, one arm knocked the head of Dr Bonner, the master of Tom's faculties and spiritual jurisdictions, who had bent down to rescue it. Blood spurted, to the horror of all present, and Bonner clapped a napkin to the wound. At that point, Agostini ran out of the room.

Tom was left feeling utterly bewildered. 'Are you all right, Edmund?' he asked Bonner.

'Yes, your Grace. It is but a scratch.'

Tom turned to Cavendish. 'What is amiss with Dr Agostini?' he asked.

Cavendish seemed equally nonplussed. 'I have no idea, my lord.'

Tom regarded him soberly for a good while. 'A bad omen,' he murmured, feeling that the physician's behaviour portended something ominous. Cavendish looked at him curiously.

Tom shook his head and said grace, then rose from the table and went into his bedchamber to pray.

Was Agostini mad? Or was he trying to tell Tom something? The cross might represent himself, and Agostini, who had overthrown it, his accusers, who would be the means of his downfall. The spilling of Bonner's blood betokened death.

Tom could not shake off the fear that he had interpreted the incident correctly and that his ruin was imminent. Had God revealed to him secret knowledge and given him a warning that these were his last days?

He returned to the dining chamber, where his chaplains were still chewing over what had happened. Fruit was served to him, but he could only toy with it. Hearing a commotion outside, he sent an usher to find Dr Agostini, thinking the physician was making an escape, but the man returned to say that he was nowhere to be seen. However, the Earl of Northumberland was downstairs in the great hall.

'You jest,' Tom said.

The usher went to the top of the stairs and looked down. 'It is the Earl himself,' he said.

It would be a social call – so many others had come to visit him.

Tom gestured to his servants. 'Leave the table set. I will go down and meet him and bring him here, and he shall join us at table. I'm sure there will be enough meat left.'

He rose and went to the stairs as Percy was coming up. He had aged, Tom thought. He looked drawn and unhappy, a shadow of the young man he had barred from marrying Anne Boleyn all those years ago.

'My lord, you are welcome,' Tom said, and embraced him, noticing that his visitor was trembling. 'A thousand apologies. We have dined, and I fear there is no more good fish to make you honourable cheer, but I can offer you such meats as we have with goodwill and a loving heart.'

Then he became aware that the Earl was being followed upstairs by Sir Walter Walshe, a member of the King's Privy Chamber, and a great company of other gentlemen, some of them armed. And in the Earl's hands were the keys to the castle.

'I bid you good day, my lord,' Percy said stiffly, in strangled tones. And in that moment, Tom knew that something terrible was afoot.

He made a valiant effort to keep up the pretence that this was one neighbour calling on another, as if he could ward off any evil. He tried to speak lightly.

'I have often wished to see you at Cawood, but I would have

hoped to receive word of your coming, so that I might have received you honourably. Nevertheless, you shall have such cheer as I am able to make you, and I trust you will accept it from your very old and loving friend. Indeed, I hope to see you more often, when I shall be better provided to receive you with choicer fare.' He was babbling, he knew it.

He seized Percy by the hand and led him into the dining chamber, the Earl's retinue following. 'My lord, you shall have my bedchamber, where there is a good fire, and there you can take off your cloak and boots. Now, I pray you, give me leave to shake these gentlemen, your servants, by the hands.'

He went around the room greeting them all, and still Percy had said nothing. Tom returned to where he stood by the hearth.

'Ah, my lord, I see that you still observe my old precept that I gave you when you were lodging with me in your youth, which was to cherish your father's servants, of whom I see you have here a great number. You have done nobly, like a wise gentleman. For they will not only serve and love you, but also live and die for you, and be true and faithful servants and glad to see you prosper in honour; which I beseech God to send you, with long life.'

He took the Earl by the hand once more and showed him into his bedchamber, leaving Cavendish within earshot at the door. Percy turned to Tom and laid his hand on his arm.

'My lord, I arrest you for high treason,' he said, so softly that Tom could hardly hear him.

Tom felt faint. He could not speak. This was it, the horror of which he had had a premonition. In the midst of his shock and distress, he found space in his heart to pity Percy, who clearly abhorred his mission and found it distasteful. It occurred to him to wonder if the night crow had made Harry send him in revenge for breaking that long-ago betrothal; but who else would the King have chosen save the most important nobleman in the region?

He found his voice. 'My lord, by what authority do you arrest me?'

'I have a commission,' Percy told him.

'Where is your commission? Let me see it.'

The Earl's voice was firm now. 'No, Sir, that you may not.'

'Well then,' Tom challenged, 'I will not obey your order to arrest me.'

Just then, they could hear raised voices in the outer chamber. 'Sir Walter Walshe is apprehending Dr Agostini,' Percy said. Tom wondered what the physician had done to deserve it.

Cavendish opened the door, and Walshe violently thrust the physician to his knees before Tom and tore off his hood.

'He tried to hide his face with that!' he spat. 'Resisting arrest!'

Tom looked down at this creature of the Boleyns.

'What has he done?' he asked Walshe, confused.

'He has abetted your treason,' Walshe replied.

'But how?'

'I am not at liberty to say.'

'No one seems to be at liberty to say anything!' Tom snapped. 'My lord of Northumberland here has arrested me for treason, but by what authority he will not tell me, nor will he show me his commission, although he says he has one. If you are privy to it, I pray you show me.'

'Your Grace, it is true that he has one,' Walshe confirmed.

'Well then, I pray you let me see it.'

'Sir, I beseech you to excuse us,' Walshe pleaded. 'Attached to it is a schedule with certain instructions that are confidential. You may not see them.'

'Why?' Tom persisted, trying to quell his anger and panic. He suspected that the commission came from his enemies and that the King would know nothing about it until he had been done to death. 'If I were made privy to them, I could perhaps help you to perform those instructions. You both know that I have been privy to weighty matters such as this, and I doubt not that I shall clear myself and prove to be a true subject, against the expectation of my cruel enemies. I am content to yield to you, Master Walshe, as a gentleman of the King's Privy Chamber, but not to my lord of Northumberland, unless I see his commission. Because for the most wicked person in the kingdom there has to be a sufficient warrant, as there has to be one to arrest the greatest peer of this realm, and then only by the King's commandment. If you have that, I am ready to comply; put the

King's commission into execution, in God's name, and I will obey his will and pleasure. I take God to witness that I never offended the King's Majesty in word or deed, and I will swear that face to face with any man alive.'

The Earl made no answer, but gestured to Cavendish to leave the room. Cavendish looked loath to leave Tom unattended, but Percy insisted. 'You must depart.'

The usher glanced at Tom, as if asking if he should obey, and Tom signalled to him to go. Then Percy called his retinue into the chamber, took the keys of Tom's coffers from him and placed him in the custody of his gentlemen.

'We leave tomorrow,' he said, 'after we have set all things in order here.'

Tom went to the window and stood with his back to them. Below, in the courtyard, he could see Dr Agostini being led away, his feet tied under his horse's belly. Tom remained there, barely able to move, wondering what to believe. What treason was he supposed to have committed?

Percy assigned two of Tom's grooms to wait on him in his bedchamber. His own men were in the outer chamber, continually keeping watch until morning. Tom rose wearily after a sleepless night, feeling frail. When were they to leave, and where were they bound? But no one came to speak to him, and he had to remain in his bedchamber under guard.

He was pleased to see Cavendish, whom Percy had sent to attend him. But soon Cavendish was called away, and Tom saw him talking with Walshe in the courtyard below. By the time he returned, Tom was in tears, for it had struck him forcibly that with his coffer taken, he was no longer in a position to reward this most faithful of servants.

Cavendish gaped at him. 'Oh, my lord . . .'

'No, George, my tears are for you. I have nothing with which to reward you for all you have done for me. And the sight of you reminds me of my other loyal servants, whom I intended to advance to the best of my power. But now, I have nothing left me to recompense any of you, for all is taken from me.'

Cavendish knelt by his chair. 'My lord, be of good cheer. The malice and lies of your enemies can never prevail against your truth, for I doubt not that you will be acquitted of these false accusations and restored to your former dignity.'

'I hope you are right, my friend,' Tom said, summoning all his fortitude. 'I have no cause to fear any man alive; for no one who looks me in the face can accuse me of any untruth, which my enemies know full well. But I still fear them. Either I shall not have indifferent justice, or they will seek some sinister way to destroy me.'

'Sir,' Cavendish said gently, 'do not doubt that the King will be your good lord, as he has always showed himself in all your troubles.'

At that point, dinner was served in the dining chamber and some of Percy's gentlemen joined them at table. But Tom ate little, unable to stop weeping at the thought of what might await him. Would he be sent to the Tower? The prospect terrified him, for few who went in there ever came out alive. Surely Harry would not demand his head or – he shuddered – the terrible fate meted out to traitors? He was a man of the cloth, and that alone should protect him. He could also plead benefit of clergy, which would exempt him from the capital punishment to which lay folk were subject. But then he remembered that benefit of clergy did not extend to high treason. The realisation chilled him to the bone, and he let out such a great sigh that everyone stared at him; some were even weeping silently. He forced himself to murmur the words of a hymn to the praiseworthy constancy of martyrs.

After dinner, he was informed that they would not be leaving that evening after all. In the morning, having passed another sleepless night, he dressed for riding, but it was not until near dusk that Percy assigned him five servants to attend him: his chaplain, his barber, two grooms and Cavendish, for which he was most thankful.

As the Earl led him downstairs, Tom asked where the rest of his servants were.

'They are here,' the Earl answered.

'Sir, I pray you, let me see them before I depart.'

'Alas, my lord,' Percy said, 'they are distressed and it will trouble you; therefore, I beseech you to content yourself with not seeing them.'

Tom rounded on him. 'I will not go out of this house unless I see them and take my leave of them.'

'As you wish,' the Earl conceded.

The servants were summoned – Tom suspected that they had been shut in the chapel – and knelt before him in the great chamber. There was not one dry eye to be seen. He tried to comfort them and praised them for their diligent faithfulness. Then, tears streaming down his cheeks, he shook each of them by the hand and walked out into the courtyard.

His mule was waiting with the horses of Walshe's party. The porter opened the gates, and they set out on their journey to God knew where. Percy was not with them; he was staying behind to close up Cawood – and no doubt search it for incriminating evidence.

As they rode through the gatehouse, Tom saw that a vast crowd had assembled outside, bewailing his arrest and his departure. There must have been about three thousand people there. Seeing him appear, someone cried out, 'The Devil take all them who have taken you from us! We pray God that vengeance may alight upon them!' and the rest shouted with one loud voice, 'God save your Grace, God save your Grace!' Then they ran after him, calling out blessings all through the town of Cawood. He was moved to realise that they loved him so much.

As they rode on, Tom turned to Cavendish, who was trotting along beside him, and asked if he knew where they were going.

'To Pontefract,' Cavendish told him.

The name struck chills into Tom, for King Richard II had been starved to death in the castle there. It was a grim place, by all accounts. His mind began to conjure up all kinds of dire possibilities.

'Alas,' he said, 'shall I lie this night in the castle, and die like a beast?'

Cavendish reached over and laid a gloved hand on his. 'Sir, you are going to be lodged in the abbey.'

'Praise the Blessed Virgin; I am so glad to hear that!' Tom said.

The next day, the party pressed on towards Doncaster, delaying their departure in order to arrive at night, because so many people were following Tom, weeping and lamenting, and crying out, 'God save your Grace, God save your Grace, my good lord Cardinal!' Some ran before him with lighted candles in their hands; others cursed his enemies. And so he arrived by torchlight at the house of the Blackfriars, where he stayed that night.

The next day, he was moved to Sheffield Park, the Earl of Shrewsbury's hunting lodge. All the way there, the people wailed and commiserated. Shrewsbury and his Countess, surrounded by their household, were awaiting his coming, as they would have done in former days.

The Earl embraced him as he wearily dismounted, stiff and saddlesore. 'My lord, your Grace is most heartily welcome, and I am glad to see you in my poor lodge, although I should have been much gladder if you had come in happier circumstances.'

To be received with such great honour nearly broke Tom's heart. 'I thank you, my gentle lord of Shrewsbury,' he replied, 'and if a sorrowful heart may know joy, I rejoice to be here in the hands and custody of so noble a person. And Sir, whatever my accusers have charged against me, I assure you and all the world that I have always been just and loyal towards my sovereign.'

'I do not doubt your truth,' Shrewsbury assured him. 'Now fear not, for I have received letters from the King in his own hand in your favour, which you shall see. And I will not receive you as a prisoner, but as my good lord and the King's true faithful subject; and here is my wife come to salute you.' Rumour had long ago had it that the former Anne Hastings had been a mistress of the King. Tom removed his hat and kissed her and all her gentlewomen, then shook the hands of Shrewsbury's servants. All he could think of was that the King had written in his favour. Maybe Harry was just going through the motions in having him arrested to pacify the night crow, and had no intention of proceeding against him.

Arm in arm, he went with Shrewsbury into the lodge, where he was accommodated in a spacious chamber at the end of a fine gallery. A glimmer of hope flickered in his heart.

Chapter 37

1530

Once a day, the Earl came to sit with him on a cushioned bench below the great window in the gallery, which was hung with tapestries depicting – appropriately, Tom felt – the Fall of Man. One afternoon, a week into his visit, when he could not hide how dejected he was feeling, his host placed a hand on his shoulder.

'Sir, I daily receive letters from the King, commanding me to entertain you as one he loves and highly favours, so you have no cause to lament. And although you are accused – in my view, unjustly – yet the King can do no less than have you tried, which is, I gather, more to satisfy certain persons than for any mistrust that he has in you.'

Tom had known it. This whole terrible episode had been brought about by the night crow, who was chief of those certain persons. 'Alas!' he burst out. 'Is it right that any man should so wrongfully accuse me to the King's person, and not let me answer before his Majesty? Oh, how it grieves me that the King should have any suspicions of me or think that I would be false or conspire any evil to his royal person!' He was weeping again, weeping to think of how he had loved Harry, and still did, and how easy they had been together. He had thought their friendship would last for ever. But he had not counted on Harry falling obsessively in love.

He looked into the Earl's shrewd eyes. 'My lord, I was in good estate and living a quiet, contented life. But then came the enemy that never sleeps, but studies and continually imagines, both sleeping and waking, my utter destruction. My good lord, will you show yourself my true friend by asking the King to let me face my accusers in his presence? Then I doubt not that I will be able to acquit myself of all their malicious accusations and utterly confound them; for they shall never be able to prove that I ever offended the King. Otherwise, I fear that they intend to dispatch me before I can come into his presence.'

Shrewsbury nodded. 'I will write to the King's Majesty on your behalf, telling him how grievously you lament his displeasure and indignation; and I will convey your request.'

Tom waited anxiously for a reply. His host tried to divert him by laying on entertainments and inviting him to go hunting in the park, but Tom always refused, preferring to remain at his prayers. But he managed to enjoy the delicious food served to him at meals, which he took in his chamber, where he was often joined by the Earl's gentlemen and chaplains.

One evening, he was served roasted pears for the final course. Cavendish stood at the table, pouring a sauce of red wine over them, and Tom ate them appreciatively. Suddenly, he felt a terrible pain grip his stomach. It was trapped wind, he assured himself, and would soon pass. But it began to spread to his chest.

Cavendish was watching him, looking concerned. He leaned over the table. 'Sir, it seems your Grace is not well. Your face has gone pale.'

Tom was praying that the pain would go. 'Indeed, I am not well.' Gasping, he described his symptoms. 'It is but wind, so pray take up the cloth and we'll finish here.' His companions made sympathetic noises, wished him a speedy recovery and departed. Cavendish went off to have his own dinner.

Tom stayed sitting at table, feeling increasingly ill. And that was how Cavendish found him on his return.

'Go down to the apothecary and ask if he has anything that will relieve wind,' Tom ordered. Cavendish sped away, and came back with a twist of paper containing white powder, which he mixed with some wine. Tom gulped it down greedily. Minutes later, he belched loudly.

'You see, it *was* wind. Thanks to this powder, I am well eased, thank God.'

He rose from the table and went to his prayer desk, as he always did after dinner. As he knelt down, he felt his bowels move and had almost to run to the close stool. Foul-smelling matter gushed out of him. He felt drained when he had finished. Dragging himself to the gallery, he sank down on a chest and began telling his rosary beads.

After a while, Cavendish appeared.

'What news?' Tom asked.

Cavendish smiled. 'The best news that ever came to you, if your Grace can take it well.'

'I pray God it is!' Tom said. 'Well?'

Cavendish looked momentarily nervous. 'My lord of Shrewsbury was so persuasive in his letter to the King that his Grace has sent Master Kingston and twenty-four yeomen of the guard to conduct you to his presence.'

Tom felt his bowels turn to water again, this time from fear. This could not be good news.

Cavendish had perceived his consternation. 'Does your Grace not wish to clear yourself before the King? Now that God and your friends have brought it to pass, will you not take it thankfully? The King has sent gentle Master Kingston to you, with men who are your old servants, and they come only to attend upon you, for the want of your own servants. His Majesty has ordered Master Kingston to escort you south with as much honour as is due to you in your high estate, and to convey you by such easy journeys as you can wish of him. Sir, I humbly beseech your Grace to be of good cheer.'

Tom was not wholly reassured. 'Very well, but I perceive more than you can imagine or know. Experience of old has taught me.'

He rose and hastened to his close stool again, for the flux had returned with a virulence. There was blood in it this time. When he returned to the gallery, his bowels felt as if they had been turned inside out, and he was sitting there sweating when Shrewsbury joined him.

'How is your Grace?'

'I will be better soon, I trust. My lord, I am grateful to you for entertaining me so well, and for writing to the King.'

'You must take heart, my lord, and be not afraid of your enemies, who, I assure you, rather fear you, for they perceive that the King is fully minded to have your case heard before him. So I doubt not but that this journey you are taking to see his Highness will be much to your advantage and bring about the overthrow of your enemies.'

'Yet Sir,' Tom said slowly. 'Master Kingston is also Constable of the Tower.'

'Yes, and what of that?' Shrewsbury asked. 'I assure you he is only appointed by the King as one of your friends and because he is worthy to take responsibility for the safe conduct of your person. For, without fail, the King bears you a secret special favour.'

Tom was finding that increasingly hard to believe. Yet if it were otherwise, would Shrewsbury be showing so much courtesy and kindness to him?

'Well,' he said, 'as God wills, so be it. I am subject to fortune, and to fortune I submit myself, being ready to accept such ordinances as God has provided for me. Sir, I pray you, where is Master Kingston?'

'I will send for him. He will most gladly see you.'

As soon as Tom saw Kingston coming into the gallery, he stood up shakily to greet him. Kingston approached him reverently and, kneeling down, saluted him in the King's name. Tom bade him rise, but he would not.

'Master Kingston, I pray you stand up, or I will have to kneel down beside you.'

Kingston got to his feet. 'Sir, the King's Majesty has asked me to commend him to you.'

'I thank his Highness,' Tom said, feeling a little more cheerful. 'I trust he is in health, and merry.'

'Yes, without doubt, and he has commanded me to reassure you first of all that he bears you as much goodwill and favour as he ever did, and he wishes you to be of good cheer. And although he has heard that you have committed certain heinous crimes against him, he thinks that to be untrue. Yet, for the administration of justice, and to avoid any suspicion of partiality, he can do no less than send you for trial, trusting that you will be able to acquit yourself of all the charges against you. You will journey towards him at your own pleasure, and I will attend you and see that you are protected from any inconvenience.'

Tom thanked him, wishing that his stomach would stop churning. He wished too that he could believe that Kingston was telling him the truth. Here he was, accused of treason and under arrest, awaiting trial. His enemies were out for his blood. Benefit of clergy would not save him. For months, the King had sent him only fair words. When had Harry ever stood up to the night crow? Never. Now the Constable of the Tower had come for him. He saw his fate clearly, like a yawning abyss opening up before him. It was like standing at the gates of Hell.

They must take him for a fool.

He managed a smile. 'Master Kingston, if I were as able and as lusty as I have been until lately, I would not fail to ride with you tomorrow. But I have a flux that makes me feel very weak.' He paused. 'I thank you for your comfortable words, although I fear that their purpose is to lead me into a fool's paradise: I know what is provided for me. Nevertheless, I thank you for your goodwill and the pains you are taking for me; and I shall with all speed try to make ready to ride with you tomorrow.'

His heart sank when he realised that Kingston was not even trying to contradict him.

That night, when the time came to go to bed, Tom began to feel very ill indeed. He was obliged to rush continually to the close stool. By morning, he had passed fifty loose motions and he felt so weak that he could barely lift a finger. The matter he had voided was black.

'If I don't get a remedy soon, I fear I will die,' he told Cavendish.

Cavendish ran to fetch Shrewsbury's physician, Dr Nicholas, who inspected what Tom had evacuated and prodded his belly. 'You cannot travel today,' he said. 'If you do, you will not live past four or five days.'

'But I must ride with Master Kingston,' Tom protested.

'No, my lord, you must tarry here, at least until tomorrow.'

He lay there, his body sore and shattered. He had never had a flux like this before. Then he had the most awful thought. Had he been poisoned? Could poison cause such symptoms? Or had it been something he ate? Those pears?

He thought not. Others had had them and not suffered any ill effects. So what had caused this?

It would be most convenient for some if he died before he could refute the charges against him in the presence of the King; before Harry felt a resurgence of the love he had had for him, and before the charges could be exposed as lies intended to bring him down. Yes, his death would be timely. But poison? How had it been done? Had the Earl's cooks or kitchen staff been bribed? Or had one of his own servants been suborned into committing murder? He did not want to believe that.

He was determined to get to London as quickly as possible, before any further harm befell him. The next day, having suffered no further attacks in the night, he dragged himself out of bed and prepared to leave with Kingston and the guard.

When Cavendish and his other attendants saw him, they looked horrified.

'My lord, you are in no fit state to travel!' Cavendish protested. 'You look ill.'

He felt ill. He felt like death. Judging by the tears in his servants' eyes, they thought he was about to breathe his last. But he took them by the hands and assured them that he was fit enough to continue his journey.

He knew, before he had gone very far, that he was anything but. The griping pains in his stomach were grievous, and he was obliged several times to dismount and hasten behind a hedge to relieve himself, to his shame and humiliation. That night, when he lodged at Kirkby Hardwick Hall, another of Shrewsbury's houses, he did not know how to lie comfortably or what to do with himself, the pain was so bad.

The next day, they moved on to Nottingham, where he had to confront the fact that he was not getting any better. Indeed, he was feeling worse and could not take any food, for fear that it would set off another attack of the flux. On the way to Leicester the next morning, he became so sick that he could hardly sit on his mule, and would have fallen off many times had it not been for the strong arm of Cavendish, who was riding beside him.

That night, when they arrived at Leicester Abbey, the Abbot and convent were waiting at the gates to receive him, their faces illumined by the light of many torches.

He barely heard the reverent words of welcome. 'Father Abbot,' he quavered, thinking he might expire at any moment, 'I am come here to leave my bones among you.'

They brought him indoors, still on his mule, to the foot of the stair that led up to his chamber, and helped him to alight, then Kingston took him by the arm and assisted him upstairs. As soon as he reached the sanctuary of his room, he fell on the bed, feeling more sick than he had ever felt in his life. He sank into a deep sleep, but when he woke, they had to bring him a chamber pot, as he was too weak to rise.

He fell asleep and dreamed, and in his dream, he was dying. An angel appeared and told him that he would be dead by eight o'clock. And he was filled with a radiant light. He thought it was the glory of God. If this was death, he welcomed it.

It was almost a disappointment when he woke up. It was yet dark. The wax lights were still burning in their pewter dishes on the cupboard and the curtains were closed. He became aware that someone was at his bedside. Seeing the shadow of a man on the wall, and being unable to turn for sheer weakness, he quavered, 'Who's there?' In that moment, he thought an assassin had come for him.

'Sir, I am here,' said Cavendish.

'How are you?' Tom croaked.

'I'd be very well, if I could see your Grace looking better.'

'What time is it?'

'It is past eight o'clock in the morning.'

'Eight of the clock?' he echoed. 'It cannot be eight o'clock, no, no; for by eight o'clock, you should have lost your master. The time draws near when I must depart out of this world.'

He heard the voice of Dr Palmes, his chaplain, murmuring to Cavendish.

'Will you be shriven, my lord?' Cavendish enquired.

Suddenly, Tom was frightened. Frightened of dying and what lay beyond. How would God judge him? Would it be Heaven – or eternal Hell?

He snapped at Cavendish, with something of his old spirit, 'Why are you asking me that? Do not presume to know the secrets of my soul!'

'Sir, Master Cavendish but did my bidding,' Dr Palmes soothed.

Filled instantly with remorse, Tom gestured at Cavendish. 'Forgive me, old friend.'

'There is nothing to forgive,' Cavendish said gently. His voice broke on a sob.

Late in the afternoon, Sir William Kingston visited Tom.

'How does your Grace?'

'I have been better,' Tom replied. He was propped up on pillows now, washed and re-clad in a clean nightgown of Holland cloth. He had suffered no fluxes this morning and felt, he thought, a little better. It had occurred to him that his illness might not just be of the body, but of the mind too, and that the one thing that might bring him back to health would be the presence of his beloved Harry – or even a kind letter from him. Without Harry's love, life was barely worth living.

He sighed and regarded his visitor.

'I fear I must trouble you with a matter that needs resolving,' Kingston said. 'My lord of Northumberland discovered an account book at Cawood that showed you had lately fifteen hundred pounds in ready money, yet not a penny of it is to be found. Naturally, he reported this to the King, and the King has written to me to ask if you know where it is, for it would be a pity if it was embezzled from you both. Therefore, I am to require you, in the King's name, to tell me the truth, so that I can report it to his Majesty.'

Tom closed his eyes for a few moments. 'Good Lord! How it grieves me that the King should think me a deceiver, when I would not deny him even one penny!' He spoke vehemently, despite his weakness. 'God being my judge, everything I had I took to be the King's goods, knowing I had the use of it only during my life. And I meant, after my death, to leave everything to his Grace. As for this money you demand of me, it is not mine, for I borrowed it from several friends to pay for my burial and to bestow small rewards among my servants. Yet if his Grace pleases to take this money, I will be content, although I would most humbly beseech him to pay back those from whom I borrowed it, for the discharge of my conscience.'

He gave Kingston their names.

'The King will not fail you,' Kingston said. 'He will do right by you.'

When Kingston had gone to have supper, Tom felt aggrieved that he had been hounded – yes, that was the word – by this demand when he was so ill. Could it not have waited until – God willing – he was better? It seemed that his enemies would never cease pursuing him. Had they ordered Northumberland to find any morsel of incriminating evidence against him? It would appear so. And yet the Earl had clearly not relished what he had to do. Could it be that the night crow still had some hold over him? Did he still cherish feelings for her, that he would undertake this skulduggery for her?

He could eat no supper that evening. As night drew in, he began to feel like death again. He had managed a little dinner earlier, but it had caused the flux to return with a deadly vengeance, and the pain in his stomach was such that he swooned with it, and thought he really was dying. Nothing gave him relief.

Cavendish was there all night, performing the most personal, often disgusting tasks for him, keeping him clean and sweet-smelling, yet being moved about was almost unbearable.

The clock had just struck four when Cavendish, seeing him lying wakeful, asked how he felt.

It was an hour since Tom had last needed the chamber pot, and the pains had lightened. He suddenly felt hungry. 'Well,' he said, 'if there is any meat, I pray you fetch me some.'

'Sir, there is none ready, but I will call up the cook to provide some for you; and will also send for Master Palmes, that you can talk with him.'

Tom was speaking with Dr Palmes when Cavendish returned with a bowl of chicken broth. Tom took two mouthfuls and laid down the spoon.

'I know I asked for meat,' he said, 'but I have just realised that it is St Andrew's Eve, a fasting day.'

'Sir, you are excused because of your sickness,' Dr Palmes assured him.

'Yes, but I will eat no more,' Tom replied. His appetite had suddenly gone. 'I would make my confession.'

Dr Palmes put on his stole and knelt by the bed. 'I am listening, my son.'

'Bless me, Father, for I have sinned,' Tom murmured. 'I have been guilty of the sins of pride, envy, gluttony . . . I fear I have been guilty of all the seven deadly sins.'

'Surely not sloth?'

Tom smiled weakly. 'Perhaps not that one. But lust, yes. I have spent the last twenty years lusting after – no, loving – one woman. Had I not been in holy orders, I would have married her. But I lived in sin with her, although even now, facing God's judgement, I cannot really see it as sin, and I can never repent of it, for I fear that I would do the same if I had my life again.' Joan's lovely face was etched on his mind.

Dr Palme was silent for a moment. 'If you do not consider it a sin, then why have you confessed it?'

'Because the world would account it a sin. I broke my vows.'

'And do you believe that God accounts it a sin?'

'If so, then why would He implant that love and those natural instincts in us? It did not feel like sin. And if God wanted retribution, then He has visited it on us both in our lifetimes. Mine has sometimes felt like a living penance.'

Dr Palme laid a hand on Tom's. 'Confess your sin, my son. I will absolve you. God will absolve you.'

* * *

Tom woke as the clock struck seven times. Then Kingston appeared and bade him good morrow.

'How is your Grace today?' he enquired kindly.

Tom could barely summon the words. 'Sir, I await the will and pleasure of God, to render my simple soul into His hands.'

'Not yet, sir!' Kingston replied with that false heartiness people liked to use about the sick. 'With the grace of God, you shall live, and do very well. Be of good cheer!'

'Master Kingston, my disease is such that I cannot live,' Tom protested. 'I have a flux with a continual fever; and from what I have seen of this kind of malady, if there is no improvement within eight days, the outcome is death. And as this is the eighth day, and you see in me no alteration, then there is no remedy, although I may live a day or two more.'

'No, Sir, you are in such a frenzied state that you are expecting the worst, which makes you feel much worse than you should, but you need not fear.'

'Well, well, Master Kingston,' Tom said wearily, his voice bitter, 'I can see – as perhaps you cannot – how the case against me has been framed. That is one reason for my illness. But if I had served God as diligently as I have done the King, He would not have given me over in my grey hairs or left me naked to my enemies. Yet this is the reward that I must receive for the pains I took to do him service, and my sin was to do it only to satisfy his pleasure, without regarding my godly duty.'

He fell silent. The effort to speak had exhausted him. He saw Kingston's shocked face and realised he had said too much. He should not have criticised Harry; he should be in charity with all men as his end approached.

He took a deep breath. 'Master Kingston, I pray you, with all my heart, to commend me most humbly to his Majesty and beseech him on my behalf to call to his most gracious remembrance all matters between him and me from the beginning to this day, and chiefly the weighty matter between him and good Queen Katherine. Then his conscience will tell him whether I have offended him or no. He is a prince of a royal courage and has a princely heart; and I know he would rather lose half of his realm than not have his will and pleasure in that matter. I assure you I have often knelt before him in his privy chamber for an hour or two, trying to persuade him from his purpose, but I could never dissuade him. Therefore, Master Kingston, if it is ever your privilege to be made a member of his Privy Council, I warn you to be well advised about what matters you put in his head, for you will never pull them out again.'

He found himself rambling on about heresies and negligent kings and the ruin of commonwealths, not quite knowing what he was saying, until he saw Kingston staring at him in alarm. And then he felt himself sinking into that place from which there would be no return.

Here was the end and fall of pride and arrogance. He had been exalted by fortune to honours and high dignities, power and glory; he had been haughtiest man in all England and had more respect to the worldly honour of his person than he had to his spiritual profession, when he should have been all meekness, humility and charity. And yet he had striven with all his heart, in these last difficult months, to put everything right and be what he should have been all along.

This was it. This was death. His life was ebbing away. Fortune – and his enemies – would be cheated of whatever fate they had had in store for him. The only tribunal he would be called to was God's. There would be no prison cell in the Tower for him, no axe descending on his neck.

'Master Kingston, farewell,' he whispered. 'I can say no more, but I wish that all the King's proceedings end in success. My time draws on fast. I may not tarry with you. Do not forget, I pray you, what I have said.'

His voice tailed away. As he closed his eyes for the last time, gladly relinquishing his spirit to God, he called to mind Joan's beloved face, and Thomas's, and those of his other little children, and wondered if they would ever know how deeply he had loved them. And then,

Harry came to him – a younger Harry, laughing and clapping his arm around his good friend, not yet made fierce by his Great Matter, not yet in thrall to the night crow. His beloved Harry.

He heard Dr Palmes speaking of Christ's passion, heard Cavendish sending for the Abbot to anoint him with holy oil as he made his passage. He felt himself slipping away – and then he could hear no more.

The clock struck eight.

Author's Note

Huge thanks go to the historian Sarah Gristwood for suggesting this book and the title. I am indebted to her for it because it has proved to be a very enjoyable project. As with all my historical novels, I have kept closely to contemporary sources, although, in the interests of keeping the narrative pacy, I have touched briefly on, or omitted, much of the politics to focus on Wolsey the man, a historical figure for whom I have a certain sympathy. In this, I have found George Cavendish's *The Life of Cardinal Wolsey* invaluable, for it is a first-hand account by a man who was close to him. I have aimed also at showing Wolsey as a statesman with an international, or European, vision, and a player and peace-broker on a world stage.

I have assumed that he was born in 1471, because in 1530, he distributed Maundy charity to fifty-nine poor men – one for each year of his age.

From numerous fragments of information, I have constructed the story of Joan (or Jane) Larke, Wolsey's mistress from *c*.1509 to *c*.1520. The life of their son, Thomas Winter, is better documented, but very little is known of their daughter, Dorothy, save that she was adopted and became a nun at Shaftesbury Abbey. These storylines in the novel are therefore speculative; I tried to imagine what Joan's life would have been like during her years with Wolsey, and how it would have felt to be hidden away to avoid scandal, and not be able to be a mother to her children. Theirs, I believe, must have been a love that knew pain. We don't know why Wolsey and Joan parted – if it all got too much for them, or if Fate intervened in some other way – but the split appears to have coincided with the scandal that erupted when Wolsey arranged an advantageous marriage for Elizabeth Blount, the mother of Henry VIII's bastard son, which excited widespread criticism. That suggested the version of events in the novel.

Joan Larke bore George Legh four children. In the novel, two of them are Wolsey's, although there is no contemporary evidence to suggest that, apart from the fact that the only boy was named Thomas. Nor is there any evidence that Urian Brereton was one of Legh's creditors. I have invented these storylines for dramatic purposes.

Wolsey was clearly aware of the weakness of the King's nullity suit, and that his marriage to Katherine was valid. Nevertheless, he strove to his utmost to obtain what Henry wanted, which I think demonstrates not only his need to cling to power, but also his love for his master.

There are conflicting accounts of what happened at Grafton in 1529, when Cardinal Campeggio came to bid farewell to the King after the disastrous culmination of the trial at Blackfriars, and Wolsey went with him. Cavendish, writing in the 1550s, claimed that when they arrived, Campeggio was led away to a comfortable lodging, but that no provision had been made for Wolsey and he was forced to sit on his mule in the courtyard until Henry Norris came and offered the use of his own room, so that the Cardinal could change out of his riding clothes before seeing the King. Another of Wolsey's servants, Thomas Alward, whose account was written five days after the event, does not mention this, but states that, Grafton being a small house, both cardinals were lodged at nearby Easton Neston. Both sources agree that when Wolsey, full of trepidation, came into the crowded presence chamber and knelt before his master, Henry's old affection for him surfaced and, smiling, he raised him and led him to a window embrasure, where they talked for some time, much to the amazement of the onlookers.

I have modernised a lot of the language from contemporary sources, especially Cavendish's *Life*. Some quotes have been used out of context. The quotes at the section headings come from Wolsey himself, Shakespeare's *Henry VIII* and George Cavendish's *Metrical Visions*.

I wish to thank my ever-supportive editors, Mari Evans and Frankie Edwards at Headline and Susanna Porter at Ballantine for commissioning this book, and my brilliant editor, Flora Rees. Warmest thanks go to the publishing teams at Headline and Ballantine for all their creative support and expertise. And to Julian Alexander for being the most amazing literary agent an author could wish for.

I want also to express my gratitude to my lovely family and friends who have been so kind and supportive during the past difficult year when I was trying to come to terms with widowhood. You have given me strength and comfort, and I am deeply grateful.

Dramatis Personae

Thomas Wolsey (Tom), later Archbishop of York, Cardinal and Lord Chancellor of England
Beaky, a master of Magdalen College, Oxford
William Waynflete, Bishop of Winchester, founder of Magdalen College
Edmund Daundy, Tom's uncle
Robert Wolsey, Tom's father
Rob Wolsey, Tom's brother
William Wolsey, Tom's brother
Joan Daundy, Tom's mother
Master Squyre, headmaster of Ipswich Grammar School
Edward Winter, Tom's neighbour in Ipswich
James Goldwell, Bishop of Norwich, Tom's benefactor
Edward IV, King of England (reigned 1461–83)
Laurence Squyre, master at Oxford
Richard III, King of England (reigned 1483–5)
Henry Tudor, Earl of Richmond, later King Henry VII (reigned 1485–1509)
Elizabeth of York, daughter of Edward IV and queen of Henry VII
Edward V and Richard, Duke of York, sons of Edward IV
Bess (Elizabeth) Wolsey, Tom's sister
Thomas, Bishop of Lydda, suffragan for John Blyth, Bishop of Salisbury
John, Leonard and George Grey, sons of Thomas Grey, Marquess of Dorset
Thomas Grey, 1st Marquess of Dorset, uncle of Henry VIII
Edward Stafford, 3rd Duke of Buckingham

Elizabeth Wydeville, queen of Edward IV, mother of Thomas Grey, 1st Marquess of Dorset
Joan Daundy's second husband, Tom's stepfather (name unknown)
Cecily Bonville, Marchioness of Dorset
Henry Stafford, 2nd Duke of Buckingham
Lambert Simnel, pretender to the throne
Oliver King, Bishop of Bath and Wells
Sir Amyas Paulet, High Sheriff of Somerset
Thomas Grey, 2nd Marquess of Dorset
Henry Deane, Archbishop of Canterbury
Margaret Tudor, daughter of Henry VII, Queen of Scots
James IV, King of Scots
Arthur Tudor, Prince of Wales, son of Henry VII
Katherine of Aragon, his wife, later first queen of Henry VIII
Henry Tudor, Duke of York, son of Henry VII, later Prince of Wales and King Henry VIII
Mary Tudor, daughter of Henry VII, later Queen of France and Duchess of Suffolk
Sir Richard Nanfan, Treasurer of Calais
William Warham, Bishop of London, later Archbishop of Canterbury
Sir Edward Poynings, Lord Deputy of Calais
Louis XII, King of France
Maximilian of Austria, King of the Romans, later Holy Roman Emperor
Mary, Duchess of Burgundy, his first wife
Philip the Handsome, his son, King of Castile
Juana the Mad, Queen of Castile
Ferdinand of Aragon and Isabella of Castile, joint sovereigns of Spain
Charles, Infante of Spain, later King of Spain and (as Charles V) Holy Roman Emperor
The Nanfan family
Dr Richard Foxe, Bishop of Winchester
Sir Thomas Lovell, Chancellor of the Exchequer
Richard Empson and Edmund Dudley, ministers to Henry VII
Thomas Larke, royal chaplain

Margaret of Austria, Regent of the Netherlands, daughter of the Emperor Maximilian
William, Tom's servant
Thomas Howard, Earl of Surrey, later 2nd Duke of Norfolk
The Daundy family
John, Edmund, Peter and William, Thomas Larke's brothers
Joan Larke, sister of Thomas Larke, later Tom's mistress
Peter Larke, her father
John Fisher, Bishop of Rochester
The Lady Margaret Beaufort, Countess of Richmond and Derby, mother of Henry VII
Henry V, King of England (reigned 1413–22)
Edward of Woodstock, the Black Prince, son of Edward III
Stillborn daughter of Henry VIII and Katherine of Aragon
Cocksparrow, Joan Larke's cat (the name is invented, but Wolsey had a cat)
Joan Larke's midwife
Thomas Winter, Tom's son with Joan Larke
Charles Brandon, later Duke of Suffolk
Mistress Barlow, Thomas Winter's foster mother
Henry, Prince of Wales, son of Henry VIII
Pope Julius II
John Kite, Archbishop of Armagh
Dorothy, Tom's daughter with Joan Larke
John Clausey, her adoptive father
Lord Admiral Sir Edward Howard
Pope Leo X
Lord Thomas Howard, later Earl of Surrey and 3rd Duke of Norfolk
Giles, Lord Daubeney
Sir Thomas Boleyn, later Viscount Rochford and Earl of Wiltshire
Elizabeth Howard, Lady Rochford, later Countess of Wiltshire, Anne Boleyn's mother
Christopher Bainbridge, Cardinal, Archbishop of York
Thomas Cromwell, a lawyer
Francis I, King of France

Louise of Savoy, his mother
A Papal emissary
Maurice Birchinshaw, Thomas Winter's tutor
John Colet, Dean of St Paul's
The Princess Mary, daughter of Henry VIII and Katherine of Aragon
Katherine of York, Countess of Devon
Agnes Tilney, Duchess of Norfolk
Lord Henry Brandon, son of Charles Brandon, Duke of Suffolk, and Mary Tudor
Sir Thomas More, later Lord Chancellor of England
Richard Pace, Henry VIII's secretary
Sir Nicholas Carew, gentleman of the Privy Chamber
Cardinal Lorenzo Campeggio, Papal legate
Elizabeth Blount, Henry VIII's mistress
Francis, Dauphin of France
Guillaume Gouffier, Lord of Bonnivet, Admiral of France
Unnamed princess, daughter of Henry VIII and Katherine of Aragon
Master Williams, one of Tom's spies
Sir Francis Bryan, Sir Edward Neville and Sir Henry Guildford, gentlemen of the Privy Chamber
Henry Fitzroy, bastard son of Henry VIII, later Duke of Richmond and Somerset
Gilbert Tailboys, husband of Elizabeth Blount
John Skelton, court poet
Sir George Legh, first husband of Joan Larke
Charlemagne, Holy Roman Emperor
Martin Luther, founder of the Protestant religion
Pietro Torrigiano, sculptor
Ellen Legh, Tom's daughter with Joan Larke
Claude of Valois, Queen of France
Piers Butler, Earl of Ormond
James Butler, his son
Anne Boleyn, daughter of Sir Thomas Boleyn
Margaret Pole, Countess of Salisbury, niece of Edward IV
Ursula Pole, her daughter

Henry, Lord Stafford, her husband; son of Edward Stafford, Duke of Buckingham
Henry Pole, Lord Montagu, son of Margaret Pole
Elizabeth Legh, daughter of Joan Larke and George Legh
Pope Adrian VI
Dr Thomas Lupset, scholar
George Cavendish, Tom's gentleman usher
Thomas Cavendish, his father
Jane Parker, daughter of Lord Morley
George Boleyn, son of Sir Thomas Boleyn
Mary Boleyn, daughter of Sir Thomas Boleyn
Thomas Ruthall, Bishop of Durham
Pope Alexander VI
Cesare Borgia, his son
Desiderius Erasmus, Humanist Scholar
Lord Henry Percy, later 6th Earl of Northumberland
Henry Percy, 5th Earl of Northumberland, his father
George Talbot, Earl of Shrewsbury
Mary Talbot, his daughter
James Melton, friend of Lord Henry Percy
Pope Clement VII (Giulio de' Medici)
Benedetto da Rovezzano, sculptor
Master Fermour, merchant of Calais
Will Somers, fool
Patch, Tom's fool
Edmund Tudor, Duke of Somerset, brother of Henry VIII
Beaufort family
Henry Brandon, Earl of Lincoln
Henry Courtenay, Earl of Devon, Marquess of Exeter
Thomas Manners, Earl of Rutland
Sir William Fitzwilliam, Lord Treasurer
Giovanni di Maiano, sculptor
Mary Legh, daughter of Joan Larke and George Legh
Dr Robert Barnes, cleric
Sir William Compton, gentleman of the Privy Chamber

Sir John Russell, courtier, later Earl of Bedford
Henry Norris, Groom of the Stool
Isabella of Portugal, Holy Roman Empress
Henry Bourchier, Earl of Essex
Anne, his daughter
George Legh's mistress
Don Íñigo López de Mendoza, Imperial ambassador
Gabriel de Gramont, Bishop of Tarbes
Henry, Duke of Orléans, son of Francis I
Thomas (Tommy) Legh, Tom's son with Joan Larke
Hans Holbein, painter
Renée of Valois, daughter of Louis XII
Sir Richard Wiltshire, Kentish gentleman
St Thomas Becket, Archbishop of Canterbury (martyred 1170)
Monsieur du Biez, Captain of Boulogne
Charles de Guise, Cardinal of Lorraine
Anne de Montmorency, Grand Master of France
Dr William Knight, Henry VIII's secretary
Gregory Casale, diplomat
Dr Edward Foxe, Henry VIII's chaplain
Dr Stephen Gardiner, lawyer
William Tyndale, religious reformer
George Heneage, Tom's servant
Cecily Willoughby, Abbess of Wilton
Isabel Jordan, later Abbess of Wilton
William Carey, husband of Mary Boleyn
Eleanor Carey, nun of Wilton
A servant of Lord Brooke, her lover
Dr Robert Shorton, Katherine of Aragon's almoner
Dr Rodrigo de Puebla, Spanish ambassador to the court of Henry VII
Thomas Abell, chaplain to Katherine of Aragon
Jeanne de Valois, first wife of Louis XII
Urian Brereton, member of the Privy Chamber
John Kite, Bishop of Carlisle
An official of the Court of King's Bench

Sir William Gascoigne, Tom's treasurer
Sir Thomas Arundell
Master Shelley, judge
Dr Agostini, Tom's physician
Dr William Butts, Henry VIII's physician
The monks of the Sheen Charterhouse
George Paulet, younger brother of Sir William Paulet and second husband of Joan Larke
Sir William Paulet, Privy Councillor
The Lord Mayor of London
Sir William Brereton, gentleman of the Privy Chamber
Sir Thomas Wriothesley, gentleman of the Privy Chamber
Eustache Chapuys, Imperial ambassador
Brian Higden, Dean of York
Dr Edmund Bonner, master of Tom's faculties and spiritual jurisdictions
Sir Walter Walshe, member of the Privy Chamber
Anne Hastings, Countess of Shrewsbury
Sir William Kingston, Constable of the Tower
Dr Nicholas, physician to the Earl of Shrewsbury
Richard Pescall, Abbot of Leicester
Dr Palmes, Tom's chaplain

Various townsfolk, citizens, schoolboys, tutors, students, nobles, courtiers, gentlemen of the Privy Chamber, councillors, officers, clerics, choristers, ladies-in-waiting, maids-of-honour, servants, physicians, ushers, grooms, men-at-arms, constables of the Tower of London, yeomen warders, Yeomen of the Guard, Gentlemen Pensioners, boatmen, heralds, trumpeters, soldiers, ambassadors, Papal nuncios and emissaries, envoys, workmen, craftsmen, engineers, merchants, apprentices, spies

Timeline

1471
- Birth of Thomas Wolsey

1482
- Wolsey a pupil at Magdalen College School, then at Magdalen College

1485
- Battle of Bosworth. Henry Tudor defeats Richard III, the last Plantagenet King, and becomes Henry VII, first sovereign of the royal House of Tudor

1486
- Wolsey awarded his degree; begins career at Oxford

1491
- Birth of Henry VIII

1496
- Death of Wolsey's father

1498
- Wolsey ordained priest

1501
- Wolsey appointed tutor to the sons of the Marquess of Dorset
- Wolsey appointed rector of Lymington
- Marriage of Arthur Tudor, Prince of Wales, and Katherine of Aragon

1502
- Wolsey appointed chaplain to Henry Deane, Archbishop of Canterbury
- Death of Prince Arthur

1503
- Wolsey goes to Calais as chaplain to Sir Richard Nanfan

1507
- Death of Sir Richard Nanfan
- Wolsey appointed chaplain to Henry VII

1508
- Wolsey appointed Dean of Lincoln and royal almoner

1509
- Accession of Henry VIII
- Death of Wolsey's mother
- Marriage and coronation of Henry VIII and Katherine of Aragon
- Joan Larke becomes Wolsey's mistress

1510
- Wolsey made a Knight of the Garter
- Wolsey takes up residence at St Bride's Inn, Blackfriars
- Birth of Thomas Winter, Wolsey's son with Joan Larke

1511
- Death of Henry, Prince of Wales, Henry VIII's infant son

1512
- Birth of Dorothy, Wolsey's daughter with Joan Larke

1513
- Henry VIII invades France
- Battle of the Spurs; Thérouanne falls to Henry VIII
- James IV of Scots killed at the Battle of Flodden
- Tournai falls to Henry VIII

1514
- Henry VIII breaks the alliance with Spain, makes peace with France and marries his sister Mary to Louis XII of France
- Wolsey begins building Hampton Court
- Wolsey appointed Bishop of Lincoln
- Wolsey appointed Archbishop of York

1515
- Death of Louis XII of France; accession of Francis I
- Wolsey made a cardinal
- Wolsey appointed Lord Chancellor

1516
- Death of Ferdinand of Aragon
- Birth of the Princess Mary, daughter of Henry VIII and Katherine of Aragon

1517
- Martin Luther publishes his ninety-five theses in Germany and inspires the Protestant Reformation

1518
- Wolsey appointed Papal legate

1519
- Death of Maximiliam I, Holy Roman Emperor
- Election of the Holy Roman Emperor Charles V
- Birth of Henry Fitzroy, bastard son of Henry VIII by Elizabeth Blount

1520
- Henry VIII meets Francis I of France at the Field of Cloth of Gold

1521
- The Pope bestows on Henry VIII the title Defender of the Faith

1525
- Wolsey founds Cardinal College, Oxford
- Henry Fitzroy created Duke of Richmond and Somerset
- Wolsey fails to raise funds for war with France through the Amicable Grant
- The Princess Mary sent to Ludlow for two years

1526
- Henry VIII in pursuit of Anne Boleyn

1527
- Henry VIII questions the validity of his marriage to Katherine of Aragon and asks the Pope for an annulment

1528
- Cardinal Campeggio, Papal legate, comes to England to try the King's case with Wolsey

1529
- The legatine court sits at the monastery of the Blackfriars in London; Katherine of Aragon appeals to Henry VIII for justice; the case is referred back to Rome
- Wolsey falls from favour
- Sir Thomas More appointed Lord Chancellor

1530
- Death of Wolsey

Reading Group Questions

- From a young age, and the novel's opening pages, we see Tom Wolsey's inquisitive intelligence and interest in how the world works – and who is in charge of it. Coming from 'humble stock' into a more rarefied life, what experiences of his youth and early adulthood cause him to long for a life at court, and where do you think his extreme ambition comes from?

- *The Cardinal* is a novel of love and power. Tom finds himself with both, yet one is private and hidden, the other public and ostentatious. His searing love for Joan is undeniable, but he has yearned to be at the heart of public life, manipulating the court and controlling the narrative. When the time comes to choose between love and power, do you think Tom should – or could – have made a different choice?

- In Joan Larke, Alison Weir has created a character who is in some ways deeply beholden to her lover, Tom, yet retains a strong self-identity throughout. How did you interpret her role in Tom's life – first as his lover, then his sounding board, then, perhaps, as the one person who could help him rein in his growing ego? What does Tom lose when he loses Joan? And what, if anything, does she gain?

- *Tom rejoiced in his affection, for he now regarded this golden young man almost as a son.* The relationship between Thomas Wolsey and Henry VIII was famously close. In *The Cardinal*, Alison Weir portrays this bond as strongly paternal, with Tom seeking to achieve Harry's aims as much from a place of love as from duty to his King. Do you feel Harry truly reciprocated Tom's affection? And how could the King justify his betrayal of his old friend?

- Throughout *The Cardinal* we witness Tom's pleasure in entertaining, and his enjoyment in 'the finer things in life', learned early on at Oxford. He uses this to develop networks of useful contacts, but seems rarely to invite true friendship. Was Tom ultimately a lonely figure, sitting under his great cloth of state? Do you see him as an outsider? Could he have trusted anyone beyond Joan?

- *He was, effectively, a king without a crown . . . his enemies could not touch him.* At his zenith, Tom has proved himself so invaluable to Henry VIII that he appears invulnerable. Yet the extent of his spy network and his need to hold so many threads of power perhaps demonstrate his true vulnerability. Do you think there was a moment when he pushed too far, for example bringing about the downfall of Buckingham, or outshining Harry himself with the works at Hampton Court? Without Anne Boleyn, would he have remained at Harry's side?

- From Thomas More to Thomas Cromwell, Katherine of Aragon to the Emperor Charles V, Tom crossed paths with some of the most significant figures of Tudor history. Whose stories did you find most fascinating, and did you see any of these people in a different light through Tom's eyes?

- The theme of loss permeates Tom's life – first the deaths of his brother and father, then the father figures he has found in his early patrons, including Henry VII. However, is losing his children the greatest sadness, especially as it comes through obedience to Harry? What impact does this sacrifice have on Tom, and on Joan? Or is, in fact, the loss of Harry's love the most painful in the end?

- *'The night crow has got at him… She seeks my ruin. He will not send for me again.'* There is a deep poignancy in Tom's realisation that Anne Boleyn has finally succeeded in breaking his bond with Harry. What are your insights into Tom's relationship with Anne Boleyn, and why does he underestimate her so very badly?

- Cardinal Wolsey holds a particular place in British history as the power behind Henry VIII's throne, whose rise was so high and fall so spectacular in its magnitude. How does Alison Weir change this narrative to show the real man behind the legendary figure? How much did you empathise with Tom Wolsey as he is shown in the novel, and do you feel his fate was, ultimately, inevitable?

ALISON WEIR is a bestselling historical novelist of Tudor fiction, and the leading female historian in the United Kingdom. She has published more than thirty books, including many leading works of non-fiction, and has sold over three million copies worldwide.

Her novels include the Tudor Rose trilogy, which spans three generations of history's most iconic family – the Tudors, and the highly acclaimed Six Tudor Queens series about the wives of Henry VIII, all of which were *Sunday Times* bestsellers.

Alison is a fellow of the Royal Society of Arts and an honorary life patron of Historic Royal Palaces.